ICONS AND THEIR HISTORY

David and Tamara Talbot Rice

ICONS

AND THEIR HISTORY

with 200 illustrations, 9 in colour

THE OVERLOOK PRESS
Woodstock, New York

Published in 1974 by
The Overlook Press
Lewis Hollow Road
Woodstock, New York 12498

ISBN 0-87951-021-8
Library of Congress Catalog Card Number:
74-78136

Printed in Great Britain by
Alden & Mowbray Ltd
at the Alden Press, Oxford
Bound by Hunter and Foulis, Edinburgh

Contents

Bibliographical Note

This bibliography, to which reference is made in the text, does not claim to be complete; only the more important works or those where full bibliographies are to be found are cited. Their full titles are given in the right-hand column, with, on the left, the abbreviated forms we have used.

Antonova/Mneva   M. V. Antonova and N. E. Mneva, *Katalog drevnerusskoy zhivopisi*, Vols. 1 and 2, Moscow, 1963

Balabanov   K. Balabanov, *Icons of Macedonia*, Skopje, 1969

Djurić   V. J. D. Djurić, *Icônes de Yougoslavie*, Belgrade, 1961

Icons   K. Weitzmann, M. Chatzidakis, K. Miatev and S. Radojčić, *Icons from South-Eastern Europe and Sinai*, London, 1968

Icônes   S. Radojčić, *Icônes de Serbie et de Macédoine*, Belgrade, 1961

Istoriya   *Istoriya russkogo iskusstva*, USSR Academy of Sciences, Moscow/Leningrad, Vol. 1, 1953; Vol. 2, 1954; Vol. 3, 1955

Kondakov 1   N. P. Kondakov, *Russkaya ikona*, Prague, 1933

Kondakov 2   N. P. Kondakov, *Litzevoy ikonopisny podlinik; Ikonografia Gospoda Boga, Spasa Nashego Iisusa Khrista*, St Petersburg, 1905

Lazarev 1   V. N. Lazarev, *Andrei Rublyov i ego shkola*, Moscow, 1960

Lazarev 2   V. N. Lazarev, *Novgorodian Icon Painting*, Moscow, 1969

Onasch   K. Onasch, *Icons*, London, 1963

Pap.   A. Papageorgiou, *Icons of Cyprus*, London, 1969

PSRL   *Polnoe sobranie russkich letopisey*, St Petersburg, 1846 onwards

Rice   D. Talbot Rice and others, *The Icons of Cyprus*, London, 1937

Venice   M. Chatzidakis, *Icônes de Saint-Georges des Grecs et de la Collection de l'Institut Hellénique de Venise*, Venice, 1962

Xyngopoulos   A. Xyngopoulos, *Catalogue of the Icons; Benaki Museum, Athens*, Athens, 1936 (in Greek)

Introduction

THE PURPOSE of this book is to provide a framework for the chronology of icons by reproducing and analysing almost all those which can be dated with any degree of precision. To establish such a canon of the relatively few dated icons is a logical first step to the dating of all the rest, and in Part III we give a brief sketch of one way in which this might eventually be done.

The study of icons, especially those of the Byzantine period, is still very much in its infancy. It is only very recently that more than a few isolated examples have become available, thanks to the remarkable discoveries in the monastery of St Catherine on Mount Sinai, and even when these are taken into consideration it still remains very hard to date them on purely stylistic criteria in view of the fact that, in any case after the sixth century, very firm rules governed the way in which the scenes and figures of the Christian faith were depicted, and the forms remained fixed throughout many centuries. It is even harder to attempt to distinguish the hands of individual painters, for once again the church authorities did not favour the type of personal expression that was to the fore in the West, and themes and styles, when once established, had to be reproduced exactly, regardless of the painter's views—if indeed he had any views other than a desire to follow the model as exactly as he could and to convey as much of the spiritual feeling of the original as was in his power. Nor has it proved possible, even in later times when the examples that survive become more numerous, to distinguish local schools with any very great exactitude; at best one can point to a few very sophisticated examples as works done in the capital or in one of the larger centres and call them 'metropolitan', as distinct from the clumsier and less accomplished works done elsewhere, which may be termed 'provincial'. But this gets one little further, for in any case from around the twelfth century work was done in practically every city, even every monastery and every larger village throughout the whole Byzantine world. At times, it is true, the subject matter of an icon may serve as a guide; certain saints were thus especially popular in certain towns or areas—the association of St Demetrius with Salonica affords a case in point—while certain subjects were particularly suited to certain communities, mounted saints being much favoured in the villages and obscure scenes in the monasteries. But further than this it is at present impossible to go, and even when terms of locality have been used, as by Professor Gabriel Millet when he distinguished the Macedonian and the Cretan schools, the distinction is a very unreliable one and has little real meaning.

Nevertheless, from about the fourteenth century onwards Greek, Yugoslav, Bulgarian and Russian work does begin to develop along distinctive lines, though it still remains hard to be sure whether that done in Yugoslavia was Macedonian or Serbian and whether icons painted in the Greek world were done in the north or south of the country, or even in Asia Minor, where there were still large Greek communities around Smyrna (Izmir) and in the Pontic region inland of Trebizond. In Russia, on the other hand, rather more progress in this matter of the distinction of schools has been made, and each locality seems to have set a rather clearer hall-mark on its products. Soviet scholars have thus in recent years progressed quite a long way in the task of assigning icons to particular groups, and the schools of a number of major centres like Vladimir, Novgorod, Pskov or Moscow can now be recognized with comparative certainty, while the experts would also claim to distinguish icons painted in remoter centres such as Tver, Yaroslavl or Suzdal. Again, individuals in Russia were accorded greater freedom than elsewhere, and the hands of a number of outstanding masters can also be recognized, notably such men as Theophanes the Greek, Andrey Rublyov, Dionysy. If study progresses with the same rapidity and seriousness it should prove possible to come to more exact conclusions elsewhere, though it must be remembered that the Russian state was made up of a number of semi-independent regional capitals, each leading its own life, whereas the areas to the south were, till the thirteenth century, all under the direct control of a centralized empire, and that, even when that empire came to an end, power was still centralized in a few cities like Salonica in the Greek world or Ochrid in the southern Slav area, and culture was less widely distributed than in Russia.

It is, however, not so much with the distinction of schools or the determination of authorship that we are concerned here, as with the problems of dating. Icons which can be firmly dated either by an inscription or some similar form of evidence are few and far between, so that there is a serious lack of fixed points around which to group the undated panels. Our aim here is thus to list and discuss such icons as do fall into the dated category, and at the same time to note a few which can be fairly firmly dated on comparative grounds or on circumstantial evidence. Sometimes a comparison of an undated panel with a dated work in another medium such as a wall-painting may afford reasonably firm evidence; sometimes it is clear that all the icons of an iconostasis were by masters of the same school, even though only one or two of them are dated. In the main, however, the corpus has been restricted to those panels on which dates are actually inscribed. The final section of the book, however, deals with some undated icons, selected in order to illustrate the problem of dating, and suggests how such icons may be dated by means of stylistic comparisons.

The main body of the book is divided into two parts, the first devoted to the Byzantine world and to those areas which were at one time or another part of the empire, and the second part to Russia. In the first chapter those icons are considered which were produced within the confines of the empire ruled from Constantinople till its fall to the Turks in 1453. The second chapter is concerned with Macedonia and Serbia, where independent work began earlier than elsewhere outside the empire itself; the modern name of Yugoslavia has been used in view of the difficulty of distinguishing between the products of Macedonia and Serbia during the prosperous years of the later thirteenth, the fourteenth and the earlier fifteenth centuries. The story of icon painting in Bulgaria, which is covered in the third chapter, is less full because little material of any but a late date has been preserved there, and what there is is mostly of very inferior quality. Greek icons, notably those painted by Cretans, are dealt with in the fourth chapter, our account being restricted to work done after the fall of Constantinople owing to the diffi-

culty of determining what exactly was done in the capital and what in such sophisticated centres as Salonica before 1453. Finally, in the fifth chapter, the icons of Cyprus are considered. They tend to be of a rather diversified nature, for Western influence played an important role there; it resulted in the frequent inclusion of donor figures and dedicatory inscriptions on the icons, so that the amount of material available for study is quite considerable, and it has proved necessary to make a selection rather than to consider every possible example.

The Russian material, in many ways the most significant both as regards variety and artistic importance, forms the subject matter of Part II. It is more individual, more distinctive, and it is easier to draw a clear line between Russian work and that of Byzantium than it is in the case of Yugoslavia or Bulgaria. Moreover, as we have already noted, it was in Russia that the most clearly defined schools were developing, and though later painting in the south Slav world was sometimes influenced by that of Russia, on the whole comparisons between Russian paintings and those done elsewhere are not very helpful in problems of dating. Though Russian painting constitutes a very definite part of the Byzantine heritage, it also developed along individual and independent lines, to form a very important national art.

We are deeply indebted to the following friends, scholars and institutions for some suggestions, and more especially for the bulk of the illustrations assembled in this book: Dr Alice Bank, Mr J. Barber, Dr M. Chatzidakis, Professor Djurić, Mrs Christopher Harris, Professor V. N. Lazarev, Dr M. Ljubinković, Dr Milković-Pepek, Dr E. A. Nekrasova, Dr I. Nikolajević, Professor Radojćić and Mr J. Stuart; the Benaki and Byzantine Museums, Athens, the Hermitage Museum, Leningrad, the Institute of Byzantine Studies and the National Museum, Belgrade, the Instituto Ellenico di Studi Bizantini di Venezia, the Tretyakov Gallery, Moscow and the Fine Arts Museum, Yaroslavl.

I ST ANNE. By Emmanuel Tsane. Benaki Museum, Athens. 106 × 76 cm. 1637

A fine example of the late Greek School. St Anne holds the child Virgin on her left arm and supports its knees with her left hand. The pose is clearly based on that of a Virgin Hodegetria, and the general appearance of the theme is closely similar to a Madonna painting. The child, however, is shown virtually as the fully-grown Virgin on a small scale. She holds a flower in her right hand. Behind her is the inscription 'The hand of Emmanuel Tsane, the priest of Rethymo', and the date, 1637. Xyngopoulos, pl. 27.

II CHRIST, ARCHANGELS AND DONORS. Byzantium. 1356. See pl. 9.

III ST JOHN THE BAPTIST. Yugoslavia. 1644. See pl. 40.

Chapter One

Byzantium

IF TRADITION may be accepted, the story of icon painting in the early Christian world begins almost during the lifetime of Christ himself, for there is an old legend that St Luke the Evangelist was a painter and that he was responsible for executing a picture of the Virgin with the Child Christ held on her left arm while she points to Him with her right hand. It belongs to the iconographic type known as the Hodegetria or Indicator of the Way and has been reproduced over the ages in many thousands of examples in East and West alike. A number of panels, both in Italy and the Orthodox world, exist which are believed by the faithful to be the original works executed by St Luke. Three of these are in Greek territory, one in the monastery of Megaspelion in the Peloponnese, one at the monastery of Kykko in Cyprus and one, which was formerly in the monastery of Sumela near Trebizond: when the Greek population of that region was expelled in the early 1920s, it was taken to Greece and is now in a little monastery known as the new Sumela, in the hills south of Salonica. There are other panels in Italy, notably one in the Pantheon, one in the Lateran known as 'the painting made without hands', one in Santa Maria Maggiore, and another in the church of the Madonna di San Luca near Bologna.

All of these are regarded as especially sacred and all are very old, though it is not possible to be very sure about their actual date, for the faces have all been considerably repainted, and moreover, the greater part of each is covered by a metal mount which obscures most of the painting, so that it has so far proved impossible to study them seriously. It is, however, most unlikely that any of them is earlier than the sixth century; that in the Lateran was certainly there in the time of Pope Stephen I (752–7), and that near Bologna dates from before 1160, when it was apparently brought from Constantinople.[1] One panel of the type has however recently been cleaned and the heads of a Virgin and Child of early date have been disclosed from beneath layers of later overpainting. The panel too was known as the Madonna di San Luca. It belongs to the Church of Santa Francesca Romana (also sometimes known as Santa Maria Nova) at Rome. Whatever its dates it is certainly one of the earliest religious paintings that have come down to us. The heads of the Madonna and Child are painted on pieces

of canvas which were apparently cut from an earlier painting or paintings and were glued to the panel, probably in the thirteenth century, when the background and the costumes were added. The two heads, which are on separate pieces of canvas of different weaves, seem to have been conceived for a work or works on a larger scale than the present one: indeed they probably represented the vestiges of two separate paintings of identical style and by the same master. The style is distinctly Hellenistic, being similar to that of the most elegant of the wall-paintings in Santa Maria Antiqua at Rome, and to some extent on the basis of this evidence Professor Kitzinger has proposed a date in the seventh or the early eighth century,[2] but this is a very conservative estimate and a sixth-century date would seem quite possible. It is very unlikely that any other of the St Luke Madonnas are of an earlier date than this. Kitzinger indeed believes that most of them should be assigned to the seventh or early eighth century, which constituted in his view an especially important period in the story of icon painting. It was probably at this time that the production of individual panels as opposed to painting on walls really came into its own, both for the purpose of Bible figures and scenes, and to serve as cult objects, but the very icon-like character of some of the wall-paintings in the Catacombs, which are dated to the sixth century, would suggest that panels were popular at an earlier date than Kitzinger supposed.

A Hodegetria[3] in the encaustic technique originating from Sinai was preserved in the Theological Academy at Kiev[4] till the Revolution while more recently a number of other icons of high quality, where delicacy of treatment and beauty of conception are to the fore, have been discovered in comparatively large numbers in the monastery of St Catherine on Mount Sinai, where there is preserved a very remarkable collection dating from the earliest times right down to the present day. Two of the finest of the early ones may be noted even though they are not firmly dated. One depicting the Virgin and Child between saints with two very Hellenistic-looking angels behind, is dated by Professor Weitzmann to the sixth, and the other of St Peter,[5] to the seventh century. He would attribute both to a workshop in Constantinople, whereas the Santa Francesca panel was more probably

IV ST GEORGE. Bulgaria. 1667. See pl. 49.
V THE ANASTASIS. Cyprus. 1563. See pl. 76.

painted in Rome. The Sinai icons are executed in the encaustic technique, where wax was used as the medium, manipulated if necessary with a hot rod. It was derived from the mummy portraits of Egypt, and was especially common at this time, though it seems to have ceded its popularity to egg tempera soon after.

Unfortunately there are no early icons at Sinai that can be exactly dated, but Professor Weitzmann has worked out what seems to be a very satisfactory chronological sequence, and he assigns an icon of the Three Hebrews in the Fiery Furnace[6] to the seventh century and a Crucifixion, which is in a less elegant style than the St Peter, to the eighth century. The latter must, he thinks, have been painted in Jerusalem where a school continued in existence in spite of the Moslem domination established in the later seventh century; the ban on figural representation which we know as Iconoclasm, which was in force from 726 till 843 at Constantinople, would not of course have affected Christians living in Moslem territory.

Though no panels that are actually dated thus survive from these early centuries, attention may be drawn to a wall painting (*pl. 1*) in the catacomb of Commodilla at Rome for it simulates a panel exactly, even to the inclusion of a painted frame. It is firmly dated by an inscription to 528 and depicts the Virgin and Child enthroned, between St Adauctus and St Felix, together with the donatrix who is called the widow Turtura. Though painted on the wall, it has to all intents and purposes the character of a panel even if it is immovable, and it may thus qualify for inclusion as the earliest example in our dated icons. It also supports the suggestion made above that panel painting was already well developed in the sixth century and was not necessarily an innovation of the seventh as Kitzinger suggests.

In the Byzantine world proper, that is to say, the area embraced by the Eastern empire, the story of icon painting falls automatically into two phases, that until about 730, when the Iconoclast ban on the reproduction of the saintly or divine form in art was imposed, and that after 843, when figural art was once more permitted; from then on development was continuous and progressive till the Turkish conquest of the mid-fifteenth century. At first the panels were primarily illustrative, their purpose being to depict the principal figures of the faith or the main scenes from the Bible story, for the edification and guidance of the faithful. But as time went on a tendency grew up to treat the icon as something more than a mere picture, first as a vehicle through which the divinity might be approached, and then as a cult object which itself had divine or miraculous power. It was here, according to the views of the purists, that danger lay in store. The frequent references to idolatry in the Old Testament point to the underlying love of image worship, and it would seem that these feelings had become especially acute early in the eighth century

when the Iconoclast ban was imposed. Those who forced it through were extremists, like the Puritans of the seventeenth century, but the movement that inspired them was widespread and it is interesting to note that at much the same date a similar attitude was adopted throughout Islam. There all representation in religious art was forbidden and the ban was to remain in force for all time; in the Byzantine world it was only firmly enforced for brief periods in the eighth and ninth centuries and in 843 was repealed, never to be reintroduced.

After 843, though the narrative aspect grew in importance as time passed, the icon took on a more definite character as a vehicle through which Christ, the Virgin or a particular Saint could be approached. Prayers were not made to the icon, but through its medium to the figure it depicted. The icon was sacred not in itself, like an idol, but as the representation of a sacred personage or because it depicted a religious theme. It could, however, not only help the worshipper in his intercession but could also aid a whole community, as happened more than once when a particularly famous icon of the Virgin was paraded round the walls of Constantinople at a time of stress, as for example when the city was beset by Arab or Russian attackers. It was not really believed that it was the icon that came to the city's aid and helped to disperse the attackers, but rather the Virgin herself, whose support was enlisted through the medium of the icon.

It may well be that the end of the Iconoclast movement brought in its wake excesses of adoration, just as Iconoclasm itself had brought a senseless destruction of all figural art; most significant was the wholesale elimination of all Iconoclast literature while the non-figural church decorations that had been set up during Iconoclasm, notably large, plain crosses in the apses of the churches, like that which still survives in the Church of St Irene at Constantinople, were replaced by figural themes. And on the less material side there can be no doubt that during the so-called Second Golden Age of Byzantine Art, which began in 843, stress on the spiritual and mystic nature of art increased considerably, and one of the forms the change took was to set greater value not only on ornate church decorations in paint or mosaic, but also on portable works which could be kept in the home or taken on journeys, and were readily available elsewhere than in the church. In the tenth and eleventh centuries we probably know such things best through the ivories of which, for some unknown reason, a comparatively large number of examples of that date have been preserved. In the mid-eleventh century, if the number of examples that survive is to be taken as a guide, the ivories began to cede place to some extent to enamels and works in metal. These, in so far as they depict figures of the saints or scenes from the Gospel story, are really icons, though the word has in general come to be applied more narrowly to refer only to painted panels, and that is the meaning given to the term here. Even the portable mosaics which became popular with the twelfth century tend to be grouped together under the heading of 'the sumptuous arts', because of their technique, rather than with the paintings, to which they are closely allied stylistically and as regards their subject-matter and purpose.

Whether it is to be attributed to a love of rich materials like ivory or precious metal in an age when luxuries were abundant or merely to the vicissitudes of fate and the destructions of time, there are today very few painted icons that can be assigned to the later ninth, the tenth and the eleventh centuries. Indeed virtually the only examples that we have are preserved in the monastery of St Catherine on Mount Sinai, and in their publications devoted to these icons Professors Weitzmann and Sotiriou have been able to attribute only three or four to this age. The most beautiful of them is a quadripartite icon depicting two seated Apostles above and four standing saints, two on each side, below, which is figured by Sotiriou[7] as a whole, while Weitzmann gives a coloured plate of one of the seated Apostles only, namely Thaddaeus.[8]

In general it would seem that the icons of this age were closely allied to the miniature paintings. Towards the end of the tenth century, however, Weitzmann notes a hardening of the style and a growing love of brilliant colouring, which he thinks may have been brought about through the inspiration of enamels. A similar influence seems to have been exercised by the sumptuous arts throughout the first half of the eleventh century, but so far as can be judged from the few paintings that remain, it would seem that thereafter the figures became slenderer and more elongated and the colours more subtle. The former factors indeed also serve to distinguish the ivories of this age from those produced in the tenth century. Weitzmann illustrates an elegant figure of St Philip and a very lovely icon of the Crucifixion as typical of this phase;[9] the medallions of saints around the borders of the latter bear out his comparison with enamels, but the figures of Christ, St John and the Virgin are imbued with a spiritual beauty which is something very distinctive, and is only to be met with in a painting of high quality. In a more prosaic way an icon depicting Sts Procopios, Demetrius and Nestor, which is reproduced by Sotiriou,[10] serves to illustrate the same approach.

A rather more monumental manner is to the fore in a great portative mosaic (*pl. 2*) which there is good evidence for dating to shortly before 1067. It is now in the church of the Patriarchate at Constantinople, but was taken there from St Mary Pammakaristos which was used as the Patriarchal Church till 1586. The icon was almost certainly made for this church when it was redecorated by John Comnenos and Anna Dalassena at

that time. It is made up of comparatively large cubes set in plaster, but is probably the earliest portative mosaic that has come down to us; later on very small mosaics, with tiny cubes set in wax, were to become very popular as the medium used for the more precious icons.

Though it can be dated only on the basis of stylistic comparison, attention may be called to another panel that is figured both by Sotiriou and by Weitzmann.[11] It is in a very different style and treats its subject, the Nativity, in a wholly narrative manner. The principal theme, the Birth itself, is accompanied by a number of subsidiary incidents, and it must have been inspired by a Gospel book in which numerous scenes from the Nativity were illustrated. There is an almost dramatic feeling for description, which contrasts quite markedly with the more restrained, more ethereal character of the icon of the Crucifixion. The two styles were to be developed independently throughout the twelfth century, the one leading to an elegant, though rather severe, linear manner, the other to a love of expressive, vivid interpretation. The former approach characterizes an icon of the Virgin and Child with figures of the Prophets on the margins illustrated by Sotiriou,[12] the latter by a tripartite icon, also reproduced by Sotiriou,[13] with the Nativity above and the Entry into Jerusalem and the Crucifixion side by side below. Neither of these panels can be definitely dated, but attention is drawn to them here because they serve to illustrate two opposing trends in icon painting which can be distinguished from this time onwards. As time went on the former manner tended to become set and perhaps over-conservative, the latter to swing too much towards the expression of emotion, though it became, thanks perhaps to the intrusion of some Western influence, the style that was dominant throughout all the Byzantine world shortly before the year 1200.

Professor Weitzmann calls attention to the development of this more dramatic style in some of the Sinai icons, notably two sections of a beam on which the Twelve Feasts were painted; he dates them on a stylistic basis to soon after 1190. Selecting two of the scenes to illustrate this style, he compares them to wall paintings at Kurbinovo in Macedonia and Lagoudhera in Cyprus, dated respectively to 1191 and 1192. These scenes depict the Anastasis (*pl. 3*) and the Ascension and are typical of the vigorous if rather crude style which was apparently to the fore at this time. He cites as an early example in the same manner an icon of the Annunciation[14] which he assigns to Constantinople, though its style is quite distinct from that of the court school that was to the fore earlier in the twelfth century.

These beams constitute a new discovery in the story of icon painting, and since Weitzmann wrote Dr Chatzidakis has discovered another, in the monastery of Vatopedi on Mount Athos.[15] They serve to show that the development of the iconostasis as an elaborate structure of several stages had already begun by the twelfth century. Large scale icons of Christ, the Virgin and the patron saint of the church had, since quite early times, been set up at the separation of the sanctuary and the nave and at a later date other registers were progressively added above, till the extreme towering structures so popular in Russia from the fifteenth century were reached. By the fourteenth, however, even in the Byzantine world a row of icons of small size depicting the principal events of Christ's life, the so-called festivals, was usually included and there was another row of larger panels known as the Deesis row, with the scene of the Deesis itself, Christ flanked by the Virgin and St John, at the centre and a varying number of archangels and apostles on either side. The painted beams from Sinai and Athos represent the first stage in the evolution of the register devoted to the festival icons. The beams stretched through the whole width of the iconostasis, and the scenes were depicted in a row upon them, one beside the other. Professor Sotiriou illustrates a number of the scenes on these beams and his plates serve to show that not all the scenes on a beam were necessarily done by the same hand. Some are in the sophisticated style of Constantinople, others are in the cruder, more dramatic manner we see in the Kurbinovo wall paintings.

Something of the same approach is to be found in a group of icons in which Dr Chatzidakis sees a good deal of Western influence. A Crucifixion on one face of a double-sided icon in the Byzantine Museum at Athens which he dates to the early thirteenth century may serve as an example;[16] there is a rather similar Crucifixion, also part of a double-sided icon, now in the Archbishop's Palace at Nicosia in Cyprus.[17] The likelihood of Western influence in these is borne out if they are compared with some panels which Professor Weitzmann has isolated and assigned to a distinct 'Crusading' school. Quite a number of examples of this group are to be found in the Sinai monastery and Professor Weitzmann thinks that the main centre of production was first at Jerusalem and later at Acre—similar work was also no doubt done in Cyprus. If he is correct a date between about 1100 and 1293, when the Crusaders were expelled from the Holy Land, is firmly established, the finest work in all probability being done in the twelfth century, before the community became unduly harassed. These paintings are in a curious hybrid style, French or Italian elements being marked, though the works are certainly to be described as icons rather than as paintings in the Western sense of the term. The painters were probably Frenchmen or Italians who had been indoctrinated in the Byzantine idiom, rather than Greeks who had been affected by Western ideas. Moreover, the iconic models were ready to hand in Palestine and Cyprus, whereas there can have been but few Western works there which could have influenced Greek masters; rather must one conclude that the Western elements remained indigenous

in the minds of Western painters who had settled in the *outre-mer*.

Contacts between Byzantium and the West were inevitably increased as a result of the Crusades, and the development of the Crusading school of icon painters was not the only effect that it produced, for in the opposite direction a rather similar hybrid style is to be seen in Italy in the work of such painters as the Pisani and Coppo di Marcovaldo. Byzantine ideas were no doubt brought back by the Crusaders, but the traffic was intensified as a result of the conquest of Constantinople by the Fourth Crusade in 1204 when so many Byzantine treasures were taken back to the West as loot.

Apart from this Crusading school, we still know but little about the icons of the twelfth century. A few examples in the Sinai monastery, most of them in the form of the Menologia or Martyria (calendars wholly given over to saintly portraits) have been assigned to the age by Professor Sotiriou[18] but they represent a rather specialized aspect of icon painting and as none is definitely dated they need not concern us here. Another painting regarding the date of which there is some circumstantial evidence, though it hardly enters into the category of the normal devotional icons, takes the form of a wooden reliquary with sliding cover; it is now in the Vatican though it was formerly in the Sancta Sanctorum at the Lateran. On the lid is the Crucifixion, while inside there are busts of Archangels above and the full-length figures of Sts Peter and Paul on either side of the incision where the relic itself was kept below. On the inner face of the lid is the figure of St John Chrysostom.[19] A comparison with the portrait of this saint in a famous manuscript in the Bibliothèque Nationale, the Homilies of St John Chrysostom (Coislin 79), suggests a rather later date than that of the manuscript (1078–81), while the rendering of the Crucifixion suggests one that is earlier than Nerez (1164). A date shortly before the middle of the twelfth century thus seems most likely for the reliquary.

Two other fine panels of the twelfth century can happily be dated more exactly. The earlier and more important is the famous icon now in the Tretyakov Gallery at Moscow known as 'Our Lady of Vladimir' (*pl. 5*). It was painted in Constantinople, almost certainly about 1130. From the artistic point of view it is of outstanding importance, for it is a truly great painting, certainly one of the finest Madonna paintings that the Christian world has produced. But it is also of great interest iconographically, for the type it represents is one that was previously extremely rare. It is known as 'Our Lady of Tenderness' (*Eleusa* in Greek; *Umileniye* in Russian) and represents the development of a new tendency towards humanism and intimacy in Byzantine art. Previously the poses most usually followed had been severe and formal, the most usual being that known as the Hodegetria or Indicator of the Way, where the Virgin holds the Child on one arm and points to Him with the other hand. Christ is here looked upon as a figure-head, symbol of the road to salvation, while the Virgin is impersonal, indeed almost aloof and divine rather than human. The character of the 'Virgin of Tenderness' represents a new outlook, more intimate and more human, and indicates a movement towards an idea that became prevalent at a later date, where the Virgin is looked upon as the epitome of loving motherhood rather than a mere symbol of the Christian faith. The Vladimir painting served as a model which was thereafter frequently reproduced over the whole Christian Orthodox world, Greek and Slav alike.

The second dated example (*pl. 4*), now at Spoleto in Italy, is a good deal less important from the artistic point of view for it has been much damaged. It too depicts the Virgin, but the pose is distinct, for the figure represents the Virgin of Supplication, in much the same pose that she occupies in the theme of the Deesis. Her right arm, covered by her maphorion, in a most clumsy manner, is stretched out holding a scroll. The whole of the blue maphorion must have been repainted, but the original painting is firmly dated to before 1185 when a certain Pietro Lifino brought it to Spoleto. It was said to have been presented to him by the Empress Irene. In so far as can be judged in view of the overpainting, the icon would seem to be a fairly conservative work, less fine than 'Our Lady of Vladimir', but nevertheless a product of a Constantinopolitan workshop.

In addition to these firmly dated panels there are a number of others that can be assigned to a late twelfth- or early thirteenth-century date, either on direct or on circumstantial evidence. Dr Chatzidakis notes an icon of St Peter in the Protaton at Karyes on Mount Athos which may be dated to around 1160. The apostle is shown frontally, the figure tall and elegant, with rather sloping shoulders, heralding the style which was to become dominant in the following century. Another icon, depicting St Panteleimon in the Lavra, is also noted by Chatzidakis.[20] It is more conservative and may well belong to the first half of the century—it bears some similarity to 'Our Lady of Vladimir', though it is more academic and lacks the sympathy of the Madonna painting. Attention may also be drawn to a fine icon of St Nicholas, with scenes from his life on the margins, in St Catherine's Monastery on Sinai, which is also probably dated to the twelfth century.[21]

There are several other icons on Sinai which may be attributed to the thirteenth century with reasonable certainty. Sotiriou cites some fifty of them,[22] one of the most interesting of which depicts Sts Sergius and Bacchus on horseback. The subject is a rare one and the icon is very decorative; the horses are suggestive of those that appear in Russian paintings of two or three centuries later, but Sotiriou's dating is probably to be accepted. Like many of the other icons which he dis-

cusses it is probably to be regarded as a local product.

In 1204 the Crusaders captured Constantinople and it would seem that painters fled the city and established themselves elsewhere in the same way that members of the aristocratic families founded minor empires at Nicaea, Trebizond and in Epirus. But the painters not only followed the Greek princes, but also went to work for Slav patrons in Serbia, Macedonia and Bulgaria. Few of the panels that survive can be associated with Greek patronage; one such is perhaps an icon (*pl. 6*) of the Virgin Orans now at Freising in Germany which can be dated to between 1235 and 1261 on the basis of an inscription on the metal mount. It is badly in need of cleaning and may have been to some degree overpainted, for the thin parallel high-lights beside the eye would suggest a rather later date. In addition to working for patrons of their own race, many Greek masters were at this time also employed by Bulgarian and Yugoslav patrons, and though very few actual panels are preserved, their character is indicated by wall paintings which seem virtually to have taken the place of icons in certain church decorations, where icons, complete with frames, are simulated on the walls. This tendency is especially conspicuous in Bulgaria where there are a number of paintings dating from throughout the thirteenth century; those at Boiana of 1259 are the finest. Although Constantinopolitan elements are present, the work here is to be classed as Bulgarian, and will be considered in a subsequent chapter. Attention, however, may be drawn to one actual icon of these years in the National Museum at Ochrid in Yugoslavia which is dated by an inscription in Greek on the reverse to 1262/63 (*pl. 20*). It depicts Christ and is perhaps to be counted as the work of a Greek master. The rendering is severe, resembling a mid-Byzantine mosaic of a pantocrator in the dome of a church. Behind the head, however, there is a halo in relief plaster work, something very unusual in the Byzantine world though it was to become common in Cyprus at a later date. Such haloes would seem to have been made in imitation of the metal ones of which there are some fine examples on other icons at Ochrid.

Another Yugoslav icon of this date, at Struga, depicts St George and also bears a long inscription in Greek giving the names of the donor and the painter, Ioannes, and the date 1266/67 (*pl. 21*). It is doubtless a local product, following a Greek model very closely. A number of other icons in Yugoslavia, notably a fine double-sided panel with the Virgin on one face and the Crucifixion on the other are more certainly to be attributed to Slav painters; they will be considered in a subsequent chapter.

Finer and more important than either of these are two other icons at Ochrid, both of them double-sided icons intended for use in processions, for they were mounted on poles for carrying. One (*pl. 7*) depicts

Christ on the obverse and the Crucifixion on the reverse, the other (*pl. 8*) the Virgin on the one face and the Annunciation on the other; both Christ and the Virgin have the special designation, 'Saviour of Souls'. There is evidence to suggest that the icons formed a pair, painted for a monastery in Constantinople dedicated to the Virgin, 'Saviour of Souls', which were presented by the Emperor Andronicos II Palaeologos (1282–1328). The emperor appointed Archbishop Gregory of Ochrid as guardian of the monastery, and in turn the archbishop employed a certain Galaction to administer it for him. Either he or the archbishop must have transferred the icons to Ochrid. Both are undoubtedly the products of a Constantinopolitan workshop, though that with the Virgin is the finer of the two—the scene of the Annunciation on the reverse is without question one of the greatest works of later Byzantine art that have come down to us. Both paintings exercised a considerable influence on the future development of painting in Yugoslavia. The icons are undoubtedly to be dated to the last decade of the thirteenth or the first decade of the fourteenth century; *c*. 1300 is as near as it is possible to go in exact figures.

With the dawn of the fourteenth century the picture changes, for very much more material of this age has been preserved. A phase of very active artistic production dawned in Constantinople, Greece and the Balkans around 1300 and it would seem that it was then that panel painting really came into its own as the most important art. Works in the sumptuous materials like ivory, enamel or precious metal were by then almost non-existent; perhaps they were too expensive; perhaps trade with the East was interrupted. But another very sumptuous art was developed at this time, that of miniature mosaic, where very tiny cubes were set in wax on a wooden panel. They began to replace the earlier portable mosaics of the eleventh and twelfth centuries where plaster was still used as the setting bed (see *pl. 2*), but it was not till the fourteenth that they began to be produced in large numbers. Iconographically and stylistically they are almost indistinguishable from the paintings, and the sketches for them, perhaps even the mosaics themselves, were no doubt made by the same men as the paintings.

Taken as a whole, the icons of this age are close in style to the wall paintings, and often it would appear that the same painters were responsible for working in both media. Thus Milković-Pepek has attributed some of the icons that were preserved in the Church of the Perebleptos (St Clement) at Ochrid in Macedonia to the painters Michael and Eutychios who signed the wall paintings in the same church. The frescoes are dated to 1295.[23] Intimate relationships between panels and manuscripts are less apparent at this time than they were in the Second Golden Age, perhaps because manuscripts of the Palaeologan period are less numerous,

but nevertheless the illustration of the Transfiguration in the Manuscript of John Cantacuzenos in the Bibliothèque Nationale (gr. 1243) is virtually an icon[24]—it is dated to between 1347 and 1355—while Sotiriou has compared an icon of Sts Peter and Paul in the Sinai Monastery to the illustrations of a manuscript at the same place (no. 152) which is dated to 1346.[25] The icon is in a rather miniature-like style, and it may even have been painted by the same hand as the illustrations to the manuscript. The tall figures, the flowing costumes and the expressive modelling, however, are all wholly Palaeologan, and also suggest a comparison with wall paintings of the most refined Constantinopolitan type, like those in the Pareclesion of the Church of the Chora (Kariye Camii) done shortly before 1320. Indeed there are quite a number of icons in this style which can be more or less exactly dated on the basis of comparison with wall paintings of the first half of the fourteenth century. One of the finest is a small panel bearing the Twelve Apostles—St Paul has taken the place of Judas— now in the Pushkin Museum at Moscow.[26] Other icons elsewhere could also be cited, for panels painted after about 1300 are to be found in quite a number of collections; in addition to those on Sinai and in Russia, work of this age is thus to be found in several collections in Greece, in the Balkans, in museums and galleries in Italy and even in a few collections in the West. And not only are panels more numerous, but also they are more frequently firmly dated, especially after about 1350.

One of the finest of the dated examples is a very unusual panel (*pl. 9*) now in Cyprus, though it is certainly to be regarded as the work of a Constantinopolitan painter. It is very tall and narrow and bears at the top a figure of Christ in a seated position, though there is no throne; below Him are the archangels Michael and Gabriel, below again a man and a woman, and at the bottom the full-length portrait of a girl, in whose memory the icon was painted. It is firmly dated to 1356. It is a work of great quality, by an accomplished master, and is of special interest, partly because of the very lovely portrait of the girl and partly because the figure of Christ serves as a key to which a number of undated icons may be compared for purposes of dating.

Next in date is a panel (*pl. 10*) of Christ in the Hermitage at Leningrad, with the portraits of two donors on the margin, and an inscription which gives their names as the Grand Stratopedarch Alexios and the Grand Primicerion John. They lived to the north of Salonica in the region of the Struma and Nestor rivers and were the founders of a church dedicated to Christ Pantocrator, which probably formed a part of the monastery of the Pantocrator on Mount Athos. The icon was painted for it in 1363. Christ's face is rather more stylized than that of the Cyprus panel, and the highlights are treated with greater severity. Two icons that were shown at the exhibition of Byzantine art at Athens in 1964 may be compared; one is in the church of St Therapon on the Island of Mitilini and the other is in the monastery of the Pantocrator on Mount Athos.[27] The highlights on these are rather more profuse and neither of them is of quite such high quality as the Leningrad panel, though they should certainly be assigned to the same workshop and to much the same date.

A problem here arises as to whether this fine icon, which is certainly a very accomplished work in the metropolitan style, was painted in Constantinople or in Salonica, where a very flourishing school existed at this time. The very fact that the patrons for whom the Pantocrator icon was painted were from the Salonica area weighs in favour of an attribution to that city, though the style is metropolitan. It is impossible to be sure. But a double-sided icon which is no less fine is probably to be assigned to Salonica, for it came from the church of St Nicholas in that city. It was included in the Byzantine exhibition at Athens in 1964.[28] As it is not firmly dated it is not included among the illustrations here; we cite it to show the high quality of work done in Salonica at this time.

Next in date, for it was probably painted between 1375 and 1384, is one leaf (*pl. 11*) of a commemorative diptych in the monastery of the Transfiguration at the Meteora, which was also shown at the Athens exhibition in 1964 (no. 211); it too is perhaps to be attributed to Salonica. At the centre is depicted a full-length figure of the Virgin, with busts of saints on the margins. At the Virgin's feet is the minute figure of the donor, Maria Palaeologina, in an attitude of *proskynesis* (reverence); she is identified by an inscription above her. She was the daughter of Simon Urus Palaeologos and was married to Thomas Preljubović, Despot of Yannina in 1367; he was murdered in 1384, so that the icon must have been painted between those years; a date close to that of the marriage seems most likely. It was presented to the monastery because Maria's brother had been its second founder. A second version (*pl. 12*) of the whole diptych is now preserved at Quenca in Spain and on the other leaf is a tall figure of Christ, with the figure of Thomas Preljubović at His feet. Here both leaves are enclosed in a sumptuous bejewelled frame, so that much of the background is obscured. It is rich and grand but the Meteora panel would seem to be superior artistically—the portrait of Maria, though on a very small scale, is both expressive and beautiful.

Her portrait is also included among the figures of the Apostles on an icon (*pl. 13*) of the Incredulity of St Thomas, also in the monastery of the Transfiguration at the Meteora (Athens Exhibition, no. 193). In a recent study, P. Mijović suggests that the icon was offered not as an *ex-dono* but as an *ex-voto* in memory of Thomas Preljubović and that it should therefore be dated to 1385, rather than to a vaguer period between 1375 and 1384, like the reliquary.[29] Here Maria is depicted in

royal costume, and she stands just behind St Thomas, in close proximity to Christ; the conception is very different from that of the excessive humility of the donor on the reliquary and for that reason also one might assign the former icon to an earlier date than that of the Doubting Thomas. The background of this icon, with its elaborate architecture, is noteworthy in itself and useful for purposes of comparisons for dating, but the main interest of the panel lies in the extremely unusual inclusion of a living person in the illustration of a Biblical scene—one indeed of the most sacred, coming as it does from the Cycle of the Passion.[30]

Another icon that should probably be assigned to Salonica is one of the Virgin Portaitissa in the monastery of St Stephen at the Meteora, dated 1389, which is mentioned by several travellers, notably Porphyry Uspensky.[31] It appears to be a fairly conventional work, and in this it contrasts very markedly with another icon (*pl. 15*) that has been claimed for both Yugoslavia and Bulgaria, though a very good case has been made out for a Salonica origin.[32] It is the famous double-sided icon from Poganovo in Bulgaria, now the glory of the icon collection in Sofia. It is comparatively large and depicts on one face full-length figures of the Virgin and St John the Evangelist and on the other the so-called Miracle of Latomos. It is firmly dated to 1395, for it was presented in that year to the monastery of St John the Evangelist at Poganovo in memory of the Despot Constantine Dejanović by his daughter Helena, as is recorded in an inscription in Greek at the bottom; the fact that it is in Greek means little so far as origins are concerned, for Greek was still the universal ecclesiastical language. Though a Bulgarian by birth, Helena had married Manuel II Palaeologos so that she was at the time Empress of Byzantium. The monumental character of the figures is characteristic of the best Byzantine work of the time, for towards the end of the fourteenth century there seems to have been a move away from the more picturesque style that predominated in the first quarter of the century towards a more dignified, more classical, approach. The attribution of the icon to Salonica may be made on three separate grounds, probability, style and iconography. In the first place it is much more likely that the Empress of Byzantium would entrust an important commission of this type to a painter of known accomplishment working at an established centre, rather than to a local man. In the second place the brilliant colouring and fine drawing are quite distinct from what seems to have been usual in provincial work. Indeed, the style is truly metropolitan, and the treatment bears little relationship to that of the few icons that can without much doubt be claimed for Bulgaria. As regards iconography, the arguments in favour of Salonica are even more convincing, for the Miracle of Latomos is firmly connected with Salonica. Though there are variations of detail, the theme broadly reproduces that of the fifth-century mosaic in the church of Hosios David there, and must have been directly inspired by it. The story of the miracle, however, belongs to a later date, perhaps the twelfth century. It refers to the setting up of the mosaic; the craftsmen had been engaged on a portrayal of the Virgin in the apse, but one morning when they came to work they found that the figure had been miraculously changed to one of Christ. Though the scene is depicted in a wall painting of the twelfth century at Bačkovo in Bulgaria and in a varied form in one of the fourteenth century at Lesnovo in Yugoslavia, it is essentially connected with Salonica. The metropolitan character of the painting is even more marked if the figures of the Virgin and St John on the other face are taken into account. The former is taken in the pose usually adopted when she appears beside the cross in the Crucifixion scene; the lovely fourteenth-century panel from Salonica to which we have referred above may be compared. Indeed the poses of both figures resemble those of the subsidiary figures in the Crucifixion; the substitution of St John the Evangelist for the Baptist is to be accounted for by the fact that the Poganovo monastery was dedicated to the former.

However active the painters of fine icons may have been at Salonica, Constantinople nevertheless remained the main centre of high-class work, and it was to workshops there that a number of commissions came not only from local patrons—a charming icon of the archangel Michael now at Pisa may be cited as an example[33]— but also from overseas. Two such commissions came from Russia. One (*pl. 14*), a lovely panel of the Virgin, was painted for the Metropolitan Pimen who was in Constantinople on two occasions, once between 1379 and 1381 and again between 1388 and 1389; it seems most likely that the icon was ordered during the first visit. The second commission was made by a Russian called Afanasy, Abbot of the Vysotsky monastery, who went there in 1387 and purchased the cell there in which he died. In 1395 he sent his Russian monastery the ten icons he had ordered for it in Constantinople. Seven of these were of single figures, intended to adorn the Deesis row of the iconostasis in the Church of the Virgin's Conception in his monastery in Russia, and three were smaller ones showing scenes from our Lord's life. The seven larger ones survive (*pl. 16*), depicting respectively Christ, the Virgin, St John the Baptist, two archangels, St Peter and St Paul. The paintings exercised a considerable influence on Russian artists. They lack the full modelling and free handling of

earlier Palaeologan work and Lazarev has compared them to some icons produced at the time in Georgia by a painter called Manuel Eugenikos (working between 1384 and 1396), who came from Constantinople.[34] Kondakov also notes that a fourteenth-century Constantinopolitan icon of Christ was transferred from the Cathedral of the Dormition in the Kremlin at Moscow to Novgorod in 1476.[35]

Another important later Byzantine painting (*pl. 17*) forms part of the famous reliquary of Cardinal Bessarion (1405–72), which he presented to the Scuola della Carità in Venice in 1463; it is now in the Accademia. The reliquary is in three parts, an inner container, a metal mount, and a sliding lid, which takes the form of an icon of the Crucifixion, with, around the border, a number of scenes from the Passion. An inscription on the reliquary itself refers to the Empress Irene, who is to be identified as the niece of Michael IX Palaeologos (1295–1320). The inner reliquary is thus probably to be dated to the early fourteenth century, but the mount and the sliding cover must be later. Chatzidakis compares the style of the Crucifixion to that of the icon of Maria Palaeologina at the Meteora, which is dated to between 1367 and 1380, and this would suggest a date around 1370 for the Bessarion Crucifixion, but it is more probably later and it is even possible that the painting was done during the lifetime of the Cardinal, perhaps while he lived at Mistra in the year preceding the Turkish conquest; there was certainly a very active and advanced school of painting there, as we know from the wall-paintings of the church of the Pantanassa done in 1438. It has even been suggested that the work may have been done by a Greek master working in Venice.

The last icon that we illustrate as Byzantine is one of Christ (*pl. 18*) now preserved in the Church of San Giorgio dei Greci at Venice.[36] It was taken to Venice by the princess Anna Palaeologina from Constantinople shortly before the time of the Turkish conquest. It must have been painted towards the end of the first half of the fifteenth century, probably about 1440. The work is delicate, but clearly lacks the strength of that done in the fourteenth century, and it already represents the decline of the Palaeologan style. In his catalogue of the Venice collection Dr Chatzidakis suggests that three other icons there, a second one of Christ and two of the Virgin, one fairly large and another rather small and partly obscured by a later metal mount, formed part of the same presentation, though the icons only came to San Giorgio at a rather later date.

5　　　6

7a　　7b

8a

8b

9

17

1 Simulated icon
*The Madonna enthroned between St Felix and St Adauctus,
with the donor, the widow Turtura*
Catacomb of Commodilla, Rome.
528

Few panels of as early a date as the sixth century survive,
but the fact that they must once have existed is borne
out by the presence of wall-paintings which clearly
represent panels, even to the inclusion of simulated
frames. The example in the catacomb of Commodilla
is especially interesting because it includes the portrait
of the woman in whose memory it was set up. Her costume is of the same purple colour as that of the enthroned Virgin, though she wears black shoes whereas
those of the Virgin are red. She holds a scroll, symbol
of the Holy Scripture. The long inscription is in verse
in her praise. The two saints are approximately of
natural size. St Adauctus has his hand on Turtura's
shoulder.

The painting was at one time loosely dated to the
sixth century, but subsequently a second inscription
bearing the exact date, 528, was discovered on Turtura's
actual tomb; her age at death was sixty years.

The painting has been quite frequently reproduced; see for
example S. Bettini, *Frühchristliche Malerei*, Vienna, 1942, pl. 71.
The basic publication is J. Wilpert, *Die Römischen Mosaiken und
Malereien der Kirchlichen Bauten Roms*, Freiburg, 1917, Vol. II, p. 938
and Vol. IV, pl. 136.

2 Portative mosaic
The Virgin and Child
Church of the Patriarchate, Istanbul.
26.7 × 16.5 cm.
c. 1060

The pose is that customary for the Hodegetria, the
Virgin being shown half-length, with the Child on her
left arm; she points to Him with her right hand.

Technically the work is still closer to that of a wall
mosaic than to the manner developed later for the small
portable panels which became so popular in the fourteenth century. As regards iconography and treatment
there is nothing to distinguish the icon from a painted
panel of the same theme. The handling is severe and
formal, and is typical of the work of the Second Golden
Age, done around the middle of the eleventh century.

The fairly early date suggested by the style is borne
out by what is known of the history of the panel. It was
brought to the church of the Patriarchate from that of
St Mary Pammakaristos when the Patriarchate was
moved from the latter in 1586 on its conversion to
Islam, and there is reason to believe that the icon was
made for the church of St Mary as part of an endowment

made by John Comnenos and Anna Dalassena. The
exact date of the endowment is not known, but she died
in 1067, so that it must have been shortly before that.
A date around 1060 seems most probable for the icon,
though one might assign it to rather earlier in the
eleventh century on purely stylistic grounds. It is, in any
case, the earliest portable mosaic that has come down
to us.

G. Sotiriou, 'L'icône de la Pammakaristos trouvée dans l'église
du Patriarchat', *Practica of the Academy of Athens* (in Greek),
VIII, 1933, p. 359. A. M. Schneider, 'Byzanz: Vorarbeiten zur
Topographie und Archäologie der Stadt', *Istanbuler Forschungen*,
Vol. 8, Berlin, 1936, p. 41. D. Talbot Rice, *The Art of Byzantium*,
London, 1958, pl. 155.

3 The Anastasis
Detail of an Iconostasis Beam. Monastery of St Catherine,
Mount Sinai.
39 × 27 cm.
c. 1191

Four scenes from the Festival Cycle are painted in
succession on the beam, namely the Crucifixion, the
Anastasis (Descent into Hell), the Ascension and the
Dormition of the Virgin. The earlier scenes belonging
to the cycle, namely the Nativity, the Baptism, the
Transfiguration, the Raising of Lazarus and the Entry
into Jerusalem, are lost. The four scenes that survive,
though on the same beam, would not seem to be all by
the same hand, for the painter responsible for the
Anastasis, and also probably the Ascension, worked in a
very distinctive, essentially dynamic, manner. In the
Anastasis Christ is thus shown striding over the broken
gates of hell to raise up Adam from the dead; Eve waits
behind. The youthful Solomon and bearded David,
together with John the Baptist, stand at the side.

The dynamic style that we see here was developed in
the last decades of the twelfth century and work in this
manner is to be found not only in the Sinai monastery,
but also characterizes some important wall-paintings at
Kurbinovo and Kastoria in Macedonia and at Lagoudhera in Cyprus, the former firmly dated to 1191 and the
latter to 1192. It would seem that the style emanated
from Constantinople, and Professor Weitzmann regards
another icon in the Sinai monastery, depicting the
Annunciation, as a metropolitan product in the same
manner. The wall-paintings are more provincial. The
style was apparently fairly short-lived, so that the Sinai
beam may be dated fairly certainly to the last decade of
the century.

K. Weitzmann, in *Icons*, pl. 33. For the icon of the Annunciation
see his 'Eine spätkomnenische Verkündigungsikone der Sinai
und die zweite byzantinische Welle des 12. Jahrhunderts', in
Festschrift von Einem. Berlin, 1965.

25

4 The Virgin
Cathedral, Spoleto.
c. 1120

The Virgin is depicted half-length, turned towards the left. Her right arm is raised and from the hand is suspended a long scroll, bearing an inscription in Greek. It is only preserved in part, but what appears to be a duplicate is embossed on the later metal mount of the panel. It takes the form of a dialogue between the Virgin and Christ and may be translated as follows:

> Accept the prayer of thy mother, O most compassion-
> ate son.
> What dost thou ask, O mother?
> The salvation of mortals.
> That is not easy for me.
> Have pity, O my son.
> But only for the converted.
> Salvation is for all.
> I grant deliverance.
> I thank thee, O Word.

The Virgin's left hand is crossed over the right and rests on her shoulder. The pose, as it appears at present, is very clumsy and contrasts markedly with the delicacy of expression and the subtle modelling of the face, where the oval eyes, the long nose and the sad, tender features attest the best Byzantine work; indeed, it would seem that the clumsiness of the rendering of the arms must be attributed to a repainting, and as the sleeve is one with the maphorion, this must have affected the whole of the Virgin's costume.

The panel is known locally as 'The Madonna of St Luke'. Happily its history can be fairly exactly reconstructed. It was presented to Spoleto in 1185 by Barbarossa, to whom it came through a certain Petraliphas or Pietrus di Alphila, who went to the Byzantine world as a Crusader at the end of the eleventh century along with Robert Guiscard. After Guiscard's death in 1085 he transferred to the service of Alexios Comnenos (1081–1118). He is mentioned as being present at the signing of a treaty between Alexios and Bohemond at Durazzo in 1108. The icon was presented to him by the Empress Irene sometime after 1100; to judge by the style, a date early in the twelfth century would seem more likely than one in the eleventh.

The icon is now mounted in a metal reliquary of Gothic type, dating from 1396, and it was removed from this to permit a close study and the taking of a photograph for the colour plate published by Professor Mercati. In this study he compares the iconography to that of some later wall-paintings, notably those at Kastoria and Staro Nagoricino, as well as to that of a panel at the Meteora known as the 'Madonna Paraklesis'. A half-length rendering of the Virgin on an icon at Freising (no. 6), dated to between 1235 and 1261, may

also be compared. On the wall-paintings the Virgin is depicted full-length, and the same is true of some other examples of the iconographical type cited by Kondakov. This suggests that the Spoleto icon may at some time or another have been cut down; in any case it was once a good deal wider than it is now. The pose was adopted for a mosaic of the seventh or eighth century in the church of St Demetrius at Salonica, but there the Virgin is shown facing St Theodore (R. F. Hoddinott, *Early Byzantine Churches in Macedonia and Southern Serbia*, London, 1963, pl. 34). The prototype was, however, probably a panel which was preserved in the monastery of the Chalkopratea at Constantinople, and the Spoleto panel was no doubt a copy of this done for the Empress Irene. The type is distinguished as the Hagiosoritissa, but a similar pose was used when the Virgin was represented along with St John the Baptist as one of the figures constituting the theme of the Deesis or Prayer of Intercession before Christ.

S. G. Mercati, 'Sulla santissima Icone del Duomo di Spoleto', in *Spoletium*, Anno III, 1956. See also N. P. Kondakov, *Iconography of the Virgin* (in Russian), St Petersburg, 1914, Vol. II, pp. 294 ff.

5 The Virgin of Vladimir
Tretyakov Gallery, Moscow.
Total ht. 100 cm and w. 70 cm. The painted area 78 × 55 cm.
c. 1131

As it now hangs in the Tretyakov Gallery the icon takes the form of a rectangular panel with very wide margins which are slightly raised above the painted area. The actual painting depicts the Virgin half-length, holding the Child on her right arm, with His face pressed against hers in affection. The pose is that known as 'Our Lady of Tenderness' (*Eleusa* in Greek and *Umileniye* in Russian). It became especially popular after the twelfth century as a new feeling for humanism began to develop in Byzantine art. The pose was not unknown at an earlier date; it is followed, for example, on a Coptic ivory of the ninth century in the Walters Art Gallery at Baltimore (*Early Christian and Byzantine Art: An Exhibition held at the Baltimore Museum of Art*, 1947, no. 160) and on a panel of the eleventh century at Chopi in Georgia (N. P. Kondakov, *Iconography of the Virgin*, Vol. II, p. 267). The full transformation of the Eleusa type is not completely accomplished in the case of the Vladimir Virgin, however, for the Mother still points to the Child with her left hand, just as she did in the old Hodegetria pose, so indicating that the painting is not only one of the Mother and Child, but rather a representation of the divine power in human form, to which the Mother pays reverence. At a later date the attitude of reverence was abandoned for one where the Virgin is conceived as mother alone; an icon of about 1350 at Dečani in Yugoslavia may be cited as an example of the fully evolved form (see M. Corović-Ljubincović, 'Deux icônes de la Vierge du Monastère de Dečani', in *Starinar*, III–IV, Belgrade, 1952/53, p. 94).

On the reverse of the panel there is depicted an allegorical theme consisting of an altar with a cross above it. This was probably added when the icon was restored under the Metropolitan Photius at the end of the fourteenth or early in the fifteenth century. The wide margins were apparently added at the same time. Previously the painted area had been set in a magnificent jewelled frame, and throughout part of its existence the icon was also fitted with a metal mount or 'riza' which obscured all but the two faces and a few other details of the figures. The process of attaching and detaching these mounts was no doubt responsible for the fact that the gesso which overlaid the panel and above which the paint was applied became seriously damaged. It is recorded that when the Mongols captured Vladimir in 1237 the mount of precious metal was torn off regardless of the damage that might be caused to the painting. The frame and mount seem to have been renewed not only as a result of this particular disaster, but on several other occasions also.

Not all the paint that is now visible is of the same date. In 1919 the painting underwent a very careful examination in the restoration workshops, and the restorers were able to distinguish no less than six phases of repair. The more recent of these involved work done in the nineteenth, eighteenth and seventeenth centuries. Most of the Virgin's costume and the lower parts of the background were shown to date from the early sixteenth century and the upper parts of the background from the fourteenth or early fifteenth. Traces of repairs done in the thirteenth were also noted. As the icon stands today, only the faces of the two figures and a small area below the Child's neck represent the original work. As these areas were always visible, whatever the nature of the mounts, they were protected by countless layers of oil and varnish, which could be cleaned off very satisfactorily.

The various vicissitudes that the icon underwent during the course of its long history are comparatively well recorded, though there is one brief interval following a fire at the Cathedral of Vladimir in 1185 regarding which there is no record. In a recent study Dr Konrad Onasch has gone so far as to suggest that the original panel was actually destroyed in the fire and that the existing one is a copy done at that time. ('Die Ikone der Gottesmutter von Vladimir in der Staatlichen Tretjakov Galerie zu Moskau', in *Wissenschaftliche Zeitschrift der Martin-Luther-Universität*, Halle-Wittenberg, 1955.) His theory has not met with general acceptance, and indeed it conflicts with the very reliable evidence accumulated as a result of the technical examination made in 1919, when a small area of repaint, in a manner stylistically attributable to the thirteenth century was

distinguished. In fact it may be accepted that the earliest portions of the painting belong almost certainly to the original icon, painted at Constantinople in 1131.

It would seem that this panel and another of the same subject were both commissioned at the same time. The second one was known as the Pirogoshskaya Virgin because it was presented to a church of that name at Vyshgorod, near Kiev. The panel 'Our Lady of Vladimir' went either to Kiev or to Vyshgorod, whence it was taken in 1155 to Vladimir by the Grand Duke Andrey Bogolyubsky and set up in the Cathedral of the Assumption there. It took on the character of protectress of the city and apparently remained there in spite of the fire of 1185 and the sacking of the city by the Mongols in 1237, though on both occasions it no doubt underwent some damage. In 1395 Vasili, Grand Duke of Muscovy, sent to Vladimir for the icon, so that it might be carried into battle against Tamerlane. Tamerlane abandoned his advance, but although the danger had passed, the Grand Duke made no attempt to return the icon in spite of petitions by the people of Vladimir; instead he sent the painters Daniil Chorny and Andrey Rublyov to Vladimir to make a copy. The copy was retained at Vladimir and the original became the property of Moscow, where it soon became a sacred panoply of the city and was feted there on 23 June each year. In 1919 its role as a wonder-working icon came to an end, though its outstanding importance as a work of art came to be more fully recognized. Today the depth of feeling and the outstanding quality of the work mark the panel as perhaps the most profoundly spiritual and certainly as one of the most beautiful Madonna paintings that have come down to us.

A. J. Anisimov, 'Our Lady of Vladimir', *Seminarium Kondakovianum*, Prague, 1928. For a summary of references to the panel that occur in the Russian chronicles see I. Grabar, *On Early Russian Art*, Moscow, 1960 (in Russian), p. 41.

6 The Virgin Orans
Cathedral, Freising, Germany.
28 × 22 cm.
1235–61

The Virgin is shown half-length, facing towards her left, with her two hands before her in an attitude of prayer. The pose is that known as the Hagiosoritissa, and the icon may be compared in this respect to that at Spoleto (*pl. 4*). In the Freising example the margin and the upper part of the background are covered with a fine metal mount, in which enamel medallions are set, together with a dedicatory inscription which mentions the name of a certain Manuel Disykatos, who was Bishop of Salonica between 1235 and 1261. The date of the mount is thus firmly established within these limits, and there is reason to date the panel to the same period, for there is no suggestion that the mount has been re-used. The way in which the highlights are indicated on the painting, however, would at first glance suggest a rather later date, but this impression may well be due to a restoration done in the fourteenth century, or even when the panel was presented to the Cathedral in 1440. It is badly in need of cleaning, and not until this is done will it be possible to be sure of the date.

Byzantine Art—A European Art, Athens, 1965, no. 214. H. P. Gerhard, *The World of Icons*, London, 1970, pl. VIII. For a discussion of the iconography see S. der Nersessian, 'Two images of the Virgin', in *Dumbarton Oaks Papers*, no. 14, 1960, pp. 71 ff.

7a, Double-sided icon; obverse,
  b Christ the Saviour of Souls;
  reverse,
  the Crucifixion
From the church of the Perebleptos, Ochrid. Now in National Museum, Ochrid.
94.5 × 70.5 cm.
Between 1295 and 1318, but more probably *c.* 1310

Christ is shown half-length, His right hand raised in blessing, His left holding a copy of the Gospels with jewelled cover. The background is obscured by a silver mount decorated with a repeat pattern in low relief. There are raised medallions on the halo, and on the margins similar medallions alternate with figures of saints in rectangular frames. The mount would appear to be contemporary with the painting.

The Crucifixion is depicted rather formally, the body firm and erect, though the head sags. The figures of the Virgin and St John on either side are tall, but at the same time perhaps unduly massive, though they are well modelled. The background is gold above, with a structure like a wall below, reaching to the level of the shoulders of the two standing figures. On this side of the panel there is no metal mount.

Though clearly not by the same hand this icon forms a companion piece to one bearing the Virgin and the Annunciation (*pl. 8*). Both apparently belonged to a monastery at Constantinople dedicated to the Virgin, 'Saviour of Souls'. The Emperor Andronicos II Palaeologos (1282–1328) put the monastery under the charge of Gregory, Archbishop of Ochrid, and he apparently brought the icons to Ochrid or ordered his agent, Progonos Sgouros, to do so, soon after 1300. The Archbishop was responsible for various additions and embellishments to St Sophia in 1317 and Sgouros was the builder of the church of the Perebleptos.

The panel bearing Christ and the Crucifixion is not of quite so high a quality as that of the Virgin and the Annunciation, but it represents good metropolitan work none the less. Like the icon with the Virgin, it was a portative icon and traces of the pole on which it was carried survive at the base.

Djurić, pl. 15, p. 24. Radojčić, in *Icons*, pls. 179 and 173. Wulff and Alpatov, *Denkmäler der Ikonenmalerei*, Leipzig, 1925, p. 140. B. Filow, *Geschichte der Altbulgarischen Kunst*, Berlin-Leipzig, 1932, pl. 45. *Obverse: Photo Kažić.*

8a, Double-sided icon; obverse,
  b the Virgin and Child;
  reverse,
  the Annunciation
From the Church of the Perebleptos, Ochrid. Now in National Museum, Ochrid.
94.5 × 80.3 cm.
Between 1295 and 1318, but more probably *c.* 1310

The pose of the Virgin is that usual for the Hodegetria, but she bears the special designation, 'Saviour of Souls'. Both she and the Child are painted with very great delicacy. The background is entirely covered with a metal mount, adorned with a pattern in low relief, though there are medallions closely similar to those of the mount of the icon of Christ (*pl. 7*). If anything the work is rather more delicate.

The Annunciation is conceived in a very decorative manner, for the Virgin sits below an ornate baldachin, and behind the angel, who is just alighting, there is an elaborate architectural composition, which forms a sort of continuation of the baldachin. The shy diffidence of the Virgin's expression is admirably rendered and the whole scene is alive and expressive, though it is perhaps the brilliance and beauty of the colouring and the lovely balance of the composition that are most distinctive. The icon is undoubtedly one of the finest products of early fourteenth-century painting that have come down to us, and represents the metropolitan style of Constantinople at its height.

For the history of this panel see *pl. 7*.

Djurić, pl. 14. Radojčić, in *Icons*, the Virgin, pl. 159; the Annunciation, pls. 161, 163 and 165. *Reverse: Photo Hirmer.*

9 (Colour Plate II) Tall panel, bearing
  Christ, archangels and donors
From the Church of the Chrysaliniotissa, Nicosia, Cyprus. Now in the Archbishop's Palace at Nicosia.
252 × 43 cm.
1356

The panel is of very unusual shape, and though two more tall panels and fragments of another exist in Cyprus (see Rice, nos. 7, 8 and 9, and Pap., pl. 38), no parallel examples are known elsewhere. At the top of this panel there is a fine figure of Christ in the enthroned position, though curiously no throne is indicated. His feet rest on a cushion, and below this are two archangels standing confronted. Below again are two lay figures on a rather smaller scale, with an inscription between them. Below again is a full-length portrait of a very beautiful girl, who is commemorated in the inscription. It records her name as Maria and the date of her death as the year of Creation 6864, that is, 1356.

The figure of Christ is dignified, yet tender at the same time. The girl wears a red robe adorned with a diamond-shaped gold repeat pattern of fish set head to head in fours. It may be compared to that on the costume of one of the figures on the back of a tomb-niche in Kariye Camii at Constantinople (the Kariye painting is dated by Professor Paul Underwood to 'soon after 1300'. See *The Kariye Djami*, Pantheon Books, 1966, Vol. I, p. 292, and Vol. III, pls. 546 and 547).

Though the form of the panel is paralleled only in Cyprus, the painting is undoubtedly to be attributed to a metropolitan artist who no doubt stemmed from Constantinople. The other panels are rather less accomplished and might well have been done by a local follower of the Constantinopolitan master.

Rice, no. 6. Pap., p. 38. Chatzidakis, in *Icons*, pl. 70. *Published by permission of the Director of Antiquities and the Cyprus Museum.*

10 *Christ Pantocrator*, with the portraits of donors on the margins
Hermitage Museum, Leningrad.
100 × 79 cm.
1363

Christ is depicted half-length, His right hand raised in blessing, His left holding a bejewelled Gospel book. The painted area is hollowed out, leaving a margin, at the bottom of which there is on either side the portrait of a donor, accompanied by inscriptions which record their names and the date 1363. The portrait to the left is badly preserved, but the inscription is legible and gives the man's name as 'The servant of God Alexios the Grand Stratopedarch'. The portrait to the right is in better condition. The inscription identifies him as 'The servant of God the Grand Primicerion John'. The names of these men are recorded as the founders of a church dedicated to the Pantocrator; it was apparently attached to the Monastery of the Pantocrator on Mount Athos. There is a related icon of the same theme in the monastery, which was shown at the Byzantine exhibition in Athens in 1964 (no. 201) and there are similar panels at Mitilini (Athens Exhibition no. 200) and at Stockholm (no. 202). They are similar to the Leningrad icon in general, but are not so close as to warrant an attribution to the same painter.

A. V. Banck, *Byzantine Art in the Collections of the USSR*, Leningrad-Moscow, 1967, pls. 265–9. P. Lemerle, 'Sur la date d'une icône byzantine', in *Cahiers Archéologiques*, II, 1947, p. 129.

11 Leaf of a diptych;
The Virgin and Child, with the portrait of a donor and busts of saints on the margin
Monastery of the Transfiguration, The Meteora.
39 × 29.5 cm.
1367–84

The central portion of the panel is hollowed out, leaving a wide margin on which the busts of saints are depicted. The Virgin, holding the Child on her left arm, occupies the central panel, with below her, to her right, the portrait of a donor who is identified in the accompanying inscription as The Pious Queen Maria Angelina Dukaena Comnena Palaeologina. She was, in fact, the daughter of Simon Urus Palaeologos, and was married to Thomas Preljubović in 1359. He became Despot of Yannina in 1367, and was murdered in 1384. Maria presented the diptych, on the other leaf of which Christ was depicted with Thomas at His feet, to the monastery of the Transfiguration because her brother John Joseph was the Second Founder of the monastery. The other leaf has perished.

The saints along the upper margin are Theodore Tyro, Theodore Stratelates, Anne and Procopios, and on the lower border Pelagia, Cosmas, Damian and Panteleimon. On the left margin are Sts Artemios, Eustratios, and Barbara; on the right Nicholas, Gourios and Samonas. Below each of them there is a small rectangular cavity where a relic of the saint was originally deposited. The cavities were once covered over by the canvas which overlaid the gesso of the whole surface.

There is a more ornate version of this diptych at Quenca in Spain; see pl. 12.

Byzantine Art—A European Art, Athens, 1964, no. 211.

12 Diptych, bearing *Christ* on one leaf and *the Virgin* on the other, together with donor portraits
Treasury of Quenca Cathedral, Spain.
Each leaf 38.5 × 27.5 cm.
1367–84

Christ is depicted full-length, His right hand raised in blessing, His left holding a Gospel book. At His feet, on a very small scale, is the portrait of Thomas Preljubović, who is identified in a fragmentary inscription. The figure of the Virgin on the other leaf is virtually identical with that on the leaf at the Meteora (*pl. 11*). In fact the two diptychs seem to be duplicates one of the other, except that in this case the entire background is adorned with a metal mount with pattern in relief and with numerous precious stones set on it in cabochon mounts. The margins bear the busts of saints. On the panel with Christ they represent at the top the Apostles Andrew, Luke, Thomas and Bartholomew and at the bottom

Sts Lawrence, Stephen the Elder, Stephen the Younger and Theodore Sykeotes. On the left margin is the sainted bishop John the Almsgiver, together with Sts Spyridon and Eleutherios; on the right are Sts Blaise, Antiphas, and Paul the Confessor. The Saints who frame the figure of the Virgin are the same as those on the Meteora panel.

Though the metal mount is both fine and precious, the actual painting here would seem to be rather more dry and stylized. There were similar small compartments for relics on these panels to those on the Meteora one.

Byzantine Art—A European Art, no. 212. Radojčić in *Icons*, pls. 196 and 197. See also his *Icônes*, pls. 50 and 51. *Photo Mas.*

13 The Incredulity of St Thomas
Monastery of the Transfiguration, the Meteora.
38 × 31.8 cm.
c. 1385

The painted area is hollowed out, leaving quite a wide margin. Christ stands at the centre, bending forward to bare His side. Behind Him is the closed door of quite an elaborate building. Five Apostles stand to His left and there are five more to His right, together with two other individuals, one of whom is probably to be identified as Thomas Preljubović and the other as his consort, Princess Maria (*see pls. 11 and 12*). She stands in the forefront behind St Thomas, wearing a rich imperial robe, with crown and veil. Her husband stands at the back so that only his head is visible. The architecture of the background is very elaborate and the tower-like building to Christ's left, with a figure standing on its roof, is unusual. But even more exceptional is the inclusion of two mortal figures as participants in a scene of especially sacred character.

In a recent article P. Mijović suggests that the icon was offered to the monastery as an *ex-voto* in memory of Thomas Preljubović; if he is correct its date would be after his death in 1384. The work is of very high quality, and the portrait of the Queen, though on a very small scale, is quite excellent.

Byzantine Art—A European Art, no. 193. A. Xyngopoulos, in *Deltion of the Christian Archaeological Society*, 1964 (in Greek). P. Mijović, 'Les icônes avec les portraits de Toma Preljubović et de Marie Paleologina', in *Recherches sur l'Art*, 2, Belgrade, 1966 (in Serbo-Croat, with a brief summary in French).

14 The Virgin of Pimen
Tretyakov Gallery, Moscow.
76.5 × 62.5 cm.
1379–81

The type is that of the Hodegetria and the Virgin is depicted half-length, with the Child on her left arm. The panel is slightly hollowed and the margin is wide.

The work is typical of the best that was done in Constantinople at the time. According to what seems to be a well-established tradition the icon was brought from there to Russia by the Metropolitan Pimen. He was in the Byzantine capital on two occasions, from 1379 till 1381 and again in 1388 and 1389. Professor Lazarev is of the opinion that the icon was probably commissioned during the earlier visit.

V. N. Lazarev, *Byzantine Painting*, Moscow, 1971 (in Russian), p. 340. *Catalogue of the Tretyakov Gallery*, no. 327, p. 374. D. Talbot Rice, *The Art of Byzantium*, 1958, pl. XLIV.

15 Double-sided icon; obverse,
the Virgin and St John the Evangelist;
reverse,
the Miracle of Latomos
From the monastery of Poganovo. Now in the Icon Museum, Sofia.
89 × 60 cm.
1395

The Virgin is shown full-length, in a pose similar to that which she normally occupies in the Crucifixion scene. She has the special title 'Katafigi', 'Virgin of Refuge'. St John, though it is the Evangelist who is depicted and not the Baptist, also resembles the portrayal of the latter figure in a Crucifixion. The Evangelist was no doubt chosen in this case because the monastery of Poganovo, for which the icon was painted, was dedicated to him.

The composition of the Miracle of Latomos on the reverse is complicated. At the top is a large 'Glory', made up of seven concentric circles of various colours. At its centre sits the Christ Emmanuel, holding a scroll on which is inscribed the text of Isaiah xxv, 9. The 'Glory' is supported by the emblems of the four Evangelists. Below this is a mountainous landscape, with below again a lake, with fish swimming in it. On either side is a figure; they appear to represent Ezekiel as an old and Habakuk as a young man.

Though there are variations, the theme on the reverse is in essence the same as that depicted in the well-known fifth-century mosaic in the church of Hosios David at Salonica. The scene there is the so-called Vision of Ezekiel, and the title, Miracle of Latomos, was apparently devised at a later date to explain a legend according to which the mosaicists who worked at Hosios David had set out to represent the Virgin, but when they returned to work in the morning they found that the central figure had been miraculously transformed into one of Christ.

The icon was commissioned by the Empress Helena, wife of Manuel II Palaeologos, as is indicated in an inscription in red letters between the two figures on the obverse. She was the daughter of the Despot Constantine Dejanović, and the icon was presented to the monastery in his memory in 1395. The style is metropolitan but it seems likely that it was done by a master from Salonica.

K. Miatev in *Icons*, pls. 102 and 103. S. Bossilkov, *Twelve Icons from Bulgaria*, Sofia, 1966, p. 6. S. Radojčić, in *Icons*, pls. 58 and 59. T. Gerasimov, 'L'Icône bilaterale de Poganovo au musée archéologique de Sofia', and A. Grabar, 'A propos d'une Icône byzantine du XIV siècle', both in *Cahiers Archéologiques*, X, 1959, pp. 279 and 289 respectively.

16 The Vysotsky Chin
From the monastery of Vysotsky, near Chudov, in Russia. Now in the Tretyakov Gallery, Moscow.
Each panel 150 × 98 cm.
c. 1390

Seven panels that formed the so-called Deesis row of the iconostasis now survive. They represent Christ, the Virgin, St John the Baptist, St Peter, St Paul and the Archangels Michael and Gabriel (four of whom are shown here). The whole series was apparently commissioned in Constantinople around 1387 by a Russian called Afanasy, abbot of the monastery. All are by the same painter. They were taken back to Russia and presented to the Vysotsky monastery in 1395. Certain additions, notably the lettering, were made in Russia at a subsequent date, but apart from these the panels represent the best Constantinopolitan work of the period. The style is close to that of the Virgin of Pimen (*pl. 14*).

V. N. Lazarev, 'New monuments of Byzantine painting of the XIV century', in *Vyzantysky Vremenik*, IV, 1951, p. 122 (in Russian). See also his *Storia della Pittura Bizantina*, Torino, 1967, p. 378 and figs. 537 and 538.

17 Cover of the Reliquary of Cardinal Bessarion; the Crucifixion
Accademia, Venice.
47 × 32 cm.
c. 1450

The reliquary is in several parts, consisting of an inner compartment of enamel to hold the relic, a border framing it, bearing three scenes on each side and one at the bottom, and a cover which slides into a groove in the border. The whole is upheld on a jewelled metal support. The cover, on which the Crucifixion is depicted, is virtually an icon, and is not necessarily of the same date as the rest, though its painting is similar in style to that of the scenes on the border. These depict the Betrayal, the Mocking of Christ, the Scourging, the Carrying of the Cross, the Deposition, and the Entombment.

The Crucifixion is shown very fully, with four women to Christ's right and a group of seven Apostles to His left; below three men cast lots for His garments. Behind the figures, and rising to the level of Christ's waist, is an architectural composition. The sky above is obscured by a metal cover, though there are spaces in this for the cross itself and for the figure of an angel on either side. The figures themselves are thin and elongated and are in a style which heralds that of work of the Cretan school; it has even been suggested that the painting was done by a Cretan master. This may or may not be so, but the cover is in any case later than the actual reliquary within, on which there is an inscription stating that it was made for the Empress Irene, who must be identified as the niece of Michael IX Palaeologos (1295–1320). The metal support was apparently added in 1463, when the reliquary was presented to the Scuola della Carità at Venice by Cardinal Bessarion (1403–72). The sliding cover with the Crucifixion must be earlier than 1463; a date around the middle of the fifteenth century seems probable.

Chatzidakis, in *Icons*, pl. 76. A. Frolow, *La relique de la Vraie Croix*, Paris, 1961, p. 563. V. N. Lazarev, *Storia della Pittura Bizantina*, p. 408 and fig. 576.

18 Christ Pantocrator, surrounded by busts of Saints
In the Collection of San Giorgio dei Greci, Venice.
110 × 70 cm.
c. 1440

Christ is depicted half-length, His right hand raised in blessing, His left holding a Gospel book on His knee, open at the text of John III, 6. This area is slightly hollowed, leaving a fairly wide margin, on which there are on each side the busts of eight saints, nearly all of whom hold books open at appropriate texts. They comprise the Twelve Apostles and four Prophets. To the left, reading downwards, they depict St Peter, St John the Evangelist, St Mark, St Andrew, an unidentified Prophet with accompanying text from Jude 15, apparently St Philip and an unidentified Prophet. To the right are St Paul, St Matthew, St Luke, St Bartholomew, St James, apparently St Thomas, a Prophet and another unidentified Prophet.

Christ's face is tender and compassionate, but the work is rather weaker than the best done at Constantinople. The icon is nevertheless probably Byzantine, and Dr Chatzidakis suggests that it follows a slightly earlier Constantinopolitan model fairly closely. The Christ on the Vysotsky Chin (*pl. 16*, of *c.* 1390) may be compared. The icon at Venice was presented by a noble lady called Anna Palaeologina, daughter of the Grand Duke Lukas Notaras. She fled to Venice from Constantinople with two sisters shortly before the Byzantine capital fell to the Turks, bringing with her a number of treasures which included this icon and another rather similar one. If the panel was commissioned as well as owned by her, a date shortly before the middle of the fifteenth century is likely.

Venice, no. 1.

Chapter Two

Yugoslavia

THE STORY of icon painting in the Orthodox parts of what is today Yugoslavia, notably the provinces of Macedonia and Serbia, is complicated by the fact that many of the paintings were actually the work of Greeks, either imports from Constantinople or Salonica made before those cities fell to the Turks, or painted in the Slav lands themselves by Greek painters who were travelling or had even settled there, to work under the patronage of Slav notables. In earlier times most of these men came from Salonica; at a later date schools peopled by Greeks working in the so-called Italo-Cretan style were established along the Adriatic coast, more especially at Kotor and Dubrovnik. Their works were imported into the purely Orthodox areas to the east and were even made use of in the Catholic churches of the coastal fringe. The books that have appeared in recent years in Yugoslavia itself, many of them admirable and extremely useful, have unfortunately tended to claim all these icons as Macedonian or Serbian, simply because they have been preserved throughout the ages in churches in those areas, and little attempt has been made to define in concrete terms the features that characterize the work done by Slavs in contrast to that done by Greeks, or in any case by those Greeks who continued to work in a conservative style. Here our object is a distinct though perhaps less ambitious one, namely to concentrate our enquiry on the consideration of those icons that truly belong to the area and that can be firmly dated, leaving those like the famous panels from Ochrid bearing Christ the Saviour of Souls on one side and the Crucifixion on the other or that with the Virgin on one face and the Annunciation on the other, to be dealt with under the heading 'Byzantium' (*see pls. 8 a and b*) for there is every reason to believe that they were imports from Constantinople.

The problem is further complicated by the fact that it is not easy to determine which parts of the area comprised today within the provinces known as Macedonia and Serbia should, in the thirteenth and fourteenth centuries, be regarded as true ethnic entities, boasting independent artistic styles of their own. In the tenth and early eleventh centuries most of Macedonia formed a part of the Bulgarian state and Ochrid was Tsar Samuel's capital from around 976 till his death in 1014. The whole area formed an integral part of the Byzantine empire

from then till about 1170, and much of Macedonia again came under Bulgarian control thereafter till 1230— it has indeed been claimed once more by Bulgaria in very recent years. From 1282 it formed a part of King Milutin's Greater Serbia, and even then, though the majority of the inhabitants were Slavs, there were still many Greeks in the area. Even before Constantinople fell before the attack of the Fourth Crusade in 1204, Greek painters seem to have taken up residence in Serbia, where they worked under the patronage of the Nemanja families, and their number probably increased as a result of the arrival of immigrants from Constantinople when the city fell to the Latins. In the fourteenth century very close cultural contacts bound Macedonia to Salonica, which was still the second city of the Byzantine empire. Painters trained there worked in the Slav areas of Macedonia and Serbia as well as in Greece; wall paintings done just before 1300 at Ochrid have been claimed for Greek masters while those in the Protaton at Karyes on Mount Athos and in some of the monasteries there have similarly been attributed to Slav painters. The one thing that is really certain is that painters and styles travelled very freely, and that work was done alike for Greek and Slav patrons by the same men. In any case till well on in the fourteenth century the Greek language was freely used for inscriptions whatever was the native tongue of the painters in much the same way that Latin was universally used by medieval artists in the West. And, to add to the confusion so far as we are concerned here, icons themselves could be transported quite easily and panels which were painted in one place often found their final home many miles away from the place where they were executed.

In spite of all this, however, the national idiom does in many cases make itself felt. Certain of the wall paintings, even in the thirteenth century, can be claimed as Serbian on stylistic grounds alone rather than as Greek, and a few of the icons that have been preserved in the churches and monasteries of Macedonia and Serbia, especially in the church of the Virgin Perebleptos (St Clement) at Ochrid, can be recognized as the work of local painters. Happily quite a number of these are either dated by inscriptions or by the evidence of documents, and it is these, and their later successors, that will form the main theme of this chapter.

Before attempting to deal with them individually, however, it will be well to try to define the features that may be regarded as characterizing them as Slav as opposed to Greek, for though the business of what may be termed ethnic aesthetics is notoriously difficult, certain clear factors do nevertheless from time to time emerge. They are to be seen both in style and in colouring. With regard to the former attention may be drawn to a large double-sided icon of the earlier thirteenth century at Ochrid bearing the Virgin and Child on one face and the Crucifixion on the other (*Icons*, pls 171–2). In the latter scene the angular movements, the concentration on rendering the intense emotion of the theme, and the sweeping forms are all clearly marked, and may be contrasted with the greater attention paid to elegance and the courtly reticence of a truly Constantinopolitan product, as it is to be observed in the fine icon from the same church noted above which bears the Virgin and Child designated as 'The Saviour of Souls'. Something of the same intensity as on the former icon also characterizes the rendering of a head of Christ at Chilandari on Mount Athos, painted about 1260, which is illustrated by Radojčić.[1] It is severe and rather sombre and again contrasts with the lighter, more delicate conception of Christ on the Constantinopolitan icon which forms a pair to that bearing the Virgin Saviour of Souls.

Even more truly Macedonian is an icon of the apostle Matthew (*pl. 22*) which must have been specially painted for the church of the Perebleptos; it is to be dated about 1295, and has been attributed to a painter called Eutychios who worked on the frescoes of the same church between 1295 and 1300.[2] The same swinging movement and rather gloomy approach are again apparent, but in this case the nature of the colouring is also distinct. The brilliant, enamel-like hues, often of a Flemish-like precision and clarity, that characterize Constantinopolitan painting are absent, and instead the colours tend to be sombre and rather thin, like a wash, and seem to have been applied with a broad brush rather than elaborately worked with a small one, as was usual in Constantinopolitan work.

Similar rather matt, wash-like colours are to be found on an icon of St John the Baptist of about 1350 which stands on the iconostasis at Dečani, and they persist in Yugoslavian work as late as the seventeenth century, as for example on an icon of St Nahum of Ochrid, now in the Skopje Gallery (*Icons*, pl. 215). Even when the colours are thicker and richer, as on a fourteenth-century icon of St Luke at Chilandari (*Icons*, pl. 187), they still have the same matt, wash-like character.

Another icon that one would unhesitatingly regard as Slav is a famous one (*pl. 28*) depicting the Virgin Pelagonitissa, now at Skopje, which was painted by the monk Makarios for the monastery of Zrze in 1421 or 1422. The curiously contorted pose is not unique; it is to be found on a number of icons produced both by Slav and Greek masters, and characterizes a distinct iconographical type. But the exaggerated oval of the Virgin's eyes, the very long nose, the very sad, austere expression, and the love of angularity for its own sake that characterize the Zrze icon are foreign to Greek art. The same love of angularity is, for example, to be found in the figure of an Annunciation on a pair of doors for an iconostasis painted in 1021 by George Mitrofanović for the monastery of Chilandari on Mount Athos.

This attempt to define some of the features that are to be regarded as typical of the southern Slav world has interrupted our consideration of the main theme of this chapter, that of surveying those icons of Macedonian or Serbian origin that can be firmly dated. Happily there are quite a number of these, and they may now be considered in chronological order.

The earliest mention of work that is of the region occurs in the twelfth century, for there are records that Stephen Nemanja (1169–96) presented icons to the monasteries of Studenica and Žiča, while Queen Beloslava, wife of the earlier Vladimir, is known to have owned more than twenty icons. None of them can be actually identified. The earliest surviving panel is probably an icon of the Annunciation (*pl. 19*) on two panels from the church of the Perebleptos at Ochrid, which is to be assigned to the second decade of the twelfth century. The panels were presented to the church by a certain Leo, who has been identified as Leo Mungo, Archbishop of Ochrid from 1108 to 1120.[3] Would it be going too far to suggest that the rather severe expression of the angel and the linear treatment of the Virgin both indicate that it was by a Slav painter? It is hard to be sure, for at this early date the features that support such attributions were not fully developed.

The earliest panel that is undoubtedly South Slav is, however, the famous 'Holy Face' (St Veronica's Kerchief), now at Laon in France, which must date from the end of the twelfth or the very early thirteenth century (*pl. 41*). It has been claimed for Yugoslavia, but is dealt with here under the heading of Bulgaria, for the inscription upon it has been defined as middle Bulgar. An icon of Christ, which, according to an inscription on the reverse, was executed under the patronage of Archbishop Constantine Cabasilas for the church of Hagia Sophia at Ochrid in 1262 or 1263, is more surely a product of Macedonia (*pl. 20*). Here the linear treatment, the staring eyes and the wash-like nature of the paint all bear out a local origin. The halo in plaster relief is, however, something very unusual in Greece or Yugoslavia, though such haloes were very popular in Cyprus. It must surely have been made in imitation of the haloes and mounts in relief metal work which are associated with so many of the Ochrid icons.

An icon of St George (*pl. 21*) at Struga, unfortunately in rather poor condition, comes next in date. It was executed by a painter called Joannes of Struga in 1266 or 1267. Though it is distinctly conservative in style, it would seem nevertheless to be a provincial work, and a resemblance to local wall paintings of the later thirteenth century has been noted by Professor Djurić.[4] It may perhaps be regarded as typical of the most polished type of local work even though, unlike the majority of the icons that we will consider below, it was not executed for a patron of great distinction. It is, however, a good deal more conservative in style than the large icon we noted at the outset as an example of the south Slav style, that with the Virgin on the obverse and the Crucifixion on the back. The latter is a very impressive work. The feeling for emotion and the heavy colouring have already been alluded to as characteristics of the Slavic school, and the figure of St John is especially noteworthy in this respect; its pose and its massive proportions recall the wall paintings at Sopoćani, of 1265, and suggest a date not very much later for the icon. Professor Djurić thinks that a painter from Salonica may have been responsible but the Sopoćani wall paintings reflect something of the excellence of Metropolitan work and it is possible that a painter from Constantinople was in part responsible for them. But by the time that they were produced local elements were beginning to make themselves felt, and it is tempting to suggest that the painters expressed themselves more fully in the icon than in the slightly earlier wall paintings.

With the last years of the thirteenth century the Slav elements had come much more to the fore, and an icon done for the church of the Perebleptos at Ochrid has already been noted as a fully fledged illustration of the new Slavonic type; it is the large one of the Apostle Matthew (*pl. 22*) painted between 1295 and 1300, perhaps by the master Eutychios. It is impressive and dignified, but is perhaps rather lacking in sympathy. A series of small icons, probably made for an upper row of the iconostasis in the same church at much the same time, are a good deal more successful artistically. They were presented by a man called Progonos Sgouros, who came from Salonica, together with an icon of the Virgin Perebleptos, of which only a fragment survives; the others, eight in number, depict the main feasts of the church. Milković-Pepek attributes all of them to the painter Eutychios, though he suggests that those of the Virgin and the Ascension are early works, whereas the others are later.[5] But Professor Radojčić does not mention Eutychios in his consideration of them, though he thinks that all the panels came from the same workshop; he accounts for any differences of style between them on the grounds that models by different painters and in differing styles were followed.[6] Balabanov attributes four of the panels, the Baptism (*pl. 23*), the Presentation, the Incredulity of Thomas (*pl. 27*) and the Anastasis, to the same painter as the St Matthew icon, though he does not accept that the painter was neces-

sarily Eutychios.[7] Djurić, on the other hand, sees the work of three painters, all distinct from Eutychios. To the most accomplished of them he attributes the Nativity, the Baptism, the Incredulity of Thomas, the Anastasis and the Nativity of the Virgin, and probably also the fragmentary icon of the Virgin which Milković-Pepek regarded as an early work of Eutychios.[8] A damaged icon of the Mounting of the Cross is assigned to another painter on the grounds of the greater elongation of the figures, and the same man was probably also responsible for a small icon from the same church depicting Pentecost. The third of Djurić's painters was less accomplished than the others, and executed the Dormition of the Virgin.[9] These diversities of view serve to indicate how difficult attributions on a purely stylistic basis actually are. One thing that is certain is that all the panels date from around 1300, while the best of them, those assigned by Djurić to his first hand, are closer to Byzantine work than are the others.[10]

Though it is established that an icon of Christ now in the Skopje Museum[11] was painted for a certain Isaac Kersak, one of Stephen Dušan's generals, while two of the Virgin in the Perebleptos at Ochrid were done for Archbishop Nicholas,[12] they cannot be more firmly dated than to shortly before the middle of the fourteenth century. The former is mounted in metal, and Balabanov points out that the mount, on which the inscription referring to Kersak appears, is not necessarily of the same date as the painting; it is made up of metal strips which were applied piecemeal and not actually fitted to the panel. Djurić notes certain Western elements in all these icons, which are especially marked in the one of the Virgin,[13] notably in the gentle features of the Child, the soft colouring and the youthful conception of the Madonna. It would seem that painters from the Adriatic coast were responsible for this icon as well as for the introduction of features of this nature, in the same way that the Western idiom was introduced into architecture and sculpture in the great monasteries of Studenica and Dečani at much the same date. Some of these men may have been Italians, others were probably Greeks, who had settled at Kotor, Dubrovnik and elsewhere in the same way that Cretan painters settled in Venice some two centuries later. They were often termed 'pictores Graeci', and they appear to have worked in a truly Greek, rather than a provincialized, Italianate style. But the majority of the Adriatic painters were more closely linked with Italy and produced work akin to the Italian dugento style; their main centre seems to have been at Split. The famous wall painting of the Crucifixion at Studenica of 1209 illustrates this style; it may be compared to the work of Ginuta Pisano.

Radojčić would also attribute to painters from Kotor our next firmly dated series of icons which were done under the patronage of the Emperor Dušan for the iconostasis at Dečani; they comprise a rather severe

Virgin and Child (*pl. 24*), an Archangel Gabriel, a St Nicholas, and a St John the Baptist.[14] All show a frank directness of approach and are executed in the flat, matt technique that has been described above as characteristic of Yugoslavia. They show a clear relationship to some of the wall paintings in the same church, an exceptionally lavish decoration in which many hands must have been involved; some of them were no doubt also responsible for the icons. The panel bearing the Virgin and Child is finer than the others, so that all of them are probably not to be attributed to the same man. But the style is broadly uniform and contrasts quite markedly with that of an icon of the Virgin and Child (*pl. 25*) from the iconostasis at Lesnovo, now in the Skopje Museum, which is firmly dated by an inscription to 1342. It follows the Hodegetria type, but the Virgin is shown in a severe frontal pose and much of the sensibility of the Dečani icon is absent. Radojčić notes its similarity to an icon in the Byzantine Museum at Athens, so that it is perhaps to be attributed to a Greek rather than to a Slav hand, but the style is provincial.[15]

Radojčić calls attention to several other icons that are to be dated to between 1350 and 1370, notably one of St Nicholas surrounded by scenes from his life in the Skopje gallery, an impressive but rather dry St Nicholas at Chilandari, and a lively presentation of the Virgin at the same place.[16] It is perhaps by the same hand as the frescoes on the outer side of the north wall of the church of the Perebleptos at Ochrid which are dated to *c.* 1365. The next firmly dated panel, however, is one of Christ (*pl. 26*) from Zrze, now at Skopje, which was executed in 1394.[17] It is signed by Bishop Jovan the Painter, and represents a very personal but also very forceful rendering of the subject, in an essentially south Slav manner. The staring eyes and the severity of expression almost savour of the Russian theme known as the Saviour of the Wrathful Eye.

Bishop Jovan was a member of a distinguished family of the region, several of the members of which appear to have been painters, and his brother Makarios produced an even more impressive panel in 1421 or 1422, the Virgin Pelagonitissa (*pl. 28*), which we have already referred to as a typically Slav work. It is now in the Skopje Gallery. The curious pose, with the Child's head twisted backwards to embrace the Mother, is repeated on several other panels, and it would seem that it was inspired by an icon specially painted for a church at Pelagonia, a village near Bitolj (Monastir). But the iconographical type was a very old one; it appears in a miniature of the thirteenth century in the Four Gospels of Belgrade, and Grabar cites other examples, tracing the origin back to Egypt.[18] But none has the same intensity of expression, the same sadness, the same depth of feeling, that distinguishes the version by Makarios. A panel from the church of St Nicholas Varos at Prilep, now in the Skopje Gallery, which is reproduced by

Balabanov[19] may be contrasted, for it is sweet, tender and charming, but far less profound and intense. The Zrze panel is an astonishingly moving work and marks out its painter as a man of genius who was able to produce a version of an old theme which was not only an exact iconographical replica but also a very personal painting, the very epitome of all that pertains to true south Slav feeling. It was done for a particular patron, Constantine Djurdjić, and there is a long prayer in Slavonic script at the base of the panel.

Though Serbian independence was brought to an end two years later on the field of Kossovo (1389) and Ochrid fell to the Turks in 1396, a few painters of the old generation continued to work for the rest of their lives. The same Makarios indeed executed a painting for the monastery of Ljubostinja between 1402 and 1405. But when these men died out the production of work of quality ceased except for a brief phase in the north, when good work was done at Krušedol under the patronage of the Brancović family between 1509 and 1512. An icon depicting St John the Baptist and the Archangel Gabriel (*pl. 29*) illustrates the work of this school; in general its products were in a very conservative vein. Nor is there anything especially new about an icon of the Dormition of the Virgin (*pl. 30*) from the Slepča monastery, now in the Gallery at Skopje, which is dated between 1537 and 1543. The work is indeed rather coarse and clumsy, but there is still some of the feeling for drama and emotion which was, for example, to the fore in the wall paintings of *c.* 1295, done for the church of the Perebleptos by Michael and Eutychios. The same is true of a few other icons at the same place done at much the same date which are mentioned by Balabanov; the most interesting are an Annunciation, an Anastasis and a Nativity of the Virgin. He illustrated the first of these[20] and attributes all of them to a painter called Dmitar Lennovo. Other work of this age includes a 'Sainte Face' of a rather Western type belonging to the Cultural Council of the Serbian State (not illustrated),[21] and a few works by Greeks like the predella by Bizamenos at Dubrovnik dated 1518.[22]

Two other paintings (*pl. 31*) of the period that follow the Byzantine heritage—they show the Annunciation, at the top of a pair of iconostasis doors—came from the monastery of Kučeviste; they are now in the Skopje Gallery and are dated 1609. The carving below is typical of the sort of work that became very popular in Yugoslavia in the course of the seventeenth century, and in many ways represents the country's most important contribution to art at this time. A panel of the Virgin and Child done for the Slepča monastery in 1607 may also be noted.[23] It is in a severe and very conservative style and may be contrasted with an icon of St John the Baptist from Krušedol (*pl. 40*) now in the Orthodox museum at Belgrade, which is dated 1645, where the extreme elaboration of icon painting at this time as practised in the more accomplished centres has reached full fruition. Here numerous baroque elements have been adopted which make of these later icons an essentially decorative art. But alongside this ornate, decorative manner there developed an art which was essentially of a peasant character: it is represented by an icon of the Three-handed Virgin (*pl. 32*) in the Slepča monastery which is dated 1627. It is a work of truly peasant art in style and conception even though other versions of this strange theme are to be found elsewhere, at Chilandari and Lesnovo as well as in Russia.

Lacking in elegance though those paintings are, however, the end of the sixteenth century was to see something of a revival, thanks firstly to the growth of a local school at Peć, the most important member of which was a man called Longinus who was active from about 1556 till 1598, and secondly to the import of Italo-Cretan icons from the Adriatic. Longinus' early work was not very distinguished and was in a truly local style; later he underwent some influence from Russia. An Epitaphios by him at Peć, dated to 1594, and a Virgin and Child of 1573/74 at Piva,[24] illustrate his earlier manner. His style exercised a good deal of influence which is to be seen, for instance, in the work of the painter Nectarius, who executed a Virgin and Child at Dečani dated 1594,[25] as well as in that of another man called Cosmas, who did a fine St George (*pl. 34*) for the monastery of Piva in 1626 (see Djurić, p. 69). A series of small festival icons at the same place, dated 1639, resemble the work of Longinus in style and colouring, though they are not signed by him. All are conservative, as an icon of the Raising of Lazarus (*pl. 36*) which we illustrate here serves to show.

Apart from the primarily indigenous revival at Peć, a new breath of life also began to penetrate from the Adriatic, where work was being done under the influence of the Italo-Cretan painters. Some of the men who worked there have already been mentioned when dealing with Crete or Venice, like Angelos Bizamenos, who worked at Dubrovnik around 1518. Constantine Tsane, Andreas Ritsos and Elias Moschos may also be noted. But others were Slavs who presumably learnt from the Greeks, and the names of a number of them are known; Kotor seems to have been their main centre. Many of the icons produced in this region found their way to the Orthodox area to the East, though quite a lot of icons seem also to have been painted for the Catholic churches of the coast lands.

The work of these men followed on the whole a very conservative manner; nor was much of it of very high quality. One of the best of them was called Jovan, who was responsible for a pair of icons of Christ (*pl. 35*) and the Virgin, surrounded by busts of the Apostles and Prophets in rectangular frames. They were done for the church of St Nicholas at Bijelo Polje in 1627 and 1628, and are closely similar to Greek work of the period,

though the inscriptions are in Slav. The same man was also responsible in 1632 for a painting of St Paraskevi at Chilandari. Another man, Giorgios Margazius, seems to have done work in an even more conservative style, for an icon of the Last Judgment (*pl. 38*) in the Orthodox church at Skradin, painted in 1647, follows almost line for line a panel by Tsanfurnari now in the Stathatos collection at Athens.

Perhaps the most famous of the painters of the littoral, however, was George Mitrofanović, who painted several icons now in the monastery of Chilandari on Mount Athos; one of the Annunciation (*pl. 33*), dated 1621, may be noted, while Radojčić illustrates one of four Warrior Saints, also at Chilandari, which is dated 1681.[26] His known work also includes icons of an Archangel (1621), the Virgin, St John the Baptist (1644), and St Sava (1645).[27] Mitrofanović was the master of two other men, John and Cosmas, and the latter executed an interesting icon of St Sava and St Simeon Nemanja surrounded by scenes from their lives in the monastery of Morača, dated 1645 (*pl. 37*), as well as a Dormition and a St George (*pl. 34*), both at Piva and dated to 1638/39.[28] Dated icons of this period are comparatively numerous and include one of St Paraskevi by the painter John, done in 1632, one of Christ by a painter called Daniel, dated 1667 (both at Chilandari), one by Radul dated 1674, ánd two by Vuičič, one of St Luke at Peć of 1673 and the other of the Doubting Thomas of 1650 at Morača.[29] Quite a number of other icons are listed by Djurić, but all are of rather secondary quality. They include a Christ of 1565/66 at Leskov, a Virgin and Child of 1568 at Sarajevo and a St Nicholas with scenes from his life of 1615–20 at Dečani.[30] It was on the whole an age of eclecticism, for in addition to Greek influence, painters were also subject to ideas from Russia and Rumania, while Greek ideas penetrated not only from the Adriatic littoral but also from Mount Athos, where the Slav painters came into direct contact with the Greek masters.[31]

The Byzantine heritage that predominates in the majority of the work may be contrasted with a typical work of the littoral like a triptych (*pl. 39*) by Franko Matkov in the village church at Sustjepan near Rijeka Dubrovačka, dated 1534/35. Matkov was one of the most outstanding of the Slav artists working at Dubrovnik. Though the Virgin conforms to Eastern iconography and his rendering of St John follows an Eastern tradition, the Evangelist's emblem, the eagle, is treated wholly naturalistically and occupies an unusual position in the composition, while St Stephen is clothed as a Catholic and wears Western vestments. This mixed style is not without charm and interest, but it marks the decadence of an old tradition and brings to an end the story of icon painting as a creative art in Yugoslavia. Any work produced after about 1700 is hardly to be classed as other than peasant craftsmanship.

25

26

27

31   32

33a   33b

34 35

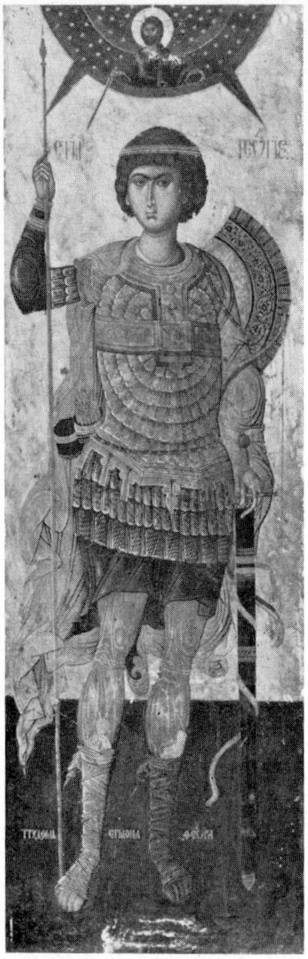

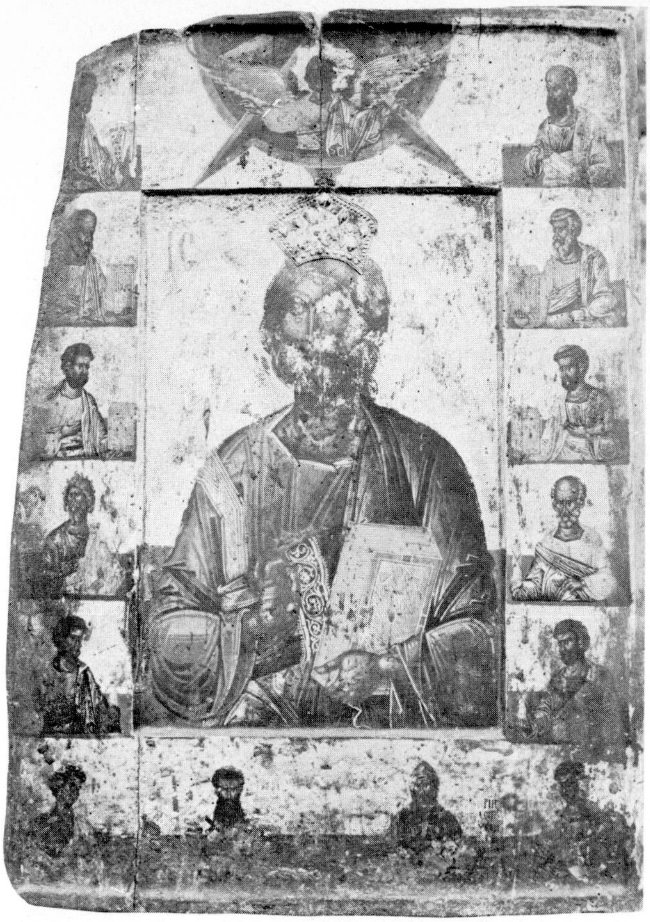

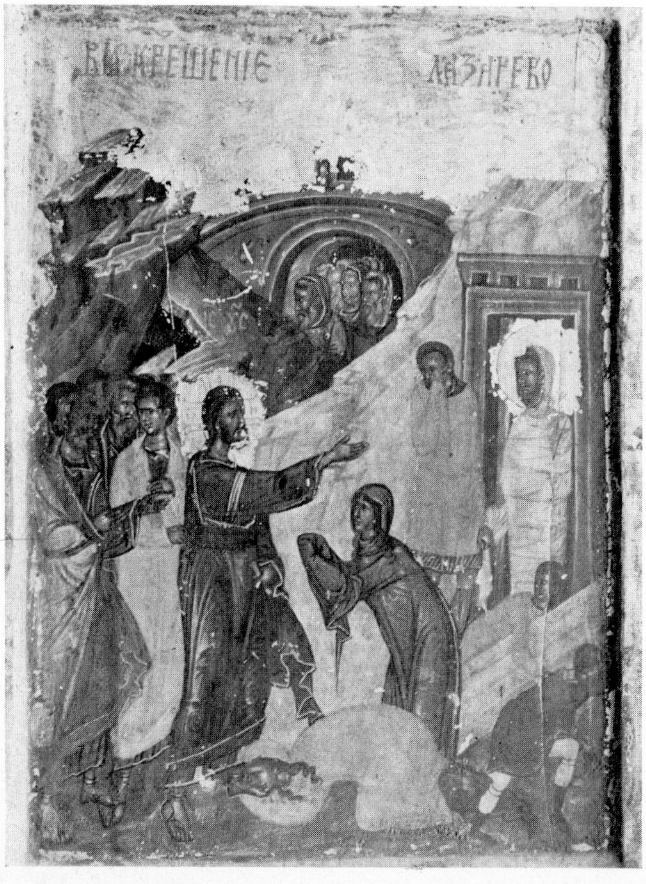

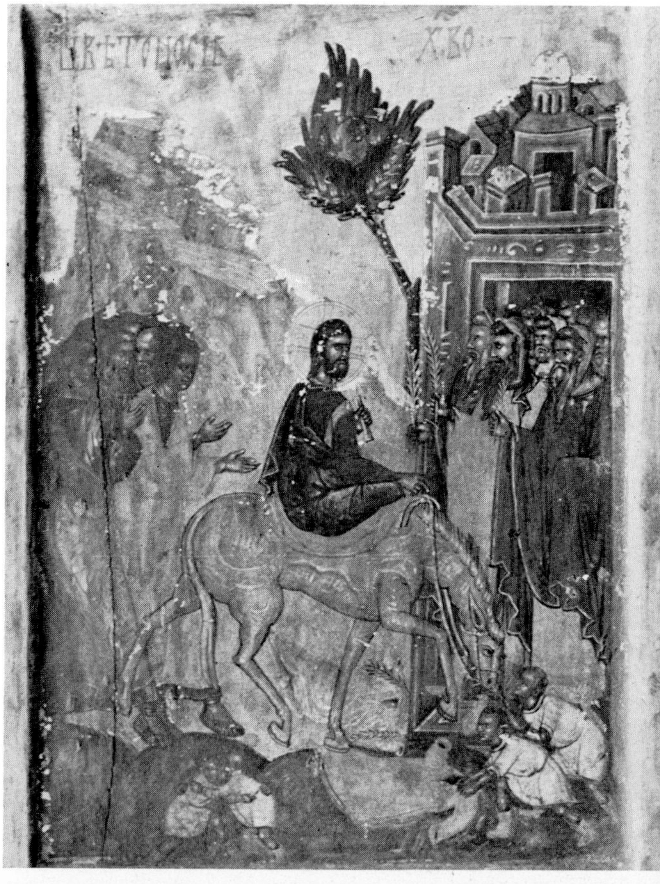

36a 36b

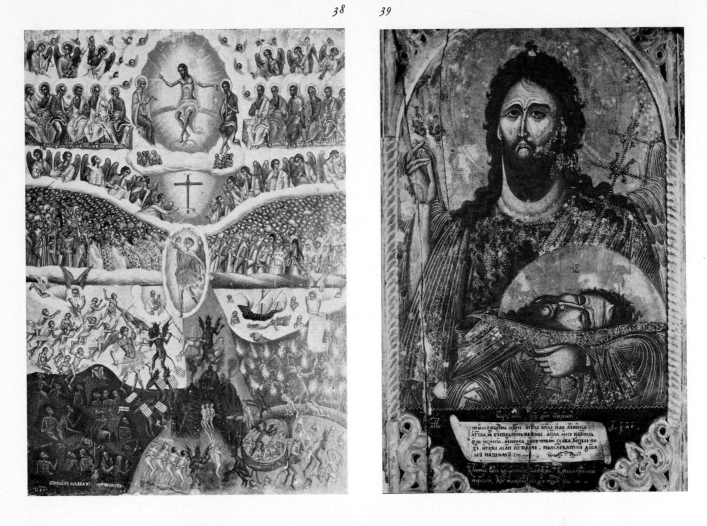

19a, The Annunciation, on two panels
b From the church of the Perebleptos. Now in the National Museum, Ochrid.
111.5 × 68 cm.
1108–20

Both panels are adorned with elaborate silver mounts decorated with a floral pattern on the main area and with figures of saints in the margins; there are five full-length figures on each side and three bust figures at top and bottom (omitted in photograph). The Virgin is seated and holds a long spindle; her expression is unusually delicate for a work of such early date, and this has led to a suggestion that the paintings may actually be later than the inscription. If so, it is probably the result of a repainting, for the inscription is clear enough and records that the icon was presented to the church by a man called Leo, who is almost certainly to be identified as Leo Mungo, Archbishop of Ochrid from 1108 till 1120.

Djurić, pls. 20 and 21. Balabanov, pl. 5.

20 Christ Pantocrator
From the church of the Perebleptos, Ochrid. Now in the National Museum, Ochrid.
135 × 73 cm.
1262/63

Christ is depicted half-length, the right hand raised in blessing, the left at His side, holding a scroll. The highlights on his costume are in gold, and behind His head is an embossed halo in plaster relief work, bearing a cross and the letters Θ N. On the back is an inscription in Greek which states that the icon was painted in the year 1262/63, during the Archbishopric of Constantine Cabasilas. It was probably presented by him to the church of Hagia Sophia at Ochrid. The style is severe and lacks the elegance of the best Byzantine work, and suggests that the icon is probably to be regarded as a local work, in spite of the Greek inscription; it is impossible, however, to say whether the painter was a Slav or a Greek. The halo in relief work is unusual in the Byzantine world, although the technique was common in Cyprus at a later date.

Djurić, pl. 2. K. Balabanov, 'Newly discovered icons of the XIII, XIV and XV centuries', in *Rasledi*, I, Skopje, 1959, p. 990 (in Serbo-Croat). See also Balabanov, pl. 15.

21 St George, a detail
By the painter Joannes
Church of St George, Struga.
146 × 86 cm.
1266/67

St George is depicted full-length and full-face. He holds a lance in his right hand while his left hand rests on the hilt of his sword. The work is very conservative, and follows the style of the Comnene period, though in a rather provincial manner. An inscription in Greek on the back records that the icon was presented by a man called John the Deacon and was painted in 1266/67 by Joannes. He also belonged to the locality, although it is impossible to say whether he was a Slav or a Greek. The frescoes at Monastir dated to 1271 that are signed by a deacon of the same name must surely be the work of this artist. Compare it with *pl. 92*.

Djurić, pl. 3. Balabanov, pl. 10.

22 The Apostle Matthew
From the church of the Perebleptos. Now in the National Museum, Ochrid.
106 × 56 cm.
c. 1300

The Evangelist is shown full-length, facing towards his left, and holding a Gospel book, half open, in both his hands. The painting is accomplished, the conception monumental, and the icon represents a typical piece of Macedonian work of the period. There is every reason to believe that it was painted at the same time that the wall-paintings were set up in the church and by most authorities it has been attributed to the painter Eutychios who, together with another man called Michael, signed the wall paintings. Their work was done shortly before 1300, and the icon must be about that date.

Djurić, pl. 8. Radojćić, in *Icons*, pl. 169. Balabanov, pl. 20. Milković-Pepek, *L'Œuvre des peintres Michel et Eutychie*, Skopje, 1967.

23 The Baptism
From the church of the Perebleptos. Now in the National Museum, Ochrid.
47 × 38·5 cm.
c. 1300

Christ, standing in the Jordan, wears a loin-cloth and his legs are crossed. Above a dove descends from a 'Glory'. St John stands on a craggy rock to Christ's right, and below him is the usual tree with the axe stuck into it, while below again is the allegory of the river. On the opposite bank are four angels, standing on similar craggy rocks.

The icon is one of a series of panels painted for the upper row of the iconostasis of the church of the Perebleptos, and presented by a man called Progonos Sgouros. Eight of them survive. All are of the same size, but not all by the same hand. Milković-Pepek is probably correct in attributing this panel to Eutychios.

Djurić, pl. 10. Radojćić, in *Icons*, pl. 180. Balabanov, pl. 14. Milković-Pepek, *L'Œuvre des peintres Michel et Eutychie*.

24a, *The Virgin of Tenderness,* a detail, and the *Archangel*
b Gabriel
On the iconostasis of the monastery of Dečani.
164 × 56 cm.
c. 1300

The Virgin stands full-length, on a red cushion; she
holds the Child on her left arm, with His head pressed
against hers in affection. The lettering is in Slavonic
script. The style is rather provincial and shows a frank
directness of approach which is distinct from truly
Byzantine work, as does the flat, rather matt, texture
of the paint.

This icon, together with several others, such as the
Archangel Gabriel in the same church, was presented
to the monastery by the Emperor Dušan (1331–55).

Radojčić, in *Icons,* pl. 193, and in *Icônes,* pl. 33.

25 The Virgin Hodegetria
From the iconostasis of the monastery of Lesnovo.
Now in the National Museum, Skopje.
1342

The Virgin is depicted half-length, in a severely frontal
position, with the Child on her left arm. The icon
is in rather poor condition and is not a work of outstanding quality, but is important as an example of local
workmanship and because it is firmly dated.

S. Radojčić, 'Die Serbische Ikonenmalerei vom 12. Jahrhundert
bis zum Jahre 1459', in *Jahrbuch der Österreichischen Byzantinischen
Gesellschaft,* V, 1956, p. 78 and fig. 18.

26 Christ Pantocrator
By Bishop Jovan, the Painter
From the Church of the Ascension, Zrze. Now in the
National Museum, Skopje.
131 × 88.5 cm.
1393/94

Christ is shown half-length and full-face. His right hand
is raised in blessing while His left clasps a book, its
cover adorned with jewels. He is designated in the
accompanying inscription as 'Saviour and Source of
Life' (Zoodotes). An inscription in red on the upper
border gives the name of the painter and the date.

Djurić, pl. 36. Balabanov, pl. 53.

27 The Incredulity of St Thomas
From the church of the Perebleptos. Now in the National
Museum, Ochrid.
56 × 22 cm.
c. 1300

Our Lord stands in the centre, before an elaborate
architectural composition. Thomas, with five Apostles

behind him, leans forward to touch our Lord's side.
On the other side of Christ are five more Apostles.

The icon belongs to the same series as the previous
one, and is probably to be assigned to the same painter,
the most competent of the men who worked on the
series. Whether or not it was Eutychios, a date around
1300 seems certain.

Djurić, pl. 11. Milković-Pepek, *loc. cit.* M. Korović-Ljubinković,
Icons of Ochrida, Belgrade, 1953, p. 3.

28 The Virgin Pelagonitissa
By Makarios the Painter
From the iconostasis of the church of the Ascension,
Zrze. Now in the National Museum, Skopje.
134 × 93.5 cm.
1421/22

The pose is that of 'Our Lady of Tenderness', but the
Virgin holds the Child on her right arm and His head
is bent round in a strangely contorted position to embrace her. The icon bears the special designation 'Pelagonitissa' and would seem to have followed an earlier
model specially painted for Pelagonia, a village situated
near Bitolj (Monastir). The same iconographical pose
is to be found in the Greek world as well as in Yugoslavia, for instance on an icon in the monastery of St
Catherine on Mount Sinai, but nowhere else is the
same intensity of feeling present. There is a long
inscription in Slavonic on the upper border which
records the icon's date and the name of the painter.

Djurić, pl. 37. Balabanov, pl. 31. Radojćić in *Icons,* pl. 191, and in
Icônes, pl. 67. *Photo Kažić.*

29 St John the Baptist and the Archangel Gabriel
On the iconostasis of the Krušedol Monastery.
93.2 × 68.5 cm.
1509–12

The two figures are shown together, full-length, and
facing towards the left. St John holds a scroll with text
in Slavonic. The association of the two together on a
single panel is rather unusual, although they normally
constitute adjacent figures on the Deesis row of an
iconostasis, but the period at which this iconostasis was
set up is firmly established, and there is every reason to
regard the panel as an integral part of it.

Djurić, pl. 67.

30 The Dormition of the Virgin
From the monastery of Slepča. Now in the National
Museum, Skopje.
36 × 73 cm.
1537–43

The circular topped sections into which this icon is divided are unusual. The large central area shows the Virgin lying on a bier with the Apostles grouped round her. Above, but below the arched top, stands Christ, with an Archangel on either side, before a mandorla or glory of great elaboration, linked up with the arched top. The section to the left contains a full-length figure of St John of Damascus that on the right of the poet Come.

Radojčić, in *Icônes*, pl. 74.

31 Pair of iconostasis doors, bearing *the Annunciation*
From the monastery of the Archangels at Kučeviste.
Now in the National Museum, Skopje.
130 × 65 cm.
1609

The Archangel is shown at the top of the left-hand door, the Virgin at the top of the right-hand one. There are elaborate architectural compositions behind both figures. The style of the painting is conservative, but the work is certainly local. The margins and the whole of the lower parts of the doors are carved with an intricate interlace pattern in low relief, in a style which became very popular throughout the country in the seventeenth century.

Radojčić, in *Icônes*, pl. 81.

32 *The Three-handed Virgin*
From the church of St John the Baptist in the Slepča Monastery.
72.5 × 48 cm.
1627

The pose is that of a normal Hodegetria, with the Child on the Virgin's left arm, but, curiously, she points to it with two hands of almost identical form. Both the Virgin and the Child have haloes in relief plaster work, of a rather rough character, decorated with a criss-cross pattern. The whole work, however, is primitive, and the icon is certainly a local product. There is an inscription, with the date, in the lower left-hand corner.

The theme of the Three-handed Virgin appears to have been quite popular in country regions in the seventeenth century, and several other examples are known; attention may be drawn to one at Chilandari. All these icons are products of popular art, and reflect the growth of superstitions and legends in an essentially peasant society.

Balabanov, pl. 69.

33a, *The Annunciation*, details
b By George Mitrofanović

In the church of St Tryphon in the monastery of Chilandari, Mount Athos.
117 × 56 cm.
1621

The scene is depicted on the doors of the Iconostasis, the Archangel on the left and the Virgin on the right door. Both figures are rendered in a very conservative manner, consistent with the rather arid character of much of the work of this period.

Radojčić, in *Icons*, pls. 210, 211, and in *Icônes*, pl. 87.

34 *St George*
By the Painter Cosmas
On the iconostasis of the Piva Monastery.
134 × 43.8 cm.
1638/39

The Saint stands full-length, holding a spear in his right hand. His round shield is strapped to his back behind his left shoulder. Above, in a semi-circular mandorla, is the bust of Christ. There is a short inscription at the bottom, giving the name of the donor, the monk Theodore, and the date.

Djurić, pl. 86.

35 *Christ and the Apostles*
By the Painter Jovan
Church of St Nicholas, Bijelo Polje.
75.2 × 55.5 cm.
1637/38

The centre of the panel displays a half-length figure of the crowned Christ. He is presented frontally, holding a volume of the Gospels in His left hand, whilst blessing with His right. The Angel of the Great Council appears in the centre of the top border with, in the left-hand-corner, a bust-size representation of St Peter, and of St Paul in the right corner. The Evangelists Mark, Andrew, Bartholomew and Philip appear below St Paul; Matthew, Luke, Simon, James and Thomas below St Peter. St Sava and St Simeon Nemanja occupy the centre of the bottom border.

There is also in the church a balancing icon, with a figure of the Virgin, by the same painter and of the same date.

Djurić, pls. 82 and 83.

36a, Double-sided icon, with on one face *the Raising of*
b *Lazarus* and on the other *the Entry into Jerusalem*
Monastery of Piva.
42 × 32 cm.
1638/39

In the Raising of Lazarus the mummy is depicted erect

in a rectangular sarcophagus which looks rather like an entrance door. Below two men remove the cover while a third stands behind, his garment held before his nose. In the centre two women implore Christ's help. Behind Him stand a group of Apostles, while a second group, composed of spectators, watch from below a sort of arch between the rocks of the background. The margin is wide, but plain.

In the Entry Christ is on His mule at the centre, with two children laying their cloaks on the ground before Him and a group of Apostles behind. A large group of elders stand in the entrance to the city, and beside it is a tall tree with one small figure amidst its branches.

These small, double-sided icons are peculiar to Yugoslavia; they were usually suspended from the large metal polycandelions on which the lamps were fixed, and these in turn were hung by chains from the dome.

Djurić, pl. 86.

37 Sts Sava and Simeon, surrounded by scenes from their lives
By Cosmas' workshop
Monastery of Morača.
1646

The saints are shown full length in the centre of the panel. The surrounding scenes illustrate the main incidents in their lives, including those of their consecration. They appear again at the top of the panel, standing on either side of Christ.

Radojčić, in *Icons*, pl. 217, for detail of the scene showing the consecration of St Sava. *Photo Kažić.*

38 The Last Judgment
By Giorgios Margazius
Orthodox Church, Skradin.
44.3 × 33.1 cm.
1647

The scene is arranged in six horizontal tiers. At the top are angels, with below them the elect and below again a second row of angels; at the centre is the Deesis above, with a cross below it; St Michael, before an oval 'glory', occupies the centre of the lower tiers, in which the righteous and the damned are depicted. The icon is signed in Latin characters in the lower left-hand corner.

Although the theme of the Last Judgment was a usual one in later Byzantine art, the details and more especially the rendering of Christ here attest a good deal of Western influence.

Djurić, pl. 63.

39 Triptych: *the Virgin and Child, St Stephen and St John the Evangelist*
By Franko Matkov
Church of St Stephen in the village of Sustjepan, Rijeka Dubrovačka.
137 × 127 cm.
1534/35

The Virgin follows a Byzantine convention, though it was one that had been universally adopted in the Adriatic region at this date. St John is again painted in the Byzantine style, though his emblem, the eagle, is shown with a feeling for naturalism which is essentially Western. St Stephen wears Western vestments and has a tonsure in the Latin manner, and there is little that is Byzantine about him.

The panel serves to illustrate very clearly the diversity of influences that characterized much of the art of the Adriatic area from the sixteenth century onwards, and is included here as a contrast to the more conservative work to be found in the Orthodox areas.

Djurić, pl. 48.

40 (Colour plate III) *St John the Baptist*
From the monastery of Krušedol. Now in the museum of the Serbian Orthodox Church at Belgrade.
63 × 42.5 cm.
1644

St John is depicted half-length, holding in his left hand a long narrow dish with his head in it, backed by a halo of half-moon shape; his staff passes up behind this, while his right arm is raised in blessing. The dish is elaborately ornamented and the whole icon is decorative in conception. The painted area is enclosed by a carved border, arched above, while at the bottom there is a flat panel painted black on which there is a dedicatory inscription, together with the date, in Slavonic script. Although late, the icon is well painted, and represents one of the finest pieces of this ornate style that have come down to us.

Radojčić, in *Icons*, pl. 213. *Photo Kažić.*

Chapter Three

Bulgaria

THOUGH NO examples of such early date survive, mention is made of icons in Bulgaria from soon after the conversion of the country to Christianity in 865. These early icons were no doubt imports, but at least by the tenth century, if not earlier, work of a sort was being done locally, for the famous pottery icon of St Theodore found at Patleina near Preslav has been dated to this time on archaeological grounds. It is made up of twenty square tiles, which were manufactured on the spot,[1] for kilns and numerous fragments of other icons have been found there. The tiles must have been made with the aid of a master drawing or painting and the painted maquette must have been specially made, even if it followed a Byzantine model. The potter, and probably also the basic draughtsman, were surely men of the locality.

At a slightly later date—in 972 to be exact—there are records that a painted icon was taken from Preslav to Constantinople by John Tsimisces after his conquest of the city, but it is impossible to say whether this was of local workmanship or an import. Even if it was an import, it had probably inspired local copies. Thereafter evidence regarding the production of local work is lacking until the later twelfth century, when an actual painting that is still preserved may be cited which is in all probability a Bulgarian product. This is the famous Sainte Face (*pl. 41*) at Laon in France. Like other icons of the same subject—the subject is often known as St Veronica's handkerchief—it purported to depict the actual grave cloth on which an impression of Christ's face had been left, and the Laon example is certainly one of the earliest paintings of the theme that survive. Other examples are to be found in the Spaso-Andreyevsky monastery in Russia and in the Cathedral of the Dormition at Moscow. The former according to legend was brought from Constantinople in 1354;[2] the latter is now in the Tretyakov Gallery.[3]

The history of the Laon panel is well attested. It was taken to the convent of Montreuil-les-Dames from Rome by a certain Jacques Pantaleon in 1249. There it was preserved till the time of the French Revolution, when it was transferred to Laon Cathedral. It was very carefully studied by Professor André Grabar in 1930, who concluded that it should be dated to the end of the twelfth or the early years of the thirteenth century.[4] He was, however, unable to decide on stylistic grounds whether it should be attributed to a Bulgarian, a Serb or a Russian master, and such circumstantial evidence as he was able to deduce added nothing to support one of these as against the others. There were Papal missions to all three countries at the time, and the icon could have been taken to Rome from any of them, while Serbian envoys visited Italy in 1200 and 1217 and a Bulgarian mission was there in 1204; any of these might have taken the panel with them as a gift. The iconography follows a Byzantine model, which could have been available anywhere in the Slav lands.

Though Grabar was unable to reach a decision as to the panel's origin, Professor Miatev has recently identified the inscription upon it as in middle Bulgarian,[5] and this lends weighty support to the claims of Bulgaria. It is therefore discussed and illustrated in this chapter rather than in those on Serbian or Russian work. A date before 1249 is certain and one around 1200 is extremely probable.

Though no other panels of these early years survive there is good evidence for their existence, if only on the testimony of what may best be termed 'simulated' icons in the wall paintings, that is to say depictions of icons, including their frames, as well as their subject matter on the walls. The earliest wall paintings of this type are those at Bačkovo which date from the twelfth century,[6] and there are others of 1230 at Tirnovo and of 1259 at Boiana. Here paintings of Christ Euergetes (*pl. 42*) and St Nicholas, the patron saint of the church, occupy the very places to right and left of the iconostasis which would normally have been filled by panels.

However, the earliest actual icon now in the country that can be counted as a truly Bulgarian work is a large double-sided panel from Nusebr (Messembria). It is to be dated to the early fourteenth century and is now in the icon museum at Sofia. It bears Christ on one face and the Virgin Eleusa on the other, with full-length figures on the margins on both sides.[7] The rather harsh colouring, with a marked predilection for red, is probably to be regarded as a characteristically Bulgarian feature; the rendering of Christ's face, dark and expressive, recalls in some way that of the Sainte Face of

Laon, though the work is not nearly as accomplished. An icon which appears to be very similar in style was presented to the monastery of Bačkovo in 1310, but it is so blackened with grime that it is impossible to be very sure as to its colouring.

The rendering of the Virgin on the double icon may be contrasted with that on a panel now in the Sofia Museum (*pl. 43*) which originally also came from Nusebr. It is much more conservative and formal. Today it is partly covered by a silver mount on which there are three inscriptions in Greek; one of them states that the icon was presented to the church of the Virgin Eleusa at Nusebr during the reign of Ivan Alexander (1331–71) and that the Tsar was responsible for the gift of the silver covering in 1342. The painting itself is thus presumably to be dated a few years before that. The expressionless faces are the result of a subsequent repainting, and give little idea of what the original was like from a stylistic point of view.

Taken as a whole icon painting in Bulgaria seems to have suffered more during the period of Turkish overlordship than that in the other Balkan lands, either because of looting or because the local populations took less care of such icons as they had, preferring to throw out the old ones when they had got into poor condition or became obscured by dirt and smoke. In any case very few icons that are earlier than the sixteenth century other than those mentioned above are now to be found and such as there are are very poor.

The next example, in chronological sequence, is a panel dated 1495 from the Bačkovo Monastery, representing the Deesis (*pl. 44*). There is an inscription in Greek at the base of Christ's throne. That the inscription is in Greek is explained by the fact that during this period the Bulgarian Church was under the direct control of the Patriarch at Constantinople. The style of the painting is essentially provincial, but we do not know enough to say whether this provincialism was universal or whether the manner is to be associated with some particular region, but it would seem that the primitive colouring, the brown background and the rather harsh drawing are all to be regarded as typically Bulgarian features. The inscription records the name of the donor, Michael Bashki, and of his wife Anna, but does not mention the name of the painter. Miatev has, however, assembled the names of quite a number of painters who were working at this time and the icon may have been done by one of them. All those he notes seem to have been Bulgars.[8]

The next icon that is actually dated belongs to the year 1541; it is a double-sided one, bearing the Virgin in the Hodegetria pose on one face and the Crucifixion on the other (*pl. 46*); it is now in the museum of the Holy Synod at Sofia. The Crucifixion is expressive and quite well painted, the Virgin rather more rigid and conventional; there are eight circular medallions of saints on the side margins in each case. An Old Testament Trinity (*pl. 45*), also in the collection of the Holy Synod, has been variously dated to 1652 or to 1597/98; the earlier date seems the more likely.[9] It too is in the collection of the Holy Synod at Sofia (no. 3332), but came from the monastery of Etropoli. It bears an inscription in Bulgarian, and is signed by a painter called Nedyalka of Loveć. The work is rather less primitive than that of the Deesis panel at Bačkovo, but the accomplishment of the best Cretan work of the period is lacking, for the bodies are badly proportioned and have little substance, while the heads are over-large. But the bright colouring, with a predominance of red, is wholly Bulgarian and the work has more real quality than most of the local products of the period.

A curious didactic icon (*pl. 47*) in a very primitive, naive style, in the monastery of Dragalevci, comes next in date, for it was painted in 1620. Its content is essentially narrative. At the top a priest stands in front of a domed church, with some peasants before him. From the mouth of one of them issues a snake, denoting that he must have made an untrue confession. There is another group of people below, to the left, approaching a second priest, while to the right a hermit gives advice to a man on whose back is a demon. The inscriptions are in Bulgarian. There is little trace here of the grand manner of the Byzantine or even of the Italo-Cretan style; indeed the icon is typical of peasant work both with regard to style and in subject matter. It has a certain charm, nevertheless, and the figures are lively and expressive.

The same local character distinguishes the next icon that may be mentioned, a spirited St George (*pl. 49*) dated 1667. It is signed by a painter called Vasili, and is now in the Sofia museum, but came from the monastery of Kremikovtsi. The brilliant colours, the prancing horse and the curled-up, serpent-like dragon, together with the group of spectators on the roof of the princess' palace, all have vigour and charm. Mounted saints, especially St George and St Demetrius, were particularly popular in Bulgaria, for they had a special appeal for the predominantly peasant population. Such icons may lack the skill and true artistic quality of the renderings of the same themes done in Russia, but they represent later Bulgarian art at its best.

An icon of the Pantocrator (*pl. 48*) in the Sofia Museum, which, on the other hand, was painted for a man called Veselin Pavle, follows a more conventional style, being based broadly on the lines of a Byzantine prototype. It comes from the village of Balćin and is dated 1642. But the painting is dry and harsh and the figure ill-proportioned and it lacks the naive vigour of the St George panel even though it is more polished and more traditional. The carved borders which frame the central figure and also enclose busts of saints and prophets on the margin are characteristic of the better

41

42   43

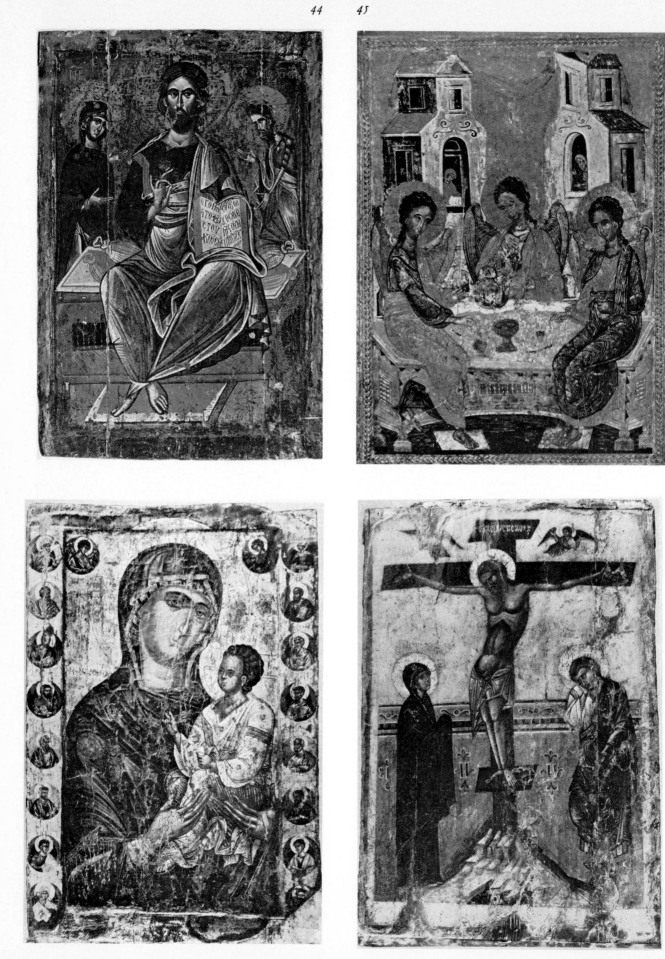

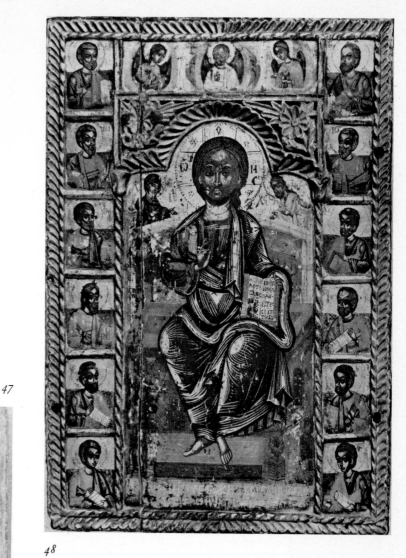

47

48

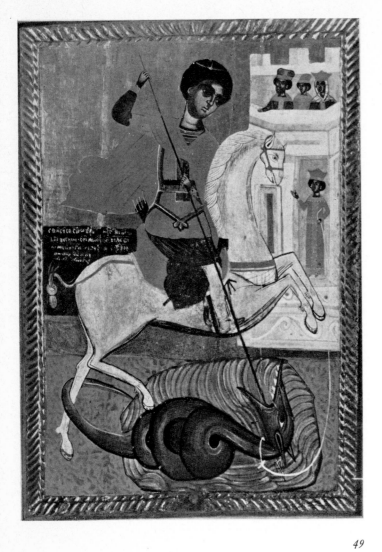 

49   50

local work. Wood carving of the type was common throughout the Balkans at the time and Bulgarian work may be compared to that found in Yugoslavia, as for example at Kučeviste (see p. 35). Both the carving and the painting must be the work of local craftsmen.

Finally attention may be drawn to an icon of St John the Baptist (*pl. 50*), surrounded by scenes from his life set in carved partitions like those on the icon of Christ from Balčin. The St John has wings and follows a model which only became popular at a comparatively late date. He is rather crudely painted, but the scenes that surround the main panel are vivacious and quite effective and serve to illustrate the interest in narrative subjects which was one of the best features of later Bulgarian art.

Though some remarkably fine wall paintings were executed by Bulgarian painters—those at Boiana are outstanding—and work which was probably equally good no doubt existed at Tirnovo, though the paintings there are now in a very poor state of preservation, the panels that are preserved, taken as a whole, seem very second-rate beside them. Whether finer work once existed and has all disappeared, or whether the Bulgarians were just not very good panel painters, it is hard to say. Certain features, notably a search for movement and expression, a love of bright, rather crude colours, and what may be best described as a peasant outlook distinguished most of the later products. This tendency towards the adoption of a wholly peasant style seems to have set in earlier and progressed more rapidly in Bulgaria than was the case in Yugoslavia or Greece. In fact, it must be admitted that later Bulgarian icon painting was a strictly minor art, which cannot compare with that work done elsewhere, least of all in Russia.

41 The Veronica or Holy Face
Cathedral, Laon.
44 × 40 cm.
c. 1200

The face of Christ is depicted in a very realistic manner surrounded by a decorative border and accompanied by a short inscription in Slavonic capitals at the bottom. It represents an early version of what was to become a popular theme, especially in Russia. Two closely similar and more or less contemporary versions are preserved there; one is now in the Tretyakov Gallery (*pl. 95*). (H. P. Gerhard, *The World of Icons*, London, 1971, pl. 33, p. 118.) The original from which they were copied purported to be the impression left by Christ's face on the grave cloth. It is usually known as the 'Veronica', sometimes as the 'Vernicle', and is associated with the saint of that name, though the word is derived from the Latin designation 'Vera-Icona' (true portrait). It was regarded as one of the most precious of the relics preserved at Constantinople, having been taken there from Cappadocia in 574, although another, and perhaps more famous, version was preserved at Edessa till 944, when it too was taken to Constantinople, to form a part of the rich treasure kept in the church of the Theotokos of the Pharos, within the confines of the Imperial Palace. The panel at Laon is certainly a Slavonic work, but the authorities are divided as to whether it was executed by a Bulgarian, a Serb or a Russian painter.

The panel was taken to Laon from Rome in 1249 by a certain Jacques Pantaleon and presented to the convent of Montreuil-les-Dames, where it remained till the French Revolution, when it was transferred to the Cathedral. How long it had been in Rome is not absolutely certain, but it is undoubtedly to be assigned to the last years of the twelfth or the earlier ones of the thirteenth century. It was no doubt either acquired in the Slav world by a member of one of the various papal missions which went there around that time, or was taken to Rome as a present; Serbian envoys were in Rome in 1200 and again in 1217 and Bulgarian ones were there in 1204.

A. Grabar, 'La Sainte Face de Laon', *Seminarium Kondakovianum*, Prague, 1934. See also K. Miatev, in *Icons*, p. xlvii, who presents the case for an attribution to a Bulgarian painter.

42 Simulated icon. Christ Euergetes (Benefactor)
Church of Boiana, near Sofia.
1259

The portrait of Christ is particularly vivid and spirited, and serves to illustrate the high quality of Bulgarian painting at this date. Although actually a wall-painting, it is situated to the north of the altar, in a place which would normally be occupied by a panel, and it would seem to have been copied from an actual panel. Although panels were undoubtedly important in Bulgaria from the tenth century onwards, no actual examples which are earlier than the thirteenth century survive, but the practice of executing wall-paintings that simulated panels seems to have been a usual one, and examples are preserved in several churches.

A. Grabar, *La Peinture religieuse en Bulgarie*, Paris, 1928, p. 120. K. Miatev, *Die Fresken aus Boiana*, Sofia-Dresden, 1961, p. 11.

43 *The Virgin Hodegetria*
From the church of the Virgin, Nusebr. Now in Icon Museum, Sofia.
131 × 107.8 cm.
1342

The Virgin, and the Child to an even greater degree, occupy rigidly frontal poses and there is little hint of sympathy or human feeling in spite of the fact that the title *Eleusa* (Tender) is written beside the Virgin. The style of the painting suggests quite a late date. The upper part of the background is, however, covered by a metal mount, which extends also over the border of the panel and the date is inscribed on this. The nature of the mount shows that it can hardly have been prepared for another panel, so it must be assumed that the painting belongs to the same period, though it must surely have been considerably affected by later restorations.

There are actually four inscriptions, all in Greek. The first records that the icon was presented to the Church at Nusebr during the reign of Ivan Alexander (1331–71), and that his son presented the silver covering for the hands. According to the second, the Tsar also provided for the restoration of the church, while the third records various treasures preserved there. The fourth states that the garland was presented during the reign of Ivan Alexander and Michael Asen, by their grand uncle, Samuel. In addition to the inscriptions two scenes, the Betrothal and the Presentation in the Temple, are depicted in repoussé work on the right-hand side and there are also medallions of the Archangels Michael and Gabriel. The Virgin's halo and the upper parts of the mount on the left-hand side are later additions.

Miatev in *Icons*, pl. 107. B. Filow, *Geschichte der Alt-Bulgarischen Kunst*, Berlin, 1932. For the inscriptions see T. Gerisimov, in *Bulletin of the National Museum*, Burgas, I, 1950, p. 253.

44 *Deesis*
Monastery of Bačkovo.
106.7 × 71.8 cm.
1497

Christ is seated on a stool-like throne in a severely frontal position. The throne extends across the whole surface of the icon from side to side and the Virgin and St John, both of whom turn inwards towards Christ, stand behind it; they are shown on a very much smaller scale than Christ. There is a dedicatory inscription to the right of Christ's footstool, in which the date is recorded. The style is extremely primitive and the icon is to be regarded as a local work, by a painter of no very great ability.

Miatev, in *Icons*, pl. 113. S. Bossilkov, *Twelve Icons of Bulgaria*, Sofia, 1966.

45 *The Old Testament Trinity*
By the painter Nedyalka of Loveč
From the Monastery of Etropoli. Now in the Collection of the Holy Synod, Sofia.
93 × 70 cm.
Probably 1597/98

The three angels are seated at a table. Behind are fantastic tower-like structures, with a red hanging suspended between them. Sarah stands in a window of the tower on the extreme left, holding a dish of food; Abraham is in the tower to the right, his hands raised in a gesture of welcome. The basic theme of Abraham's encounter at the oak of Mamre has thus been discarded, and the background adopted is that usually associated with a scene taking place inside a building. The painter's ideas must thus have been somewhat muddled, but the bright colours are gay and attractive, though the conception is closer to peasant art than to the true Byzantine tradition.

The date is included in an inscription below the table, but there has been some difference of opinion as to its interpretations. Miatev suggests 1652, but Bossilkov gives it as 1597/98, reading 7105 after the year of Creation, and his reading would appear to be correct.

Miatev, in *Icons*, pl. 133. S. Bossilkov, *Twelve Icons of Bulgaria*, no. viii.

46a, Double-sided icon; obverse,
b *the Virgin and Child*;
reverse, *the Crucifixion*
From the church at Sozopol. Now in the Church Museum, Sofia.
105 × 70.5 cm.
1541

The Virgin, who bears the special designation, Phaneromeni, is depicted rather severely and the severity of the rendering is enhanced by the very formal medallions of saints on the borders, eight of which appear on each side. The epithet Phaneromeni presumably refers to an icon of that designation in the church of the same name at Nicosia in Cyprus; though considerably restored it is perhaps to be assigned to the eleventh century. (D. Talbot

Rice, *The Icons of Cyprus*, London, 1937, no. 27.)

In the scene of the Crucifixion, on the other hand, the body of Christ is depicted with great feeling and delicacy as it hangs limply on the cross. St John is also expressive, though the Virgin is more severe, and the formal character is enhanced by the wall-like structure which occupies the lower portion of the background and cuts the icon virtually in half.

The work is much finer than much of that to be found at this time in Bulgaria, but still falls short of the better work being done in Yugoslavia and Greece.

Miatev, in *Icons*, pls. 122, 123 and 124.

47 Icon bearing a didactic theme
Monastery of Dragalevci.
106 × 77 cm.
1620

The composition is made up of a series of separate scenes. At the top, to the left, a group of five peasants moves towards a priest, who stands below a ciborium. To the right four more men are tempted by the devil to drink from a hogshead while a fifth man is driven towards them by a demon. At the centre is a stylized hill, and below it, to the right, a monk gives advice to a peasant on whose back is a demon; to the left another group approaches a priest to make their confessions. At the top of the panel Christ appears in clouds, and there is an inscription, with the date, on the mountain, and another in the bottom right-hand corner. The work is very primitive and the conception wholly that of a peasant society so that the icon has an essentially local significance.

Miatev, in *Icons*, p. 137.

48 *Christ Pantocrator*, framed by busts of Saints and Prophets
From the village of Balčin. Now in the museum of the Holy Synod, Sofia.
77 × 53 cm.
1642

Christ is seated in a frontal position on a throne with a high back. The figures of the Virgin and St John, on a much smaller scale, rise up from behind it, thus transforming the theme into a rudimentary Deesis. At the top there is a bust figure of Christ, conceived as The Ancient of Days, with an Archangel on either side. On the margins there are busts of Apostles in rectangular frames, six on either side. They are separated from the main composition by a carved border and the whole icon is framed by a band of similar carving, though here it is rather wider. There is an inscription below Christ's footstool giving the date of the icon and the name of the donor, Veselin Pavle. Christ's head is very out of proportion, and the icon is not a work of any artistic consequence.

Miatev, in *Icons*, pl. 131.

49 (Colour plate IV) *St George*
Signed by Vasili the Monk
From the Monastery of Kremikovtsi. Now in the Icon Museum, Sofia.
88 × 63 cm.
1667

The saint holds a long lance in his tiny hands, with which he spears the dragon, writhing in a pool below his toy-like horse. There is a cord round the dragon's neck, the end of which is held by the Princess, who stands in the door of her palace, and on the ramparts above are three men who watch the events. Behind St George is an inscription in cursive script, which mentions the date and the name of the painter and the donors, Petko, Peter and Todor.

The saint's red cloak gives the icon gaiety, as does the idiotic horse, but the work is naive in the extreme.

Miatev, in *Icons*, pl. 135. Bossilkov, *Twelve Icons of Bulgaria*, no. IX.

50 *St John the Baptist*, with fourteen scenes from his life
From Vraca. Now in the Archiepiscopal Museum, Sofia.
93 × 65 cm.
1694

The Baptist, who is shown with wings, is depicted almost three-quarter length, his left hand holding a scroll and staff, his right hand raised in blessing. The figure occupies over half of the full extent of the panel and is bordered by a carved moulding, outside which there are three scenes from his life above and below, and four on either side; the final one depicts the Baptism of Christ.

The rendering in this case is very conventional and rather less crude than is the case with most of the later Bulgarian icons.

Miatev, in *Icons*, pl. 130.

Chapter Four

Greece

THE TERM GREEK, so far as icon painting is concerned, has a dual connotation. On the one hand it may be applied to describe icons which are known to have been executed on Greek soil, even if they date from Byzantine times, that is to say from before the Turkish conquests of the mid-fifteenth century. On the other it may be used purely chronologically, to describe the icons produced for Greek-speaking peoples of the Orthodox East after the end of the Byzantine empire, whether those peoples lived in the area now called Greece or in regions which were then mainly inhabited by Greeks, though they had already become part of the Turkish empire, notably in the region of Smyrna or in the Pontus.

So far as localization is concerned, it still remains remarkably difficult to determine on stylistic grounds alone where icons were painted. Those that are in a wholly provincial style may, it is true, sometimes be associated with a particular area simply because they are so poor that it is impossible to believe that there was ever any desire to remove them from the region where they were painted. Many such icons are to be found in small towns and villages especially in later times; at an earlier date they are rare, because in the villages the dangers of destruction were very considerable so that few have survived. Others again, which are rather finer artistically, are in so very individual a style that it seems possible to attribute them to a restricted area. A panel of this type from Patmos, now in a private collection in Athens, is reproduced by Chatzidakis.[1] It depicts the Raising of Lazarus and is probably to be dated to the early twelfth century. The colouring, where blue predominates, the red background, and the rather clumsy figures are all distinctive. It must have been one of a series of small icons depicting the feasts of the Church, the major events of our Lord's life. Another panel, on which the Transfiguration is represented, is clearly by the same painter and must have belonged to the same series of festival icons; it is now in the Hermitage Museum at Leningrad.[2] It is uncertain when it arrived in Russia, but the very fact that two icons from the same place and by the same painter are to be found as far apart as Patmos and Leningrad serves to show how little reliance can be placed on the present whereabouts of icons as a guide to their original home.

In so far as the finer, more sophisticated icons are concerned, that is to say those sponsored by the nobility or painted for the larger churches, what one may term the Metropolitan style was universally influential, and, as we have already noted, quite a number of panels can be cited which can, with a reasonable degree of certainty, be assigned to workshops both in Constantinople and in Salonica. Salonica had from quite early times been the second city of the empire, and its inhabitants included a considerable number of rich and prosperous citizens, who could well afford the best. How hard it is to distinguish the work done there from that of Constantinopolitan masters is proved if the mosaics in the church of the Holy Apostles there, executed around 1315, are compared with those of much the same date in Kariye Camii at Constantinople; we have already called attention to two icons which fall into the same category namely a Crucifixion and a bust figure of the Archangel Michael, which might equally well have been painted in either city. They are now in the Byzantine Museum at Athens.[3] The former is certainly one of the most beautiful and spiritual icons ever produced in the Byzantine world, whether it was painted in the one city or the other.

Though one day it may become possible to attempt some form of classification on the basis of locality, that day has not yet arrived, and for that reason we are using the term Greek in this book in its purely chronological sense, and in this chapter propose to deal only with icons that were painted in the Greek-speaking world after the year 1453.

It is not possible to say very much about Greek painting in the years immediately following the Turkish conquests, but it must be remembered that the Greek areas fell under Turkish domination gradually, so that the inhabitants of the various regions had time to accustom themselves to a foreign overlordship which was at the outset by no means unduly oppressive. The larger churches were, it is true, mostly converted to the worship of Islam, but the smaller ones were left to the Christians and as time went on the construction of new ones was permitted, provided that they were not on too impressive a scale. Moreover, monastic institutions like those at the Meteora or on Mount Athos were hardly interfered with by the conquerors at all, and life in these places probably flourished just as vigorously as it had before the Turkish conquest—in many cases the monasteries were even more prosperous, for they provided a sure home for Christians and a refuge from the upsets and turmoils of everyday life. Icons were required for these monasteries and for the churches that remained in Christian hands, and it is probable that at this time there was also an increased demand for them in the home, so that private intercession might be made through them for support against the Moslem overlords. In fact the demand for icons was accelerated rather than diminished as a result of the conquests. The highly sophisticated patronage of the upper nobility and members of the court circle may have come to an end, but a new and even wider, if more modest, demand took its place, which tended to be more universal and was less centralized around the products of a few metropolitan workshops.

As we have stated, research has not yet gone far enough to permit any exact distinction of schools as is being done in Russia, but it is nevertheless possible to say that painting in the north of Greece seems to have been a good deal less progressive than that done in the more westerly islands, and more especially in Crete. Crete did not fall to the Turks in the mid-fifteenth century like the rest of Greece, for it had already been taken over by the Venetians, and it remained a Venetian colony till the seventeenth century. Many Greek painters from Constantinople appear to have migrated thither, and in spite of the differences between Catholic and Orthodox which had divided the Christian world in the fourteenth and earlier fifteenth centuries, the situation in the Islands seems to have been much more satisfactory; the Orthodox population was allowed to develop with greater freedom than under Turkish rule, which in the rest of Greece gradually tended to become more and more oppressive. More important, the Christian population there gradually became more isolated, being cut off from the rest of Europe in a way which was not the case in Crete. There, the West abounded and the Orthodox Christians were treated with the greatest liberalism. It was thus in Crete that the finest work in the way of icon painting was done after about 1500, for the Cretan painters were the direct inheritors of the true Constantinopolitan style. Elsewhere local elements were more to the fore and the art was on the whole less sophisticated. This does not apply to Venice, where a large Greek colony existed under most favoured conditions.

Nevertheless, quite good work was produced on the Greek mainland and in those parts of Asia Minor where there were large Christian populations such as the Pontic area or even Constantinople itself, and many of the icons which are to be found in private collections in the West today belong to these regions, having come into the market in the twenties of the present century, when the Greek inhabitants of Turkey were exchanged with the Moslem ones of Greece; only on very few occasions were these Greeks permitted to take their personal possessions or even the furnishings of their churches with them and much of what they left found its way into the bazaars of Constantinople.

Occasionally the painters of Constantinople and the mainland signed their panels and inscribed dates upon them, though this practice was not usual before the seventeenth century. One of the few such men that we know by name was called John the Priest and he worked in the village of Zarkha near Trikkala in 1621, as well as doing several icons for the monastery of Barlaam at the Meteora, some of which are dated 1628. He had at least two sons who were also painters and who worked with him on the wall-paintings of the same monastery.

Another was the monk Pegasios, who executed an icon of the 'glorification' in the Benaki Museum dated 1600, while a painter called Iamblikis Romanos, who worked on Mount Athos, signed a copy of a famous icon in the monastery of Iviron, dated 1648. It was made for the Archimandrate of Iviron and presented to Tsar Alexei Michaelovich of Russia in 1654. The original icon is virtually invisible; the copy represents a conservative Hodegetria adorned with an elaborate mount or 'riza', and was, in 1915, in the monastery of the Virgin.[4]

In Crete and the western islands, where contacts with the West were responsible for the introduction of new ideas, signatures and dates were much more frequently added, just as they were by Western painters. Most of the men who signed in this way were natives of Crete, even if they worked for a time elsewhere; but a few others came from the western islands of which Corfu was the most important—it had fallen to Venice as early as 1386. It is the icons that these men produced both at home and in Venice that form the basis of this chapter. It was probably also as a result of contacts with the West that the Cretan painters began to claim a place as individual artists. In earlier times the painters had all been anonymous, and if any name was recorded it was that of the patron. In Crete the names of the painters tended to become more important than those of the donors and it would seem that patrons began to value the work of particular men and to commission paintings by them quite early in the sixteenth century.

These icons are today usually described as Italo-Cretan or Italo-Greek, more because the painters worked mostly in places which were under Italian domination, or even in Italy itself, rather than because there was anything very Italianate about their products, in any case at the outset. Their paintings are essentially icons and follow an icon-painting tradition in style, technique and iconography, even if a few Western or baroque elements intrude. They are quite different from the so-called primitives produced in Italy slightly earlier.

Sometimes the paintings are simply described as Cretan without the addition of the word Italo, but the word Cretan when used alone is a rather confusing one, for it has several different meanings. It was first coined by the French Byzantinist Gabriel Millet to describe a group of wall-paintings produced from the fourteenth century onwards which stood apart from those of another school, centred in northern Greece, which he termed the Macedonian. The work of this Cretan school was distinguished from the Macedonian by brighter colouring, a lighter touch and a different iconographical system; it represented a direct descent from the style which dominated in court circles in Constantinople, whereas the Macedonian manner was more dramatic and rather less sophisticated. The products of this Cretan school were by no means limited to Crete, any more than the work of the Macedonian school was restricted to Macedonia; rather they represented two families of paintings, as similar and as different from one another as, say, the Florentine and the Venetian schools in Italy. In the fourteenth century the finest work of the Cretan school was probably that done at Mistra, in the Peloponnese, which remained an outpost of Constantinople till it fell to the Turks in 1463. This use of the term Cretan should thus be distinguished from its application to the icon painters of the sixteenth and seventeenth centuries, nearly all of whom were born in Crete itself. They nevertheless worked at times overseas; most of them spent quite a considerable portion of their working lives in Venice while others were responsible for many of the later wall-paintings in the monasteries of Mount Athos.

The icons that can be ascribed to the Italo-Cretan painters are very numerous. There are large collections in the Byzantine and Benaki museums at Athens and in the church of San Giorgio dei Greci at Venice or in the museum attached to it, while numerous icons are dispersed throughout the churches of Greece, in Dalmatia, and sporadically in collections all over Europe; those at Ravenna, in the Vatican and in the Hermitage Museum at Leningrad are the most important of them. The collection in the Hermitage was mostly assembled by the Russian scholar Likhachev and the icons were illustrated in his great album entitled *Materials for the History of Icon Painting*, published at St Petersburg in 1906. The collection at Venice has been fully published by Dr Chatzidakis and that in the Benaki Museum by Professor Xyngopoulos; the numbers in brackets after the icons refer to their catalogues, to the inventory of the Byzantine Museum at Athens or to Professor Djurić's book *Icônes de Yougoslavie*.

The earliest of the Italo-Cretan icons that is actually signed and dated that has come down to us is a panel depicting the Last Supper (*pl. 51*) hanging on the iconostasis of San Giorgio dei Greci at Venice.[5] It is dated to 1517. Were it not for the date it would be tempting to assign it to the end of the century, for it shows certain Italianate traits such as a circular table with the Apostles seated on both sides of it; according to the Byzantine tradition, the table was shaped like a capital D, with the figures assembled around the curved side, facing the spectator. The icon was presented to the church by a Serb called Bozdar Vuković though the painter was a Cretan working at Venice.

This panel predates by a year a predella at Kolomać in Dalmatia (*pl. 54*), dated 1518, signed by another Cretan painter called Angelos Bizamenos, who worked for a time at Dubrovnik as well as in Venice. The form of this panel is more Western than Greek, while certain of the details, notably the horseman to the right, also savour of Italian art, though these Western traits are by no means universal, and do not necessarily appear in other works by the same painter which are usually more truly Byzantine in style; one formerly in the Russian museum at Leningrad (no. 2986) may be noted which is dated 1532. Bizamenos seems to have spent the greater part of his working life at Venice, and either he or Donatos Bizamenos, who was probably his brother, also spent some time at Otranto in the very south of Italy where there was also quite a considerable Greek population; it had been established since early times, unlike the colony at Venice. Quite a number of icons by Bizamenos seem to have found their way to Dalmatia, where they were used in the Catholic as well as in the Orthodox churches. A date of 1536 on an icon in the Benaki Museum[6] has been wrongly interpreted; it is in fact a work of the eighteenth century.

Only slightly later in date are two sets intended for the Deesis row of an iconostasis; one is made up of five panels, Christ, the Virgin, St John the Baptist, St Peter and St Paul (*pl. 52*), and is at the monastery of Dionysiou on Mount Athos; the other, consisting of seven panels, is in the church of the Protaton at Karyes, also on Mount Athos. Both sets are dated 1542 and the former is signed by a painter called Euphrosynos.[7] His figures are rather ungainly, with large heads and sloping shoulders, while those on the other series of panels—they include two Archangels (*pl. 53*)—are more elegant, more academic, and closer to the style followed by most of the so-called Cretan fresco painters on Athos. Another panel (*pl. 55*), bearing the main figures of the Deesis alone (Christ, the Virgin and St John) is in San Giorgio dei Greci at Venice; it is dated 1546. It includes at the bottom the portrait of the donor who commissioned it, Joannes Manises, and there are inscriptions both in Latin and in Greek. Though the date is given there is no mention of the painter's name. The rendering of the Deesis itself is wholly Byzantine in spite of the Latin inscription, but the donor and the figures of men on horses at either side of the inscription are Western. Many of the Cretan painters, though they normally worked in a wholly Byzantine style, seem to have been able to adopt a Western idiom at will, but owing to the firm rules laid down by the Orthodox Church no liberties could be taken with regard to the religious scenes even if new styles were followed for such things as donor portraits.

The most important of the Cretan painters working towards the end of the sixteenth century was Michael Damaskenos, who is revered in Greece today as their greatest painter; he is sometimes even called 'the friend of El Greco'. He was born in Candia about 1550, and went to Venice in 1574. Later he returned to Crete. The earliest icon that can be attributed to him is one of the Virgin (pl. 56) in the Loverdos Collection at Athens, dated 1570. Slightly later is a Presentation on Mount Sinai, dated to 1571. He was responsible for no less than twenty-three of the icons in the church of San Giorgio at Venice, for he was commissioned to paint the whole iconostasis and most of the work was done in time for it to be presented to the church in 1574, though a few of the panels were added later, in 1582. Dr Chatzidakis, in his study of the icons of San Giorgio, notes that the painter's style had changed markedly during these eight years in Venice. The earlier panels are thus very traditional but the later ones show the intrusion of a good many Italianate features. The change was no doubt due to the atmosphere of Venice, where the painter came into contact with a good many Italian masters, but when once he had returned to Crete Damaskenos reverted to his earlier manner. The changed style in the icons of 1582 is clearly illustrated if the Epitaphios of 1582 (pl. 58)[8] is compared with the Baptism done in 1574 (pl. 57).[9] There is no doubt that Damaskenos' more conservative work is, artistically speaking, the more satisfactory.

An intrusion of Italian elements similar to those that we see in Damaskenos' work can be observed in the paintings of several of his contemporaries. The most important of them was probably George Klotzas, also a native of Candia. His icons are well represented in San Giorgio as well as in several collections both inside and outside Greece. He was especially active between 1567 and 1576. Though none of his icons seem to be exactly dated, one at Venice entitled 'In Thee Rejoiceth' (pl. 59) may be noted both because of the interest of the subject and because of the quality of the work. The subject was one that was hardly known in Byzantine times though it became very popular later, especially in Russia. The theme is abstract rather than direct and represents the Glorification of the Virgin, who is shown at the top of the panel surrounded by a mass of figures arranged as a sort of geometric composition. In Klotzas' painting the figures seem almost innumerable, but every one is beautifully painted and the icon is a work of very high quality, even if it can perhaps be best appreciated as a series of details.[10] The poses and appearance of some of the figures, notably the Magi in the scene of the Adoration, show something of the freedom of Italian

art, but the picture is essentially an icon and an icon of high quality even if the miniature-like treatment contrasts markedly with the more selective style of earlier Byzantine art. Klotzas was especially adept at this type of miniature work and other icons in the same style are to be found in several collections. Another man, called John Apakas, seems to have been much influenced by Klotzas. He executed two icons in the Venice collection,[11] neither of which is exactly dated; otherwise little is known about him.

Italian influence is rather less marked in the work of the next man we must consider, Johannes Kyprios, who executed a small panel of the Annunciation (pl. 60) now in the Benaki Museum.[12] It is dated 1585. There is nothing particularly Cypriot about it, in spite of the painter's name. In actual fact he seems to have been trained at Venice, where he studied for a time under Tintoretto, though he always remained faithful to the Byzantine idiom. An Ascension[13] and a Noli me Tangere,[14] both in Venice, must be dated to the last decade of the century. They are in a rather poor condition.

The work of the generation of painters that succeeded these men—it belongs in the main to the first quarter of the seventeenth century—is on the whole rather conservative and shows less evidence of Italianate influence, even though the painters were just as closely associated with Venice as were those of the preceding generation. The phase is best represented by three men, Emmanuel Lombardos, Emmanuel Tsanfurnari and Beninos Emporios, though there were numerous other painters, many of whom we do not know by name.

One of Lombardos' earliest works is an icon at Venice (pl. 61)[15], of St John the Evangelist dictating to his assistant Procoros. It is dated to 1602. He seems to have been especially distinguished as a painter of Madonnas and there are examples in several collections; one at Venice[16] is perhaps as early as 1602; one in the Benaki Museum is dated 1609 (pl. 62); one in the Sinai monastery is dated 1626 and one at Padua 1647. His earliest work is probably an icon of the Burning Bush in the Loverdos collection at Athens, dated 1593. An icon of St Catherine in the Benaki Museum[17] dated 1622, and a Noli me Tangere at Dubrovnik (pl. 63)[18] dated 1603, may also be noted. The painter was a native of Rethymo in Crete, but most of his work seems to have been done in Venice.

In addition to Emmanuel there were three other painters called Lombardos, while another man, called Emmanuel Lamprados, must also be distinguished. Of the three called Lombardos one, Joachim, is known from a document preserved in the Isle of Zante; another, John, painted an icon of St Gregory now in the Benaki Museum;[19] the third, Peter, executed a painting of the Saviour at Corfu, a head of St John the Baptist in the Byzantine Museum at Athens[20] and an icon of Christ as High Priest in the Benaki Museum.[21] All of them worked in the early seventeenth century. Emmanuel Lamprados was more important than any of these men. He is sometimes known as Lampra, and is represented by a Nativity in the Byzantine Museum at Athens[22] and an icon now in the Hermitage which was first published by Likhachev.[23] An icon in the possession of Lord Melchett is also probably by him; it is dated around 1650.[24]

The most outstanding figure of this age, however, just as Damaskenos was that of the preceding one, was Emmanuel or Manuel Tsanfurnari who painted an elaborate Death of St Spyridon in San Giorgio dei Greci (pl. 64).[25] The arrangement of the scene follows that which had been established many centuries earlier for the Dormition of the Virgin and was followed for death scenes in general. Tsanfurnari seems to have been attracted by the composition, for he did at least one painting of the Death of St Ephraim Syrus which is now in the Vatican, the arrangement of which is virtually identical with the St Spyridon. The St Spyridon picture is dated 1636 and it is probably one of the earliest of his works, though there are a good many icons signed by him distributed throughout a large number of collections. There are three in the Benaki Museum, an Annunciation, an Ascension and a very elaborate Nativity;[26] all are signed but none is exactly dated. Unlike so many of the painters of the age Tsanfurnari was not a Cretan but came from Corfu. Most of his work was, however, apparently done at Venice, and he assimilated there a good many Western ideas.

Beninos Emporios, who did wall-paintings in the church of San Giorgio, was one of the first Cretans to spend virtually his whole life in Venice. Like Klotzas he favoured a minute, miniature-like style, as can be seen in his rendering of the Last Supper at Venice (pl. 66),[27] which is dated 1606. It takes the form of a double panel, made to fit a special place on the wall, and the Apostles are depicted seated behind a rectangular table of very Western appearance. The painting is not a work of great distinction, but is nevertheless interesting as a transitional piece.

Another Cretan who lived nearly all his life in Venice was Emmanuel Tsane, sometimes called Boniales. He was a priest and though he served in the church of San Giorgio for many years he also found time to paint a surprisingly large number of icons, perhaps because he lived to the age of eighty, being born in Crete in 1610 and dying in Venice in 1690. Tsane was especially happy when confronted with lively subjects and his work is to be seen at its best in the rendering of vivid scenes. There are fifteen icons by him in San Giorgio, many of them dated, while elsewhere an icon of St Spyridon (pl. 65) in the Correr Museum at Venice, dated 1636, and one of St Anne (frontispiece) dated 1637 and one of St Demetrius dated 1672 both in the Benaki Museum,[28] may be noted. A Tree of Jesse in San Giorgio[29] dated 1644 and other panels dated 1660, 1667, 1677 and 1686

illustrate the development of his style over the years, as do three panels in the Byzantine Museum at Athens which date from 1661, 1671 and 1680.[30] One of Sts Cosmas and Damian in the National Gallery in London is more accessible to Western students; it must date from about 1680, while a Virgin dated 1681 is figured by Likhachev (op. cit., pl. 96). Many other dated examples of his work could be cited. His single figures tended to be conservative, but in the rendering of scenes he searched for greater originality, and this irrespective of the date at which they were done. But a love for ornate baroque detail was especially to the fore in his later work. His brother Constantine was also a painter, but he was less prolific in output and he died some years before Emmanuel. There are three dated icons[31] by his hand in San Giorgio, an Apostle Thomas of 1670, the Saints of January the Twenty-second (pl. 67) of 1682, and a portrait of an ecclesiastic in a wholly Western style, dated 1675.

Another well-known name of this age was that of Philotheus Scouphos, who painted a large icon of the Presentation (pl. 68)[32] now in the Byzantine Museum at Athens, dated 1669; it is characterized by very striking colouring which is of the type to be found in the best work illustrating the Byzantine heritage, even though, in 1662, he too had been a priest of San Giorgio dei Greci. The icon marks Scouphos out as a painter of considerable ability.

More famous among collectors of today, however, is the painter Theodore Poulakis, who was born in Crete in 1662. He seems to have worked in Venice on two occasions, the first between 1644 and 1650, the second from 1670 till 1675. He died in Corfu in 1692. His icons were widely spread all over Greece and the western islands during his lifetime. Their style is somewhat eclectic, Italianate baroque features frequently being present. He is probably to be seen at his best in his more conservative work. None of his icons would seem to be exactly dated, but the more austere ones appear on the whole to be early, the more baroque ones later.

A greater degree of conservatism characterized the work of the last of the great Cretans, namely the man known as Victor; he seems always to have signed with what was presumably his Christian name, and his surname is not known. He first worked in the western islands, but was apparently in Venice between 1674 and 1676, and two of his icons[33] in San Giorgio are dated to 1674; one represents Jesus the Vine of Life and the other the Tree of Jesse (pl. 69). In 1675 or early in 1676 he adorned with religious scenes a banner which Francesco Morosini flew from his ship in expeditions to the Morea in 1676 and 1693. An icon in the Hermitage is dated 1660 and may serve to illustrate his earlier style.

By the end of the century Crete had fallen to the Turks and the continuity of the flow of painters to Venice was broken. Nor were any of the men who

54

55   56

57

58

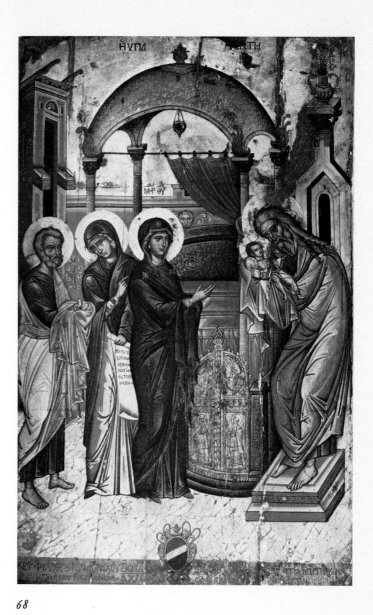

67

68

worked at the end of the seventeenth or early in the eighteenth century of anything like the same importance as those working earlier. The names of a few of them who produced exactly dated paintings may, however, be noted. Elias Moschos painted an Anastasis in the Benaki Museum,[34] a St Tryphon at Donja Lastva near Cattaro dated 1658,[35] and an icon of Christ (*pl. 70*) at Recklinghausen dated 1653. He must not be confused with John Moschos who worked at a rather later date; one of his earliest icons seems to be a Virgin and Child in the Benaki Museum (no. 39), dated 1681, but most of his product belongs to the next century. George Chryso-loras and Parthenos Kangularis, whose work is also represented in San Giorgio, belong to the eighteenth rather than to the seventeenth century. A very nice icon of St Catherine in the Byzantine Museum at Athens, dated 1692, but not signed, may also be noted.

By this time painters who were not Cretans or even from the western isles had also begun to sign and date their work more freely. One of the earliest seems to have been Nicholas the Peloponnesian, who painted an icon of an archdeacon in the monastery of St Stephen at the Meteora, dated 1659. A man called Makarios the monk executed an Ascension in the Byzantine Museum at Athens[36] dated 1663; John Metaxas of Kalabaka painted a St Nicholas in the cathedral at Trikkala dated 1665, and Stephanos Tsankarolas a large icon of St Jacob dated 1688, now in the Benaki Museum at Athens.[37] None of these paintings are of very great artistic quality.

Other men, some known by name (see Appendix I), but many more of them anonymous, continued to paint throughout the eighteenth century. Most of their products represent the work of journeymen, but they maintained the old traditions of icon painting and it is often very difficult to be sure of the dates of their products, for earlier models were followed very exactly. It is this adherence to tradition that makes the icons of this period interesting and puts them in a class that is perhaps higher than that of the second-rate painters in the West, where some degree of originality was believed to be more essential. But in spite of the innate conservat-ism of icon painting, several new themes become popu-lar in these later years, the most important of which was the cycle of the Apocalypse. It was especially popular in wall paintings, and was frequently used for the adorn-ment of monastic refectories, but an interesting icon (*pl. 71*) devoted to the subject, dated to 1625, is pre-served in the icon museum at Recklinghausen; it shows the Four Horsemen of the Apocalypse. The subject was a favourite theme for wall paintings in monastic refec-tories, but it is seldom found on icons. It was probably introduced from the West by way of a woodcut, but it is treated on this icon with real feeling for decoration. Russian work of the so-called Stroganov school was very similar.

51 The Last Supper, flanked by Sts Stephen and Michael
San Giorgio dei Greci, Venice.
122 × 54 cm.
1517

Christ and the Twelve Apostles are seated at a large round table. Christ is shown blessing and St John is bent down before Him. The arrangement, although it is not unique in Byzantine work of the fourteenth century, represents something of an innovation, for the D-shaped table, with Christ at the end, was still usual. The in-clusion of a standing figure at either end, St Stephen in deacon's robes to the left and the Archangel Michael to the right, is also something new, as are certain details of a baroque character in the foreground. The architectural background, made up of tower-like structures with a hanging spread between them follows, on the other hand, a very old convention, while the profusion of vessels on the table is paralleled in many of the Athos wall paintings of the same period. The styles that influenced the painter were thus diverse, though the technique, especially as regards the use of highlights, is typical of the best Cretan work.

The icon was presented to San Giorgio by a Serbian patron called Bozdar Vuković, who was a native of Podgoritsa, though he also owned a printing-press at Venice. He seems to have been an admirer of the work of Greek icon painters, and, as the inscription at the base of the panel attests, he commissioned this icon from one of them in 1516/17. The gold background and certain details are the work of a restorer and belong to the nineteenth century.

Venice, pl. 6. *Photo Alinari*

52 St Paul
By the painter Euphrosynos
Monastery of Dionysiou, Mount Athos.
114 × 84 cm.
1542

The icons of the Deesis row of the iconostasis at Dionysiou are five in number; in addition to the Deesis itself they depict St Peter and St Paul. All the figures are shown half-length and St Peter holds a scroll and St Paul a closed volume. The features are all rather con-ventionalized, St Paul's ear being indicated only as a white outline, and the highlights being very exaggerated. But the figures are strong and powerful, with large heads. The style is closer to that of the earlier Mace-donian work as we see it in the wall paintings of the Protaton at Karyes, but the painter, who did all five icons, was called Euphrosynos, and was a Cretan by birth, although up to now none of his work has been found in Crete.

Dr Chatzidakis compares these icons to those of another Deesis row, this time consisting of seven panels, in the Protaton (no. 54), which date from the same year, though here the name of the painter is not known. His figures are more elongated and his work more elegant, and closer to that of the Constantinopolitan school. He too was probably a Cretan.

M. Chatzidakis, 'The Painter Euphrosynos', in *Critica Chronica*, I, Heraklion, 1956, p. 18 (in Greek). *Photo M. Chatzidakis.*

53 The Archangel Michael
Church of the Protaton, Karyes, Mount Athos.
94 × 67 cm.
1542

The Deesis row in the Protaton is made up of seven icons, the Deesis itself, two Archangels and Sts Peter and Paul. We illustrate here the icon of the Archangel Michael. The painting is on a fine hollowed panel and the work is typical of the Cretan style of the period, more so, indeed, than the contemporary work by Euphrosynos at Dionysiou (*pl. 52*).

M. Chatzidakis, 'The Painter Euphrosynos' in *Critica Chronica*, I, Heraklion, 1956, p. 280. *Photo Ph. Zachariou.*

54 Predella, with four Saints
By Angelos Bizamenos
Church of Kolomać, Dalmatia.
31.5 × 168 cm.
1518

The predella is divided into five compartments by columns topped by an arcade. There is one figure in each compartment. To the left is St Nicholas, before a background of houses; next is St John the Baptist, holding a staff with the lamb at its top and a text 'Ecce Agnus Dei' in Latin; in the central panel is St Blaise, patron saint of Dubrovnik; to his left is St Jerome on his knees before a landscape background and with a red cardinal's hat and a lion beside him; and finally, to the right, is St Martin, cutting his cloak with his sword. The names are in Greek characters, except for St Martin's, which is a later addition in Latin. Two fragments bearing the Pentecost are all that survive of the remainder of the painting for which this formed the predella. The iconography is of a very mixed character, indeed more so than was usual in the work of the Cretan masters.

The contract for the making of the predella, drawn up between Bizamenos and the council of the church of Kolomać, is preserved at Dubrovnik. It is dated 1518.

Djurić, pl. 53. He gives a list of the various periodicals in which this unusual panel is mentioned.

55 Deesis, with donor portraits
Church of San Giorgio dei Greci, Venice.
119 × 89 cm.
1546

Christ sits on a simple throne with no back, His right hand raised in blessing, while His left supports a book on His knee, open at the text of John VIII, 12, 'I am the Light of the World'. The Virgin and St John the Baptist turn towards Him in attitudes of intercession. All three figures are impressive and dignified, and the work is of high quality. A donor is shown kneeling between Christ and St John. The portrait is full of expression and shows that the painter was a master of portraiture in the Western style as well as of conventional icon painting.

At the bottom of the icon there is a sort of predella, at the centre of which is a panel bearing inscriptions in both Greek and Latin. They give the names of the donors as Joannes Manises and his brother, George, and the date, 21 April 1546. The kneeling figure on the icon itself depicts Joannes, and he appears again on the predella to the left, leading a horse, while his brother George is shown to the right, with his horse behind him. The Western character of the predella again serves to indicate the ability of the painter in a Western as well as a Byzantine idiom.

Venice, pl. 8.

56 The Virgin and Child
By Michael Damaskenos
Loverdos Collection, Athens.
1570

The Virgin is shown half-length in the Hodegetria pose. Thus she designates the Child with her right hand and supports Him on her left arm whilst He blesses with His right hand and holds a scroll in His left. The style adheres to the grand Constantinopolitan tradition, but the use of broad high lights on the faces is characteristic of the sixteenth-century Greco-Venetian school. The use of numerous rather harsh lines of varying density to indicate folds in the garments is also not unusual although the lines are rather more pronounced in this painting than is customary.

The panel's semi-circular top reflects Western influence.

57 The Baptism
By Michael Damaskenos
Church of San Giorgio dei Greci, Venice.
225 × 215 cm.
1574

The icon forms one of a series of eleven done for the iconostasis. Christ stands in the water, though it reaches only to just below His knees. There are fish in the river, and the personification, holding a vase from which the water gushes, is crouched at the bottom. Above, on the bank, is the tree with the axe stuck in it (Matt. III, 10) and above again a rock on which the Baptist stands, his hand outstretched to touch Christ's head. On the opposite bank are five angels holding towels, while craggy rocks rise above on both sides. At the centre the Holy Spirit, in the form of a dove, descends towards Christ. The figures depicted are those that belong to the basic iconography of the scene, and the general character of the icon is very conservative, though there is a feeling for decoration which, combined with the excellence of the figures, marks the icon as a work of real quality.

Venice, pl. 31. Photo Toso.

58 Epitaphios
By Michael Damaskenos
Church of San Giorgio dei Greci, Venice.
283 × 295 cm.
1582

The painting is on several boards and forms a sort of revetment to the eastern wall of the Prothesis. It is thus on a more monumental scale than the rest of the paintings in the church. Christ's body is depicted lying on the top of a stone sarcophagus. The Virgin, seated at its end, supports His head on her knee. Behind her is Mary of Cleophas, while Mary Magdalene is behind the sarcophagus, raising her arms in lamentation. St John kisses Christ's hand, while St Joseph, at the end, bends sorrowfully over Christ's feet, ready to wrap the grave cloths round the body. Beyond him is Nicodemus, in an attitude of great sorrow. Above angels hold a cross in the sky.

The iconography in general corresponds to that usual in the so-called Cretan wall-paintings of Mount Athos, though Mary of Cleophas and the angels above are additional. Damaskenos' panel is, however, more spiritual and more profound than is the case with the general run of paintings of the scene, and the contrasts between the calm of the figures in the foreground and the greater emotion of those behind adds greatly to the depth of expression. The influence exercised by Venetian art on Damaskenos' work is clearly apparent here, though it does not in any way make the painting eclectic or derivative. It is to be counted as one of the artist's most important works.

Venice, pl. 48.

59 'In Thee Rejoiceth'
By George Klotzas
Church of San Giorgio dei Greci, Venice.
71.5 × 47 cm.
1567–76

The theme is one which was only developed at a fairly late date, and no comparable earlier rendering is known in the Greek world. It is not one, like the Epitaphios, that called for great depth of feeling; it sought rather to convey delight and joy by means of brilliant colour and a composition of an almost abstract character, based to a great extent on geometric forms. Thus a series of concentric circles, all crammed with a mass of rejoicing figures, surround the Virgin, who sits enthroned at the centre with the Child on her knees. In the first of the surrounding circles are cherubim, in the second angels, and in the third the signs of the zodiac. The outer zone, wider than the others, contains scenes of the Akathistos hymn, while below are the Twelve Feasts and above a symbolic rendering of the Crucifixion. Below the main composition there are two horizontal bands, crowded with the figures of saints and prophets.

Venice, pl. 50.

60 The Annunciation
By Johannes Kyprios
Benaki Museum, Athens.
225 × 175 cm.
1585

The two figures of the scene are ranged before an elaborate architectural background, at either end of which is a towering structure, with a colonnade linking them one to the other. In the middle a large pine-tree, treated very realistically, grows from the tower behind the Virgin. She is depicted with great tenderness. In her left hand she holds a book, while the right is raised in a gesture of humble submission. The angel, who has just alighted on the ground, is shown as a rather more massive figure. Between the two figures is an inscription giving the painter's name and the date, 1585. Apart from the unusual background the composition is conservative, and the effect is spiritual as well as decorative.

Xyngopoulos, pl. 7.

61 St John the Evangelist and Procoros
By Emmanuel Lombardos
Church of San Giorgio dei Greci, Venice.
113 × 65 cm.
1602

The two figures are seated in a cave, St John to the left, turning his head to look behind for inspiration, while his disciple Procoros faces him, writing the first words of St John's Gospel 'In the beginning'. Between the two figures is a strangely shaped lectern with a scroll spread out at its top, on which is a text from Acts II, 1. Implements for the manipulation of parchment lie on a shelf half-way up the lectern. Above, silhouetted against the black void of the cave, is a box containing eight rolled scrolls. At the top left-hand corner the Hand of God appears from a 'glory', from which rays also descend towards the Evangelist. In earlier renderings of the subject the figures are more often shown in a building than in a cave, or even before a landscape background; the idea of placing them in a cave was only developed with the sixteenth century. The treatment is truly Cretan and the icon is a typical example of Lombardos' dry but very competent style.

Venice, pl. 55.

62 *The Virgin and Child*
By Emmanuel Lombardos
Benaki Museum, Athens.
108 × 81 cm.
1609

The Virgin holds the Child on her right side, His face pressed against hers in affection, but the pose is different from that of the normal Eleusa and should bear the name Vrephokratousa. At the top of the icon are bust figures of the Archangels Michael and Gabriel. The icon is signed and dated at the bottom. Like most of Lombardos' works it is firm and accomplished, but somewhat hard and lacking in sympathy.

Xyngopoulos, pl. 13.

63 *'Noli me Tangere'*
By Emmanuel Lombardos
Orthodox Church, Dubrovnik.
100 × 69 cm.
1603

Christ stands to the right, looking with compassion at Mary Magdalene, who kneels at His feet. Behind her is a jagged mountain, with the tomb shown as a cave at its side. A tall tree grows out from beside the tomb and there is another smaller tree behind Mary. She and the tomb are identified by inscriptions, and between her and Christ is a text from John XX, 15. The icon is signed and dated on the lower margin. There is a closely similar panel in San Giorgio dei Greci at Venice (*Venice*, no. 96); it is neither signed nor dated, but may well be a work of the same painter.

Djurić, pl. 59. For a full study of the icons depicting this scene see A. Calliga-Yeroulanou, 'The scene Noli me Tangere' in Deltion of the *Christian Archaeological Society*, vol. G, 1962, Athens, 1963, p. 203 (in Greek).

64 *The Death of St Spyridon*
By Emmanuel Tsanfurnari
Church of San Giorgio dei Greci, Venice.
60.5 × 42.8 cm.
1595

The death of the saint is shown at the centre of the panel, and there are five scenes from his life at either side and two each at top and bottom. The death scene follows a formula in common use, similar to that established over many centuries for the Dormition of the Virgin. The body lies on a bier, with the principal mourners at either end and a group of subsidiary figures behind. Here a five-domed church occupies the background and above, in the sky, are the Archangels Michael and Gabriel, who receive the saint's soul, while Uriel and Raphael open the gates of heaven. In the foreground are two figures on a smaller scale, one waving a censer and the other holding a book on which is the inscription 'The Soul of Holy Spyridon'.

The scene on the margin to the left depicts the saint's ordination, his appearance to the king in a dream, baptizing a heathen, overturning the idols in a temple and a river ceasing to flood because of his prayers. At the top he changes a serpent to gold and attends the Synod, while at the bottom he saves a man and his wife from death at the hands of Mohammedans and stops an excess of rain. To the right he refutes Arian teaching, the king renders him homage, he brings a girl to life, he encounters robbers taking corn and offers a goat to some thieves. The scenes depict the events set out in the monthly church calendar, but the painter has rendered them freely, and some of the lay figures wear contemporary costumes. Many of them are very vivid studies, as for example the final scene where thieves drive away flocks. Moreover, the subjects chosen for illustrations are those that give the greatest scope for rendering life and movement.

The icon is signed 'The hand of Emmanuel Tsanfurnari' and is dated 1595. It is thus a comparatively early work of the painter, and shows a happy combination of Western and conservative elements.

Venice, pl. 62.

65 *St Spyridon*
By Emmanuel Tsane
Correr Museum, Venice.
1636

The Saint is shown full-length, blessing with his right hand and holding an open book in his left. He wears the bee-hive-like head-dress that is habitual and his vestments are unusually elaborate. There are four scenes from his life depicted on either side. To the left they represent the changing of a serpent to gold for distribution among the poor, the turning back of a river in flood, the Saint talking to an official's wife and curing Constans, son of Constantine. The top scene on the right is unidentifiable; below it the Saint attends the Council of Nicaea, visits the official's daughter and resuscitates her.

Joseph Myslević, *Ikona*, Prague, 1947, pl. 11.

66 a, The Last Supper
b By Beninos Emporios
Church of San Giorgio dei Greci, Venice.
235 × 362 cm.
1606

The painting has been contrived to fit a particular space surrounding the central door of the iconostasis. The table is shaped like a square bracket laid on its side, the two ends that extend downwards being depicted in inverted perspective. One Apostle sits at each end, three on the outside of each downward projection, and the remaining four face forward from behind the main table, with Christ at the centre. The composition is thus both original and ingenious and surmounts the problem with considerable skill. M. Chatzidakis proposes that the arrangement may have been suggested to the painter by an engraving of Marc Antonio Raimondi, but it may equally well have been the original conception of Emporios, modifying the conventional D-shaped table of Byzantine art to suit the space at his disposal.

The figures are painted in a broad, slightly Westernized, style, but the faces are somewhat stereotyped and the effect is more satisfactory as an ingenious composition than because of the detail.

Venice, pl. 70.

67 The Saints of January 22nd
By Constantine Tsane
Church of San Giorgio dei Greci, Venice.
60 × 49 cm.
1682

The Saints are ranged in three formal rows against a plain gold background, with a figure of Christ above, before an elaborate 'glory'. To His right is an inscription reading 'Prayer of the servant of God the priest Gregorios Moras' and on His opposite side is a coat of arms and an inscription reading 'St Joseph Samakos of Crete and the saints celebrated on the same day, January 22nd'. There is the signature of Constantine Tsane and the date 1682 at the bottom. The names of the saints in the lower row are written on the haloes; they are Leo the Prelate, Timothy the Apostle, Joseph Samakos, who is depicted as a monk holding a scroll, a second, unidentified monk, and St Vincent. Immediately behind are St Parados, St Sissinios and St Gabriel. The names of the figures in the upper row are written on the background; they represent Leo the Martyr, St Devolis, St Emmanuel, St Peter the Prelate and St John the Martyr.

Venice, pl. 122. *Photo Toso.*

68 The Presentation in the Temple
By Philotheus Scouphos
Byzantine Museum, Athens (no. 328).
20 × 64 cm.
1669

The priest, St Simeon, stands to the right holding the Child. The Virgin stands before him, while the Prophetess Anne is behind, holding a scroll, and St Joseph brings in the offering of doves. A large ciborium occupies the middle portion of the background and there are tower-like structures on either side. At the bottom is an inscription reading, 'The hand of Philotheus Scouphos, the monk, abbot of the monastery of Kydonia, 1669'. The icon is a good example of later Cretan work still in a pure Byzantine style.

G. Sotiriou, *Guide du Musée Byzantin d'Athènes*, Athens, 1932, p. 110 and fig. 66.

69 The Tree of Jesse
By Victor
Church of San Giorgio dei Greci, Venice.
52 × 41 cm.
1674

At the bottom Jesse is depicted as an old man sleeping on the ground. A tree rises above with the Virgin at its centre, holding the Child Christ. The various ancestors of Christ are shown as full-length figures on the branches, each holding a narrow scroll with his name upon it.

A second icon, entitled 'The Vine' forms a pendant to it and is of the same shape and date, and by the same painter. Here the central figure represents Christ.

Venice, pls. 129 and 128.

70 Christ Pantocrator
By Elias Moschos
Ikonenmuseum, Recklinghausen.
1653

Christ sits on a marble throne with a very elaborate carved base. His right hand is raised in blessing and with His left He supports a book on His left knee, open at the text 'I am the Light of the World'. Above are the usual initials IC XC and two decorative devices, and the icon is signed 'The hand of Elias Moschos' in the bottom right-hand corner.

N. P. Gerhard, *Welt der Ikonen*, Recklinghausen, 1957, p. 91 and fig. 18; *The World of Icons*, London, 1971, p. 84 and pl. 20. *Photo Wiemann.*

71 The Four Horsemen of the Apocalypse
Ikonenmuseum, Recklinghausen.
1625

The riders are depicted on prancing horses, crushing a number of figures before them. It is probable that this icon was modelled on a Western woodcut of the type executed by Dürer. It is interesting because of its rarity and because of the effective colouring.

H. Skroboucha, *Die Botschaft der Ikonen*, Ettal, 1961, pl. 132.

Chapter Five

Cyprus

THE ICONS of Cyprus present a rather special problem, firstly because of the very large number of firmly dated icons that were produced there in the sixteenth and seventeenth centuries and secondly because of the great diversity of influences that were at play in their creation at this time. Nearly all of them are in a very distinctive style in which Western elements have an important role, most notably in the inclusion of the portraits of donors clothed in more or less Western costumes; they look very like the portraits so frequently found on Flemish paintings towards the end of the fifteenth century. At an earlier date on the other hand such icons as survive present no such distinctive characteristics, for as often as not they bear close relationships to those of the Byzantine world; some must actually have been imported from there, while others must clearly have been brought from the West, notably the great panels of the Virgin at Nicosia or St Nicholas at Kakopetria, which are wholly Romanesque in character. A small panel depicting St Andrew with a wide margin on which there are scenes from his life and a number of coats of arms is also a Western work but in the Gothic style.[1] Two early processional icons, depicting Christ and the Virgin, in the Hermitage of St Neophytos, which Mango and Hawkins date to the early thirteenth century, probably represent local works in the Byzantine style,[2] while a tall panel, with Christ at the top and donors below, dated to 1356, is either an import from Constantinople or by a Constantinopolitan painter who was working in Cyprus; it has already been discussed in the chapter on Byzantine painting (see p. 14, *pl. 9*). Two other complete panels of similar form, on the other hand, are more likely to be local works, done to match the Byzantine import. They are of rather later date and should probably be assigned to the later fourteenth century; while a fragmentary panel of the same form bears the portraits of two donors confronted who resemble those on the Byzantine panel of 1356 so closely that it is probably to be assigned to the same date and even the same workshop.[3]

The story of Cypriot painting proper is probably to be begun shortly before the close of the fifteenth century, with an icon of St Demetrius on horseback[4] in the church of the Chrysaliniotissa at Nicosia. Though it is

certainly a local product it is still in a very Byzantine style except for the inclusion of donor portraits between the horse's legs. An impressive icon of the Virgin and Child (*pl. 72*) from the same church[5] may also be noted here. It bears a long inscription requesting prayers for Maela the deaconess, daughter of Nicholas, Bishop of Nicosia. A Bishop of that name is noted in the year 1472 and though at first glance the icon might appear to be rather later, it seems likely that it should be associated with the Bishop and assigned to a date towards the end of the fifteenth century. It is stylistically akin to a long series of Madonna paintings done in the sixteenth century and is to be counted as one of the earliest exemplars of the series that have survived.

The number of actually dated icons of the sixteenth century so far recorded amounts to no less than thirty-one, and more than a dozen are known from the seventeenth century. As researches continue these numbers are likely to be increased. It is thus something of a problem to know which of them to select for reproduction here. We have therefore chosen both some of the most typical, and some of the finest from the artistic point of view, together with a few which are probably to be attributed to identifiable painters, even if their names are not always known. Most of them have been described and illustrated in *The Icons of Cyprus*, but the plates in that book are not always very good, for the photographs were all taken before the icons could be cleaned. There are much better reproductions in Mr Papageorgiou's book, but the coverage there is less complete, though a number of panels not noted in the earlier book are there reproduced, for they represent subsequent discoveries. A few other Cypriot icons are to be found outside the island, notably one dated 1618 which was on exhibition at Recklinghausen in 1963; it is a rather baroque-looking two-sided panel, with the Virgin and Child on one face and Christ on the other, with six scenes below.[6]

Of the long series of post-fifteenth-century Cypriot panels that are illustrated here one of the earliest is a Crucifixion in the monastery of Kykkos, dated 1520 (*pl. 73*).[7] It is still broadly Byzantine, but the faces and the proportions of the figures savour somehow of the West and are somewhat suggestive of an earlier group of icons classed together by Professor Kurt Weitzmann under the heading of *The Crusading School*.[8] It flourished at Jerusalem and Acre in the twelfth century, so there can be no direct connection and such similarities as there are must be attributed to independent Western elements in both. There is a kneeling figure of a donor in priestly costume at the bottom of the Cypriot icon, and there are two separate inscriptions, one on either side of him. The date appears at the end of the one behind him.

Icons of Christ and the Virgin are, as one would expect, more numerous than those of other subjects, and it is with them that the donor figures are most frequently associated. An icon of Christ, with three donor figures below, may be illustrated as a typical example of the work of this period; it is dated 1521 (*pl. 74*).[9] It was included in the Byzantine exhibition at Athens in 1964,[10] being loaned from the Metropolitan Museum at Kyrenia, though its original home was the village of Kharcha. The presence and appearance of the donors distinguishes it as a Cypriot work, but the Pantocrator is closely akin to those favoured by painters of the Italo-Cretan school at much the same date, and the Cypriot icon may well have been modelled on a panel imported from there or more probably from Venice.

To represent the characteristic Madonna icons of this age we illustrate an unusually elaborate one with the donors ranged below in front of a church of Italianate type (*pl. 75*).[11] There is an inscription giving the names of two of them, a man called Vana and his wife, and it also includes the date, 1529. Once again the rendering of the main figure follows an Italo-Cretan model, but the church is wholly Western and the blending of styles is truly typical of Cypriot work.

Another panel which is close to the work of the Italo-Cretan school is a large icon in three tiers now in the Archbishop's Palace at Nicosia (*pl. 77*).[12] At the top is the Deesis, at the centre St Peter and St Paul face one another before a decorative architectural background; at the bottom four Saints are shown full-length, though they are on a rather smaller scale. There is no inscription, but a comparison with the icon considered above, which is firmly dated to 1529, supports a closely similar date. Here the colours are perhaps rather more brilliant than is usual in Cypriot painting, but this effect is to some extent deceptive, for the icon is in a particularly good state of preservation, it is not overlaid by dirty varnish, and the colours keep their original freshness.

To represent the next decade, 1540 to 1550, three icons have been selected, an Annunciation of 1540, an Entry into Jerusalem of 1546, and a Pantocrator of 1549. In this case the choice has been made because of the general interest of these icons[13] rather than because they are typically Cypriot. The first (*pl. 78*), comes from the church of Hagios Lukas at Nicosia. There are a number of kneeling donors at the bottom, but the scene itself is in the Italo-Cretan manner; the icon is nevertheless to

be regarded as a Cypriot product, though the painter must have been familiar with Italo-Cretan work. The Entry into Jerusalem (*pl. 79*) is, from the artistic point of view, a much finer painting; it is, indeed, a work of very high quality, the colouring being very effective and the faces alive and expressive. It is to be counted as one of the finest of all the mid-sixteenth-century icons preserved in Cyprus. The third panel, depicting the Pantocrator (*pl. 81*) comes from the church of Hagios Johannes near Nicosia and is dated 1549. The treatment is a little harsh in comparison to that of the Entry, but it is a thoroughly competent piece of work, and the donor portraits, especially those of three women to the right in costumes of a Venetian type, are very well done. The icon represents Cypriot work at its best, and its high quality is apparent if it is compared with another Pantocrator by the hand of a painter named George, dated to 1554, which is reproduced in colour by Papageorgiou.[14]

The icons painted in the second half of the sixteenth century—some ten dated examples are known—tend on the whole to be rather less interesting than those done during the first half, but four may be noted to give a comprehensive idea of what was being done at this period. They comprise a full-length figure of the Virgin and Child of 1556, an Anastasis of 1563, a triptych of 1595 and a St George of 1599. The icon of the Virgin and Child has been chosen because it represents a type that was not very common in the Orthodox world, for the Virgin is shown full-length (*pl. 80*).[15] Figures of the Virgin and Child enthroned or half-length are to be found in practically every church, but full-length ones are few and far between, and the example we illustrate is the only one we encountered in the island. The half-length panels are again unmistakably Cypriot, either because of the rather limited, dry colouring which distinguishes much of the work done for the villages, or because the Madonnas wear a very distinctive type of costume made from richly decorated materials, usually Venetian silks or velvets (*see pl. 84*).

The composition of the Anastasis (*pl. 76*)[16] is unusual, for the figures of Adam and Eve do not rise from the graves, as was normal in Byzantine renderings of the scene, while the mandorla behind Christ is of unwonted size; also a banner of St George floats in the sky above and this is presumably an innovation due to Western influence. In spite of this hybrid character, the icon is a work of considerable quality, and it represents the Cypriot school at its best. An inscription records the name of the donor, Menikos Pelekanos, and the date 1563, but there is another inscription on the lower margin which states that the icon was restored in 1808. The restoration would not seem to have affected the panel very greatly, for it has now been cleaned again and a comparison of a recent photograph with one taken in 1936 suggests that the removal of the later additions has produced little change. The main difference seems to have had regard to the epigraphic nature of the title.

The triptych bears the Deesis on its central panel, with St Nicholas on the left and St Athanasios on the right wing (*pl. 82*).[17] No donor portraits are included, but there is a commemorative inscription reading 'prayer of the servant of God Christophios' and giving the date 1595. The prayer is followed by eight letters which appear to read I C I N O I; this is perhaps to be interpreted as εἶς τὴν πολίν 'from the city', meaning of course Constantinople, but whether this refers to the original home of the donor or to that of the icon it is impossible to say. But as the style is very conservative and the colours are unusually brilliant for Cyprus the latter seems a possibility.

As has already been stated, icons of mounted saints were almost as popular in Cyprus as they were in Bulgaria, and one of the best of them, depicting St George, is in the church of Hagios Cassianos at Nicosia. Unfortunately a small portion behind the horses is missing (*pl. 83*).[18] A commemorative inscription refers to a man called Markos, who died on Friday 18 August 1599.[19] The painting has a curious naive charm rather than real artistic quality, but the brilliant colouring distinguishes it from the general run of icons of the mounted saints to be found in the villages. The painting is on canvas, which appears to have been mounted on the present board at some date later than that of the actual painting.

Among later icons an interesting one depicting the Virgin enthroned with the Child on her knee with both hands raised may be noted, as the iconographical type is rather unusual; it is one that was indeed rare both in Cyprus and throughout the Byzantine world; it was distinguished by Kondakov as the Cypriot type though it was of course not restricted to Cyprus.[20] In this case there are full-length figures of St Nicholas and St George on either side of the Virgin, and below there are portraits of no less than six donors, with an open book depicted between them on which is a dedicatory inscription (*pl. 85*).[21] The inscription registers a prayer for the souls of three men, who died respectively in 1604, 1532 and 1600. The icon is presumably to be assigned to the latest of these dates, for the inscription seems to be all of a piece, and the costume of the foremost of the donors supports this conclusion, for it is rather different from those that are worn by donors of the mid-sixteenth century. The colours are brilliant and gay and the icon is well painted. Though it is now in a village church, the style and high quality of the work show that it was certainly not done by some village craftsman, but rather by an accomplished master from some progressive centre.

As has already been noted, icons of the Virgin and Child constitute what is probably the most common theme among the Cypriot painters. Many of these icons follow a conservative rendering, where the Virgin wears the conventional plain purple maphorion. But very frequently in Cyprus her robe is made of a richly patterned material, apparently of silk or velvet, the patterns comprising a number that were popular in Venice, as well as a few that might well have been produced on the looms of Bursa in Turkey. The costume on a Madonna at Pera dated 1609 thus possibly reproduces a Turkish material, while those on icons at Monagri (1563), Nisou (early seventeenth century), Kaleana (early seventeenth century) and Eylenja (1609) depict Venetian textiles.[22] The Monagri icon (*pl. 84*) is typical and has been chosen for reproduction because it is particularly well preserved. The Virgin actually forms the obverse of a double-sided processional icon, with the Crucifixion on the reverse; it is here that the date appears, but there is no reason to suppose that it does not also apply to the obverse. Rich costumes of this type are not known elsewhere in the Byzantine world; they were no doubt adopted in Cyprus as a result of the close contacts maintained with Venice. The island was occupied by Venice from 1489 till 1571, when it fell to the Turks, but trading links with the West were not wholly broken off, and the Venetian fashions, when once established, probably did not die easily.

The above survey has not included a number of the finest and most interesting icons to be found in the island simply because they are not exactly dated. But it will, it is hoped, have served to show that the story of icon painting in Cyprus has a dual character; on the one hand there were many imports, which were faithfully copied locally; on the other a truly local style was developed which was not without considerable qualities of its own. Of the imports a few were Western products but the majority were of Byzantine or Italo-Cretan origin; with a few exceptions most of the examples of this type are not actually dated. It was the local painters, following a custom introduced from the West, who liked to include dates and donor portraits. Many of these men were very accomplished, and probably worked in such centres as Nicosia; the truly village painters produced much poorer work, which has not been mentioned here more than occasionally. But even in these poorer works something of the grand tradition lived on, and the tradition was maintained in a way which was, for example, never the case in Bulgaria. There a new, essentially peasant art grew up; in Cyprus the old models were followed faithfully reflecting the sophisticated styles of the Byzantine world, of Crete or of Venice, and such innovations as were introduced consisted in the addition of donor portraits, coats of arms or similar features to the conventional subject matter.

73

74

75

76

77

78   79

80

81

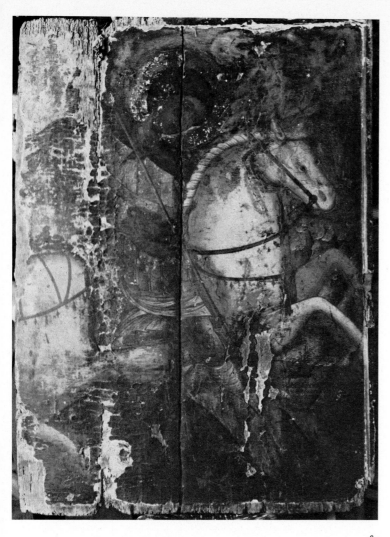

83

84

72 The Virgin and Child, with donors
Church of the Chrysaliniotissa, Nicosia, Cyprus.
209 × 122 cm.
c. 1490

The type is that of the enthroned Hodegetria, but the Virgin has a special designation, Kamariotissa, 'of the Chamber', and the Child rests on the Virgin's right arm instead of her left knee. Above are two Archangels, and below the Child three donors are portrayed, with an inscription giving the name of one of them as Maela, daughter of the deceased Lord Bishop of Nicosia, Nicholas. A second inscription mentions a man called Eustathius and his daughter Elena. The work is rather clumsy and is clearly to be attributed to a local painter. The inscription above the donors on the opposite side names Eustathius and his daughter Elena as well as Iotibras and George.

A Bishop Nicholas of Nicosia is noted in 1473, and it is probably this man who is referred to in the inscription. As he was already dead when the icon was painted, a date around 1490 seems likely.

Rice, pl. 64. Pap., p. 68, pl. A.

73 The Crucifixion, with donors
Monastery of Kykkos, Cyprus.
89 × 59.5 cm.
1520

The conception of the scene is essentially decorative and the style rather baroque, especially with regard to the rendering of the wall that occupies the lower part of the background. The figure of Christ, however, is rather conventional, as are those of the Virgin and St John, both shown as rather dumpy figures. Above the cross are weeping angels, while the sun and moon are shown on an unusually large scale. A priestly donor in a white robe kneels at the foot of the cross and there is an inscription in cursive characters behind him and another on a sort of panel before him; the date, 1520, is included in the former.

Pap., p. 91.

74 Christ Pantocrator, with donor
Church of the Archangels, Kharcha, Cyprus.
106 × 80 cm.
1521

Christ is depicted full-face on a throne with an elaborately lobed back. He holds a book on His left knee and His right hand is raised in blessing. His feet rest on a footstool, and a male donor and a boy kneel beside it to Christ's right, and a woman to His left. There is a dedicatory inscription recording the date, 1521. The

paint is rather thin and the style is typical of local, Cypriot work.

Rice, pl. 102. *Byzantine Art—A European Art*, Athens, 1964, no. 208.

75 The Virgin and Child, with donors
Church of Hagios Cassianos, Nicosia, Cyprus.
150 × 96 cm.
1529

The painting is in two separate registers, a half-length figure of the Virgin above in the Hodegetria pose, with, below, a church of basilical type, which extends right across the icon from side to side, while its tower rises up to the top register, beside the Virgin. At either end of the church is an angel, and at its centre there is a small panel on which the Virgin and Child are once again depicted. Below this is an inscription, and disposed symmetrically on either side are the kneeling figures of the two donors, a man and a woman. The Virgin and Child in the upper register follow a Byzantine tradition, but the inclusion of what is virtually the view of a church of Western type is something very unusual and attests a good deal of Western influence. Italian renderings of the theme known as the Virgin of Loreto may be compared; an example in the church of the Capuchins at Saroca in Sicily is especially close. (See R. van Marle, *Italian Painting*, The Hague, 1924, I, fig. 274, p. 443.)

Rice, pl. 58.

76 (Colour plate V) *The Anastasis, with donor*
Church of the Chrysaliniotissa, Nicosia, Cyprus.
121 × 62.5 cm.
1563

The massive figure of Christ stands before a dark mandorla of oval form. He raises Adam from the grave with His right hand and Eve with His left. The mandorla is supported by two Archangels, one on either side. It is so large that little space is left for the other subsidiary figures usually associated with this scene. Rocks, however, rise up above on either side and in the centre is a white flag with a red cross on it. Between Adam and Christ's leg is the kneeling figure of a male donor and a dedicatory inscription giving his name as Menikos Pelekanos and the date, 1563. A second inscription states that the icon was restored in 1808, but a supplementary cleaning which the icon seems to have undergone since its first publication in 1936 and its republication by Papageorgiou in 1969 suggests that the restoration of 1808 had little effect other than to alter the form of the letters of the inscription.

The inclusion of the banner, presumably that of St George, is a very unusual feature, while the arrangement of the figures shows considerable deviation from the normal Byzantine system. The icon is certainly a Cypriot product, but the painter must have been submitted to a number of diverse influences, more especially from the West.

Pap., p. 102. Rice, pl. 23.

77 *The Deesis and Sts Peter, Paul, Nicholas, Timothy, George and Marina, with donor*
Church of the Chrysaliniotissa, Nicosia, Cyprus. Now in the Archbishop's Palace.
120 × 75 cm.
c. 1529

The icon has a rounded top and is in three registers; above, and extending to just below the bottom of the rounded portion, is the Deesis; in the middle section St Peter and St Paul are confronted with a domed building between them and with a building on a smaller scale at either side. In the bottom register Sts Nicholas, Timothy, George and Marina are shown on a smaller scale, but full-length. In the corner, below St Nicholas, is a kneeling figure.

The work is more accomplished than is often the case with local products in Cyprus and the colouring is rich. The panel is not actually dated, but the close similarity in style that it shows to one of the Virgin in Hagios Cassianos (*pl. 75*) firmly dated to 1529, supports a similar date for this icon as does the donor's costume.

Pap., p. 109. Rice, pl. 14.

78 *The Annunciation, with donors*
Church of Hagios Lukas, Nicosia, Cyprus.
91 × 62 cm.
c. 1540

The two figures, which are tall and elongated, stand before an elaborate architectural background; the donors kneel at the very bottom of the panel, a woman below the Virgin and two men before the Angel. The style of the painting is close to that of the Cretan school and Western elements are striking by their absence. There is no dedicatory inscription, but a date close to 1540 is supported by the costumes of the donors.

Rice, pl. 17.

79 *The Entry into Jerusalem, with donors*
Church of the Chrysaliniotissa, Nicosia, Cyprus.
124 × 82 cm.
1546

In contrast to the usual representations of this scene, the city of Jerusalem is placed to the spectator's left and Christ approaches from the right, with a group of

Apostles behind Him. A tree with three youths amidst its branches occupies the central part of the background. There are rocks behind Christ, balanced by a very ornate rendering of Jerusalem on the opposite side. At the bottom of the panel no less than six donors are depicted, four men to the left and two women to the right, all facing inwards; the two groups are separated by the minute figure of a youth laying a cloth before Christ's mule. Below him is a fragmentary inscription, but the date, 1546, happily is legible. The work is accomplished and the icon is a fine one in spite of the crowded nature of the composition.

Pap., p. 103. Rice, pl. 22. *Published by permission of the Director of Antiquities and the Cyprus Museum.*

80 *The Virgin and Child*
Monastery of the Panaghia Aragha, at Lagoudhera, Cyprus.
104 × 45 cm.
1554

The Virgin is in the Hodegetria pose, but is depicted full-length, something which is very rare not only in Cyprus, but in Byzantine panel painting in general. There are no donors or subsidiary details; simply an inscription giving the date. The icon is impressive and dignified, and represents good local work.

Rice pl. 46.

81 *Christ Pantocrator, with donors*
Church of St John the Baptist, near Nicosia, Cyprus.
105 × 75 cm.
1549

Christ is depicted rather more than half-length, seated, with the very massive back of his throne behind Him. Below kneel five donors, a man and his wife to the left and three women, presumably their daughters, to the right. They are clothed in very fashionable costumes of Venetian style. Between the two groups is a short inscription recording the date. Christ's face is somewhat wooden, but His costume is elaborately picked out with gold highlights. The panel represents Cypriot work at its best.

Pap., p. 93. Rice, pl. 101.

82 Triptych, depicting the *Deesis* on the central panel, with *Sts Nicholas and Athanasios on the wings*
Church of St George, Lagoudhera, Cyprus.
Central panel 60 × 42 cm.
1595

The scene of the Deesis is inset, with a pointed arch above, the spandrels of the arch being adorned with relief carving. The figures are shown full-length, as are the saints on the side panels. They are well painted in a truly Byzantine style. The triptych form was a very popular one, especially in Greece, and the fine work and bright colours suggest that the icon may well have been imported from the Greek mainland. An inscription at the bottom of the central panel, recording the date, 1595, and the name of the donor, Christopher, is however, certainly Cypriot.

Rice, pl. 108.

83 St George
Church of Hagios Cassianos, Nicosia, Cyprus.
133 × 97 cm.
1599

The saint is shown mounted, with a spear in his raised right hand, with which he strikes at the dragon below the horse's belly. A commemorative inscription above the dragon's head records the name of the deceased donor as Markos and the date of his death as 1599. (Papageorgiou gives the date as 1559, but there can be little doubt that the penultimate letter is ?, representing 90, and not N representing 50.) A portion of the panel is missing on the left. The icon is a good example of a theme which was popular in the villages of Cyprus.

Pap., p. 110. Rice, pl. 82.

84 Double-sided icon; obverse,
the Virgin and Child;
reverse, *the Crucifixion* (not illustrated)
Church of the Panaghia Damaskenos, Monagri, Cyprus.
104 × 62 cm.
1569

The Virgin is shown half-length, in the Hodegetria pose. The most distinctive feature of the icon is her rich costume, made from a patterned Venetian velvet or silk. The haloes are in relief plaster work, something that was very popular in Cyprus; a metal plaque of recent date has been added to that of the Virgin. Ornate costumes of the type depicted were comparatively common in Cyprus, and it is often possible to suggest dates for the icons on the basis of the designs of the textiles which the costumes copy.

The obverse of the panel is not dated, but there is a dedicatory inscription, with the date 1569, associated with the Crucifixion scene on the reverse, and there is every reason to regard the two faces as contemporary.

Rice, pl. 34. The Crucifixion is numbered 119.

85 The Virgin and Child enthroned, between St Nicholas and St George, with donors
Church of St George, Vatili, Cyprus.
130 × 109 cm.
Probably 1604

The Virgin is seated on a high-backed throne, the Child, with both hands raised in blessing, posed on her left knee. The saints stand on either side of the throne. Below are the bust figures of six donors, three to the left below St Nicholas and three on the right, below St George. They hold between them an open book, on which is written a prayer for their souls, naming them as Francis, Florence and their children George and Francis, who died in 1604. The others, whose names are illegible, died in 1532 and 1600. Papageorgiou dates the icon to *c.* 1500. Although it is just possible that the inscription is a later addition, the manner of its painting does not support this, and it seems preferable to accept the most recent of the dates, 1604, as that at which the icon was painted.

Pap., p. 74. Rice, pl. 57.

Chapter Six

Russia

Introduction

IN 843 the Regent of Byzantium lifted the ban on figural representations in religious art in the name of her six-year-old son, the Emperor Michael III. The prohibition had been in force for the best part of a hundred years and had proved especially frustrating to the artists concerned with the production of portable objects of a devotional nature, symbolic motifs having proved less readily adaptable to small-scale works than to large compositions. With the raising of the ban artists were able to resume the production of icons, whether in the form of painted panels or of plaques made of metal, ivory or some other precious material. The fervour with which they infused their figural representations was to endure for centuries to come, fostering the determination of generations of painters to invest the human face and form with intense spirituality and with characteristics of a manifestly celestial nature. Ever since that day the Orthodox Church has celebrated the abolition of Iconoclasm on the first Sunday in Lent as the Triumph of Orthodoxy.

Although few examples survive it would seem that by the end of the tenth century the Byzantine output of icons had become quite considerable, the panels playing an even more important part in the people's religious life than had been the case in pre-Iconoclast times. Kievan Russia's conversion to Orthodoxy in 988–89 coincided with the period when the firm roots which figural art had re-established in Byzantium had brought about a Second Golden Age in the Empire's art. That golden age was approaching full fruition at the time of Russia's conversion and Russia was to benefit greatly from that synchronization, since church furnishings of fine quality had to be imported from Byzantium to the newly converted districts in considerable quantities. The majority took the form of portable objects, with icons heading the list. Large-scale works in the forms of mural paintings and mosaics were at that stage put in hand in Kiev, the country's capital, by Byzantine artists who had gone there for that purpose, but mural paintings were also done at the time at Novgorod and such important regional capitals as Chernigov and the like. In the eleventh century some of the Greek artists working in Kiev established workshops there, employing in them Russians as pupils and assistants. One of the most important of the icon workshops belonged to the Kievo–Pecherskaya Lavra (the Monastery of the Caves) situated on the capital's outskirts. It had been established by the Greek artists who were engaged in 1073 in adorning the Lavra's cathedral. According to the Lavra's records these artists stayed on in Kiev when their work in the cathedral ended. At their deaths their cartoons must have passed into the Lavra's possession.

Within a generation the Lavra's workshop had produced a Russian artist who was so much admired by his Kievan contemporaries that the Monastery's chronicle contains several references to him. He was called Alipy and was one of the Lavra's monks. He had trained under a Greek master and executed some of the mural paintings in the Lavra's cathedral. Later in life he had an assistant of his own, a fellow monk called Gregory, who is referred to in the chronicle as the painter of numerous icons, and who may well have been trained by Alipy. The chronicler was at pains to describe Alipy's industry, his kindliness, humility and goodness —attributes which were thought in medieval times to be well-nigh essential to a religious painter of distinction, since it was assumed that only a man verging on sanctity could possess the insight and piety necessary for infusing an icon with the deep emotional content essential to a truly holy painting, an adjective which must be accepted as synonymous with that of great. It is worth noting in this connection that the icons which came to be most revered and admired in Russia, and credited with miraculous powers, are also among the finest from an aesthetic point of view. Alipy must have possessed the qualities considered essential to a great icon painter to a very high degree, for his fellow monks became so jealous of him that, on one occasion at least, they refrained from telling him that he had been asked to paint a five-figure Deesis cycle. Although Alipy was in the habit of dividing his earnings into three equal parts in order to give one to the poor and another to his monastery, whilst using the third to buy the painting material he required, the monks told no one that the icons had been paid for in advance. It is said that their omissions were noted in heaven and some angels therefore descended to earth to save Alipy's good name by painting the icons for him. Later, when the artist was close to death and unable to complete an icon of the Dormition they once again came to his aid, finishing it by the date on which he had promised to deliver it. He died around 1114.

The icons which were produced in Russia before 1240, when the Mongols captured Kiev and the greater part of central and eastern Russia, retaining control over these areas for over two centuries, were almost always intended for use in a church. They were of the type known as devotional (*molennya*) to distinguish them from those which came to be privately owned and termed domestic. To begin with the Church was so much in need of icons that it absorbed most of the available supply. Members of the reigning families, great prelates and some wealthy notables must also have acquired a few personal icons, but even they were more likely to place such panels in their private chapels than in their homes. Even the great cathedrals cannot at first have owned many icons. They probably displayed them on lecterns for at that period icons were not standardized in size. Their dimensions depended upon those of the best boards available to the artist. It was not until the introduction of the multi-tiered iconostasis that the sizes of icons were established to correspond with the respective tiers of the iconostasis—a development which led to the growth of a thriving panel industry.

The multi-tiered iconostasis was developed at a relatively late date. Indeed, it was not until the tenth or eleventh century that the Byzantine altar screen gave way to a low, embryo iconostasis made either of wood, marble or stone. The local icons were displayed between its posts; they were placed at waist height against a curtain backing. The festival icons were ranged above the local ones at a height which enabled them to be changed with ease and the whole structure was then surmounted at its centre either by a cross or by a painting of the Crucifixion set between icons of the Virgin and St John the Forerunner, the theme known as that of the Deesis. Later the Crucifixion was replaced by an icon of Christ, the three representations, whether presented on a single panel or on three separate ones, coming to form the central section of the Deesis cycle. The extended Deesis cycle consisting of five, seven, nine or more figures made up of the two archangels, the Apostles and Fathers of the Church developed from it. Recently evidence has come to light pointing to the existence in the twelfth century of a wooden iconostasis at Mount Sinai and of another at the monastery of Vatopedi on Mount Athos, but there is nothing to indicate their heights. They must have been among the earliest in use. At the time Russia's contacts with Byzantium centred chiefly on Mount Athos and Salonica rather than on Constantinople. The earliest Russian iconostasis to be mentioned in the records is the one which was erected in 1341 in the Cathedral of

St Sophia at Novgorod; it was almost certainly a three-tiered one with the lower tier containing the local icons, the second tier those of the Deesis cycle and the third tier panels depicting the Church's festivals. Had wooden multi-tiered iconostases been in general use in Byzantium in the twelfth and thirteenth centuries it is inconceivable that the Russians, with their centuries-old skill in carpentry and their unlimited supplies of excellent wood, would have waited for a couple of centuries before introducing them into their own churches, yet it was not until the fifteenth century that the many-tiered wooden iconostasis, the logical descendent of the embryo type, was in general use not only in Russia, but also in Bucovina, Moldavia and on Mount Athos. The next earliest Russian examples to be mentioned in the chronicles were that which was installed in 1405 in the Cathedral of the Annunciation in Moscow's Kremlin and that erected in 1427 in the masonry cathedral of the Trinity at the Troitse-Sergeyeva Lavra, at what is now Zagorsk. The latter church was built to serve both as a mausoleum and as a memorial to St Sergius of Radonezh, the monastery's founder and first abbot. According to the chronicle the icons for the Moscow iconostasis were painted by 'Theophanes, the Greek icon painter, by Prokhor, the monk, and by the monk Andrey Rublyov'. By that date the Deesis tier generally displayed the extended cycle, the figures being usually shown full-length instead of half-length or as mere heads, as had formerly been the custom. The change is ascribed by Professor Lazarev to Theophanes, the Greek artist. Two glorious icons in the Tretyakov Gallery at Moscow are of the latter kind, both displaying the heads and shoulders of the three central personages on a single, rectangular-shaped panel (*pl. 90*).

The cost of fitting out a fair-sized iconostasis was by no means inconsiderable. Novgorod's *Sofiyskiy Vremennik* (the chronicle compiled by the clerics of the Cathedral of St Sophia) for the year 1482 records that 'Vasian, Bishop of Rostov, gave one hundred roubles to the painters Denis, the priest(s?) Timothy, Tars and Koni, to provide the New Church of the Holy Virgin with paintings of the divinities with the festivals and prophets', that is to say for the icons required for a five-tiered iconostasis. In 1509 the Novgorodian Chronicle recorded the painting of a similar set of icons for the town's Cathedral of St Sophia, the work being carried out by 'Andrew, son of Lavrenty, and Ivan Dermoyartzev'. These statements imply that, at any rate by that date, multi-tiered iconostases were being installed in all churches of importance. It had by then also become the rule for the first tier of an iconostasis to display the local icons, the second tier the Deesis cycle which, depending upon the width of the church, varied in number, the third tier to contain anything from twelve to nineteen festival icons—therefore generally showing a larger number than was customary in Byzantium—the fourth tier to present the prophets with the Virgin and Child at its centre and the fifth tier the Fathers of the Church with a Paternity icon set above that of the Virgin and Child. By that date the local tier often included a baptismal icon done to mark the birth of a local prince or notable, known as a 'measured' (*mernaya*) icon (*pl. 152*) because its height corresponded to that of the newly born infant; it displayed a full-length representation of the baby's patron saint.

At the centre of the iconostasis the Royal Doors had also become a feature of great importance; they led to the sanctuary and only clerics were entitled to pass through them. They were made of two rectangular sections each of which was surmounted by an ornate curved or otherwise shaped panel. Each of the rectangular sections was divided into two squares on which it was customary to portray the four evangelists although they were sometimes replaced by Fathers of the Church. The ornate top panels almost invariably depicted the Annunciation, the Archangel on one leaf of the door, the Virgin on the other, whilst the architrave above the doors displayed a painting of the Crucifixion.

By the sixteenth century the number of icons belonging to a church even of secondary importance had become so great that, in addition to filling its iconostasis, many had to be placed in the body of the church. Monasteries had by then also acquired a large number of icons, partly because a monk retained possession of his personal icons on taking his vows but bequeathed them at his death to the foundation. By the sixteenth century private ownership of icons for use in the home as vehicles of worship had also not only become general but so extensive that, in the more prosperous households, the 'red corner' of each room displayed one with a light burning before it. When Paul of Aleppo visited Moscow in 1665 he commented with surprise on the number of icons which he saw there. By that date memorial icons were being widely used. They were either placed above the tomb of the person they commemorated or, in the manner of an English church plaque, on a wall close to it. The origin of the custom is to be traced back to early Christian times, to portraits such as that in the Commodilla catacomb (*pl. 1*) or to that in the Calixtus catacomb where a mural portrait of a second- to third-century Christian simulates a panel painting.[1] They represent a survival in Christian times of the Coptic use of mortuary portraiture, a form of painting from which icon painting developed. Although the tradition does not seem to have been widely followed in Byzantium in early times the splendid commemorative icon which is now in Nicosia (*pl. 9*) proves that it was still in force there in the fourteenth century. In Russia memorial icons must have been popular at an earlier date than that of the one which was placed above the tomb of Maksimov, Metropolitan of Vladimir, at his

death in 1305;[2] according to its inscription, it was commissioned by Maksimov for the purpose in 1229. By the fifteenth century embroidered portrait hangings, like the one of St Sergius of Radonezh which was worked by the Grand Duchess of Moscow and her embroidresses, were often substituted for the painted panels.[3] This hanging appears to have set a precedent for such portraits in Muscovy; they also became popular in Rumania where it became usual to commemorate sovereigns and notables by means of embroidered or appliqué worked portrait hangings. Some fine examples are now preserved there in the monastery of Putna. Back in Russia in the seventeenth century interest in true portraiture first expressed itself in panels which, like those of the Boyar, Prince Skopin-Shuysky (*pl. 154*)[4] or Tsar Feodor, were executed in a style which presents a blend of the iconic convention and the naturalistic.

The custom of adorning icons with precious stones or elaborately worked and bejewelled metal sheets was of Byzantine origin. It was adopted at Kiev where the icon of the Virgin of Vladimir (*pl. 5*) was lavishly adorned. Chroniclers commented on this and the Mongols were quick to strip the icon of its valuables when they conquered Russia. During the long Mongol occupation the subjected territories were, however, so impoverished that few worshippers other than an occasional prince, great prelate or rich merchant could express their attachment to a particular icon in so expensive a manner. With the growth of the country's economy and a corresponding increase in its prosperity the situation altered, and the custom of embellishing icons gradually became widespread and eventually excessive. By the end of the seventeenth century many icons were literally plastered with gems and metal work. Peter the Great found their appearance offensive and, on becoming tsar, instructed the clergy to remove any excessive adornments. Although icon painting had by that time ceased to be an art, it nevertheless often still continued to display fine workmanship. Peter the Great's Westernizing reforms were to have the effect of lowering the standards even further so that icons of true artistic merit were produced increasingly rarely and eventually the art deteriorated into a craft.

Byzantium's religious art made such a deep impression on the early Russians that their own works were moulded by it for centuries to come. The same is true to some extent of such Western schools of art as the Ottonian or early Italian, more especially of the Sienese and Venetian schools, but whilst the Orthodox paintings were invariably closely linked to the cult, the Western paintings were not created in order exclusively to serve as vehicles of worship. Inventiveness therefore quickly succeeded in establishing itself as the motive force inspiring the West's religious artists but the Russians, together with their Slav co-religionists—owing perhaps to the relatively late date of their conversions—remained so absorbed in Orthodoxy that they do not seem ever to have wished to give free rein to their imaginations and personalities. Instead, they remained content throughout the centuries to express the burning intensity of their faith in the manner which the Eastern Church had prescribed in early Christian times. They not only willingly conformed to the iconographic rules which the Church established between the fifth and seventh centuries, but they also readily complied with its desire that the chief personages appearing in their works should be depicted in such a manner as to be easily recognizable, either by their appearance or as a result of some attribute or emblem. Nor were they perturbed by the ancient convention which encouraged artists to work for God's glory rather than their own, that is to say anonymously. The vast majority of Russia's artists willingly did so until the seventeenth century when the worldlier outlook of the West penetrated to Moscow and started to affect their own attitude. Prior to that the observance of anonymity was seldom broken, but in 1294 the painter of a very fine icon of St Nicholas the Miracle Worker (*pl. 96*) disregarded it and, by inscribing it, he provided us with a unique example of a signed Russian icon of a very early date. The scarcity of signed works and the lack of information concerning even the best-known artists not only renders the dating of icons extremely difficult but also severely hampers attempts to distinguish between the regional schools, and even more so, between the major workshops. The complexities of these problems are well illustrated by the fact that whilst many eminent Soviet scholars regard the icon of The Great Panaghia, formerly described as of Yaroslavl (*pl. 88*), as a thirteenth-century work of that school, the compilers of the Tretyakov Gallery's catalogue of icons assign it to Kiev and about the year 1114.

In some cases legends or traditions can be used as guide lines for dating purposes. However, since sceptics are entitled to question conclusions founded on such premises it is fortunate that a small number of icons exist which are dated with considerable exactitude, either by the possession of a dated inscription or because they are mentioned in a chronicle or similar near contemporary text or, as in the case of an early icon of the Veronica (*pl. 95*), because a dated painting in another medium, in its case a book illumination, provides a terminal date. Datable references to particular icons or to legends relating to them occur quite often in texts ranging in date from the eleventh to the seventeenth centuries. An incomplete index compiled by the Academician N. K. Nikolsky lists no less than 1,158 such entries.[5] Although they rarely indicate the date at which the icons were painted, they often provide information which helps scholars to deduce it.

The readiness with which Russian artists accepted the dictates of the Orthodox Church has often led

Westerners to question the vitality of their inspiration, the quality of their creative powers and their intellectual adventurousness. To do so is to fail to appreciate the essence of iconic art. It is made up of the artist's willingness to express a spiritual experience by means of an immutable figural composition in preference either to a personally devised one or, as demanded by the iconoclasts, by means of a no less stereotyped abstract or symbolic design. In orthodox eyes a fixed composition—that is to say the iconographic form prescribed by the Church for each scene drawn from a carefully established cycle—had the immense advantage of instantly indicating the key, in other words, the setting and content of the event portrayed. By doing so it left the artist free to concentrate on investing his painting with religious fervour. In addition, although no two icons are truly identical, the sameness in each rendering of each scene helped to endow the icon with abstract qualities and, by doing so, to transfer the event from the terrestrial world in which it had occurred to the celestial, to which the persons concerned had been transported. Such multiple illusionism—that is to say blending of realism, of abstraction as a vehicle for the expression of emotion, of religious fervour and of belief in the celestial world all combine to form the core of iconic art. The Russian mentality, indeed, the Slavic mentality was perhaps better fitted to blend these elements into a balanced entity capable of producing more truly rapturous images than those volved by the more incisive, more cerebral and also more dramatic Greek mind. Certainly these elements are nowhere consistently better integrated, nowhere expressed with a greater economy of detail or a more telling pictorial directness, nowhere infused with gentler yet firmer persuasiveness than in Novgorodian icons of the fourteenth and fifteenth centuries. They represent the classical phase in Russia's religious art. They possess a religious fervour which dispels all doubts, a tranquillity which contains no touch of tameness, a tenderness which avoids the melodramatic. Although a comparable humanism is seldom encountered in Russia's turbulent and violent history it runs through its literature, appearing as clearly in such ancient literary compositions as *The Lay of Igor's Men* as in such recent ones as the poems of an Akhmatova or Pasternak.

Icons were not only revered in Russia—from an early date they were also cared for, the most loved being subjected to overpainting and repair every hundred years or so. Under the Muscovite tsars a special treasury called the *Obraznaya Palata* (The Repository of Holy Images) was established in the Kremlin for the preservation and restoration of icons. By that time Russian panels were also sought after in other parts of the Orthodox world. Thus in the seventeenth century the Phanar at Constantinople possessed some icons of Muscovite workmanship; so did the Sinai Monastery and some of the monasteries on Mount Athos, that of Simopetra owning over a hundred. In Russia the Old Believers were zealously collecting and preserving their sect's icons, whilst the publication in 1687 by Jean Mabillon in his *Museum Italianum* of the icon of the Veronica which is reputed to have been sent to Pope Urban IV in the thirteenth century led the Catholic world to take an interest in icons. It proved short-lived, but Likhachev[6] has drawn attention to six engravings of icons published in the West between 1723 and 1755. However, these developments were due to religious rather than to artistic fervour, and as a result the West quickly forgot about icons whilst the Orthodox world continued to cherish them for their religious content. Their artistic qualities were ignored in Russia until the nineteenth century, when the ban which was passed on the Old Believers in 1856 aroused the sympathies of certain wealthy merchants, industrialists and bankers, leading them to collect the sect's icons. Their activities encouraged other art-lovers to take an interest in icons for artistic and patriotic reasons. Archaeological studies and Slavophil aspirations helped to extend the range of connoisseurship and artistic perceptiveness. By 1862 a small museum in Moscow exhibited alongside its antiquities some icons, thought at the time to be ancient, but which were later found to date from the eighteenth and nineteenth centuries. The icons quickly attracted the attention of art-lovers and two years later the Rumyantzev Museum was able to sponsor the founding of The Society of Ancient Russian Art. In 1863 scholars started to study the panels seriously and a considerable number of people began collecting them. By 1890 the Archaeological Congress meeting in Moscow felt justified in devoting six of the eleven halls of the exhibition it had organized in the Russian Historical Museum to icons, drawing largely on the Uvarov, Silin, Postnikov and Egorov collections for the purpose. Although the number of collectors rapidly increased Tretyakov and Ostroukhov soon proved the most discerning and important. They chose their icons for aesthetic reasons rather than for the purpose of tracing the art's development. They were prepared to pay considerable sums for icons of high quality. Between 1890 and 1892 Tretyakov is reputed to have spent over one hundred thousand roubles for those which he acquired from Silin and Egorov; these panels constitute roughly half the number of those which he bequeathed in 1896 to the museum which he founded in Moscow, and which still bears his name. Ostroukhov was to become their curator. By 1894 he had himself acquired forty-four splendid icons which now form part of the Tretyakov Gallery's collection. In 1905 Likhachev catalogued the Tretyakov icons; in 1914 Muratov did the same for the Ostroukhov ones; the two catalogues led Russians to regard icon painting as a branch of the fine arts. A first step towards its recogni-

tion by Europe was taken in 1911 when Manet came to Moscow at Mr Shchukin's invitation. Although Shchukin collected contemporary French painting he fully appreciated the aesthetic qualities of Russia's icons and was anxious that Manet should also do so. He therefore arranged for Ostroukhov to show Manet the Tretyakov Gallery's icons. Manet was so genuinely impressed and enchanted by them that thirty-five years later he was still writing of them with admiration and enthusiasm, yet it is only within recent years that Western art-lovers have responded to their beauty.

The publication in Moscow of the catalogue of the Tretyakov Gallery's icons, a task undertaken by M. V. Antonova and N. E. Mneva, marks a notable advance in the study of Russian icon painting. The authors have subtitled their monumental work 'An Attempt at a Historical and Stylistic Classification of the Panels'. Their catalogue is indispensable to all serious students of Russian painting. Much of the information in this section is drawn from it and the writer's debt to the two cataloguers cannot be overstressed.[7]

In Poland the appreciation of icons as works of art dates only from the post-war years. The first important exhibition of icons from Poland was held at Recklinghausen in 1966. It included two icons dated to 1631;[8] six others dated by their inscriptions to the years 1687, 1698 and 1699 are recorded. These panels are of so late a date and their number is so small as to make it necessary, at any rate for the time being, to exclude Poland from this survey. Similar reasons are responsible for the omission of Rumanian icons from this study which, as a first attempt of its kind, will inevitably prove far from comprehensive. It is, however, to be hoped that this volume will provide a starting-point for a complete catalogue of all dated icons of quality, together with those which can be dated by documentary evidence, and that the very interesting Polish and Rumanian schools will come to be represented in it beside those of their Slav co-religionists.

Russian Icons

At his conversion to Christianity in 988 Vladimir, Grand Duke of Kievan Russia, gave instructions for all the idols in his country, including an especially impressive one of the god Perun which he had himself recently set up, to be flung into the nearest rivers and for all objects associated with paganism to be destroyed. The thoroughness with which these orders were carried out, together with the damage wrought over the years by time and a rigorous climate, have resulted in the well-nigh total disappearance of Russia's pre-Christian arts and culture. Yet even in the absence of material evidence the quality of the earliest icons to survive is such as to encourage the belief that painting must have been quite widely practised by the Eastern

Slavs in pagan times. It is most unfortunate that nothing survives to indicate the nature of the pictorial works they may have produced, for the oldest icons known to us date from no earlier than the twelfth century and closely follow the Byzantine style and tradition. Since the men who painted them had been carefully grounded by Byzantine masters the strongly Byzantine appearance of these works cannot come as a surprise. What should surprise, however, is the realization that even the earliest of these icons display a very different imprint from their Byzantine prototypes and retain no tentative or un-comprehended elements in their execution. Instead even the earliest icons possess the directness and assurance of well-conceived masterpieces, and even those in which the persons portrayed retain the pear-shaped faces and elongated noses associated with Greece, in place of the rounder heads and features of the Russians, can seldom be mistaken for Greek works. Nor is there a parallel in Byzantine art for such lyrical and rhythmical representations as the icon of the Archangel Gabriel which is distinguished by the name of The Golden-Headed Angel (*pl. 176*), a beautiful work which scholars regard as a twelfth- to thirteenth-century painting of the Novgorodian school. In contrast to it the heads of the two archangels set in roundels placed on either side of the upper sections of the impressive presentation of The Great Panaghia (*pl. 88*) possess a Byzantine austerity and faces of the Greek shape and type, yet the icon's feeling for linear rhythm, the contrast between the curved and circular lines of its composition and the rectangular folds of its draperies, together with the markedly graphic treatment of the archangels' hair, are features which appear constantly in paintings of the Russian school and are characteristic of it.

Prior to the Mongol invasion three major schools of painting quickly developed in Russia. All three were essentially metropolitan in character although only one centred on the Kievan court. Of the remainder one evolved in Novgorod and the other was to establish itself in the Vladimir-Suzdalian district and to flourish especially under Andrey Bogolyubsky (third quarter of the twelfth century), when Vladimir had succeeded Kiev as the country's virtual capital. This school of painting quickly extended its influence over Yaroslavl and Rostov the Great, both of which also became important artistic centres. To begin with the Kievan court school must have been the most important of all, to judge by the mural paintings and mosaics which survive there; it was probably also the most closely linked to the Byzantine. The disappearance of all its panel paintings makes it impossible to form any idea of the character of Russia's first icons. In their absence the Byzantine icon of the Virgin of Vladimir (*pl. 5*) must be regarded as representing the aesthetic standards which prevailed in Kievan court circles at the time when the policy which had been inaugurated by Yaroslav the Wise

(died 1054) was being followed by Vladimir Mono-machos (1113–25) in order to ensure that Russia retained its place in the consort of Christendom.

Kiev's admiration for the icon of the Virgin of Vladimir and such allied representations as that of the Bogolyubovo or Feodorovo versions, to name but these from other comparable compositions featuring the Virgin and Child or the Pantocrator, was to persist in Russia throughout the centuries. Variations on the theme of the Virgin and Child are too numerous for all of them to be enumerated here, but sixteen from among the most important should perhaps be distinguished. In addition to the Virgin of Vladimir they consist of the following, listed here alphabetically rather than chronologically:

1 The Bogolyubovo Virgin, painted in Vladimir *c.* 1158. She stands with arms raised in supplication, holding a scroll in one hand; her head is turned to the right to face a half-length figure of Christ in the act of performing a blessing, seen in the top right-hand corner of the panel.[9]

2 The Virgin of the Don carries the Child on her right arm whilst His feet rest on her left one. He performs a blessing with His right hand and rests His left on her knee.

3 The Golubitskaya (of the dove) Virgin includes a dove in its composition. The type became especially popular in Novgorod, where its appearance has been ascribed to Western influence.

4 The Iverskaya Virgin, so called after one in the Georgian Monastery of Iviron on Mount Athos. Here the Virgin's left hand touches the Child's left hand as He looks towards the left. His feet are joined, but His left knee is slightly raised. It is closely related to

5 The Virgin of Jerusalem, of which there are two variants. The more usual closely follows the iconography of the Tikhvin Virgin, but shows the Child seated on the Virgin's right arm; He looks to the left and holds a scroll in His left hand which He rests on His left leg. The Virgin is presented frontally, pointing to the Child with her left hand. The variant presents the scene in reverse with the Virgin looking at the Child, who turns His left shoulder and arm inwards, resting His left hand, which continues to hold the scroll, on His hip whilst grasping a flower in the other hand.

6 The icon of the Virgin of Kazan was so widely revered in Russia that the Calendar of the Russian Church lists no less than nine miracle-working versions of the painting. The original icon was painted *c.* 1579 in Kazan and eventually came to be lavishly adorned. In 1612 Prince Pozharsky carried it into battle against the Poles and after his victory it was kept in Moscow. In 1679 a church was built

in its memory at Kazan and dedicated to it. In 1821 the icon was moved from Moscow to the newly completed cathedral of Kazan in St Petersburg. It disappeared from there in 1918 when it was supposedly being sent to Moscow; its subsequent fate is uncertain although New York claims to possess it. On it the Virgin and Child were presented full-face with the Virgin holding the Child, who performs a blessing with His right hand, seated on her right arm; neither figure shows its left hand. Of the remaining eight miracle-working versions the Kazanskaya-Kaplunovskaya manifested its powers in 1689; it was probably painted shortly before that date. Other miracle-working icons doubtless similarly date from shortly before the first miracle ascribed to them.

7　The Virgin of Khorsun derives its name from the town of Chersonesus in the Crimea whence the original is thought to have reached Kiev. Its iconography resembles that of the Virgin of Tenderness, but its Byzantine prototype must have been very ancient when it reached the Russians for it had already been darkened by age and dirt; as a result the Russian versions are always very dark in colour.

8　The Petrovskaya Virgin being a bust-size rendering of the Virgin of Kazan, neither of the figures' hands are shown on it.

9　The Virgin of Pimen is a Byzantine half-length representation of the Virgin. The original shows her supporting the Child with both hands although He is seated on her right arm. Christ's head and shoulders are presented frontally, but His legs are shown from the side, with both feet touching. He blesses with His right hand and holds a scroll in the left (*pl. 14*).

10　The Virgin of Smolensk closely resembles the Iverskaya, but presents the Child full-face.

11　The Strastnaya or Virgin of the Passion is a late variant which probably derives from Italy. It presents the Virgin frontally with the Child seated on her right arm holding her thumb in both His hands. His right leg passes under His left to reveal a sandal-shod foot. He turns His head upwards to look at some angels which are seen in the sky with the instruments of the Passion.

12　The Virgin of Tenderness is the name given to the Virgin of Vladimir presented in reverse, that is to say with the Child seated on the Virgin's right arm as she designates Him with her left hand. His left arm encircles her neck and their heads touch. The Child extends His right hand whilst His left leg passes beneath the right to reveal the sole of its foot.

13　The Virgin of Tikhvin shows the Child seated on the Virgin's right arm. She is shown full-face in the act of indicating Him. He performs a blessing with His right hand. His right leg passes beneath the left to reveal the sole of its foot.

14　The Vsygranie or Playful Virgin became very popular in Moscow in the sixteenth and seventeenth centuries. The Child is shown either playfully clutching His mother's chin, a pose which some scholars ascribe to Gothic influences, or else He touches another part of her body, in doing so often turning His back to the worshippers.

Older than most of these types, and perhaps even more fervently revered, was the icon of the Virgin of Znamenie or of the Sign, which was often also termed the Great Panaghia. The Russian panel reproduced a Byzantine icon which was kept in the church of the Blachernae at Constantinople, where it was venerated as the palladium of the city. The Russian version took the form of a double-sided icon presenting on the reverse St Peter and St Natalia praying to the Saviour; the latter painting has partially survived whilst that of the Virgin and Child on the panel's face is almost obliterated. Both are of Novgorodian workmanship and were already revered in 1169, when the Novgorodians carried the icon into battle when attacked by Andrey Bogolyubsky's Suzdalians. In the mid-fifteenth century, when Moscow was attempting to annex Novgorod, the Novgorodians remembered the protection which the icon had extended to them three centuries earlier and once again invoked its aid, this time against Moscow. They did so by depicting the earlier incident on an icon; a parallel for this is to be found in Moldavia where, at an only slightly later date, the Moldavians symbolized the fall of Constantinople to the Ottomans, and their own subjection to them, by including a far earlier siege of Constantinople among the mural paintings with which they decorated the exteriors of some of their churches.

Three icons exist illustrating the Suzdalian attack on Novgorod; all are very similar, and all three date from about the middle of the fifteenth century. One is preserved in the Tretyakov Gallery in Moscow, one in the Russian State Museum at Leningrad and the earliest of the three in the Museum of History and Architecture at Novgorod. Their iconography was specially evolved for the purpose. Each icon is divided into three horizontal registers (*pl. 100*), the two upper ones showing the Novgorodians carrying the icon of the Virgin of the Sign from the Church of the Saviour, where it was kept, to the Kremlin's battlements, where it afforded them its protection.

Icons of the Virgin and Child of the types just listed, with other closely related ones, ensured the survival into modern times of the grand and monumental representations both of the Virgin and Child and of the Pantocrator which the Byzantines had conceived. These portrayals stemmed from Constantinople. From the start they were greatly revered and admired in the Kievan world, where the influence of Salonica, and even more so of Mount Athos must have been as quickly felt. The link with Athos was especially close partly because the Kievo–Pecherskaya Lavra owed its existence, at any rate in part, to the encouragement afforded to it by the Holy Mountain, partly too because the Kievans established a monastery of their own there in 1016 and another in 1169, both of which Russians were in the habit of visiting. No paintings survive to reveal the nature of the influence which Salonica exercised over Kiev's artists, but one relatively early icon exists which may possibly throw some light on the nature of the monastic school which developed in the Kievo–Pecherskaya Lavra in the twelfth century, when the monastery was still run on Athonic lines, although it was soon after to adopt the rule of Constantinople's Studite monastery. For centuries the Lavra was to serve as the centre of Russia's religious life, learning and the arts, to be paralleled in the north only in the late fourteenth century by the Troitse-Sergeyeva Lavra, founded at what is now Zagorsk, by St Sergius of Radonezh.

The Kievo–Pecherskaya Lavra's workshops were staffed to begin with by Byzantine artists, but within a few years Russian artists of distinction were manning them. Foremost among them was Alipy. His name is linked by tradition to an icon known as the Virgin of Svensk (*pl. 86*) after the monastery of that name, a dependency of the Lavra's, founded in the icon's honour in the neighbourhood of Briansk. The icon shows the Virgin seated on a throne with the Child on her knee. To her right stands Feodosy, whose life as a hermit in a cave on the outskirts of Kiev led to the founding of the Lavra, on her left Anthony, Feodosy's disciple and successor as the Lavra's abbot (1062–74). According to the records the icon, whilst still belonging to the Lavra, was brought to Briansk in 1288 in answer to the prayers of its prince, Roman Mikhailovich, who had recently lost his sight. The cataloguers of the Tretyakov Gallery's icons have tentatively assigned the icon of the Great Panaghia (*pl. 88*) to Kiev; many scholars feel unable to agree with them; if that suggestion is set aside, the icon of the Virgin of Svensk stands out as the only painting that is linked to Kiev and attributed by tradition to Alipy. Nevertheless scholars agree in refusing to date it to the start of the twelfth century, preferring to regard it as a work of late thirteenth-century date. Even so, there can be little doubt that the icon which restored the prince's sight and survives to our day presents a faithful copy of an earlier prototype, and thus almost certainly of the one which Alipy evolved; the latter was probably the first Russian painting to introduce a new iconographic type to the long list of existing portrayals of the Virgin and Child. The style of this icon, the earliest rendering of the type to survive, differs sharply from those followed in either the great mural works which survive in Kiev's cathedrals or in the panels which reached Kievan Russia from Byzantium. It savours more of monasticism than of courtly taste and displays a remarkable degree of humanism in its portrayal of the two monks. Here we are on the threshold of that trusting, childlike, credulous yet real and carefully observed world of the medieval monk and pilgrim, a world which was several centuries later to create, in response to a growing awareness of its surroundings, what can best be described as 'founder' icons, that is to say icons depicting the founder of an important monastery against a detailed rendering of its buildings as they were at the time at which the first version of the icon had been painted, not as they were when he first founded it.

Kiev's court style is probably reflected in the patrician style which flourished in the Vladimir–Suzdalian principality following Kiev's decline. The Vladimir–Suzdalian school occupies a foremost place in the history of Russian art, for until the invading Mongols put an end to its first phase it possessed unique vitality and true originality. In the pictorial works that survive, the dignified reserve of imperial Byzantium is tempered by a gentler refinement and controlled by the Russian fondness for decoration. The treatment is marvellously lucid and poetic, yet forthright. The style is to be seen at its severest in its icons and at its most imaginative in the damascene panels forming the south and west doors of Suzdal's Nativity Cathedral. They date from about 1230–33 and are the last works of major importance to have been completed in the principality before the Mongols conquered it. This is not the place in which to attempt to assign the panels to their rightful position in European art, yet these fresh, freely and vividly rendered scenes set the mind wondering about the road which Russian art might have followed, had not the Mongol occupation left the Church and its flock determined to ensure the survival of Orthodoxy by staunchly adhering to all its ancient canons, not least to its iconographic style.

Four extremely fine icons of pre-Mongol invasion date are assigned by many scholars to the school of Vladimir–Suzdal; they are less eclectic and less Western in style than the damascene door panels, but this is only to be expected in icons. They possess the patrician qualities which are characteristic of that period and school to an unusual degree. Two of the four icons are familiar to Western art lovers, but the two others are virtually unknown to them. All four belong to the Tretyakov Gallery. One of the two better known paintings presents the full-length figure of the Virgin with a medallion of Christ on her breast and the two archangels shown in roundels in the two top corners of the painting; it is known as the Great Panaghia (*pl. 88*). Although many eminent scholars consider the painting to be a thirteenth-century work of the Rostov-Suzdalian or Yaroslavl schools the authors of the Tretyakov Gallery's catalogue of icons suggest that it should be assigned to Alipy and dated to about 1114. It seems unlikely, however, that a Russian monk would have produced so majestic and sophisticated a painting at such an early date, whilst from the latter half of that century art was at a standstill in Kiev. The icon's style bears marked similarities to that belonging to the second icon in this group, the no less monumental and refined representation of St Demetrius of Salonica shown seated on a throne and holding the sword which served at the time in Russia as the symbol of princely authority (*pl. 87*). Demetrius is portrayed as a valorous and upright prince, a warrior saint rather than a martyr. When the panel was undergoing cleaning and conservation the cypher of the Grand Duke Vsevolod-Dmitri, the Great Nest (1176–1212), was found on the right side of the back of the saint's throne. It is an indication that the icon was painted for the Grand Duke and it provides the panel with a terminal dating. It is one which confirms the conclusions put forward by earlier scholars on stylistic grounds and therefore lends support to their views concerning the origin and probable date of the icon of the Great Panaghia.

The correctness of the conclusions reached by earlier scholars regarding the date of the icon of St Demetrius helps to sustain those which they have put forward regarding the two less well-known panels in this group. Both are exceptionally beautiful; both depict on a single, fairly narrow rectangular panel the heads and shoulders of the three central figures of the Deesis cycle; on both icons these figures display fortitude, profound humanism and compassion. The more conventional of the two (*pl. 90*) depicts Christ as a mature, although still young man; the Virgin and St John appear on either side of Him. Because of the marked similarity between the Virgin's face as it appears on this panel and that of the severely damaged twelfth-century Bogolyubovo Virgin this icon is thought to date from the latter half of the twelfth century and to belong to the same school. The second Deesis icon[10] resembles the first stylistically, but possesses exceptionally lyrical and poetic qualities. It too displays three heads on a rectangular shaped panel, but in this case the artist has reverted to a very early iconographic form by representing the Deesis by the young Christ Emmanuel and the Archangels Gabriel and Michael. The cataloguers of the Tretyakov Gallery's icons have tentatively assigned the painting to Novgorod and dated it to the middle of the twelfth century, basing their suggestion for its Novgorodian origin on the surely not very close resemblance of the rendering of Christ Emmanuel to that to be seen on the Ustyug Annunciation (*pl. 174*), as well as between that of its archangels and the Golden-Headed Angel (*pl. 176*), yet here there is a delicacy in the rendering of the archangels' faces, more especially in the treatment of the Archangel Michael's face and eyebrows, a nobility in the young Christ Emmanuel and a patrician quality which must surely support the opinions of those who assign the icon to Vladimir–Suzdal. All scholars agree in dating it to the mid-twelfth century. Rublyov must surely have seen this painting, or others closely resembling it, when he was in Vladimir, for his own work clearly reflects something of its style and spirit.

The patrician element made itself felt for only a short time in Novgorod and was never predominant there. However, its presence is to be discerned in two icons of St George which are believed to have been painted for Novgorod's princes at the time when the town's sturdy, independent-minded inhabitants were evicting them first from the Kremlin enclosure, then from the city in order to govern themselves on near republican lines. One of the panels presents a full length of the saint (*pl. 91*), the other a half length (*pl. 92*). Both possess a touch of the spirit which permeates the icon of St Demetrius (*pl. 87*). The full-length icon of St George is thought to have been brought to the Dormition Cathedral in Moscow, together with the Ustyug Annunciation, from the cathedral of St George in the Yuriev Monastery; this cathedral was built in 1119 on the outskirts of Novgorod by the master builder Peter for Prince Vsevolod, who had been expelled from the Kremlin, and for the Abbot Kiriak. The icon is believed to date from about 1140, when the monastery's cathedral was dedicated. The half-length icon of St George is associated with George, a younger son of Andrey Bogolyubsky, who became Prince of Novgorod in 1170. As on the full-length panel the saint is pictured as a sturdy, doughty warrior who firmly grasps the sword symbolizing his princely sovereignty. The treatment is in both cases earthier than the Byzantine or Vladimir–Suzdalian. This, together with the strongly graphic treatment of their hair and the blend of gentleness and firmness in their expressions, clearly proclaims their Russian origin. The ambiguity of Novgorod's political organization at this period, when it stood mid-way between being a principality and a republic, helps to account for the portrayal in both icons of a warrior saint who, although of rustic origin, yet possessed a touch of the patrician in his make-up. In both paintings the dignity associated with a court art blends with the candour which was to characterize Novgorodian painting of the fourteenth and fifteenth centuries.

Until the Mongol invasion and for a short time after it, patrician conventions still continued occasionally to manifest themselves in the paintings produced in the country's major regional capitals. It is, for example, to be discerned in the very damaged, splendid double-sided icon with the Virgin of Tenderness of the Feodorovo type[11] on its face and St Paraskevi on its reverse. In both figures only the faces and hands survive from the original works. Tradition links the panel with Vasili

Yaroslavych, Prince of Kostroma (1272) and it is especially valuable as an approximately datable example of the type of quality work being done before the Mongol occupation had set a term to the early medieval period in the history of Russian art and slowed up its further development. In the districts which the Mongols controlled, life was to stagnate throughout the fourteenth century and it is unlikely that any masterpieces were produced in them until the Mongols had been defeated on the Field of Kulikovo (1380).

The first interesting datable icon to survive from the fourteenth century is that in the Yaroslavl Museum which displays a half-length version of the full-length painting of the Virgin of Tolg (*pl. 89*). It was done by a monk of the Tolg Monastery and is distinguished by the name of The Second Tolg Virgin (*pl. 93*) for it is a copy of the earlier work. It is dated to the year 1314. Its style differs as sharply from those to be found in icons of pre-Mongol invasion date as from near contemporary and slightly later Novgorodian ones, but follows quite faithfully that of the full-length version known as the First Virgin of Tolg. The latter shows the Virgin seated on a throne with the Child standing on her lap in order to embrace her and with the sky above them containing two standing angels. Its style is accomplished, but it does not savour of Russia. The suggestion that the icon is of Georgian origin and is the one which was brought from Ossetia to Yaroslavl in 1278 by Prince Feodor Rostislavych, the Black, seems thoroughly convincing.

Novgorod was not conquered by the Mongols and also succeeded in defeating the westerners who attacked it in the hope of benefiting from Russia's collapse. Novgorod was therefore able to develop and prosper at its own pace. Although the Dnieper route to Byzantium was no longer safe, contacts with Byzantium were to some extent maintained whilst trade with Western Europe was expanded. In addition Novgorod succeeded in extending its authority beyond its immediate boundaries till its rule and influence embraced a large tract of north-eastern Russia, in addition to the neighbouring small, though important, individualistic and creative satellite town of Pskov. In the autonomous Novgorodian lands the arts quickly recovered their original vitality and were soon flourishing as splendidly as in the early Christian period. An icon of St Nicholas the Miracle Worker from the church of St Nicholas on the Lipna at Novgorod, now preserved in the museum at Novgorod (*pl. 96*) has the distinction of being the earliest signed and dated example of Russian religious art to survive. The inscription tells us that it was painted in 1294 by Aleksa, son of Peter, for one Nikolay Vasilievich to present to the church. Its graphic features are a characteristic of the Russian school and are even more pronounced in this painting than in such undated, yet definitely earlier icons as, for example, those of the Golden Headed Angel (*pl. 176*) and the two St Georges

(*pls. 91 and 92*). They are even clearer in the earlier, double-sided icon displaying the Veronica on the front and the Adoration of the Cross on the reverse (*pl. 95*), which now belongs to the Tretyakov Gallery. Although the compilers of the Gallery's icon catalogue assign the latter work to the school of Vladimir–Suzdal, Professor Lazarev argues convincingly that it is a Novgorodian painting and proves that it was in existence in 1262 when details from it were used as a chapter heading for the Novgorodian manuscript, the *Zakharievskiy Prolog*,[12] which bears that date.

A hundred years later the Russian feeling for colour, line and the exclusion of the non-essential had fused into the distinctive style which was to endow Novgorod's paintings with their compelling, individual type of beauty. It is already to be seen in its fully evolved form by 1377, when the icon of the two martyred princes Boris and Gleb (*pl. 97*) is believed to have been painted for the Novgorodian church which was built and dedicated to them in that year. There is no mistaking the icon's Novgorodian origin. Its linear, rhythmical features, its use of vivid yet harmonious colours, its robust elegance and lucidity are typical features of the Novgorodian school. Yet in addition to these native elements many Novgorodian icons of fourteenth- and fifteenth-century dates also reflect the influence of the contemporary Constantinopolitan school, for although contacts with Byzantium had been impaired by the Mongol conquests to the south they had not been severed. Byzantine elements are so prevalent in some of the icons which Vasili, Archbishop of Novgorod, commissioned that Professor Lazarev suggests that certain of these may have been painted by 'Isaiah, the Greek', the artist who, so the chronicle states, was employed by the Archbishop in 1338 to execute the murals in the church of The Entry to Jerusalem at Novgorod. The copper gilt Royal Doors which, according to the records, Archbishop Vasili commissioned in 1336 for the cathedral of St Sophia at Novgorod are the earliest datable works to reflect the influence of Constantinople's Palaeologue style.[13]

Since Archbishop Vasili is the first true patron of the arts to be represented by some of the works which he commissioned, a few words about him may not be out of place here, more especially since he was very much a man of his city at the very time when it was entering on the period of its greatest power and prosperity. Like many of his future parishioners Grigori Kalika, as Vasili was called until he took his vows, was a travelled man for in his early manhood he had visited Constantinople and the Holy Land.

He came from a humble home and his sympathies were always to lie with the poor of his see. In becoming a member of the white clergy—the section from which village priests, who were permitted to marry, were drawn—he was appointed priest to the church of Sts

Cosmas and Damian at Novgorod. They were the patron saints of the city's blunt and enterprising merchants, who are therefore thought to have worshipped there, yet in the rising of 1342 Vasili was to side with the democrats. He had, however, ceased to be a priest well before that date, having in the interval taken his vows and been appointed archbishop as far back as 1330. He was respected in his diocese as an able politician of independent views.

By the second decade of the fourteenth century Moscow's star was in the ascendant and Vasili recognized this. In contrast to Novgorod's merchants, he thought it wise to establish good relations with Moscow's ambitious, ruthless and wily ruler. In 1335 he therefore got in touch with Ivan Kalita, Grand Duke of Muscovy, and ten years later he invited the latter's successor, Semeon Ivanovich, the Proud, to Novgorod. The Archbishop's conduct was always governed by his unshakable devotion to his faith and his pride in his native city. These sentiments led him to refuse to receive a deputation sent by King Magnus of Poland for the purposes of debating on the relative merits of Orthodoxy and Catholicism since, Vasili asserted, his attachment to his own church was so profound as to be permanent, rendering such an exchange of views pointless.

Vasili was a writer of distinction, but it was as an enlightened patron of the arts that he made his greatest contribution to Novgorodian culture. The palace which he built for himself in the precincts of the cathedral of St Sophia was the most advanced secular building to be found at the time in Russia. The church of the Annunciation which he erected in Novgorod in 1342-3 and that of the Resurrection at Derevyanitza on which work started in 1348, although more traditional in style than his residence, were elegant and well proportioned. His interest in painting was as keen as his love of architecture. He established an artist's workshop in his palace. Those whom he employed in it were known as 'the Archbishop's lads' and it was they who, in 1341, painted the icons for the cathedral of St Sophia's newly completed, many-tiered iconostasis, perhaps the earliest of the kind to be installed in Russia.

The introduction of the many-tiered iconostasis presented artists with a problem of considerable complexity, for it obliged them to produce a sequence of icons each of which, whilst retaining all the characteristics essential to individual paintings, had at the same time to blend harmoniously with all the panels displayed in the iconostasis, all of which had to combine in creating a sufficiently colourful effect to attract a worshipper's attention as he entered the church and then to continue to hold it, both collectively and individually. It is impossible to establish how successfully Vasili's lads overcame this difficulty, but it had certainly been generally mastered by the start of the following century.

It is unfortunate that nothing is known about the way in which Vasili's workshop was run, for the information could have helped to determine when the narrow specialization which was eventually to reduce icon painting from a fine art to a craft was first resorted to. In Moscow it was gradually to lead to the division of the painters into three groups, the first consisting of the *znamenshchiki* or emblazoners who, with the aid of apprentices and assistants, did the gilding, silvering and ornamentation of the backgrounds; the *dolichniki* (non-facial), who specialized in figural work and the pictorial details in the backgrounds, and the *lichniki* (facial) who painted heads and faces, a division of work which did much to kill true inspiration. Lazarev is surely right in asserting that some sort of collaboration between master and assistants existed from the start, as it did in Rublyov's day, but it is unlikely that that system differed substantially from that followed by the early Italian masters and their apprentices. This assumption is borne out by the fact, to mention but this example, that Lazarev's penetrating stylistic analysis of the icons painted in 1405 for the iconostasis of Moscow's Annunciation Cathedral enabled him to distinguish between those which were painted by Andrey Rublyov and those done by Prokhor of Gorodetz. Even Dionysy, the layman who became the finest of Moscow's late fifteenth-century religious artists, is unlikely to have encouraged narrow specialization in the large and thriving workshop which he ran, and in which his sons were probably trained. As accomplished artists they worked with their father on the murals of the Ferapont Monastery's church, but there is no sign of their having resorted to the narrow specialization which was to become usual a century or so later.

It is tempting to think that the paintings stemming from Archbishop Vasili's workshop came to be admired not only in Novgorodian lands, but also as far afield as Constantinople, and that the stimulating and cultivated climate which the Archbishop created in his see persisted after his death and helped to encourage artists such as the great Constantinopolitan painter Theophanes, the Greek, to abandon their crumbling capital in order to seek a better life in Novgorod. Like El Greco, Theophanes was to become known as 'the Greek' in his adopted country, like El Greco's his superb style was to acquire a new facet—in his case a Russian one—there. In return Theophanes brought with him to Russia the contemporary Constantinopolitan style, using it with the skill and assurance of a great and fully-formed artist. The Russians were quick to appreciate his genius; their chroniclers thought it right to record some of his activities and more important commissions whilst his personality and artistic methods impressed all those who came in contact with him. He is brought to life for us by a letter sent by the distinguished writer Epiphanius, a monk of the Troitse-Sergeyeva Lavra, in 1415 to Cyril,

VI THE GREAT PANAGHIA. Russia. *c.* 1224. See pl. 88.
VII ST NICHOLAS THE MIRACLE WORKER. Russia. 1294. See pl. 96.

Abbot of the Spas-Afanasiev Monastery near Tver. The letter deserves to be quoted in full, for it not only records all that is known about Theophanes, but—indirectly—it also throws some interesting light on the way in which average Russian icon painters of the period worked. The circumstances which led up to the letter occurred in 1408–9 when Yedigei, Khan of the Golden Horde, marched on Moscow. His route led past the Troitse-Sergeyeva Lavra and he had no hesitation in besieging the monastery which served also as an outer defence of Moscow. Epiphanius managed to escape just before the attack; taking some of his best-loved books he sought refuge in Cyril's monastery, which was situated in the safer district of Tver. One of his books contained a picture of Constantinople's cathedral of St Sophia, the mother church of Orthodoxy. Cyril must have been impressed by the picture, for six years later, when Epiphanius was once again living in his own monastery, Cyril asked him for fuller information about it. Epiphanius sent him the following letter in reply:

'You saw Constantinople's Church of Sophia in a book of mine, a Gospel known to the Greeks as a tetra-evangelion. . . . And this is how it befell that that building came to be pictured in our book. When I was living in Moscow there lived there a most delightful sage, a cunning philosopher, one Theophanes, a Greek by birth, a fine book illuminator and one outstanding among icon painters, who with his own hand had adorned a large number of stone churches, over forty of them, in the towns of Constantinople, Chalcedon, Galata, Kaffa (Theodosia), and also in Novgorod the Great and Nizhni Novgorod. In Moscow he painted three churches, that of the Annunciation,[14] that of St Michael[15] and another.[16] In the church of St Michael he painted a town on one wall, carefully colouring it; in Prince Vladimir Andreievich's palace he painted a view of Moscow on one stone wall; he also adorned the Grand Duke's *terem* (apartment) with a most novel, remarkable painting, and in the stone church of the Annunciation painted a Tree of Jesse and an Apocalypse. Whilst he was delineating and colouring these scenes no one ever saw him consult a model as do some of our icon painters who, in their bewilderment, constantly turn to one, gazing hither and thither, and are not so much engaged in painting as in studying their models. He, however, seemed to create his paintings with his hands, yet he was constantly on the move, conversing with visitors, his mind occupied with learned and lofty thoughts, his wise, perceptive eyes perceiving goodness and sweet reason. This wondrous and famous man deigned to express a liking for my worthlessness; and I, unworthy and senseless, found great courage within myself and often went to converse with him, for I enjoyed his talk.

'Whosoever conversed with him could not fail to wonder at his wisdom, at his parables, at his ingenuous arguments. When I found that he liked me and did not scorn me, then I added shamelessness to my daring and said to him: 'I beg of your kind understanding to record for me in colour the outlines of the great and holy Sophia of Tsargrad (Constantinople) which the great Justinian built, likening in this the wisdom of Solomon; some say that in its quality and size it equals the inner part of Moscow's Kremlin; that if a traveller should enter it and wish to visit it without a guide, then, whatever his intelligence, he is unlikely to emerge from it without having lost his way amidst its profusion of columns and piers, of ascents and descents, of passages and galleries, and of various chambers and chapels, staircases and treasuries, tombs, offices of diverse sorts, windows, corridors and doors, entries and exits, and also of stone columns. Also paint for me that same Justinian seated on a horse and holding a copper apple in his right hand, in size, they say, being such as to hold two and a half buckets of water,[17] and all these things depict for me on a leaf of a book so that I can mount it at the start of a book and, whilst remembering your work and gazing on that temple, I may be able to imagine myself in Tsargrad.' He, however, sagely replied to me in his wisdom: 'It is impossible', he murmured, 'either for you to obtain or for me to provide all you ask, but because of your insistence I will paint a part, a part which is less than a hundredth part, a particle of its immensity, yet even the little that I depict will suffice to enable you to imagine and comprehend the remainder.' Having spoken, he resolutely seized a sheet of paper and quickly outlined a church identical to the actual Constantinopolitan temple and handed it to me. The painting has proved of immense use to Moscow's icon painters as many of them have copied it for themselves, vying and contending with each other. Following their example, I too ventured in my capacity of icon painter to paint four versions of it which we placed in four sections of our book, one at the start of the Gospel of Matthew, beside Justinian's column and a portrait of Matthew, the second at the start of the Gospel of Mark, the third before Luke's and the last before the Gospel of John; I painted these four pictures of the temple and those of the Evangelists which you saw when I, in fear of Yedigei, fled to Tver and found refuge with you in my grief, and showed you all the books which were left to me after my flight and ruin. It was then that you saw the picture of the temple which, after a lapse of six years, you asked me about last winter.'

From all the information which is available today Professor Lazarev concludes that Theophanes was born in the 1330s,[18] that he died sometime between 1405 and 1409, and that he reached Novgorod the Great before 1378 when, according to the chronicle, he executed the murals in the church of the Transfiguration. A few fragments of these paintings survived the last war to

VIII THE OLD TESTAMENT TRINITY, by Rublyov. 1422–27. See pl. 118.

IX VIRGIN AND CHILD. Greece. 14th or 15th century. See pl. 163.

attest to Theophanes's skill as a mural artist. By 1395 he had moved to Moscow from Kostroma where he was working in 1390. Although Theophanes must have painted many icons in addition to his mural compositions most scholars agree in assigning only nine to him; some, however add a couple to this figure, some deduct a couple. The icons which are indisputably assigned to Theophanes consist of a Saviour in Glory, a Virgin, a St John Chrysostom, an Archangel Gabriel, a St Paul, St Basil and St John the Evangelist, all of which were painted in 1405 for the Deesis tier of the iconostasis in Moscow's Cathedral of the Annunciation. Lazarev argues convincingly that these icons escaped damage in the fire which ravaged the cathedral in 1482, and that the burns to be seen on them occurred during the no less disastrous fire of 1547. A much-damaged head of Christ (*pl. 109*) is questioned by some experts, although its style bears the mark of Theophanes. It is even more difficult to concur with Lazarev's doubts concerning one of the finest icons in existence, that of the Transfiguration from Pereslavl–Zalessky, and his inclination to class it as a workshop painting. The cataloguers of the Tretyakov Gallery's icons must surely be right in ascribing it to Theophanes himself; they date it to about 1403. Lazarev supports his own opinion by the fact that the icon is inscribed in Russian, not in Greek, scarcely a conclusive reason in the case of a man who had spent the last twenty-five years of his life in Russia and was providing the icon for a church situated in a comparatively small and remote, although thriving and important regional town. The compilers of the Tretyakov Gallery's icon catalogue do not share Lazarev's doubts. (*Pl. 108*.)

Lazarev also questions the attribution of the greatly revered icon of the Virgin of Don on its face and the Dormition on its reverse to Theophanes; but most experts agree that the Greek master painted it in 1392, when living at Kolomna, for that town's Dormition Cathedral. If this is so, then the icon is the earliest of Theophanes's panels to survive. Legend, in this case far from convincingly, assigns the icon to an even earlier date by asserting that it was commissioned by the Don Cossacks as a gift for Dmitri Donskoy in order that he might carry it into battle when engaging the Mongols on the Field of Kulikovo. The Grand Duke is then supposed to have placed the icon in the Dormition Cathedral at Kolomenskoe, where Ivan Kalita had built a country palace for himself and his heirs. If this were so the icon is hardly likely to have been moved to Kostroma by 1552 yet it was there that Ivan IV, the Terrible, paused to pray before it when setting out to besiege Kazan. On his return, after capturing Kazan, Ivan IV transferred the icon from Kolomna to the Annunciation Cathedral in Moscow, with which it was henceforth to be associated. In 1591 Giray, Khan of the Crimean Tartars, attacked Moscow; the icon was carried to the battlefield and enabled the defenders to ward off the attack. In gratitude for its intervention the tsar founded the Monastery of the Don in Moscow. Finally, in 1598, the Patriarch Jove used the icon at Boris Godunov's coronation.

Lazarev is reluctant to assign the icon of the Virgin of the Don to Theophanes partly because its flesh tints are executed in the Russian technique of *ochrenie* where light and dark flesh tints are imperceptibly fused, and also because the Dormition on the panel's reverse, although clearly by the same hand, is depicted with an economy of detail, with that almost poster-like simplification which characterize the works of the Novgorodian school. Indeed, if we recall that in Byzantium Theophanes worked as a mural artist and that the sweeping, powerful brushwork best suited to large-scale work is inapplicable to icons, the argument seems convincing enough, but the sweep in the Pereslavl–Zalessky icon of the Transfiguration, although responsible for much of its glory, is as well controlled as is to be expected from an artist who, according to Epiphanius, was also a fine book illuminator. Comparison of the face of the Virgin in the icon of the Virgin of the Don with that of the undisputed Virgin in the Deesis of Moscow's Annunciation Cathedral's iconostasis goes far towards convincing us that both panels are by the same hand. After the years he had spent in Novgorod Theophanes could surely have learnt to admire the restraint and exclusion of subsidiary details of Novgorodian works and come himself to strive for the telling directness which renders the Dormition on the reverse of the Virgin of the Don so impressive a painting. If so, it is the concision in Novgorodian art which must be seen as having most affected Theophanes's art during the years which he spent in Russia, making him as much a Russian artist as El Greco is a Spanish one. There is an additional reason for ascribing this double-sided panel to Theophanes. When the icon was undergoing cleaning and conservation the restorers found that lapis lazuli had been used for its blue shades. Even in Byzantium the use of this precious and expensive ingredient was reserved for paintings of special importance. In Russia it appears to have been used only once by a Russian, by Andrey Rublyov, who must have obtained it from Theophanes in 1405, when working as his assistant. Rublyov must have treasured the colour throughout the remainder of his life for he used it towards the end of it when painting his masterpiece, the Old Testament Trinity, as a memorial to his first abbot and kind patron, St Sergius of Radonezh.

In 1405 Rublyov and Prokhor of Gorodetz worked on the murals of Moscow's Annunciation Cathedral as fully established artists, although as Theophanes's assistants. Association with as great an artist as Theophanes must have done much to quicken Rublyov's genius, yet the influence which so experienced and accomplished an older man as Theophanes could have exercised over as modest a younger one as Rublyov was not to prove as profound as might reasonably have been expected from such an association. A comparison of the much-damaged head of Christ from the Deesis tier in the Annunciation Cathedral's iconostasis (*pl. 109*), although not universally attributed to Theophanes, yet which is widely regarded as his, and that painted by Rublyov for the Vysotsky Monastery in about 1420 (*pl. 118*)—it is, alas, in almost an equally damaged condition—reveals the extent and the limits of that influence. The impact made on Rublyov by the late twelfth- and early thirteenth-century mural and panel paintings of the Vladimir–Suzdalian school, which he must have been able to study carefully when he was himself engaged on painting murals for the cathedral of the Dormition at Vladimir, seems to have exerted a far stronger influence on him than did Theophanes. Rublyov's inspiration quite clearly stemmed from Russia, the Russia represented by the early Vladimir–Suzdalian school; it sharpened his imagination as it did that of his near-contemporary fellow artists living in Yaroslavl and Rostov. Representative of the latter is the icon of the Transfiguration from the church of that name in the village of Spas-Podgorie near Rostov the Great which is dated by an inscription to the year 1395.[19] Rublyov was moulded by the same traditions as that artist, but his genius enabled him to transcend the achievements of his contemporaries and to win a following for himself which was responsible for the development in the course of the fifteenth century of the school now known by his name.

Although Rublyov's name appears several times in contemporary records nothing is known about his origin, his early life or his artistic schooling. The Soviet Government celebrated the six-hundredth anniversary of his birth in 1960, yet most scholars place it as much as a decade later. Rublyov must have taken his vows early in life for it seems certain that he was a monk of the Troitse–Sergeyeva Lavra when St Sergius of Radonezh (1322–92) was still its abbot. St Sergius's piety, goodness and wisdom no less than his accomplishments cannot have failed to act as a formative influence over the young monk. Nor can it be doubted that St Sergius quickly came to appreciate the young artist's excellence and spoke well of him in court circles. As a close friend of Dmitri Donskoy and his family St Sergius often acted as the Grand Duke's adviser and was godfather to the latter's son, Prince Yuri of Zvenigorod. It can only have been due to St Sergius's intervention that Rublyov was entrusted with important commissions by Vasili, Dmitri Donskoy's elder son and successor on the Muscovite throne, and by Vasili's brother, Prince Yuri. There is reason to think that Rublyov worked for Prince Yuri in the 1390s. By 1400 Rublyov had become a monk of the Andronikov Monastery (now the Rublyov Museum at Moscow), and he was no longer connected with the Troitse–Sergeyeva Lavra in 1405, when he was given work at Vladimir; by 1408 he had returned to the

Andronikov Monastery and although he may have temporarily gone back to the Lavra when painting the icons for its new cathedral of the Trinity, he remained attached to the former foundation till his death as an old man in 1430.

Contemporary records start by linking Rublyov's name with that of Prokhor of Gorodetz, but later they associate him with Daniil Chorny. In each entry Rublyov's name is placed second to theirs, suggesting thereby that both were older than Rublyov. Daniil Chorny is not mentioned in the records until 1408, but from then onwards his name is always linked to Rublyov's and they seem to have become regular colleagues. All three artists sought anonymity and never signed their works but surviving documents show that Prokhor and Rublyov were acting as assistants to Theophanes in 1405, helping him to adorn the walls of Moscow's Cathedral of the Annunciation with murals and to provide icons for its iconostasis. Professor Lazarev assigns the icons of the Annunciation, the Nativity, the Virgin's Purification, the Baptism, the Transfiguration, the Raising of Lazarus and the Entry of Jerusalem to Rublyov, and those of the Last Supper, the Crucifixion, the Entombment, the Descent into Hell, the Ascension, the Descent of the Holy Ghost and the Dormition to Prokhor.

Having distinguished himself by his work in the Annunciation Cathedral at Moscow Rublyov was sent to Vladimir in 1408, this time with Daniil Chorny, in order to execute some mural paintings in the Dormition Cathedral. Lazarev attributes the following icons in its iconostasis to Rublyov—Christ in Glory with the Virgin and St John from its Deesis tier, all three of which now belong to the Tretyakov Gallery. Comparisons with Theophanes's full-length Deesis, done three years earlier for Moscow's Annunciation Cathedral, when Rublyov was working on the same church, show how much the two artists differ in style, outlook and temperament. Rublyov's icon of the Ascension is also assigned to 1408, his version of the Virgin of Vladimir to 1409 when, according to some scholars, he may have been living for a time at the Troitse–Sergeyeva Lavra. Lazarev thinks that it was in about the year 1410 that Rublyov painted his finest icon of Christ in Glory and the accompanying half-length representations of the Archangel Michael and the Apostle Paul; he suggests that they were done for the Savin-Storozhevsky Monastery at Zvenigorod, but the cataloguers of the Tretyakov Gallery's icons believe that they were painted for the Voskressensky Vysotsky Monastery and subsequently moved to Zvenigorod, and they therefore assign the three icons to the 1420s. Lazarev sees the influence of the Constantinopolitan style reflected in these paintings and ascribes its presence to the arrival in Moscow some time between 1387 and 1395 of the Byzantine Deesis group of icons known as The Vysotsky Chin (*pl. 16*).

The date of Rublyov's masterpiece, the Old Testament Trinity, is hotly debated. Lazarev places it in about 1411, when a wooden church dedicated to the Trinity was built at the Troitse-Sergeyeva Lavra to contain St Sergius's coffin. Rublyov must at the time have been at the height of his powers, but some scholars, including the cataloguers of the Tretyakov Gallery's icons, make a good case for assigning it to some time between 1422 and 1427 when Nikon, St Sergius's successor as the Lavra's abbot, became extremely anxious to replace the wooden church of the Trinity, which had been destroyed when Yedigei's troops captured the monastery, with the masonry one which survives to this day. According to the records Nikon felt that his life was drawing to a close. He accordingly wrote to Rublyov and Daniil Chorny begging them to come to the Lavra in order to help to decorate the new church and provide the icons for its iconostasis. Although the surviving icons are obviously the work of several artists Lazarev and most other scholars agree in attributing to Rublyov those of the Baptism, the Archangel Michael, St Paul and possibly also that of St Peter. Although they were painted a few years before Rublyov's death and are the last works to be assigned to him they show no trace of declining power; their lines are as delicate yet firm as in his earlier works, the spirituality remains as intense, the colours as luminous, delicate and harmonious. It is therefore quite possible that the later of the two dates suggested for the icon of the Old Testament Trinity is the most likely of all. Nikon died in 1427; Rublyov's death occurred three years later and attracted little notice, a sad omission in the case of an artist of European calibre, the founder of the early Muscovite school, the greatest of Russia's medieval painters, its counterpart for Italy's Fra Angelico. Rublyov's humility and piety had won him the obscurity he desired. Only Moscow's leading patrons of art had appreciated his genius in his lifetime yet after his death the number of painters who came to be influenced by him steadily increased. In the course of the fifteenth century they enriched Russian art by an important number of icons adhering to the Rublyov tradition. The features in Rublyov's work which they set out to retain were the firm and fluid lines which provide his figures with narrow, sloping shoulders, his frequent use of the circle which was thought at the time to symbolize God's circular movement, his habit of offsetting these curved outlines by the angular folds of his draperies. These linear features forming, so to speak, the painting's skeleton, were cloaked by Rublyov in lyrical, strong yet pastel-toned colours of celestial hues. They reflected the serenity and happiness within him and were attuned to the sense of buoyancy felt throughout Russia at the defeat of the Mongols at Kulikovo, a victory which did much to restore Russia's pride and faith in its future. Rublyov expressed all these sentiments with admirable felicity in his painting of the Old Testament Trinity, which he represented in the persons of the three angels seated at Abraham's table. To symbolize eternity he disposed them within an imaginary circle, setting the central angel slightly back from the others; the difference in spacing is so slight as to be almost imperceptible yet it is sufficient to invest the figure with a touch of aloofness which is perhaps intended to indicate that this angel personifies God the Son; since, like the angel to the worshipper's right, he inclines his head, seeming with his companion to be listening to the words of the angel placed on the left, the latter may represent God the Father and, in that case, the third angel must personify the Holy Ghost. Each appears as the counterpart of the others, as laid down by the scriptures, yet each possesses its own individuality.

Rublyov's style, as has been suggested, was a compound of the early Vladimir–Suzdalian, of the later twelfth-century Byzantine as represented at Vladimir and of that branch of the Palaeologan Constantinopolitan school which produced such paintings as those of The Vysotsky Chin. When fused with the style of the contemporary Suzdal–Rostov school it was to form the basis of the Muscovite, doing so at the very time when the less subtle but more dynamic Novgorodian school was producing its great series of masterpieces. It is unfortunate that no dated Novgorodian icons of the period exist to set beside the Suzdal-Rostov and Muscovite works of the first half of the fifteenth century. Only one Novgorodian icon of quality is dated (*pl. 98*); according to its inscription it was painted in 1467, only eleven years before Novgorod's annexation by Moscow. It is therefore representative of the final years of Novgorod's great school of painting, for although standards were maintained during several decades following its integration into Muscovy yet, on being deprived of its autonomy, Novgorod's art lost much of its impetus. The icon is divided into two horizontal bands; the lower contains the figures of seven donors; it is they who give the panel its title of the Praying Novgorodians. Commissioned by Antip Kuzmin, it portrays six of his relations; it is tempting to identify one of them, Timofei Kuzmin, as the boyar of that name who, in 1476, attended a reception held in honour of Ivan III, Grand Duke of Muscovy.

The early Muscovite age (1340–1550) witnessed a great expansion of monasticism. Many existing foundations were to increase considerably in size and wealth during those years; this enabled them to establish outposts in some remote, heavily wooded places. A number of new monasteries, some of them of great size and considerable importance, were also founded during this period. One of the most impressive and influential was established to the north-west of Moscow by St Cyril of Belo-ozero, a disciple of St Sergius of Radonezh. Large foundations such as this possessed their own artists among their brethren and set up special workshops for them, using their products as a means of combating paganism, pockets of which survived in certain isolated communities. The monks who lived in these remote areas often responded both to the humanistic outlook which was beginning to manifest itself in Moscow and also to the earthier local humanism as reflected in the region's folk lore and peasant crafts. In icon painting these elements encouraged the depiction of the local flora and fauna as well as of details drawn from contemporary life. Such features are especially marked in the 'founder' icons. These primitivist, curiously touching paintings are comparatively rare; although seldom of great artistic merit they paved the way for the transition which was about to take place from the otherworld outlook of medieval Russia to Moscow's more mundane and self-seeking one. In former times, when artists were deeply, almost exclusively concerned with the celestial world and the need of fitting their souls for admittance to it, the terrestrial settings of the scenes they depicted were of so little concern to them that they instinctively represented their personages as far larger in size than the supporting details in their backgrounds, but when the painters' interest in terrestrial ideas and events obtruded on these thoughts the figures in their paintings became smaller, the architectural elaborations in their backgrounds increased in size, contemporary furniture and costumes came to be portrayed, and animals and flowers, whilst still being kept of minute size, made their appearance in their paintings.

The transition was not completed until the very end of the sixteenth century and start of the seventeenth. In the interval the early Muscovite style reached its full development under Dionysy who, although a layman, was a painter of sacred subjects of great religious intensity. There is nothing in his work to suggest that he wished to break free of the iconic convention but his paintings reflect an interest in aesthetics unusual at that period. It is especially evident in his striving to endow his works with a sense of movement and to use draperies in such a way as to outline the flesh and muscles which they cover. Some scholars ascribe these elements in his art to the influence of the Italian architects who came to Moscow in the latter quarter of the fifteenth century to work for Ivan III. However, Dionysy was essentially a religious artist, not a secular one, and he attempted to convey the religious fervour which inspired him by elongating his figures more than had been done previously, even poising them on tiptoe, as if to stress their passionate desire to reach heaven.

Dionysy was probably born in about 1450 and must have died soon after 1515. He is first mentioned in the entries for the year 1467 when, together with the monk Mitrofan, he was executing the murals of the Parfuntiev-Borovsk Monastery. Between 1481–86, when his sons Feodosy and Vladimir were sufficiently accomplished to be described as his assistants, as was the monk Paisiy, Dionysy was executing the murals and also the icons of the iconostasis of the Church of the Dormition in the Joseph Volokolamsk Monastery. In 1500 Dionysy signed the icons which he painted for the iconostasis of the Trinity Cathedral at the Pavlov–Obnorsky Monastery. Between that date and 1502 he and his sons were decorating the Ferapont Monastery's church with mural paintings and providing icons for its iconostasis. It is also thought that Dionysy worked in the Resurrection Cathedral at Volokolamsk in 1510 and in the Dormition Cathedral at Moscow in 1515.

The icons which are attributed to Dionysy consist of a Virgin Hodegetria painted in 1482, a St John the Forerunner of 1484–86 forming the central panel of a triptych, a Christ in Glory and a Crucifixion done in 1500 and, when working with his sons, he appears also to have been responsible for some of the panels in the Ferapont Monastery's iconostasis, notably a Virgin, a St John, an Archangel Michael, the Apostles Peter and Paul and a St Demetrius of Salonica.[20] The icons of the Metropolitans Peter and Alexei which many scholars ascribe to Dionysy, surely correctly, and that of the magnificent Apocalypse were done shortly after 1502. The last icon attributed to him is dated to 1510 and illustrates the Virgin's Birth.

Dionysy lived at the time when Muscovy's strength and importance first came to be generally realized in Europe, when Russia first saw itself as the champion of the Orthodox communities living under Ottoman rule and when a cleric referred in his sermon to Moscow as the third Rome. Dionysy sensed this spirit of ascendancy, one that was new to Russia, and expressed it with superb felicity in his biographical icons of Russia's two Metropolitans, Peter and Alexei. He painted their icons following the transfer in 1479 of Peter's mortal remains to the new Dormition Cathedral which Ivan III had built in Moscow's Kremlin on the site of an earlier cathedral of that name. Dionysy was fascinated by the monumental and succeeded in expressing it in these panels even more forcefully than in his mural works or even in his splendid icon of the Apocalypse, which is now to be seen in the Annunciation Cathedral at Moscow. The impact he made on his contemporaries was as great as that achieved by both Theophanes and Rublyov. It is reflected in such fine, anonymous icons as that of the Deposition from the Cross in the Tretyakov Gallery[21] which is assigned to the end of the fifteenth century and, tentatively, to Novgorod. In it an extremely forceful and dramatic effect is obtained by daringly contrasting sloping, almost circular lines and sharp, rectangular ones—a harsher juxtaposition than Dionysy would have resorted to, but one which was to appear with increasing frequency in icons of the Muscovite school.

From the late fifteenth century onwards Moscow's taste was becoming increasingly eclectic. To begin with, the elements stemmed from Russia itself, from places such as Novgorod, Yaroslavl, Suzdal, Rostov, Tver, to name but these, and also, until Byzantium's collapse, from Constantinople. Then, first with the arrival of foreigners in Moscow in the fifteenth and sixteenth centuries, then with the recapture from Poland of the Ukraine in 1654 and of Kiev in 1667, they were to stem both directly from Western Europe and also, via the latter outposts, from central Europe. By that time Eastern, that is to say Islamic, influences were also making themselves felt in Moscow. The use which Ivan III had made of Italian architects in the latter half of the fifteenth century had first directed Russian eyes westward. Following the establishment of Moscow's Foreign Quarter Western books and illuminations began to reach the capital in increasing quantities. Some fell into the hands of artists who were fascinated and enchanted by them, and unconsciously responded to them. An interest in naturalism started to develop. As a result even the artists who were not tempted by it became dissatisfied with existing iconographic themes and, whilst still adhering wholeheartedly to the iconographic style, started to evolve new ones. To begin with their themes remained based on scriptural texts. Typical of them is that of 'In Thee Rejoiceth', which is found on an icon dated to 1629.[22] More important was the tendency which quickly became established of depicting a sequence of events upon a single panel instead of, as formerly, presenting only one event even if, as in a Nativity, it illustrated all the major incidents connected with it. The unity of place and time which had until then been unconsciously preserved gave way, probably just as unconsciously, to a narrative portrayal of a string of events associated to a greater or lesser degree with the main incident. This enabled artists to display ingenuity in the presentation of these scenes, encouraging them to divide the panel into a number of compartments or divisions which served to break up the surface of the panel in a novel manner. The Council of the Stoglav or One Hundred Chapters which met in 1550/1 to codify the Church's laws and eradicate errors from its services and texts was opposed to all forms of iconographic innovation. To put an end to them it drew up careful rules for the guidance of artists, but it omitted to deal conclusively with such matters as the creation of narrative icons or with the tendency to adopt didactic themes in addition to the scriptural or with the substitution of symbols for figural representations. Deacon Ivan Mikhailovich Viscovati therefore raised these points at a meeting of the Holy Synod held in 1553/4, but that body decided to give its approval to the narrative paintings even though such compositions were not ideally suited to serve as vehicles of worship. However, their acceptance enabled artists to depict in them many aspects of contemporary life, a development which was to pave the way for the introduction of genre scenes in religious mural paintings, notably at Yaroslavl.

The Council of the Stoglav had advised artists to look to the older icons, and more especially to those of the Novgorodian school, for guidance and inspiration. This is precisely what was being done in the north-east of the country, at Solvychegodsk, near Perm, by the end of the century. The Stroganovs, a family of Novgorodian origin, lived there. They had become extremely rich, chiefly as a result of the salt trade. Like most Russians of the period the Stroganovs were devout and godfearing, but unlike the majority of their fellow countrymen they were also cultivated and loved the arts. One of them, Nikita, was no mean painter of icons. Their interests and inclinations led them to establish an icon painting workshop on their estate. At their wish it looked to Novgorod for guidance, but since the Stroganovs were discerning art lovers its artists were also expected to satisfy the exacting demands and tastes of a family made up of true connoisseurs, in whose eyes artistic merit ranked as scarcely less important than religious sentiments. As a result elaborate compositions gradually replaced the sharp, poster-like representations favoured by Novgorod and, situated as was Solvychegodsk within relatively easy reach of Persia, by degrees the miniaturist's technique also received encouragement. Since the Solvychegodsk artists worked for a small group of patrons they ceased to pursue personal anonymity and many made a practice of signing, dating and even of inscribing their patrons' names upon their icons. The leading artists quickly became known by name in Moscow, where many members of the Stroganov clan were living. Their works came to be admired in the capital and some of the best artists moved to Moscow. Soon they were working for the tsar and his courtiers. Outstanding among them were Prokopy and Vasili Chirin and Istom, Nazary and Nikifor Savin.[23] They were especially admired by Moscow's merchants and received many commissions from them, but by 1620 they had lost the Stroganov stamp; when this happened the Stroganov artists merged with those of the Armoury and their school's existence came to an end. In the past the two schools have often been confused, but in recent years Soviet scholars have succeeded in distinguishing between their works.

Court patronage became important in Moscow under Ivan III and remained so until the transfer of the capital to St Petersburg at the start of the eighteenth century. By the sixteenth century the artists employed by the tsar and his family were known as 'the tsar's iconographers'. By Ivan IV's day the Armoury had lost much of its original military importance and it came instead to serve as the country's most vital and artistic centre. Workshops of every type were established within its walls. The painters staffing its studios worked for the tsar and his family and therefore continued to be known as the tsar's iconographers. Boris Godunov, perhaps in an effort to atone for some of the sins attributed to him by his contemporaries, made a practice of commissioning icons to serve as gifts to various monasteries such as the Troitse-Sergeyeva Lavra or the Ipatiev. Sometimes he commissioned copies of famous icons as in the case of that of The Old Testament Trinity dating from 1598; a kinsman of his, Dmitri Godunov, did the same in 1586 in the case of the twelfth-century icon of St Demetrius of Salonica belonging to the Dormition Cathedral at Moscow; the differences in the styles of these copies and the versions on which they were based, although glaringly obvious today, were hardly noticeable then. By that time the court style was flourishing in Moscow alongside the Stroganov. Both produced figures having very small heads; these came to be greatly admired and much sought after, commanding higher prices than icons featuring figures with the old type of larger head. However, the court painters made a practice of using deep, rich colours and, above all, a profusion of gold. They used gold for the 'assides' or highlights, for robes and items of regalia, such as crowns, as well as for various decorative details, in addition to retaining the gold backgrounds. These colour schemes are well in evidence in the icon which the Metropolitan of Moscow presented with his blessing in 1586 to Ivan IV's son, Tsar Feodor.

The Armoury artists were divided into two classes. Dr Mneva states that the first was made up of the best artists available in the country. They were given permanent employment and paid an annual salary. The second group consisted of men of considerable skill, although perhaps less talent. Between 1642–44 many of the latter were occupied in painting the murals in Moscow's Dormition Cathedral. Artists of this group were employed on a part-time basis and, although provided with board and lodging when at work, received no other form of payment. When their services were not required they were expected to fend for themselves and to earn their living as best they could. Some were obliged to do so by becoming gardeners, coachmen, agricultural labourers, even innkeepers.

The Armoury workshops expressed the taste of Moscow's rulers as interpreted by the country's leading artists. Their output was at its best when the workshops were directed by Bogdan Matveyevich Khitrovo (1650–80). He stood for all that was most enlightened in the Moscow of his day. A man of remarkable abilities, he served his country as soldier, diplomat, judge and administrator, but his interests lay in the arts. He proved an inspired patron of architecture, for although he delighted in Russia's medieval buildings he was also keenly appreciative of contemporary trends. In painting he was in favour of naturalism at a time when the Patriarch Nikon was in passionate opposition to it. This was unfortunate both for Russia and for Khitrovo, who was obliged to decide on what was traditional in contemporary Russian art in the light of Nikon's reforms.[24]

Nikon was the son of a village priest and began his own career in the Church as one. Later he took his vows and in 1648 he was appointed Metropolitan of Novgorod. His profound admiration for Novgorod's religious art may well date from that period in his life. In 1652 gentle Tsar Alexei raised Nikon to the Patriarchate, a position which he retained till 1666. As Patriarch, Nikon proved an ardent devotee of Greece, one bent on enforcing a Byzantine type of discipline on his clergy and flock, and on retaining its church ritual unchanged in his own Church. He therefore set out to cleanse Russia's religious texts of what he termed 'its Slavonic errors' in order to bring them into line with the older Byzantine works. For similar reasons he forbade in the architectural field the building of tent-roofed churches, insisting on the retention of the dome which he associated with Byzantium. In painting he was an ardent traditionalist and, as such, he firmly resisted the naturalistic trends reaching Muscovy from the West. Although he allowed his portrait to be painted he forbade all signs of naturalism in religious art, going to the length of destroying icons which he regarded as Frankish and then publicly burning them in Moscow's Dormition Cathedral. Peace-loving Tsar Alexei (1645–76) did not venture to oppose the fierce prelate even though his own sympathies lay with the Westernizers. Nikon's pro-Greek policy and the measures which he took to amend the Russian liturgy and religious texts, together with his views on painting, aroused intense opposition alike among clerics and laymen. In 1654 the controversy between them developed into a schism, the breakaway section of the population joining the sect of Old Believers led by Nikon's chief opponent, the Archpriest Avvakum. Although ostracized, and eventually anathematized, the Old Believers survived to modern times, but in Nikon's day the atmosphere resulting from this theological battle encouraged controversy. Controversy led to heresies and to the invention of new iconographic themes which ceased to be based on scriptural texts, as had formerly been the case, but strove to express abstract theological ideas. The Old Believer icons, however, continued to adhere to the ancient traditions, some of which Nikon considered wrong and wished to destroy. Although these icons are generally aesthetically inferior to those provided for the established Church they are often extremely interesting from an iconographic point of view, and for this reason it is especially to be regretted that it has not as yet proved possible to find any dated examples.

The Armoury style was created primarily by such artists as Dmitri Terentiev, Kvashin, Feodor Kozlov, Vasili Leontiev, Ivan Maksimov, Yakov Kazanets, Feodor Evtikhiev Zubov and Nikita Pavlovetz, many of whom also worked for the Stroganovs and other wealthy Moscow merchants. The style was, however, epitomized by Simon Ushakov (1626–86). He was far more gifted than his colleagues and was immensely admired by his contemporaries, especially by those who were attracted by the West's naturalistic style. Their admiration was not misplaced for Ushakov was a man of many talents. His religious paintings present a blend of the iconic and naturalistic styles and seem debased to us today, but they were acclaimed in their own day, whilst his secular works enchanted and intrigued his contemporaries.

Ushakov was appointed court painter at the early age of twenty-two. As such he was not only expected to produce mural paintings and icons, but also banners and tents, to delineate maps, to provide plans for fortifications and to accompany Tsar Alexei on his campaigns in order to act as his defence adviser. In addition Ushakov was asked to furnish designs for metal articles and even to turn his hand to portraiture. He was able to meet all these demands and also to gain recognition as a writer whose enquiring mind enlivened his clear and well-thought-out ideas. In 1667 he wrote a treatise on aesthetics which he addressed to all art lovers (*Slovo k Lyubitieliam Ikonogo Pisaniya*). This was in itself an innovation, but its text shows that Ushakov had studied anatomy, and this was also unusual at the time. More surprising still is the stand which Ushakov assumed in it of a firm supporter of the West's naturalistic style in art. His arguments in favour of it aroused the violent opposition of the strongly conservative upper clergy but won Ushakov the support of many of his fellow artists. When Ion Pleshkovich wrote a treatise on icon painting, clearly in refutation of Ushakov's Joseph of Volokolamsk, a warm supporter and friend of Ushakov's, who had painted some of the murals in Moscow's Archangel Cathedral in 1652 and had worked on those in Rostov's cathedral in 1654, replied with a passionate defence of Ushakov's views. There was still need for it, for even as late as 1690 no less a person than the Patriarch Joachim was adding a codicil to his will imploring the tsar to adhere to the Greek style in painting. Yet naturalism was gaining in impetus. It expressed itself with ever greater insistence in the memorial icon, where it had made its appearance as far back as the second quarter of the seventeenth century. By blending with the iconic it had produced a style which stands mid-way between that of true portraiture and the iconic. Works of this type are therefore known in Russia by the name of *parsunya* which derives from 'persona'. The earliest example to survive is the panel (*pl. 154*) which was painted in about 1630 to hang above the tomb of Prince Mikhail Skopin-Shuysky. The prince was born in 1587 and died in 1610. Unless his *parsunya* was painted immediately after his death it is unlikely on political grounds to have been painted before 1620 or after 1630. It is perhaps a trifle ironic that the art of the icon, which developed from that of the Egyptian tomb portrait, should have started to die out in Russia with the memorial icon, for naturalism, quite as much as the passing of time, the acceptance of a new way of life and of a new attitude to it, and Russia's rise to the position of a power in world affairs, all had a hand in killing icon painting. By the end of the seventeenth century it was moribund; it succumbed under the impact of Peter the Great's Westernizing reforms.

86

87

95a   95b

86 The Virgin of Svensk
By a follower of Alipy's
The Tretyakov Gallery, Moscow.
Lime board 67 × 42 cm.
c. 1288

The Virgin is shown as a small, foreshortened figure seated on a backless throne. She holds the Child upon her knees, presenting Him frontally. His hands are extended in the act of blessing, as on the icon of the Great Panaghia. Both figures create a remote and detached impression, and the composition gives the impression of being derived from some foreign model, quite possibly one stemming from Athos. In this connection it is worth noting (*see note on pl. 89*) that Professor Lazarev thinks that representations of the Virgin Enthroned are alien to Russia. The figures standing on either side of the Virgin and Child are conceived in another spirit. That on the Virgin's right portrays Feodosy, the founder of the Kievo–Pecherskaya Lavra, the cowled one on her left Anthony, Feodosy's disciple and successor as abbot. In their case the treatment is elegant; their very elongated, slender figures contrast with the Virgin's dumpier one poised well above them; there are elements of true portraiture in their sensitive, well-rendered faces. If the Virgin and Child follow the Lavra's monastic style, the figures of the two saints reflect in their refinement something of the Kievan court's patrician taste. The colours are sombre, truly monastic, ranging from browns, reddish-browns and dark to pale blues, but they are relieved, above, by a gold ground; below, by a delicate green one.

According to the Svensk Monastery's records the icon was brought to Briansk in 1288 from the Kievo–Pecherskaya Lavra at the request of Prince Roman, the son of Prince Michael of Chernigov, who had lost his sight. Its restoration was ascribed to the icon's intervention and the panel was retained in Briansk until a monastery had been built for it at Svensk as a dependency of the Lavra. The records state that it was painted by Alipy of Kiev and although scholars feel unable to date the icon prior to the thirteenth century, they agree in regarding it as a Kievan work. It probably faithfully copied that done by Alipy early in the twelfth century.

Antonova/Mneva, no. 12. *Istoriya*, Vol. 1, p. 224, pl. 223. Onasch, pl. 3.

87 St Demetrius of Salonica
From the chapel of St Demetrius of Salonica in the Dormition Cathedral at Dmitrovo, built in 1714. Now in the Tretyakov Gallery, Moscow.
Lime board 156 × 108 cm.
Vladimir-Suzdal school 1154–1212

The Saint is presented seated on a large throne, holding his partly drawn sword in both hands at waist height. He wears a princely coronet, military clothes and bejewelled slippers. His throne recalls the shape of that of the first Virgin of Tolg (*pl. 89*). Originally it was red in colour, the ground behind it silver. Here, as in the icons of the Great Panaghia and the first Virgin of Tolg, the floor beneath it is covered with a carpet, a feature seldom found in icons of any school; in this case the carpet's design consists of a floral device set in rectangles disposed in rows, suggestive of a Seljukid origin.

The Saint's face is treated asymmetrically, a feature which is usually associated with the early Vladimir–Suzdalian school, although its presence in the icon of the Veronica (*pl. 95*), dating from prior to 1262, has not prevented V. N. Lazarev from assigning the latter work to Novgorod. Here the linear treatment of the eyes, eyebrows and the face in general is unmistakably Suzdalian, and is closely similar to that of the face of the Great Panaghia (*pl. 88*). Tradition has long associated this icon with Grand Duke Vsevolod-Dmitri, the Great Nest (1176–1212). His cypher appears to the right of the back of the throne; like other sections of the icon, it dates from the sixteenth century, yet it is unlikely to have been added fortuitously at that time and it is highly probable that it reproduces one which, almost obliterated by that date, was still discernible. Today only the saint's head, bust, right arm and hand, left hand, sword, feet and the cross which he wears, as well as the figure of the Saviour in a cloud in the top left-hand corner of the panel, date from the twelfth century; the rest of the painting, including the angel in the top right-hand corner, was repainted in the sixteenth century.

Antonova/Mneva, Vol. 1, no. 10. *Istoriya*, Vol. 1, pp. 52–3, pl. 22. H. P. Gerhard, *Welt der Ikonen*, Recklinghausen, 1957, pl. 26. Onasch, pl. 4.

88 (Colour plate VI) The Great Panaghia, sometimes incorrectly designated as the Yaroslavl *Virgin Orans*
From the store room of the monastery of the Saviour at Yaroslavl. Now in the Tretyakov Gallery, Moscow.
Lime panel 194 × 120 cm.
Yaroslavl school. *c.* 1224

The Virgin is presented full-length, standing with her arms raised, like the Virgin Orans, in the position of supplication, but unlike the Virgin Orans, she displays on her breast the half-length figure of the Child, in this respect resembling the Virgin of the Sign. The Child's arms are extended in much the same position as hers as He performs a blessing with each hand. Although the Virgin's legs are turned slightly towards the spectator's right, the upper part of her body is presented frontally. She stands on a rug the designs of which recall some of the motifs found on early Seljukid carpets. The draperies of her robes are severely regulated, foreshadowing in this respect the Russian delight in graphic art. Similar tendencies are also evident in the treatment of the draperies belonging to the half-length renderings of the Archangels in the roundels placed in the two top corners of the panel. Here the contrast attained by the juxtaposition of circular and curved lines and the rectangular folds of the draperies are even more marked than in the central composition. Throughout, the treatment of eyes and eyebrows also reflects a feeling for graphic art. Although the Archangels' features are Byzantine in type, the painting's style, and also its decorative details, are essentially Russian. The church for which the icon was painted was consecrated in 1224, and there is every reason for thinking that the icon was indeed painted for it at that date.

Antonova/Mneva, no. 3. *Istoriya*, Vol. 1, pls. 190 and 191. Onasch, pl. 6.

89 *The Virgin Enthroned*, known as the first Tolg Virgin
From the church of the Raising of the Cross in the Tolg Monastery near Yaroslavl. Now in the Tretyakov Gallery, Moscow.
Cyprus board 140 × 92 cm.
Some scholars have ascribed the painting to Georgia, an attribution which derives support from the nature of the wood on which it is painted. Prior to 1278.

The Virgin is shown seated on a splendid, bejewelled throne with a double row of rectangular, oval-topped openings cut into its back. The Child, whom she holds with both hands, stands on her lap in order to encircle her neck with His right arm so as to draw their faces together. Above, an angel stands on either side, its hands concealed by a cloth.

Although the Virgin of Svensk (*pl. 86*) is also depicted enthroned V. N. Lazarev has shown (*Studies in the Iconography of the Virgin*, Art Bulletin, Vol. XX, no. 1, 1938) that, in Russia, it was very unusual for her to be presented in this way, but that it was customary to do so in Georgia. This fact, seen in conjunction with the nature of the board and, above all, the painting's unusual style has led scholars to regard the icon as having formed part of the booty which, according to the Simeonovskaya Chronicle, Prince Feodor Rostislavych, the Black, brought back from Ossetia to Yaroslavl in 1278. Since the icon cannot have been painted in Ossetia it is more than likely that it was done in Georgia.

Its colours are splendid, its details extremely decorative. Blues, brownish reds, ochre, red and white predominate, standing out against the icon's silver background. The Virgin's robe is trimmed with pearls and silver thread; her cushion is made of a sumptuous green fabric and her feet rest on a carpet, traces of which are just discernible. The style, if not instantly appealing, is monumental and very accomplished.

Antonova/Mneva, no. 162. *Istoriya*, Vol. 1, p. 497. P. Schweinfurth, *Geschichte der russischen Malerei im Mittelalter*, The Hague, 1930, pl. 57.

90 *The Deesis*
From above the tomb of the Metropolitan Philip II in the Dormition Cathedral, Moscow. Now in the Tretyakov Gallery, Moscow.
61 × 146 cm.
Vladimir-Suzdal school. Undated. Not mentioned in the records, but probably late twelfth century.

Christ, the Virgin and St John the Forerunner are presented on a rectangular panel. Only their heads and shoulders are shown. Christ is represented as a young man. His face is rendered in a manner closely resembling that of the St Demetrius of Salonica (*pl. 87*), bearing the cypher of the Grand Duke Vsevolod-Dmitri. The influence of Constantinople, as represented by the mosaic of the Virgin in the south gallery of the cathedral of Hagia Sophia there, is evident in this painting, but its resemblance to the severely damaged Virgin Bogolyubovo in the museum at Vladimir is even more marked and it is because of this that the two icons are assigned a similar origin and date; so too is the very similar, even lovelier panel on which the Deesis is represented by Christ Emmanuel and the two Archangels. (Antonova/Mneva, no. 6.)

Antonova/Mneva, no. 8. *Istoriya*, Vol. 1, p. 472.

91 *St George*
From the cathedral of St George in the Yuriev Monastery, Novgorod. Now in the Tretyakov Gallery, Moscow.
Lime board 230 × 142 cm.
Novgorodian school. *c.* 1130

The Saint is shown full-length, standing firmly on the ground. Although little remains of the original paint the outlines of the figure, its pose and robust build survive unaltered. The Saint stands in space against a gold background holding a lance in his right hand whilst resting his left on the sword symbolizing princely power. His shield is slung on his back. His head is encircled by a princely coronet. The figure is massive, sturdy, a trifle squat.

The icon is believed to have been painted to serve as the cathedral's principal icon; because of its dimensions V. N. Lazarev thinks that it was a 'pier' icon. The cathedral was built by the master-builder Peter in 1119 and consecrated in either 1130 or 1140.

Antonova/Mneva, no. 1. Lazarev 2, pl. 3.

92 St George, the Warrior
Dormition Cathedral, Moscow.
174 × 122 cm.
Novgorodian school. Dated by tradition to *c.* 1170

This half-length version of St George presents the Saint as a robust youth holding a lance in his right hand and prominently displaying in his left the sword which served at the time in Russia as the emblem of military strength and princely sovereignty. He wears armour over a robe made of a stuff patterned with an arrow-head design enclosed in diamonds very reminiscent of some found on Seljukid carpets of much the same date; the sword sheath is adorned with a device or cypher which may also derive from an animal form of nomadic, basically Central Asian origin. The Saint's hair is treated very graphically whilst his eyes and eyebrows recall those of the Great Panaghia (*pl. 88*) and those of St Demetrius of Salonica (*pl. 87*).

The icon is believed to have been painted for Andrey Bogolyubsky's youngest son, Georgy Andreyevich, who became Prince of Novgorod in 1170 and was driven from power in 1174. The panel is thought to have come to Moscow together with that of the Ustyug Annunciation (*pl. 174*) from the cathedral of St George in the Yuriev Monastery at Novgorod.

Lazarev, 2, pls. 4 and 5. *Russian Icons*, published by UNESCO, 1958, p. 6.

93 The half-length version of the Virgin of Tolg, known as the Virgin of Tolg II
From the monastery of Tolg, near Yaroslavl. Now in the Yaroslavl Museum.
Lime board 61 × 48 cm.
1314

This shortened version was painted in the monastery to which it belonged. It does not show the Virgin's throne, but in other respects it adheres to the iconography of the original icon, although here the Virgin's right hand assumes the pose belonging to the Virgin Hodegetria. The painter had clearly set out to follow the style of the Georgian prototype, yet his highlights are typical of his own day, not of the thirteenth century, when the first Virgin of Tolg was painted. His robes also adhere to the taste of his day and he has treated the Child's hair in the graphic manner that is essentially Russian.

A third version of the icon, dating this time from the middle of the fourteenth century, is to be seen in the Russian State Museum, Leningrad.

N. V. Rozanov, *Rostov-Suzdal Painting of the 12th–16th century,* Moscow, 1970, pl. 13 for the Virgin of Tolg II, pl. 14 for the third version.

94 The Virgin of Tolg with a border of twenty-four scenes
From the monastery of Tolg at Yaroslavl. Now in the Yaroslavl Museum.
157 × 122 cm.
1655

The iconography has undergone minor changes in the intervening centuries. Thus this three-quarter-length rendering of the Virgin suggests that she is standing, rather than enthroned, and that the Child is not standing on her knees but is poised on her left arm, as on the second version. Here too the Virgin's right hand assumes the pose of the Hodegetria. Although both faces adhere to those of the prototype they are rendered more naturalistically, yet the treatment of the eyebrows and hair follow the Novgorodian tradition.

The scenes which form the borders are historical in content, and thus of unusual interest; they illustrate the building of the monastery of Tolg, the architecture of which is rendered in very much the same manner as on contemporary 'founder' icons.

The panel is inscribed on the reverse, the text stating that the 'icon was completed on the first day of the month of August in the year 7163' (1655).

Yaroslavl Museum Catalogue, no. 55.

95a, Double-sided icon; obverse,
b the *Veronica*;
reverse, the *Adoration of the Cross*
From the Dormition Cathedral, Moscow. Now in the Tretyakov Gallery, Moscow.
77 × 71 cm.
Novgorodian school. Prior to 1262

The two paintings are by different artists. On the face of the panel Christ's head is surrounded by an ochre halo containing three arms of a white cross, the whole set against an ochre ground. His head is imbued with the patrician quality which characterizes the early works of the Vladimir–Suzdalian school. The treatment of His eyes and the asymmetric rendering of His face also recall the style of that school. It is doubtless for these reasons that the cataloguers of the Tretyakov Gallery's icons have assigned the painting to it. Nevertheless, the graphic treatment of Christ's hair and beard points to Novgorod, and V. N. Lazarev discovered that the icon was reproduced in 1262 as an illumination on the first page of the Novgorodian manuscript known as the Zakharyevsky Prolog. He therefore asserts, surely correctly, that the icon is hardly likely to have been put to that purpose had it not ranked as a Novgorodian work of distinction, one already greatly revered at the period by Novgorodians. Lazarev feels that the painting may in fact date from as early as the second quarter of the twelfth century.

The painting of the Adoration of the Cross on the reverse of the panel is rather later in date. It shows the cross decked with the crown of thorns erected on the summit of Golgotha with St Michael standing on one side of it and St Gabriel on the other, both holding the instruments of the Passion. In the sky are two cherubim, two seraphs and medallions containing the sun and moon. This painting has a bejewelled look, as if it had been inspired by a cloisonné enamel or book illumination, but its colours are typical of the Novgorodian school, featuring the lemon yellows and raspberry pinks which were to predominate in Muscovite decorative art, as well as cinnabar, sky-blue and white. Lazarev compares the angels to some appearing in the murals of the Novgorodian church at Spas Nereditza, which was destroyed in the last war; they dated from 1199, and it therefore seems probable that this painting is to be assigned to a similar date. His belief that both paintings are Novgorodian works seems to be fully justified.

Antonova/Mneva, Vol. 1, no. 7. Lazarev 2, pls. 8 and 9.

96 (Colour plate VII) *St Nicholas, the Miracle Worker*
By Aleksa, son of Peter
From the church of St Nicholas on the Lipna, Novgorod. Now in the museum of History and Architecture, Novgorod.
177 × 129 cm.
Novgorodian school. 1294

The iconography is traditional, showing the Saint half-length holding a volume of the Gospels in his left hand and blessing with his right. According to legend the book was presented to him by the Saviour, Who is seen in the sky, to the right of the Saint, holding it, when St Nicholas was languishing in gaol for opposing the Arian heresy. Opposite the Saviour is the Virgin, who presented St Nicholas at the same time with the omorphion (stole), which he is generally shown wearing. Both the Saviour and the Virgin stand in space on cushions. The side margins of the panel contain small, full-length figures of saints; the top margin displays bust-size representations of the prophets with, at the centre, the empty throne flanked by two Archangels, the three symbolizing the Deesis. The style is essentially graphic and, in view of the icon's early date, makes unusually great use of decoration, thereby reflecting the influence of folk art.

The inscription forming the lower border states that the icon was painted in 1294 by Aleksa, son of Peter, and donated by Nikolai Vasilievich. Wulff/Alpatov (*Denkmäler der Ikonenmalerei in Kunstgeschichtlicher Folge*, Leipzig, 1925, pl. 31–2) question the authenticity of the inscription without giving a reason. I. Grabar (*O Drevnerusskom Iskusstve*, Moscow, 1966, p. 148) supports it on the strength of the following entry in the Novgorodian Chronicle (St Petersburg, 1879, p. 203):

In the year 6802 (1294), in the reign of Prince Andrey Aleksandrovich and in that of Archbishop Clement of Novgorod and Pskov, and in that of Burgomaster Andrey Climentovich this icon of the great miracle worker Nicholas of the Lipna Monastery was painted at the order and cost of God's servant Nikolai Vasilievich in honour and glory of Nicholas the Wonder-Worker... and in the year 7064 (1556), in the reign of the great Tsar and Grand Duke Ivan Vasilievich, Autocrat of Russia, and in the reign of Archbishop Pimen of Novgorod the Great and Pskov, at the order and expense of Abbot Antony of Nikolsk, this image of the great miracle worker Nicholas of the Lipna Monastery was restored.

Russian scholars accept the earlier date as authentic.

Lazarev, 2, pl. 16. Lazarev, *Russkaya srednevekovaya zhivopis*, Moscow, 1970, pp. 126–7.

97 *St Boris and St Gleb*
Probably from the church of Sts Boris and Gleb at Novgorod. Now in the museum of History and Architecture, Novgorod.
160 × 92 cm.
Novgorodian school. *c.* 1377

This icon is believed to have been the 'local' icon of the church which was built in Novgorod and dedicated to the two Saints in the year 1377. It is carried out in tones of ochre, light brown and brilliant reds, and is redolent of medieval pageantry. The princes wear clothes of identical cut but different colours, made of sumptuous brocades. They wear armour and their horses are splendidly caparisoned, the chased and embossed silver background adding another rich touch. The faces are dark, with highlights round the eyes, on the chins, along the top of the nose and across their necks. The treatment is highly stylized and strongly graphic. They ride through a mountainous countryside, with the Almighty blessing them from the top right-hand corner of the panel.

Lazarev 2, pl. 21.

98 *Praying Novgorodians*
Now in the museum of History and Architecture, Novgorod.
109 × 82 cm.
Novgorodian school. 1467

The icon is divided horizontally into two sections. The upper presents a seven-figure Deesis with the Saviour seated on a large, oval-backed throne; His feet rest on a rectangular stool; He blesses with His right hand and holds an open volume of the Gospels in His left. On His right stand the Virgin, the Archangel

Michael and St Peter, on His left, St John, the Archangel Gabriel and St Paul. Grabar sees a faint trace of Theophanes's influence in their faces, but the unsubstantial nature of their figures seems rather to foreshadow Dionysy, both as regards their elongation and their rhythm.

The lower register contains the figures of seven donors and two of their children; it is they who provide the icon with its title. Although they are of heavier, earthier build than the divine personages represented in the upper register, their figures have also undergone the elongation which heralds the approach of a new stylistic trend. They wear contemporary dress, high leather boots and the woman a head shawl. True portraiture is lacking in all, excepting perhaps the second figure from the left, yet the faces are alert. The pose, that of supplication, is, however, static. The inscription separates the two registers; it reads 'God's servants, Grigory, Yakov, Stefan, Yevsey, Timofey, Olfim and children (the woman, presumably their mother, is not named) pray to the Saviour and the Holy Virgin for their sins.' The Kuzmins were a local boyar family, some of whom are mentioned in the chronicles. The inscription along the base of the icon reads '(Painted) in the summer of 6975 [1467] of the fifteenth indiction by order of God's servant Antip Kuzmin for veneration by Orthodox believers.'

Lazarev 2, pl. 49. Kondakov 1, part 2, p. 21.

99 *The Archangel Gabriel*
From the church of St Nicholas in the Gostinopolsky Monastery. Now in the Tretyakov Gallery, Moscow.
Lime board 164 × 54 cm.
Novgorodian school. *c.* 1475

According to an inscription on one of the monastery's bells, the church to which this icon belonged was founded in 1475. Although the monastery was dissolved in the seventeenth century the following icons from the church's iconostasis survive—panels of the Virgin, St John, St Peter, the Archangel Michael and St John Chrysostom from its Deesis tier, as well as its Holy Doors with, in addition, icons of the Holy Women at the Sepulchre, the Prophet Daniel and the Dormition (Tretyakov Gallery, nos. 99, 98 and 100) as well as a version of the Battle between the Novgorodians and Suzdalians (*pl. 100*) in the Russian State Museum at Leningrad. Like the church's murals, they are known to date from the year of the church's consecration.

The Deesis figures are presented full-length against a gold background. The Archangel Gabriel is shown striding forward, the sense of movement being well rendered. The draperies are robustly modelled and include some angular folds which help to offset the composition's numerous curved lines. Decorative

subsidiary details are almost entirely absent, but the hair and eyebrows are strongly graphic in treatment. The highlights on the face and hands are characteristic of the school at this period.

Antonova/Mneva, Vol. 1, no. 101. For the St Michael, St John the Forerunner and the Holy Women at the Sepulchre see Lazarev 2, pls. 54–56.

100 *The Battle between the Novgorodians and the Suzdalians* and the *Miracle of the Icon of the Virgin of the Sign*
Probably from the church of St Nicholas in the Gostinopolsky Monastery on the upper Volkhov. Now in the Russian State Museum, Leningrad.
88 × 66.5 cm.
Novgorodian school. Last quarter of 15th century.

There are three early versions of this icon, the oldest of which is not thought to have been painted before 1460; it is now in the museum at Novgorod. The one illustrated here is assigned by the authors of the Tretyakov Gallery's catalogue of icons to the last quarter of the fifteenth century, and so too is the version belonging to that Gallery.

The icon is divided into three registers. Local topography is followed in the top register, where the story unfolds from right to left. As the icon of the Virgin of the Sign is being carried out of the church of the Saviour on the Ilyin Street at Novgorod, where it was kept, and taken across the bridge spanning the river Volkhov to the Kremlin, it is met by the faithful emerging from the Kremlin, hatless and in contemporary dress, to receive it. The dome of the cathedral of St Sophia is at the centre of the Kremlin enclosure. In the second register Novgorodian warriors stand on the town's battlements with the icon beside them, whilst their spokesmen ride forward to parley with the Suzdalians. In the third register the battle rages; the Suzdalians turn in defeat after one of their arrows, as shown in the second register, had struck the icon. On this version the Novgorodians are led by Alexander Nevsky, St Boris, St George and St Gleb. The scene is painted in a style which can be compared to Uccello's.

Antonova/Mneva, Vol. I, no. 103 or Lazarev, 2, pls. 60–63.

101 *Selected Saints*
From the church of Sts Boris and Gleb at Novgorod, built in 1536–7. Now in the Tretyakov Gallery, Moscow.
Lime board 78 × 64 cm.
Novgorodian school. 1560

The icon is divided into two registers, the lower being the principal. At the centre of the upper register is a painting of the Virgin of the Sign in a glory with, on her right, half-length figures of Barlam of Khutin and St

Sergius of Radonezh and, on her left, Sts Sozima and Savaty, founders of the Solovetsk Monastery, all performing a blessing with their right hands. Below two Muscovite saints and two Novgorodian ones are represented full-length, the two on the left holding volumes of the Gospels, the other two scrolls and all four performing a blessing. They are, from left to right, St Nicholas, St Nikita of Novgorod, St John of Novgorod and St Alexander of Svirsk. Four pairs of saints occupy the side margins; they are, from top to bottom, the sainted Grand Duke Vladimir and an unidentifiable saint, Sts Boris and Gleb, Sts Cosmas and Damian, Sts George and Demetrius.

The inscription at the foot of the panel reads 'On the 15th of October in the year 7069 [1560] this icon was painted at the order of God's servants the Orthodox Christians and members of the Guild of the Zapolie and Koniushenaya streets for worship by all Orthodox Christians'. According to an entry for the year 1536–7, the church in which it was set up was built in order that Novgorod's Muscovite guests, as well as the local townsmen, might worship in it. (*PSRL*, Vol. VI, St Petersburg, 1853, p. 300.)

The interest taken in vestments at this date is clearly reflected in this painting. The use of highlights on the foreheads, above the eyebrows and along the cheek bones as well as the feeling for symmetry and linear design are also characteristic of the period.

Antonova/Mneva, Vol. 2, no. 366.

102 St Nicholas, the Miracle Worker

From the Morozov collection. Now in the Tretyakov Gallery, Moscow.
Lime board 127 × 99 cm.
Novgorodian school. 1526

The icon follows the customary iconography by displaying the half-length figure of the Saint with his right hand performing a blessing and the left holding a volume of the Gospels. A roundel to his right displays a bust of Christ holding the copy of the Gospels, that on the left a bust of the Virgin holding the stole. In addition, beneath them are half-length representations, beneath Christ, of St Vlasy, beneath the Virgin, of the Blessed Nikita, doubtless the patrons of the man who commissioned the icon. An almost obliterated inscription on the icon's lower rim dates it to 1526.

Antonova/Mneva, Vol. 2, no. 344.

103 St Nicholas

Possibly from the neighbourhood of Narva. Now in the Tretyakov Gallery, Moscow
Lime board 107 × 83 cm.
Novgorodian school. 1587

The icon follows the customary iconography, showing a half-length figure of the saint performing a blessing with his right hand and holding the Gospels book in his left. Three-quarter-length figures of the Saviour and Virgin appear on either side of the Saint's head, holding the gifts they intend for him. The authors of the Tretyakov Gallery's icon catalogue trace the large oval-topped frames enclosing them, and more especially the two rows of wavy lines which adorn these, to the influence of folk art.

The all-over, almost dazzling pattern of the Saint's robe, although perhaps a trifle more obtrusive than is customary, nevertheless conforms to the taste of the period. The markings on his forehead and the highlights on his cheeks are especially characteristic of the latter half of the sixteenth century; so too is the treatment of his eyes and nose, and the shape of his ears, whilst his beard is rendered in a particularly marked linear style.

The inscription runs along the top of the icon and reads: 'On the 29th of June in the year 7095 [1587] this icon was painted in the reign of the Orthodox Tsar and Grand Duke of all Russia Feodor Ivanovich and that of Alexander, Archbishop of Novgorod, at the wish of God's servant Mikhail, son of Constantine.'

Antonova/Mneva, Vol. 2, no. 377.

104 Biographical icon of St Nicholas

From the cathedral of St Nicholas in the Nicola-Ugrezhesk Monastery, near Moscow. Now in the Tretyakov Gallery, Moscow.
Lime board 94 × 69 cm.
Moscow school. *c.* 1380

St Nicholas's portrait shows him half-length, blessing with his right hand and holding a volume of the Gospels in his left. The ground behind him is gold. The border illustrates nineteen scenes from his life, six being shown along the top, but only five along the bottom. The scenes selected for the purpose are the following: (top border, from left to right) his birth, his christening, the miracle of the woman with the withered hand, praying before a well, exorcizing a serpent (two scenes, which the cataloguers of the Tretyakov Gallery's icons trace to an apocryphal account of the Saint's life), and, finally, his ordination as a deacon. Immediately below the last scene St Nicholas's ordination as a priest is illustrated. The account then switches to the left border where he is shown appearing before the imprisoned men, Constantine and the eparch, and saving three men from execution. The story then moves to the right-hand border, showing the Saint restoring a lunatic to sanity, evicting demons from a well and saving Dmitri from drowning. The scenes along the bottom border show, from left to right, the miracle of the

Kievan youth, restoring the rug to the elder's wife, the miracle with Agricola's son, Nicholas's death and the transfer of his remains.

The icon is an early Muscovite painting; the colours, consisting of browns, dull reds and dark greens, lack the brilliance of Novgorodian works. The faces are dark ochre in colour, the Saint's hair chestnut brown. There are few highlights on the faces; the treatment is austere, monastic.

According to tradition the icon appeared before Prince Dmitri Donskoy during his campaign against Mamai; for this reason it is dated to *c.* 1380, a date which is supported by its style.

Antonova/Mneva, Vol. 1, no. 214.

105 Biographical icon of St Nicholas
From the chapel of St Nicholas, church of the Dormition in the village of Meletovo, near Moscow. Now in the Tretyakov Gallery, Moscow.
Pine board 128 × 108 cm.
School of Pskov. *c.* 1465

According to tradition St Nicholas is presented half-length, performing a blessing with his right hand and holding a volume of the Gospels in his left, but the ancient custom of including in the sky bust or half-length figures of Christ and the Virgin has been abandoned. Scenes from St Nicholas's life form a border to the Saint's portrait. Those along the top, seen from left to right, show his birth, his arrival at school, his ordination as a deacon and his ordination as a priest. In the side borders the scenes are ranged horizontally disposed in pairs; from left to right they show Christ presenting a volume of the Gospels to St Nicholas and an angel instructing a Lycian notable to appoint Nicholas Archbishop of Myra; the Saint saves three men from execution and evicts devils from a well; he restores a drowned youth to life and returns him to his parents by transporting him to the cathedral of St Sophia at Kiev, and appears outside the cathedral at Myra with Paul of Rodopi and Theodore of Ascalon; he releases three men from prison and saves some men from drowning. The scenes along the lower border illustrate his Miracle with the three maidens, the Virgin presenting St Nicholas with his stole, the Archangel Michael appearing before the Saint and Nicholas's death. The scenes are set against simplified architectural backgrounds.

It is interesting to compare this painting with that dating from 1380 (*pl. 104*) in order to note the different types of highlights used on each of the faces. On this panel the squat nature of the figures featured in the side scenes are less typical of the period than they are of the Pskov school.

The Pskovian Chronicle for the year 1461 records the building of the church to which this icon belonged and notes that its pictorial decorations were completed in 1465. These entries provide terminal datings for the icon.

Antonova/Mneva, Vol. 1, no. 156.

106 'Wisdom has built itself a House'
Probably from the Kirillov Monastery at Novgorod.
Now in the Tretyakov Gallery, Moscow
Lime board 146 × 106 cm.
Novgorodian school. *c.* 1548

Based on a saying of Solomon, the iconography of this icon is extremely complex. It is divided into two registers, the lower of which, being the more important, is the larger of the two. A single-domed, six-aisled church fills the lower part of the upper register; it symbolizes the seven Oecumenical Councils, each accompanied by a medallion containing its angel, shown half-length and holding a scroll.

Below, to the worshipper's left, Sophia, the Holy Wisdom, is represented in the guise of an angel within a triple glory, the two outer rims of which contain the symbols of the Evangelists and the seven angelic orders. A palace rises in the distance with King Solomon leaning out from one of its towers. Below, servants are killing a lamb, filling vessels with wine and distributing food and drink to the needy. To the right and above them St John of Damascus stands holding an open scroll. An enthroned Virgin and Child within a glory are seen in the sky.

The icon is associated with an icon of the Ascension in the museum at Novgorod which has the date of 1542 inscribed on it; the latter belonged to the Kirillov Monastery which, according to an entry in the second Novgorodian Chronicle, was burnt out in 1548. The icon of the Ascension is known to have been saved from the fire and this one is presumed to have been saved also. Interest in composition and movement, and in didactic themes, the introduction of the narrative element and the breaking up of the panel's surface in a novel manner—features all of which are present in this icon—were tendencies that were to become more widespread as the century advanced.

Antonova/Mneva, Vol. 2, no. 365. V. N. Lazarev, *Iskusstvo Novgoroda*, Moscow/Leningrad 1947, p. 122.

*107 Double-sided icon; on the obverse, the Virgin of the
a, b Don*; on the reverse, *the Dormition*
By Theophanes the Greek
From the Dormition Cathedral at Kolomna. Now in the Tretyakov Gallery, Moscow.
Lime board 86 × 68 cm.
c. 1392

On the face of the icon the Child is shown seated on the Virgin's right arm with both feet resting on her left wrist. She inclines her head so that their cheeks touch as she gazes sadly at Him. The Child's right hand is raised to perform a blessing whilst His left hand holds a scroll as it rests on His left knee; His feet are bare and so are His legs to just above the knees. The style adheres to the grand Constantinopolitan, but the Virgin's face expresses greater sorrow and tenderness than is usual even in Palaeologan art, thereby perhaps conforming to Russian taste. Lapis was used for the Virgin's stole and sleeve.

On the reverse side of the panel the Virgin is shown laid out on a high bier. A candle burns before it. According to the Apocrypha of John of Salonica the Virgin lit it herself when an angel had informed her that her death was imminent. Christ stands behind the bier holding the Virgin's soul in the form of a small child. A seraph appears in the sky above Him. Gathered round the bier are the Apostles, headed on the left by Peter, on the right by John. A saint stands behind each group, each holding a book. The colours are sombre and impressive, as befits the scene, ranging from purples to browns and ochres relieved by touches of cinnabar and lapis lazuli.

Antonova/Mneva, Vol. 1, no. 255/6. V. N. Lazarev, *Feofan Grek i ego shkola*, Moscow, 1961, pp. 63–7. Onasch, pl. 87–90.

108 *The Transfiguration*
By Theophanes the Greek
From the church of the Transfiguration at Pereslavl-Zalessky. Now in the Tretyakov Gallery, Moscow.
Lime board 184 × 134 cm.
1403

Christ stands on the summit of a hill in a glory containing a white star. He blesses with His right hand and holds a scroll in His left. His figure is elongated and ethereal. As on the icon of the Anastasis attributed to Rublyov (*pl. 111*) He is represented as a man in the prime of life, but in place of the benignity with which Rublyov invests Him, Theophanes depicts Him as one inured to suffering. He turns His head towards Moses who holds the Ten Commandments in both his hands. Elias stands opposite Moses; both are represented as of solider, earthier build, as well as smaller in size, with less ascetic faces than the Saviour's. Below, blinded by the rays of the vision, are Peter, John and Jacob. Midway up the mountain are two caves. Christ emerges from that on the left to lead the Apostles up the mountain; on the right He is seen descending from it with them.

The full magnificence of this painting can only be appreciated by seeing the original. The colours are particularly lovely; they are admirably attuned to the theme, ranging from whitish blue to pale blue flecked with bluish-mauve highlights; ochres of various shades, delicate greens, navy blue, lemon yellow, pink and gold complete the colour scheme.

Antonova/Mneva, Vol. 2, no. 217. Lazarev, *Feofan Grek i ego shkola*, Moscow, 1961, pp. 101–2, pls. 120–21.

109 *The Saviour*
By Theophanes the Greek. A detail
From the Annunciation Cathedral, Moscow.
81 × 103 cm.
1405

In 1397 a cathedral was built in the Kremlin in Moscow which was dedicated to the Annunciation. It is indeed fortunate that the icons which were painted for it in 1405 by Theophanes the Greek were preserved for use in the iconostasis of the cathedral which replaced it on the same site in 1484. The head of Christ illustrated on this plate is a detail of the Christ in Glory which Theophanes the Greek painted for the centre of its Deesis tier in 1405. This powerful, meticulously drawn, exquisitely coloured icon reveals both the mastery of Theophanes and the characteristics of his style. It is interesting to compare it with Rublyov's head of Christ (*pl. 118*). Theophanes made use of the rare and expensive lapis lazuli blue in this icon as he had done in that of the Dormition (*pl. 107, b*).

V. N. Lazarev, *Feofan Grek i ego shkola*, Moscow, 1961, pp. 86–95, pl. 89–90.

110 *The Virgin*
By Theophanes the Greek. A detail
From the Annunciation Cathedral, Moscow.
211 × 120 cm.
1405

As with the preceding icon and eight others which, together with this one, form the Deesis tier of the iconostasis of the Annunciation Cathedral at Moscow, we have the evidence of Moscow's chronicler and of Epiphanius to prove that they were painted by Theophanes in 1405. The same elaborate and very careful use of highlights provides the modelling of the Virgin's face as it does that of Christ (*pl. 109*), but whilst Christ's face reflects no more than a touch of compassion, the pity and sorrow in the Virgin's is more pronounced than in any contemporary Constantinopolitan work. Once again it is interesting to compare this icon with a very similar one by Rublyov (*pl. 112*).

V. N. Lazarev, *Feofan Grek i ego shkola*, Moscow, 1961, pp. 86–95, pls. 91, 92 and 93.

111 The Anastasis

From the iconostasis of the Dormition Cathedral, Vladimir, which was sold to the village of Vasilievskoe-Shuyskoe in the eighteenth century. Now in the Tretyakov Gallery, Moscow. By Andrey Rublyov and Daniil Chorny; such pieces are often ascribed to Rublyov's workshop.
Lime board 124 × 94 cm.
1408

This icon belongs to the series which the two artists painted when executing the murals in the Dormition Cathedral, Vladimir. Christ is shown raising Adam and a very small Eve from their tomb. A group of righteous men stand behind them. A similar group is assembled opposite to them. It includes John the Baptist, David and Solomon whilst Simon, according to the Apocrypha, God's adopted son, is among the figures standing behind Adam and Eve. The painting lacks the assurance, directness and majesty of Rublyov's work and Lazarev is surely correct in assigning it to his workshop rather than to either Rublyov or Daniil Chorny, yet Christ's face bears a closer resemblance to that of Theophanes's Christ in his icon of the Transfiguration (*pl. 108*) than do any of the others that are assigned to either Rublyov or his workshop.

Antonova/Mneva, no. 225. Lazarev 1, pp. 131–2, pl. 125.
The icon was also exhibited at Burlington House—'Russian Painting from the 13th to the 20th Century', London, 1959, no. 5.

112 Four figures from a fifteen-figure Deesis tier

a, b, By Andrey Rublyov and Daniil Chorny.
c, d, The Deesis tier, seven icons of which survive, was painted by the two artists for the iconostasis of the Dormition Cathedral at Vladimir. Some time between 1768–75 the iconostasis was sold to the village of Vasilievskoe-Shuyskoe in the district of Ivanovskoe. They are now in the Tretyakov Gallery, Moscow.
Lime boards. The central panel of Christ in glory 314 × 220 cm; the side ones *c.* 313 × *c.* 106 cm.
Moscow school. 1408

Christ is shown enthroned in majesty against an oval-shaped glory peopled with seraphs, the projecting triangles at its corners displaying the symbols of the Evangelists. He blesses with His right hand and holds an open volume of the Gospels in His left. His feet rest on a footstool adorned with the three rings symbolizing the throne of one of the nine angelic orders. His figure is elongated and ethereal, yet solid. The curve of His shoulders is not as pronounced as in Rublyov's later works.

The Virgin on Christ's right was subjected to some repainting in the eighteenth century when the position of her left hand was slightly altered. Here the curved

lines which are so characteristic of Rublyov are more pronounced than on the central panel. St John, placed on Christ's left, is in the traditional pose, but his figure is more bent, his silhouette more rounded than in most representations of an earlier date. The icon of St Gregory, although also subjected to some later repainting, is largely original. He wears an ornate robe and holds a book, the splendid binding of which is studded with jewels. His gentle expression and rounded shoulders are in the Rublyov tradition.

Antonova and Mneva assign all seven surviving icons to Andrey Rublyov and Daniil Chorny. Lazarev has attempted to distinguish between them and attributes the Christ in Glory, St John the Forerunner and the St Paul to Rublyov. The icon of the Virgin is clearly of slightly inferior quality, but that of St Gregory in no way falls short of those singled out by Lazarev.

Antonova/Mneva, Vol. 1, no. 223. Lazarev 1, 119a.

113 The Annunciation

From the iconostasis of the Dormition Cathedral, Vladimir. Now in the Tretyakov Gallery, Moscow.
Lime board 125 × 94 cm.
Rublyov and Chorny workshop. 1408

The iconography adheres to custom, but it shows the Archangel approaching the Virgin with unusual impetuosity while she shrinks from him to a degree rarely encountered in portrayals of the scene. Indeed, she seems neither prepared to welcome his tidings nor able to hear them without profound distress. The architectural background is fairly prominent and shows as much striving for symmetry as is to be seen in the accompanying icon of the Anastasis (*pl. 111*). Like the latter, it lacks the splendid rhythm and balance of Rublyov's works, features which are well in evidence in the paintings with which he was adorning the interior of the Dormition Cathedral at Vladimir at this date. Lazarev is surely right in regarding it as a workshop piece.

Antonova/Mneva, no. 225. Lazarev, 1, no. 123.

114 The Ascension

By Andrey Rublyov and possibly also Daniil Chorny
From the iconostasis of the Dormition Cathedral, Vladimir. Now in the Tretyakov Gallery, Moscow.
Lime board 125 × 92 cm.
Moscow school. 1408

The Virgin stands in the centre pressing one open hand against her breast, indicating with the other the group of Apostles standing to her right; the others are grouped on her left. Two angels, garbed in white, stand behind her with their arms raised towards the sky where, above a hilly background, two angels, shown in the position of classical victories, fly upwards as they raise the figure of Christ seated within a glory. Christ blesses the Apostles as they do so.

Lazarev asserts that Rublyov followed in this icon the composition chosen by Prokhor of Gorodetz for the icon of the Ascension which he painted in 1405 for the cathedral of the Annunciation at Moscow. They are, indeed, well-nigh identical, but Rublyov has made his figures a trifle shorter, a shade more substantial and also slightly more animated.

Antonova/Mneva, no. 225. Lazarev 1, pl. 128.

115 *The Virgin of Vladimir*
By Andrey Rublyov
Painted for the inhabitants of Vladimir, it is now in the museum there.
Lime board 101 × 69 cm.
Between 1395 and not later than 1410, *c.* 1409 being the more likely date

The icon is a faithful copy of the famous Byzantine icon of the Virgin of Vladimir (*pl. 5*). This was essential, for Rublyov was instructed to paint it to take the latter's place and thus placate the inhabitants of Vladimir for the removal of their deeply revered icon to Moscow. The exact date at which the Byzantine panel was transported to Moscow has not been ascertained, but the quarrel over its removal raged from the 1380s until Rublyov's copy reconciled the people of Vladimir to the loss of the earlier icon. It seems logical to assume that Rublyov painted his version when working in Vladimir's Dormition Cathedral. It was certainly in existence by 1410 when the Tartars raided Vladimir and seized its precious adornments. The Chronicle (*PSRL*, Vol. 22, p. 130) refers to a copy of the Byzantine work, possibly to this one. as in existence in 1395.

Lazarev 1, pl. 126/7. I. E. Grabar, *Voprosy restavratzii*, Vol. 1, Moscow, 1926, p. 103.

116 *Christ in Glory*
By Andrey Rublyov
From the Sevastianov Collection in the Rumyantzev Museum, Moscow. Now in the Tretyakov Gallery, Moscow.
Pine board 18 × 16 cm.
Moscow school. *c.* 1411

This, the smallest of Rublyov's three surviving icons of Christ in Glory, is also the finest. Its iconography follows traditional lines. Christ is presented seated on a cushion placed on the seat of a fine throne with a semicircular back. His feet rest on a rectangular footstool

accompanied by the symbolic rings. He holds a copy of the Gospels in His left hand open at the text 'Come ye all unto me . . .' His right hand performs a blessing. His throne is encircled by a glory containing six-winged seraphs whilst triangles at the corners of the panel display the symbols of the Evangelists.

The style, although to some extent miniaturist, is at the same time also monumental. The fragility which is associated with Rublyov—erroneously for it is found in the works of certain of his followers rather than in his— is absent here; the Saviour is determined and purposeful, almost austere, yet truly compassionate.

Antonova/Mneva, Vol. 1, no. 227. Lazarev 1, pl. 140.

117 *Lintel above a royal door with scenes of the Eucharist*
By Daniil Chorny
From the wooden church of the Annunciation near Zagorsk. Once in the Troitse-Sergeyeva Lavra, now in the Tretyakov Gallery, Moscow.
Lime board 75 × 111 cm.
c. 1411

The scene is painted on a board, originally rectangular in shape, with the archway cut into it. The scene to the left shows the Communion with bread, that on the right with wine. In each scene Christ stands behind an altar within a domed building with the Apostles advancing along a stone or marble path. The group on the left shows Judas holding his bowl, his inclusion being based on the Gospels of Luke and John. The icon is believed to have been painted for the wooden church to which it belonged; it was built in 1411.

Antonova/Mneva, Vol. 1, no. 226.
The icon was exhibited in London in 1959 in the Burlington House Exhibition of 'Russian Painting from the 13th to the 20th Century', catalogue no. 6.

118 *Three icons from the Deesis tier of an iconostasis:* The Saviour, the Archangel Michael and St Paul
By Andrey Rublyov
The icons were done for the Deesis tier of the Vysotsky Monastery's iconostasis, but were transferred in the eighteenth century to the Savin-Storozhevsky Monastery, and are therefore sometimes incorrectly ascribed to the latter. Now in the Tretyakov Gallery, Moscow.
Lime boards—The Saviour, a fragment 158 × 106 cm.; The Archangel 158 × 108 cm.; St Paul 160 × 109 cm.
Moscow school. *c.* 1420

The icon of Christ formed the centre of the Deesis tier. He appeared on it three-quarter length and it is just possible to discern that He held a copy of the Gospels in His left hand. The Archangel is also depicted three-quarter length, holding a staff in his left hand and extending his right in a gesture of supplication. He is non-terrestrial and ethereal in appearance yet of solid build. St Paul, who is also shown three-quarter-length, has the massive body of a countryman, the furrowed brow of one who has experienced many trials.

In these three paintings Rublyov is seen at the height of his powers. It is interesting to compare this deeply moving head of Christ with the no less powerful one by Theophanes the Greek (*pl. 109*) and, whilst doing so, to assess the style and quality of each of these masters. The Archangel bears a marked affinity to the angels of Rublyov's Old Testament Trinity (*pl. 119*) and the two icons must be close in date. The Archangel's inclined head and sloping shoulders, and the gentle folds of his draperies all combine to emphasize the importance of the composition's curved and circular lines. The influence of Constantinople, noted by Professor Lazarev in the rendering of St Paul, is very evident although the Apostle's figure is more robust than those of the Vysotsky Chin (*pl. 16*) and most other Constantinopolitan works.

Antonova/Mneva, Vol. 1, no. 229. Lazarev 1, nos. 128–32.

119 (Colour plate VIII) *The Old Testament Trinity*
By Andrey Rublyov
From the Trinity Cathedral at the Troitse-Sergeyeva Lavra, Zagorsk. Now in the Tretyakov Gallery, Moscow.
Lime board 142 × 114 cm.
Moscow School. Either *c.* 1411, or, more probably, between 1422–27

The Angels symbolizing the Trinity are shown seated at Abraham's table. The table may well represent the one believed to have belonged to Abraham which was venerated as a relic in the Cathedral of Hagia Sophia at Constantinople, but in medieval times it was thought to represent the Saviour's coffin. The latter was used for the first celebration of the Eucharist and became the prototype of the Christian altar. Rublyov must have regarded it as such for he has provided it with the small opening often found in the coffins of saints to enable worshippers to see their remains.

The central angel is slightly recessed and is also a little larger in size than the two others; these details, and the more elaborate nature of his robe have led the cataloguers of the Tretyakov Gallery's icons to conclude that he symbolizes Christ, more particularly since he wears the stole which they regard as one of the Saviour's attributes. Together with the angel seated on his left he inclines his head towards the third angel, as if listening to him; the latter angel is therefore thought to represent God whilst the second personifies the Holy Ghost. All three angels hold measuring rods.

Detail is reduced to the minimum here. The meal is symbolized by a single vessel containing the head of the sacrificial lamb. Abraham's house is unobtrusively set in the background and is counter-balanced by a hill and the oak tree. This is Rublyov's masterpiece. The lines are delicate yet firm, the colours, which include lapis lazuli, are translucent yet glowing.

Antonova/Mneva, Vol. 1, no. 230. Lazarev 1, no. 136.

120 *St Cyril of Belo-ozero*
By Dionysy of Glushytsk
From the Kirillo-Belozersky Monastery. Now in the Tretyakov Gallery, Moscow.
Lime panel 28 × 24 cm.
Ascribed by some to Novgorod, by others to Moscow.
1424

This small panel portrays St Cyril, the founder and first abbot of the Kirillo-Belozersky Monastery. He was a friend and disciple of St Sergius of Radonezh and is represented as a small, hunched-up old man. There is a marked striving for portraiture both in the rendering of his face and of his figure. The painting stands mid-way in time between the two icons of St Nicholas, respectively of the Pskovian and Muscovite schools (*pls. 104 and 105*); already highlights play a prominent part here in the saint's face, but they are less numerous and less pronounced, also less schematic, than those on the later of the two St Nicholas panels.

In the seventeenth century this panel was used to form the central section of a diptych dedicated to St Cyril. An inscription carved at the time along the top and bottom of its frame indicated that the central panel was painted by the Reverend Father Dionysy of Glushytsk in the lifetime of St Cyril, in the year 1424, whilst the side panels were painted in 1614.

Dionysy of Glushytsk was born near Vologda in 1362. His numerous paintings were greatly admired by his contemporaries who also thought highly of his carvings. He was likewise noted as a calligrapher, a skilled worker of iron and copper, and a splendid basket maker. He derived his cognomen of Glushytsk from the monastery which he founded close to the river of that name. He was its first abbot. (N. P. Kondakov, 2, illustrates on photographic pl. 40 a miraculous icon of the Veronica from the Resurrection Cathedral at Romanov-Borisoglebsk in the district of Yaroslavl, which tradition ascribes to the same painter. Its silver 'riza' dates from 1850.)

Antonova/Mneva, Vol. I, no. 236. Lazarev, *Iskusstvo Novgoroda*, Moscow/Leningrad, 1947, pp. 124–45.

121 *The Virgin of Yaroslavl and selected saints*
From the Church of the Prophet Elias in the village of Sandyry near Kolomna, formerly a property of the

Princes Sheremetiev. Now in the Tretyakov Gallery, Moscow.
Lime panel 35 × 30 cm.
Moscow school. 1491

The icon forms the centre panel of a triptych. The Virgin looks to the left and holds the Child seated on her right arm, her left supporting His shoulder. Both His legs are extended to reveal His bare feet. He rests His cheek against hers and touches her chin with His left hand and her breast with His right one. Both figures are enclosed in a double glory filled with seraphs. Above them the Old Testament Trinity is represented with, at each corner of the panel, medallions containing half-length representations of the Archangels. The roundels in the bottom corners contain the half-length figures of St Alexey, God's Servant, and St Thecla.

Comparison of the Virgin and Child's faces with those of Dionysy's Virgin Hodegetria (*pl. 123*) illustrates the way in which artists of the period interpreted the grand Byzantine style as it had been handed down to them by the Virgin of Vladimir or the Virgin of Pimen.

An inscription dating from 1814, which assuredly reproduced an original text, dates the icon to 1 December 1491 and its restoration to 23 March 1814.

Antonova/Mneva, Vol. 1, no. 273.

122 Four icons from a seventeen-figure Deesis Cycle—
a, b The *Archangel Michael, St Peter, the Virgin and St John the*
c, d *Forerunner.*
By Dionysy and his sons Feodosy and Vladimir
From the church of the Virgin's Birth in the Ferapont Monastery. Now in the Tretyakov Gallery. The Archangel Gabriel from the same iconostasis is in the Russian State Museum, Leningrad.
Lime boards all *c.* 155 × 61 cm.
Moscow school. 1500–02

All the icons of this Deesis tier adhere closely to the tradition for the full-length figures established by Theophanes the Greek and followed by Andrey Rublyov. However, Dionysy's figures are even more elongated than those of earlier artists; in all but the Virgin's case, their draperies are more billowy and, in the case of the Archangel and of St Peter, a sense of movement is achieved both by raising the heel of one foot from the ground and by treating the Archangel's wings asymmetrically. Outlines are heavier than in the works of Theophanes or Rublyov and religious fervour perhaps slightly less in evidence, but the delicacy of the faces is unmarred by any trace of effeminacy.

Antonova/Mneva, Vol. 1, no. 278. *Istoriya*, Vol. 3, Moscow, 1955, pp. 526–7.

123 The *Virgin Hodegetria*
By Dionysy.
From the cathedral of the Ascension in the Ascension Monastery of the Moscow Kremlin. Now in the Tretyakov Gallery, Moscow.
An old lime panel 135 × 111 cm.
Moscow school. 1482

In 1407 the widow of Prince Dmitri Donskoy built the cathedral of the Ascension on the site of her late husband's palace within Moscow's Kremlin. An entry in the Second Sophia Chronicle records that, in the year 1482, 'in Moscow, in the stone church of the Ascension, an icon of the Hodegetria, a glorious, holy Virgin of the Greek school, was destroyed by fire, and one of the same size, as glorious as that from Tsargrad, was painted . . . on the panel which survived the fire; and it was the icon painter Dionysy who painted it on that panel in an identical form.'

Indeed, on this panel Dionysy clearly adhered closely to the outlines of the Byzantine prototype as well as to its iconography, yet the expressions on the two faces, for all the Greekness of their features, are those sought for in the Moscow of his day. Bust size figures of the Archangels Michael and Gabriel appear in the icon's upper corners.

Antonova/Mneva, Vol. 1, no. 274. *PSRL*, St Petersburg, 1853, Vol. 6.

124 Christ in Glory
By Dionysy
From the Trinity Cathedral of the Pavlov-Obnorsky Monastery, near Vologda. Now in the Tretyakov Gallery, Moscow.
Lime panel 192 × 130 cm.
Moscow school. 1500

This panel was painted for the central position in the Deesis tier of the iconostasis of the church of the Holy Trinity belonging to the monastery founded in 1414 by Paul Obnorsky, a disciple of St Sergius of Radonezh. The original church was replaced between 1505–16 by a stone one built at the wish of Vasili III, but the icons of the earlier structures were retained in the later one.

On this panel Dionysy closely followed Rublyov's icons on the same theme, but although the iconography is well-nigh identical and the disposition of the figure very similar Dionysy's version is less spiritual, the figure more tense, but an impression of movement is achieved through the position of Christ's right foot and the treatment of the draperies.

An old, almost obliterated inscription on the back of the panel was transcribed on it in the 1530s. It dates the icon to the year 1500 and ascribes it to Dionysy.

Antonova/Mneva, Vol. 1, no. 276. *Istoriya*, Vol. 3, Moscow, 1955, pp. 500 and 528.

124

125

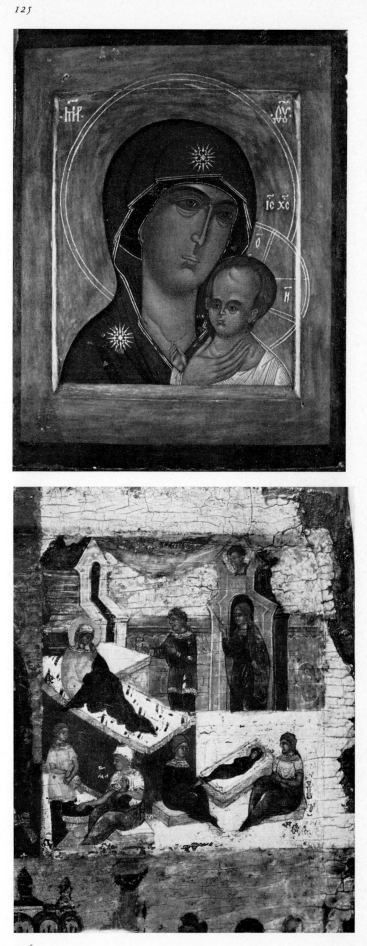

126

145

146

148   149

151 152

154

155

125 The Virgin of Petrov
By Ierofey, the Sinful
From the Zubalov Collection. Now in the Tretyakov
Gallery, Moscow.
Lime panel 31 × 25 cm.
Moscow school. 1561

Instead of being rendered half-length, as on the prototype, the figures of the Virgin and Child are of bust-size.
The cataloguers of the Tretyakov Gallery's icons note
that shortening of this sort was resorted to in the
fifteenth century in the case of many renderings of the
most revered Russian icons of the Virgin and Child.
The treatment of the eyes on this icon is distinctive for
the Virgin's lids are indicated by two light lines and her
eyes are underlined by two semi-circles, features which
Antonova and Mneva regard as characteristic of the
mid-fifteenth-century Muscovite school. In this case,
therefore, the artist was working in a style which had
by his day become outdated. The panel is inscribed on
the back.

Antonova/Mneva, Vol. 2, no. 453.

126 A September-November icon. A detail
From the Joseph Volokolamsk Monastery. Now at the
Tretyakov Gallery, Moscow.
Lime panel 56 × 45 cm.
Monastic school. 1569

This illustration shows the upper scene of the September
section of the icon. It illustrates the Virgin's birth, an
event celebrated by the Church in September. Although
the figures lack the refinement of a metropolitan work,
both they and the architectural details featured in the
background have been subjected to some elongation,
and thus kept in step with trends current at the time in
Moscow. Some of the faces, such as those of the maids
engaged in bathing the infant Mary, are markedly
naturalistic and were probably based on life. The
costumes are also contemporary in style. The inscription
on the back of the panel states that the icon was painted
in the year 1569 'in the reign of the Orthodox, Christ-
loving Tsar and Grand Duke Ivan Vasilievich, Autocrat of Russia, and his noble descendants, the Tsarevich
Ivan and the Tsarevich Feodor, and in the reign of the
saintly Metropolitan Kiril'. The latter held that office
from 1568 to 1572.

Antonova/Mneva, Vol. 2, no. 554.

127 Liturgical icon on the text of '*All ye Cherubim*', *with
donors*
From the Annunciation Cathedral at Solvychegodsk.
Now in the Tretyakov Gallery, Moscow.
Pine panel 197 × 153 cm.
Stroganov school. 1579

The icon figures in the Monastery's inventory of 1579,
but from 1584 it was displayed in the Annunciation
Cathedral which had been built in that year at the expense of the Stroganovs. Its text is taken from the
Liturgy of St John Chrysostom.

This symbolic composition shows the liturgy being
celebrated within a five-aisled, five-domed church.
Within it, high in the main dome, the Paternity is
represented by God the Father, shown here enthroned,
with God the Son and the Holy Ghost appearing
against a circular glory filled by a choir of angels. Below,
Christ stands behind an altar surrounded by angels and
saints with, on either side, angels performing an oblation.
Christ appears for a second time at the centre of the
bottom register with angels approaching from His right,
celebrating the liturgy as they do so, whilst other angels
emerge from a side chapel carrying the naked body of
the dead Christ. On the right are a group of donors and
their patron saints—on the extreme right is Nikita
Grigorievich Stroganov, the chief donor, who died
childless in 1619; he presses his right hand to his breast;
his patron saint, the Warrior Nikita, stands behind him,
beneath a canopy with a tent-shaped top. Nikita
Stroganov's heirs stand in front of him; they consist of
his uncle Semeon, who died in 1587, and his two sons
Andrey and Petr with members of both their families.
Simeon Stylites, standing beside Christ, completes the
composition.

Donor icons are extremely rare in Russia. This one,
with its close association with Nikita Stroganov, is a
good example of the pure, early Stroganov style. The
heads of the figures are still fairly large, the bodies not
yet elongated, the decorative features still restrained.
The white highlights and general colour scheme, based
on ochre shades, are also characteristic.

Antonova/Mneva, Vol. 2, no. 643, where the donors are identified.

128 The Old Testament Trinity
From the Ipatiev Monastery at Kostroma. Now in the
Tretyakov Gallery, Moscow.
Cedar panel 150 × 110 cm.
Godunov school. 1586

This icon is the central panel of a quinquepartite icon
recounting the history of the theme. The Old Testament Trinity sets out to follow that of Rublyov as
closely as possible, both iconographically and stylistically, but the artist could not resist devoting more
attention to the background than Rublyov had done,
including more vessels on the table and investing the
angels with worldlier expressions. Yet, by and large,
he remained quite faithful to Rublyov's version and it is
only on the side panels that he followed the style current
in the Moscow of his own day. Nevertheless, comparison
of the two icons shows how much the style even of a

faithful copyist had altered in the course of two centuries or so.

A silver plate fixed to the centre of this panel states that it was commissioned by the Boyar Dmitri Ivanovich Godunov in the second year of the reign of Tsar Feodor Ivanovich and of the Tsarina Irina, and placed in the Ipatiev Monastery in the year 1586 in memory of his own soul and that of his parents.

Antonova/Mneva, Vol. 2, no. 547; for illustrations of two of the side panels see pls. 49 and 51.

129 The Annunciation and St Basil
Details from a travelling church.
Now in the Tretyakov Gallery, Moscow.
Some sections painted on pine, some on lime panels; this section 70 × 19 cm.
Vologda school. *c.* 1598

The travelling church to which this icon belongs is made up of eleven panels each measuring 70 cm in height and all but the centre one, which is 35 cm wide, measuring 19 cm in width. The style of the painting is a trifle heavy, but delightfully alert, with the facial markings and highlights attempting to follow trends fashionable at a somewhat earlier date in Moscow. The love of decoration which was expressing itself at the time both in folk and in Muscovite art is also reflected in these paintings, which are additionally enlivened by certain iconographic innovations. Thus, in the scene of the Annunciation, the angel is shown alighting from heaven and not, as was customary, advancing towards the Virgin after having done so; in addition, he wears a contemporary robe instead of the usual draperies. The icon's treatment foreshadows the work of the later Palekh school and, ultimately, of the artists who are at present engaged in making the extremely decorative papier-mâché objects being produced in the USSR.

The name of John, Archbishop of Vologodsk, is inscribed on the back of this travelling church. He was appointed to Vologodsk in 1589 and transferred to Rostov in 1603.

Antonova/Mneva, Vol. 2, no. 630.

130 Nikita, the Warrior
By Prokopy Chirin, son of Ivan
From the Annunciation Cathedral at Solvychegodsk.
Now in the Tretyakov Gallery, Moscow.
Lime panel 29 × 22 cm.
Stroganov school. 1593

This panel formed the centre of a triptych, the side panels of which are by a different hand. The saint is shown standing on the left of the panel; his figure is elongated, his heels raised slightly from the ground,

whilst the upper part of his body is slightly inclined towards the Virgin and Child seen in the panel's top right-hand corner. The Saint's head is large, his features carefully drawn, his gold armour treated in a miniaturist technique. Some light colours are included, but it is the gold and darker shades which were soon to predominate in Moscow, that prevail.

The inscription on the back of the panel reads: 'In the year 7101 [1593] this image was painted in Moscow by the Novgorodian icon painter Prokopy. It was given a chased silver-gilt cover and adorned with gems and pearls on 15 September 1598 at the order of Nikita Grigorievich, son of Stroganov.' Prokopy Chirin was a Stroganov painter who was appointed a Tsar's iconographer in 1620–1 and who also worked at times for the Patriarch Filaret. He died before 1650, when his place in the Armoury workshop was conferred on another artist. This painting is an early work executed in the Stroganov style. His fairly numerous known works include an icon of the Veronica with the Blessed Maxim, mentioned by Kondakov, 2, pl. IX; a St John, the Warrior in the Russian State Museum, Leningrad, illustrated by Wulff/Alpatov on pl. 89; and a triptych of the Virgin of Vladimir with Festivals and heads of saints exhibited at Burlington House in 1959 in the Exhibition of 'Russian Painting from the 13th to the 20th Century', no. 10.

Antonova/Mneva, Vol. 2, no. 803. *Istoriya*, Vol. 3, Moscow, 1955, p.648.

131 The Birth of St Nicholas and scenes from his Life
By Semeon Borozdin
From the Nikolsky Edinoverchesky Monastery, Moscow. Now in the Tretyakov Gallery, Moscow.
Lime panel 36 × 30 cm.
Stroganov school. 1601

The largest scene, that on the left of the top register, depicts the birth of St Nicholas with, to its right, the blessing of the newly born. Below we see his baptism, his presentation to the temple and the start of his schooling. The scenes are not partitioned off, but each is set against a different architectural background; the buildings serve to divide the panel into sections, but the device is not wholly successful and the difference in size between the main scene and the subsidiary ones strikes rather a discordant note. There are two inscriptions on the back of the panel. One states that 'In 1601 this domestic icon of the Cathedral of the Annunciation of the Holy Virgin at Solvychegodsk was placed there at the order of Nikolay Grigorievich, son of Stroganov'; the other states that it was 'painted by Semeon Borozdin'.

Antonova/Mneva, Vol. 2, no. 779.

132 'Glory Unto Thee'

Formerly in the Silin Collection. Now in the Tretyakov Gallery, Moscow.
Lime panel 157 × 125.
Moscow school. 1602

The panel is divided into four sections to correspond with each of the hymn's four verses. The inscriptions display the texts of other hymns extolling the Virgin. In each section the Virgin occupies a central position and stands against a glory differing either in shape, colour or content. She is in each case surrounded by worshipping angels, saints and divines; in the lower, right hand scene the latter are accompanied by two men and two women wearing contemporary clothes. The full-length figure of saints appear on the side margins, those on the left represent the Archangel Gabriel, Pope Clement, the Archdeacon Stephen, the Martyr Prokopios, St Maxim and the Martyr Matrena; opposite are Christ's brother, Jacob, St George, Roman, the singer, the stylite Daniel, the Martyr Agafia and the Blessed Efrosinia.

This type of symbolic, liturgical icon was very popular in Moscow in the seventeenth century. The style is typical of the period and school. The inscription at the bottom of the panel states that 'this icon was painted in 7110 [1602] at the order of Semeon, the Deacon of Ivan Bykov, for himself and his parents'.

Antonova/Mneva, Vol. 2, no. 692.

133 St Simeon, the Stylite

Now in the Tretyakov Gallery, Moscow.
Lime panel 92 × 58 cm.
Moscow school. 1605

This strongly stylized, impersonal, somewhat dry and aloof representation of the Stylite is executed in the style popular in Moscow at the time at which it was painted. The use and shape of the highlights are also characteristic of the period and school. The graphic element is strongly marked; only the colours are unusually bright for their day, featuring the distinctive shade of pink so popular in the decorative arts of the late sixteenth and early seventeenth century, notably in the enamels. The medallions show, as is customary in icons of St Nicholas, but unusual in other instances, the Saviour holding a volume of the Gospels and the Virgin a stole. The dedicatory inscription at the bottom of the panel dates the painting to 7 May 1605.

Antonova/Mneva, Vol. 2, no. 694.

134 A triptych of the Bogolyubovo Virgin and selected saints

By Istom Savin
From the tomb of the Grand Duke Sergei Alexandro-vich in the Chudov Monastery. Now in the Tretyakov Gallery, Moscow.
Oak panel 35 × 15 cm each.
Stroganov school. Late sixteenth or early seventeenth century

In the centre panel the Metropolitan Peter, standing with the Metropolitans Photius and Macarios and the Blessed Maxim and John, adore the Virgin and Child appearing to them in the upper left-hand corner of the panel; on the left-hand panel the Metropolitan Alexei, the taller of the four, the Metropolitans Cyprian and Philip, and St Stephen of Perm venerate the Virgin, who appears before them standing on a cloud and holding a scroll, whilst Christ blesses them from above; on the right-hand panel the Virgin appears once again standing on a cloud, but this time she displays the Child to Basil the Blessed and the Metropolitans Gerontius, John and Feognost. She holds the Child on her left arm and supports His feet with her right hand. The style is miniaturist and ornate, devoting great attention to detail; there is some striving at portraiture; figures are elongated and white highlights are used on the faces.

There are two inscriptions on the back of the icon, both enclosed in circles; one reads: 'This painting from the tomb of Peter, Metropolitan of Kiev and Moscow, the miracle worker of all Russia'; the second states: 'This icon of Maxim Yakovlev, son of Stroganov, painted by Istom Savin.'

Antonova/Mneva, Vol. 2, no. 785.

135 The Bringing of the Veronica

By Pervusha
From the Nikolsky Edinoverchesky Monastery, Moscow. Now in the Tretyakov Gallery, Moscow.
Lime panel 40 × 34 cm.
Stroganov school. First quarter of seventeenth century

King Abgar of Edessa's splendid palace occupies the background of this painting. The ornate buildings are coloured in the characteristically Muscovite shades of luminous yellow, pink and green which are seen at their clearest in Muscovite enamels of much the same date. Their elaborate window surrounds and roofs are of gold. Abgar's bed fills much of the foreground. To the left of it the painter Ananius displays the Veronica which cured the king, who is shown risen from his sick bed to give thanks for his recovery. His subjects crowd behind him. Abgar is depicted as larger in size than his subjects. Christ's head follows the style of earlier Novgorodian paintings of the Veronica, but the highlights on all the faces are in the form of splodges rather than lines, as was typical of Moscow's seventeenth-century painting.

Antonova/Mneva, Vol. 2, no. 783. M. Farbman, ed., *Masterpieces of Russian Painting*, London, 1930, pl. LXVI.

136 The origin of the wood of the True Cross
By Istom Savin
From the Egorov Collection. Now in the Tretyakov Gallery, Moscow.
Lime panel 40 × 31 cm.
Stroganov school. Early seventeenth century

A religious procession advances from a large town; it includes a tsar and tsarina, many clerics and a large crowd. They gather on either side of a large well with a cruciform opening to it. An angel is descending from heaven to fit a cross into it. At the bottom of the icon the ill and deformed gather at the water flowing from the well which, thus sanctified, has acquired curative powers. The scenes include many details derived from contemporary life; the town's ornate buildings also reproduce contemporary architectural features. The type of white highlights which are characteristic of the period appear on all the faces.

The inscription on the reverse states that the painting was executed 'at the order of Maxim Yakovlevich Stroganov by his man Istom'. Istom Savin was also one of the Tsar's iconographers.

Antonova/Mneva, Vol. 2, no. 789. Kondakov, Vol. 4, text p. 2, pl. 283.

137 The Miracle of the Blind Man
By Istom Savin
From the Soldatenkov Collection. Now in the Tretyakov Gallery, Moscow.
Lime panel 40 × 36 cm.
Stroganov school. Late sixteenth or very early seventeenth century when Istom Savin was still living, although the date of his death is not known.

The outer walls of Jerusalem face a mountainous countryside; it is there that the Saviour, who is accompanied by the Apostles, meets the blind man and performs the miracle. To the right, the man, having regained his sight, washes at a well. The figures are elongated yet vigorous; much use is made in their faces of white highlights. The wide margins are characteristic of the Stroganov school.

The inscription is on the reverse of the panel; it is written in decorative lettering and is enclosed in a circle, and accompanied by two stylized floral devices; it reads: 'This image belongs to Maxim Yakovlev, son of Stroganov. Painted by his man Istom'.

Antonova/Mneva, Vol. 2, no. 784.

138 The Petrov Virgin
By Nazary Savin
Now in the Tretyakov Gallery, Moscow.
Lime panel 36 × 30 cm.
Stroganov school. *c.* 1614

A head-and-shoulder representation of the Virgin and Child. The Child is seated on the Virgin's left arm. He blesses with His right hand and holds a scroll in His left whilst the Virgin indicates Him with her right hand. Three of Moscow's Metropolitans appear in the margins, Peter to the left, Alexei to the right and John below.

The artist has closely followed Novgorodian versions of the monumental Byzantine renderings of the Virgin and Child and has reproduced the Metropolitans' vestments with that attention to detail which was characteristic of Russia from the sixteenth century onwards.

The inscription on the reverse of the icon states that 'on 5 December in the year 7123 [1614] this image of the Virgin with the Metropolitan Peter was exchanged in Kazan by Nikita Grigorievich Stroganov with Nazary, the son of the icon painter Istom, for fifty roubles'. Stroganov must have greatly admired this icon, for on another occasion he paid Nazary only twenty-two roubles for an icon. Nazary, a son of Istom Savin, also worked for the Tsar in Moscow, as well as for close friends of his master, painting murals in churches and palaces in addition to icons. He died in *c.* 1629.

Antonova/Mneva, Vol. 2, no. 790. *Istoriya*, Vol. 3, 1955, p. 666.

139 The King of Kings
By Nazary Savin
From the Afanasiev and Chirikov collections. Now in the Tretyakov Gallery, Moscow.
Lime panel 40 × 34 cm.
Stroganov school. 1616

Christ sits enthroned wearing bishop's robes whilst the Virgin, dressed as a tsarina, stands on His right and St John, clothed in the traditional sheepskin, stands on His left. The Archangels Gabriel and Michael stand between them, just behind the Saviour. Decorative details of the type much admired in court circles abound here, appearing not only on the textiles and trimmings used for the garments of both Christ and the Virgin, but also for the cushion and upholstered, sofa-like back of the Saviour's throne; the latter appears to be made of Spanish leather. Gold prevails in a colour scheme including pale pinks, greens and browns. Wide margins of the Stroganov type create a frame-like effect.

An inscription on the back reads: 'Nazary Istomin, son of Savin, painted this image for Nikita Grigorievich Stroganov in 1616.'

Antonova/Mneva, Vol. 2, no. 791.

140 The Veronica
By Simon Ushakov
From the church of the Trinity in Nikitniki, Moscow.
Now in the Tretyakov Gallery, Moscow.
Lime panel 55 × 48 cm.
Armoury school. 1658

It is interesting to compare Ushakov's version of the Veronica with the early Novgorodian one (*pl. 95*) in order to see how this artist adapted the naturalistic style to the iconographic convention.

The icon is inscribed along the bottom, the existing lettering being a repainting of the original; the text reads: 'The Tsar's iconographer Simon Feodorov Ushakov painted [this image] in the year 7166 [1658].'

Antonova/Mneva, Vol. 2, no. 910. Kondakov, 1, Vol. 4, text, p. 2.

141 St Sergius of Radonezh
By Simon Ushakov
From the Troitse-Sergeyeva Lavra. Now in the Tretyakov Gallery, Moscow.
49 × 39 cm.
Armoury school. 1669

This half-length figure of St Sergius shows him blessing with his right hand and holding a scroll in his left. There is an attempt at true portraiture in his face, more especially in the treatment of his eyes and in the extended area of a lighter coloured flesh tint. Nevertheless the inherent Russian instinct for the graphic style is strongly reflected in the handling of his beard and hair. His ears and eyebrows accord with the style already current in the sixteenth century and which is to be seen in the icon of St Nicholas (*pl. 103*).

The inscription is to be found on the bottom margin; it reads: 'According to the promise of the Boyar and Armourer Bogd . . . Matveevich Khitrovo. Painted by Pimen, son of Feodorov, known as Simon Ush[a]kov for the life-giving Trinity at Sergeyevo' (the original name of Zagorsk). The date of 1669 appears on the left, at the bottom of the background.

Antonova/Mneva, Vol. 2, no. 916.

142 The Old Testament Trinity
By Simon Ushakov
Now in the Russian State Museum, Leningrad.
123 × 92.7 cm.
Armoury school. 1671

Ushakov has retained the oak tree which in earlier versions of the scene symbolizes the Grove of Mamre, but has depicted Abraham's house as a mansion of the classical style and included a church and a classical temple in the background, emphasizing this Greek element by inscribing the icon's title in Greek. Although he has followed Rublyov's model for the three angels he has seated them on ornate thrones at a highly decorated table laid with a cloth and rich vessels. His colours are those found in contemporary book illuminations and comparison with Rublyov's masterpiece (*pl. 119*), even

with that of the Godunov school (*pl. 128*), shows the extent to which Ushakov had been affected by the West's naturalistic style.

Onasch, pl. 135.

143 The Annunciation
By Simon Ushakov
From the Church of the Virgin's Protection in the village of Bratzevo, near Moscow. Now in the Tretyakov Gallery, Moscow.
Lime panel 56 × 43 cm.
Armoury school. 1673

This painting is perhaps to be numbered among Ushakov's best, possibly because he remained more faithful in it to the iconographic style whilst successfully modifying it by showing the Virgin standing behind a lectern displaying an open book instead of seated at her spinning wheel. He also shows the angel descending from heaven on a cloud instead of walking towards her. Both faces adhere fairly closely to the iconic style although the light areas on each are more extensive than on the traditional works. Western influence is also reflected in the architectural style of the buildings and the striving in them for true perspective.

The inscription beneath the clouds enfolding the angel states that: 'This was painted in 1673 by Pimen Feodorov . . . alias Simon Ushakov.'

Antonova/Mneva, Vol. 2, no. 918.

A quite considerable number of Ushakov's works survive. Among the more important are:
1 The Virgin of Vladimir and the Planting of the Tree of Russian Autocracy, 1668, Antonova/Mneva, Vol. 2, no. 912.
2 A Veronica of 1673 in Kondakov 2, pl. 25.
3 The Almighty, *c.* 1680, probably commissioned by the Tsars Ivan and Peter, Kondakov 2, pl. III (in colour).
4 A Saviour of *c.* 1680, Kondakov 2, pl. IV (in colour).
5 A Veronica, signed and dated 1676 from the Gallery at Perm, in *Pamiatniki Cultury*, Vol. I, Moscow, 1959, pp. 176–86, B. V. Filatov, *Restavratzia isvetsnogo proizvedeniya S. Ushakova.*

144 The Council of Nicaea
Now in the Tretyakov Gallery, Moscow.
Lime panel 41 × 36 cm.
Perhaps a work of a Muscovite monastery. *c.* 1666

The Emperor of Byzantium in his role of Christ's vicar on earth is seated on a throne in a great temple. Grouped on his right are leaders of the established Church, on his left those of the heretical Arian creed with their leader, Arius, in contemporary dress, seated in a pavilion below them. On the opposite side Christ stands in another pavilion with Peter of Alexandria kneeling below Him. In the lower register the Emperor is shown once again, this time standing between representatives of both creeds, each upholding his beliefs. The figures are static, elongated, small-headed, the architectural compositions varied and elaborate. The icon has a silver border with a chased floral design; the Old Testament Trinity is shown at the centre of its upper rim.

The inscription is on the reverse; it reads: 'On the 25th day of February 1666 the Pope Sava presented this image to the Great Celestial Ruler.'

Antonova/Mneva, Vol. 2, no. 766.

145 The Virgin in the Enclosed Garden
By Nikita Pavlovetz
From the Sherbatov Collection. Now in the Tretyakov Gallery, Moscow.
33 × 29 cm.
Armoury school. c. 1670

In earlier times the garden symbolizing Paradise was depicted as round in shape, but the latter half of the seventeenth century witnessed the growth in Russia of a great interest in landscaped gardens. Peter the Great's father, Tsar Alexei, was very much wrapped up in his Muscovite estates, and laid out exceedingly impressive grounds such as those at Izmailovo, where the alleys radiated in a star formation from the main entrance gate; its orchards were also much admired, and so was its parterre of flowers. This was the Laleli or Tulip Age in Turkey and it may have been due to Turkish influence that the Tsar and his courtiers were particularly fond of tulips and carnations.

Pavlovetz has placed his Virgin and Child in just such a garden as Tsar Alexei's parterre, enclosing it with the type of ornate wooden palisade which retained its popularity in Russia into modern times; he also placed oriental, in this case Persian-looking, urns at its ends, but he must have looked to Western art for the landscape that unfolds beyond this celestial garden. In contrast, the Virgin's robe seems to be made of a fine Turkish velvet or brocade rather than one of Italian make, yet both her crown and Christ's reflect Western influence; nevertheless their faces adhere fairly closely to the iconic tradition.

The inscription along the top reads: 'Image of the Holy Virgin in the Enclosed Garden'; that along the bottom: 'This image was painted by the icon painter Nikita Ivanov, son of Erofey Pavlovetz.' Nikita was a serf of Prince Cherkassky who was appointed an Armoury artist in 1668 and died nine or ten years later. He and his father derived their surname from their native village of Pavlov Perevod, near Novgorod.

Antonova/Mneva, Vol. 2, no. 892.

146 The Purification of the Virgin
By Andrey . . .
From the church of the Virgin's Protection at Bratzevo, near Moscow. Now in the Tretyakov Gallery, Moscow.
Lime panel 56 × 37 cm.
Armoury school. 1673

The church of the Virgin's Protection in the village of Bratzevo, near Moscow, was built in 1672 by the Boyar Khitrovo. He must therefore have also provided it with its first icons. These must include both the icon illustrated here and that by Ushakov (pl. 143), for both adhere, at any rate so far as the figures are concerned, to the ancient iconographic tradition whilst displaying, as a result of Western influences, less dark faces. Another concession to change in the icon under discussion is to be found in the architectural styles of its buildings and in a striving after Western perspective. The workmanship is accomplished, the handling dignified, yet truly deep religious emotion is lacking.

The inscription in white lettering appears at the bottom of the panel; it mentions the painter Andrey and the year 1673. (The compilers of the Tretyakov Gallery's icon catalogue have traced four artists answering to the name of Andrey in the Armoury list, but cannot ascertain which of the four painted this icon.)

Antonova/Mneva, Vol. 2, no. 877.

147 The Virgin's Festivals
By Nikita Pavlovetz
From the church of the Dormition in Apukhtina Street, Moscow. Now in the Tretyakov Gallery, Moscow.
Lime panel 32 × 27 cm.
Armoury school. 1675

We look into a building as if into a doll's house. Within it we see, starting from the top, Joachim and Anne praying for a child; the large scene immediately below it illustrates the Virgin's presentation to the temple, her birth being depicted immediately below it with, to the right, Joachim waiting for news of the child's safe delivery. The bathing of Mary is shown at the bottom of the panel with a shepherd driving his flock beside it. These scenes are surrounded by an ornate, frame-like border suggestive of the side wings of a house; standing on one side of the border is St Gregory, the Evangelist, and on the other St Paraskevi. A cartouche at the centre of the lower border states that the icon was painted in 1675 by Nikita Pavlovetz. It is an admirable example of Pavlovetz's skill as a miniaturist and his great feeling for and understanding of the decorative.

Antonova/Mneva, Vol. 2, no. 895. Kondakov 2, pl. XI, ill. 20, reproduces an icon of the Saviour which was painted on 31 November 1677 for Tsar Feodor Alexeevich by Pavlovetz and his comrades.

148 King of Kings
By Nikita Pavlovetz and others
From the Smolensk Cathedral at the Novodevichy Monastery, Moscow. Now in the Tretyakov Gallery, Moscow.
Lime panel 84 × 130 cm.
Armoury school. 1676

Here we have an example of an icon painted by several hands. It is impossible to establish either the number of the artists engaged on this work or the sections for which each was responsible, but it seems probable that one did the figures, another the heads, another the lettering and that Pavlovetz contributed all the decorative features. The icon follows the traditional iconography, showing Christ enthroned, wearing a bishop's vestment, the Virgin dressed as a tsarina and St John the Forerunner wearing a sheepskin.

The inscription runs along the base of the painting and reads: 'On the eleventh day of the month of November in the year 7185 [1676] this icon was painted at the order of the Orthodox Tsar and Grand Duke Feodor Alexeevich, ruler of the whole of Great, Small and White Russia, and the painter Nikita Pavlovetz and his comrades did the work.'

Antonova/Mneva, Vol. 2, no. 896.

149 St John the Forerunner, Angel of the Wilderness
By Tikhon Filatiev
From the church of the Metropolitan Alexei in Glinishchy, Moscow. Now in the Tretyakov Gallery, Moscow.
174 × 107 cm.
Armoury school. 1689

This large panel displays a very tall figure of St John the Forerunner. He is presented frontally, holding the Eucharistic chalice on his left arm whilst indicating it with his right forefinger. He holds an open scroll in his left hand. Much of the background consists of sky, but a lush, undulating landscape unfolds below it, extending to less than a third of the icon's total height. Nevertheless some of the trees are very large. A river is included in the scene which is rich with bird and animal life, for the term 'wilderness' is not used to describe a desert but to refer to a remote district, luxuriating in fauna and flora, and untouched by man, one more akin to a jungle. The birds include storks; when compared with the animals they seem disproportionately large for the latter include a camel and elephant in addition to a hare, a wolf and a stag.

The white lettering in the panel's lower left-hand border dates the icon to 1689 and ascribes it to Tikhon Ivanov, son of Filatiev; he was a native of Yaroslavl and became an Armoury artist. His known works were produced between 1675 and 1709.

Antonova/Mneva, Vol. 2, no. 926.

150 The Prophet Elijah with twenty-six scenes from his life
By Semeon Spiridonov, son of Kholmogoretz
Now in the Yaroslavl Museum.
145 × 113 cm.
Armoury school. 1679

Elijah stands in a hilly, densely wooded landscape, framed by an arch resting on square capitals placed on piers adorned with decorative devices, the whole framed by a rectangular border containing a Biblical text. Scrolls decorate the triangular spaces between the top of the border and the curves of the arch, an arrangement which must derive from a book illumination. The Prophet has a slender, greatly elongated body and fairly small head. He holds a scroll in his left hand and extends his right in supplication towards the Saviour who appears enthroned in the sky, seated within a cloud and accompanied by a choir of angels. Twenty-six scenes illustrating events from the Prophet's life are portrayed with a wealth of detail, and are especially remarkable for their architectural settings and feeling for landscape. The latter is also well in evidence in the central scene. This interest in nature is expressed in other icons of a contemporary date, notably in Tikhon Filatiev's. (See Filatiev's icons in Antonova/Mneva, Vol. 2.)

Semeon Spiridonov was a native of Kholmogory, but worked in Yaroslavl where he appears to have established a workshop. He owed his appointment as an Armoury artist to Ushakov, as did Gury Nikitin, both being listed as such in 1679.

Yaroslav Museum catalogue no. 50. Burlington House, 1959.

151 St John the Forerunner in the Wilderness with scenes from his life
By Tikhon Filatiev
From the church of Sts Cosmas and Damian on Kadasha in the Large Field at Moscow. Now in the Tretyakov Gallery, Moscow.
Lime panel 142 × 122 cm.
Armoury school. 1685

Once again the central figure, that of St John the Forerunner, occupies almost the entire height of the icon. It has been subjected to even greater elongation than was usual among artists of the Stroganov school (see Antonova/Mneva, Vol. 2, no. 803). In contrast, the landscape and buildings in its background, regardless of their importance and size, are on a greatly reduced scale. So too are the animals, but not the birds. St John gazes upwards where the Saviour is to be seen in the right-hand corner of the sky. Meanwhile, below, in the centre of the panel we are shown the interior of a house —this represents an iconographic innovation since, in early times, a drapery slung between two towers sufficed to indicate an interior. Within the house we witness St

John's birth. In the foreground his truncated head is held outside the building in which it was severed. Both buildings are shown in correct perspective, that on the right having surely derived from an Italian picture. The inscription beneath the cartouche reads: 'Painted by the icon painter Tikhon Ivanov, son of Filatiev, in the year 1689.'

Antonova/Mneva, Vol. 2, no. 927.

152 Theodosia the Blessed
By Kiril Ulanov
From the Ascension Convent in the Kremlin at Moscow. Now in the Tretyakov Gallery, Moscow.
52 × 16 cm.
Armoury school. 1690

This is the baptismal icon which was done for Theodosia, the infant daughter of Tsar Alexei, and its measurements correspond to the baby's on the day of her birth. The panel shows the Tsarevna's patroness, St Theodosia, dressed as a nun, holding a cross in her right hand and blessing with her left. The highlights on her face reflect Western influence. Inset above her head is The Old Testament Trinity. The inscription in white lettering appears below the hillock on which she stands; it reads: 'Painted on the 7th day of June by Kiril Ulanov.'

Ulanov was appointed to the Armoury in 1688. With the transfer of its workshops to St Petersburg in 1710 he became a monk of the Krivoe-Osero Monastery, taking the name of Karion. The last of his known icons is dated to 1728.

Antonova/Mneva, Vol. 2, no. 904.

153 A biographical icon of the Prophet Elijah
By John and Boris
Now in the Tretyakov Gallery, Moscow.
Lime panel 146 × 122 cm.
A northern monastic school. 1690

Elijah is seated in the mouth of a cave situated in a wilderness. He looks up towards the raven which is flying towards him, bringing him food. The mountains are strongly stylized whilst the rendering of both the river and the vegetation reflects the influence of folk art. The prophet's figure is elongated, the treatment of his hair and robe essentially linear. The scenes unfold from left to right. They portray the prophet's birth; two angels feeding him with the sacred flame; his powers of divination being foretold by a sage; God the Father, appearing before him; Elijah predicting three years of drought; his meeting with a widow at the town gates; conversing with her; returning with her to her house where her son lies ill in bed; his meeting with a king; curing the woman's son; soothsayers disputing with him; Elijah sacrificing to God; destroying the sooth-

sayers' idol; praying for rain; detecting Ahab; releasing the queen's slaves; meeting Elisha; anointing Elisha and blessing him as he guards his flock; Elijah and Elisha cross the Jordan; Elijah ascends to heaven in a fiery chariot.

The inscription in white letters states that the icon was painted on 25 March 1690 by the icon painters John and Boris.

Antonova/Mneva, Vol. 2, no. 976.

154 Parsunya of Prince Mikhail Vasilievich Skopin-Shuysky
By a tsars' iconographer
Until 1870 the panel was placed in the Archangel Cathedral in Moscow's Kremlin; it was then transferred to the Historical Museum, Moscow. Now in the Tretyakov Gallery, Moscow.
Lime board 41 × 33 cm.
Painted either in 1610 or between 1620–30, more probably the latter

This is a good, early example of the *parsunya*—a striving after portraiture within the iconic idiom in memorial panels. The young man's features are rendered with considerable fidelity and much greater use of white is made in his face than was customary in traditional icon painting. He wears contemporary dress. Antonova and Mneva draw attention to the Veronica occupying the centre of the icon's upper border, noting that it is rendered in the style which was used at the time on painted standards.

Antonova/Mneva, Vol. 2, no. 854.

155 The Annunciation
By John Matveev, son of Bobyleov
From the Church of Smolensk in the Bogoyavlensky Monastery, Uglich. Now in the Tretyakov Gallery, Moscow.
Lime panel 119 × 76 cm.
Monastic school. 1696

Both the shape and the style of this icon strongly reflect Western influence. Although the angel appears before the seated Virgin from the traditional direction and to a large extent in the traditional manner the lily which he holds in his left hand is of Western origin; so too is the placing of the Virgin within a tent which is suspended from the beam of a loggia. The building's perspective derives from the West as does the towel hanging from a hook on the loggia's wall. The cloud which descends from heaven is also Western in conception. It contains a bust-size rendering of the Almighty watching the angel as he flies earthwards holding the lily. The inscription in white lettering states that John Matveev, son of Bobyleov, painted this panel in the eighth month of the year 1696.

Antonova/Mneva, Vol. 2, no. 978.

Chapter Seven

Pointers to Dating

IN THIS section an attempt will be made to distinguish certain details which can serve as pointers in the dating of icons although, ultimately, the final assessment depends upon a feeling for style which, in its turn, is the result of long practice. The problem of dating will be simplified if several versions of a specific iconographic theme are compared. Four such themes have been selected for the purpose, the choice falling on icons depicting the Virgin Hodegetria, the Annunciation, the Veronica and the Old Testament Trinity.

When considering representations of the Virgin Hodegetria it is convenient to start the survey by referring to the twelfth-century Byzantine icon of the Virgin of Vladimir (*pl. 5*), for although its iconography differs from that of the Virgin Hodegetria it possesses many of the characteristics that are associated with the Palaeologan age to which the majority of our earliest icons of the Virgin and Child are to be assigned. The painting is remarkable for its use of subdued colours which nevertheless succeed in personifying the divine, for its restrained, almost severe draperies and for the great depth of feeling expressed in it. On it features remain classical, the Virgin retaining the pear-shaped face and long nose of the Greeks, the Child still displaying the chubbiness of infancy as visualized by Hellenists. The Virgin's eyebrows are, like the Child's, delicately curved, the eyes of both are almond-shaped, with the lids heavily shaded and with some shading also appearing below the eyes. No white highlights are used on the faces, the modelling being carried out in dark flesh tints slightly tinged with red, the deeper tones having a greenish basis. By the thirteenth century Palaeologan artists were imbuing their works with deep poignancy, but in Macedonia, to judge by the icon of the Virgin Hodegetria in the National Museum at Ochrid (*pl. 156*) the Child was being depicted with greater naturalism than in Byzantium, His hair lacking the curls of Hellenistic origin which are almost the rule in Byzantine paintings. Here modelling of the faces is achieved by applying lighter flesh tints smoothly over fairly large surfaces, already the bridge of each nose is marked by a continuous highlight, the eyebrows have become more prominent and linear, and the almond-shaped eyes are set in almond-shaped sockets. The

curious, angular brush-stroke used to accentuate the eyes is more marked than is customary, but the icon's other stylistic features are paralleled in a number of fourteenth-century panels. They recur in the painting of the Virgin Hodegetria which is associated with Thomas Preljubović and which therefore dates from between 1367–84 (*pl. 12*), and is thus our earliest dated example of this type of work. The same methods were used with equal subtlety on the icon of the Virgin of Pimen (*pl. 14*), a near contemporary panel since it is known to have been painted in Constantinople sometime between 1379–81. On both these Byzantine masterpieces the highlight on the Virgin's left cheek is considerably smaller than that on her right, the latter being extended to form the outlines of her rounded chin; an inverted half-moon shaped shadow serves to separate the point of the chin from her lower lip. Similarly, in both icons, the shading of the Virgin's right eyelid is prolonged in a straight line to mark the top of her cheek and to extend down its side to form its contour.

It is interesting to compare these panels with a very similar, though undated icon of the Virgin Hodegetria in the National Gallery of Ireland (*pl. 163*). Although the Dublin icon expresses less compassion than the two paintings which have just been examined its workmanship is equally refined, but the frontal presentation adopted by the artist for both figures creates a more formal, perhaps even austere, effect than does the slightly inclined pose of the Virgin of Pimen. Like other paintings of this group the Dublin panel displays the same type of facial modelling even though the artist made great use of whitish highlights, disposing them in parallel lines round the eyes—a method which is already present on the icon of Christ in the Hermitage Museum (*pl. 10*) which is dated to 1363. Highlights of this type had come into use as much as a century earlier and were to become increasingly frequent in the course of the fifteenth century, when they were used over larger areas. Similarly the use of gold lines to indicate the folds of the Child's garment is also encountered in the thirteenth century and was likewise to persist in centuries to come. In contrast, an older, more sober way of rendering folds is seen here in the Virgin's robes. Thus the treatment of the garments provides little clue to the dating of this panel and guidance has to be sought in the modelling of the faces which, together with that of the two archangels pictured in the panel's upper corners, conforms to the method followed in Constantinople in the latter part of the fourteenth century. It is one that differs from that employed for the faces of the figures occupying the icon's margins: their largish flesh tints, rounder heads and smaller eyes are suggestive of the fifteenth century, a dating which is confirmed by the inclusion of hats, no less than by their styles.

Two fine icons of the Virgin Hodegetria in the National Museum at Ochrid illustrate the way in which artists working in the grand fourteenth-century Constantinopolitan manner treated eyes and handled facial highlights. One of the panels bears the designation of the Virgin Saviour of Souls (*pl. 158*), the other of the Virgin Perebleptos (*pl. 159*). On both the eyebrows take the form almost of straight lines, although they are rendered in a pictorial rather than in a graphic style. On both paler flesh tints extend along the cheeks and a highlight outlines the bridge of each nose. The dark setting of the eyes is emphasized on both by the use of a light border to the pouches below the eyes; this line is especially pronounced on the icon of the Virgin Saviour of Souls, but on that of the Virgin Perebleptos it is combined with highlights disposed in thin parallel lines. On both paintings white flecks at the corners of the eyes add to the intensity of the round pupils set in oval-shaped surrounds. On the Virgin Perebleptos the shading beneath the eyes is achieved, as was customary at an earlier date, by a single brush-stroke, in that of the Virgin Saviour of Souls by precise, almost geometrical outlines. The geometrical treatment of the large eyes is even more marked in a painting of the Virgin and Child in the Benaki Museum (*pl. 160*), a painting which is remarkable for its psychological intensity and patrician nobility. It too is a fourteenth-century work and although the flesh tints on the cheeks are more extensive on this painting than on either of the two preceding icons the nose is highlighted in a similar manner; so too are the chin and mouth although the Virgin's lips remain small. The schematic treatment of the eye pouches is absent from another icon belonging to the National Gallery of Ireland (*pl. 157*) although the Virgin bears a close resemblance to that of the Virgin Saviour of Souls. However, the alert, almost perky expression of the Child is something wholly new and as a result, regardless of the icon's close stylistic resemblance to the Ochrid panel, the Dublin painting must be considered to be at least a century later in date than the Yugoslav example.

If we are to judge by the icon of the Virgin Hodegetria in the Phaneromeni collection at Nicosia (*pl. 161*), highlights in the form of parallel lines were not being used in Cyprus in the fourteenth century, yet there is such a close stylistic resemblance between this icon and that of the Virgin, Saviour of Souls that it too must have been painted in the fourteenth century. The embossed and decorated haloes are typical of Cypriot work and so too is the choice of a contemporary garment for the Child.

The monumental type of Byzantine icons and the stylistic mannerisms followed in them in later Byzantine times were still being adhered to in Bulgaria in the sixteenth century. The icon of the Virgin and Child designated as Phaneromeni at Sozopol (*pl. 46*) is dated to 1541, but it follows an older style so closely that were it not inscribed it would be tempting to regard it as an earlier work. Yet the double shading under the Virgin's eye and its inverted, comma-shaped outline, seen in conjunction with the shading on the right side of the nose should give cause for reflection and suggest a later dating than that which seemed likely at a first view of the panel. The massive shoulders and build of the figures in the medallions serve as a pointer to the painting's non-Byzantine origin. In Venice in the latter half of the sixteenth century (*pl. 162*) lighter flesh tints were being used to produce rounder and fuller faces. It was also usual then for the forehead to be highlighted, sometimes intersected or modelled into a shape (*as on pl. 165*) or a semicircle whilst the pouches below the eyes were stressed by a light, often half-moon or almond-shaped line. But here, when painting the Virgin's face Damaskenos adhered to the earlier tradition of highlighting the top of the nose, the upper lip and chin, although he extended the areas of highlights to produce a rounder chin and shorter, fuller face.

In Russia the grand Byzantine style was intentionally adhered to for the monumental icons although in these the Virgin's face is not as elongated as in the Byzantine prototypes. Generally, rather than follow the pose adopted for the Virgin of Pimen, artists preferred the frontal presentation which is the more characteristic of the Byzantine forms. Typical of such works is the impressive icon of the Virgin of Smolensk (*pl. 164*) which the cataloguers of the Tretyakov Gallery's icons assign to the fourteenth century. Here the treatment closely follows the Byzantine, but the Virgin's face has been subjected to some foreshortening; however, it still retains the long Greek nose; light flesh tints are rendered by highlights in the form of thin, parallel lines which, as has been noted, were widely used at the time in Byzantium, having made their appearance there by the thirteenth century. Although these lines are often found in groups of three a larger number is not in itself sufficient to suggest a later dating. This is evident from an examination of two fourteenth-century icons of very distinctive character and markedly individualistic styles. In one the light lines are chiefly grouped in threes (*pl. 165*) whilst in the other the lines are more numerous, but still concentrated to form areas of lighter coloured flesh tints (*pl. 166*). On both panels the Virgin's face is similarly shaped and is similar in expression yet the slightly pouting mouth is something new and of a kind hardly likely to be found prior to the later fourteenth century, and it is apt to acquire prominence in the fifteenth century. Both paintings possess a candour and directness that is first encountered in Russia in early Novgorodian work of post-Mongol invasion date, yet they are also present in a provincial Byzantine rendering of the Virgin and Child thought to be of fourteenth-century date (*pl. 167*); it too displays highlights in the form of parallel lines and eyebrows rendered in a strongly linear manner. The whites of the eyes are clearly marked, the eyes being accentuated by means of double pouches whilst the lips are allowed to protrude. On all three examples the prominent, half-moon-shaped shadows under the eyes help to broaden the long eyes, a device which did not come into general use before the fourteenth century. Prior to that, as in the case, for example, of the icon of the Virgin of Svensk (*pl. 86*), where the pouches are unusually prominent for so early a work, their purpose was to elongate the eye.

In the fourteenth century Muscovite artists engaged in painting monumental icons continued to strive closely to adhere to Byzantine prototypes. An icon of the Virgin Hodegetria in the Tretyakov Gallery (*pl. 168*) is a good representative of the style, but the grouping of the highlights on the Child's cheekbones together with a tendency to set the Virgin's eyes rather closer together than was formerly the custom suggest a date at the end of the fourteenth century rather than one in the earlier part of it.

The icon of the Virgin of the Don which most scholars ascribe to Theophanes the Greek (*pl. 107*) is universally assigned to the year 1392. On it pale highlights are reduced to a minimum, those that appear being concentrated round the eyes and on the chin where they take the form of parallel lines, whilst a single, small brush-stroke highlights the tip of the nose. However, the eyes of both figures are heavily underlined, those of the Virgin by one full-length curve designed to elongate them, then by a shorter curve intended to widen them. Whilst in most icons the second curved shadow either fails to merge with the dark modelling of the nose and cheek or else merges with that forming the side of the face, here it tends to link with the shadow extending along the right side of the nose and cheek; a parallel for this occurs on the rather earlier Byzantine icon of the Virgin Saviour of Souls (*pl. 158*).

In the early fifteenth century there was a proneness, already noted in the case of the late fourteenth-century icon (*pl. 168*) to narrow the space between the eyes so that, occasionally, an almost cross-eyed or squint effect was created; fortunately this style was soon abandoned. Later in the century (*pl. 125*) there was a tendency to return to the almond-shaped eye, often now outlined on the lid by two pale-coloured lines and under-

lined by two full-length, slightly curved ones. Now too foreheads were often highlighted and some modelling was introduced by means of a single, slightly curved brush stroke. The Virgin's face also began to acquire a certain flatness owing to the elimination of highlights on the cheekbones. These features had become fairly general by the end of the sixteenth century (*pl. 169*). Dionysy and his followers had by then introduced the markedly elongated figure, setting a fashion which reached the southern Slavs (*pl. 170*); in icons of the Virgin and Child it often resulted in Jesus being portrayed as an older child rather than as an infant, but this was by no means universal as is evident from a rather later version of the Virgin of Tikhvin (*pl. 171*). On the latter highlights take the form of patches formed by delicate brush strokes; they now appear on foreheads, round the eyes, on the nostrils, round mouths, on chins and also on necks. This icon is typical of the type of work being done in the seventeenth century by conservative artists whilst innovators such as Ushakov were extending the areas of lighter flesh tints along the sides of faces in an effort to blend the iconic style with the naturalistic as it appeared in Western woodcuts rather than in actual paintings (*pl. 172*).

Let us now consider some icons of the Annunciation. One belonging to the monastery of St Catherine, Sinai, is assigned by Weitzmann to the twelfth century (*pl. 173*). It is painted almost in grisaille and its style is strikingly unusual, as are certain details in its composition. Thus, although it was customary to present the scene against an architectural background, indicating by means of a hanging suspended between two buildings that it was taking place indoors, there is little suggestion of this in the present icon. Instead the Virgin's throne is placed beside a building where a curtain drawn back from a doorway serves the same purpose. In contrast to this, doubtless in order to symbolize the Archangel's celestial abode, his figure has the sky as a background—a detail which recurs in an icon of Ushakov's (*pl. 143*). The outlines of buildings, perhaps of a town, appear in the distance, their roofs being almost on a level with the feet of the two figures. A similar although far less extreme division of earth and sky recurs in the much later icon of St John (*pl. 151*). The foreground is occupied by a river epitomizing, according to Weitzmann, the description of the Virgin as a 'life-giving stream'. Water fowl swim in it and walk amidst the flowers growing on its bank. A similar Virgilian feeling for nature led the artist to depict a landscape or roof garden on the upper floor of the Virgin's house. Such an interest in nature is seldom encountered in icon painting; this is in fact not only a rare example of it, but a well-nigh unique one in an icon of such an early date. It cannot therefore serve as a guide to dating. Indications have to be sought in stylistic details, but here the remarkably characteristic faces of the two figures provide another difficulty for no other known icon portrays the Virgin as past her first youth, whereas here she appears as such, nor can a parallel be found for the Archangel's lean, stern face, tense figure and twisted pose. The clue lies in the agitated folds of his robe; such folds appear on a mural painting of the Annunciation at Kurbinovo in Yugoslavia, which is dated to 1191, and they also occur in a slightly modified form on a damaged mural of the same scene in the church of Hagia Sophia at Trebizond, where the frescoes are dated to the mid-thirteenth century on stylistic, technical and historical considerations.

A virtually contemporary icon of the Annunciation from Ochrid (*pl. 19*) follows the more conventional iconography, although the Virgin, who is seated at her spinning, is presented almost frontally instead of turned towards the Archangel who approaches from the left. The Virgin's long, pear-shaped face, aquiline nose, carefully worked eyes with their rounded pupils offset by whitish highlights and the regular eyebrows also conform to the period's characteristic style.

The Annunciation (*illustrated on pl. 8*) is among the finest Orthodox paintings of the scene to have come down to us. This superb Byzantine icon is permeated by the humanism characterizing Palaeologan art. The icon is very close in date to the mosaic panels in Kariye Camii at Istanbul and has much in common with them. On the icon the drapery which is slung between two buildings is given a subsidiary, largely decorative role. The Virgin's throne is placed almost on the building's threshold; it is backless, but stands beneath a portico which rests on the backs of two diminutive, Atlas-like figures squatting on the capitals topping two short columns. The inclusion of these figures is most surprising and can equally well be attributed to Western influence as to the Palaeologan interest in the culture of classical Greece. This detail, assessed in conjunction with the modelling in depth which distinguishes this painting, with its feeling for movement, with the proportions of its figures and that intangible element which determines a style point to the early fourteenth century as the panel's most likely date.

Three iconographic versions of the Annunciation were current in Russia from early times. One is represented by the Ustyug Annunciation (*pl. 174*), so called after the monastery near Novgorod for which it is thought to have been painted. Iconographically it is the least usual of the three for it shows the two figures standing side by side with a celestial ray symbolizing the immaculate conception pointing to the Christ-child in the Virgin's womb. This Novgorodian version must assuredly follow a Byzantine prototype. Although it is a most accomplished work the figures are heavier and squatter than would have been the case on a Byzantine painting of similar date. Nevertheless, the Archangel's draperies are handled in a way which suggests that the artist was acquainted with classical sculptures. The Archangel's face bears a close stylistic resemblance to the Novgorodian icon of the Golden-Headed Angel (*pl. 176*); both are attributed on stylistic grounds to the twelfth century. By the latter part of the sixteenth century this version of the Annunciation (*pl. 177*) was being presented against a very elaborate background which often included contemporary features, such as sculptured cornices, the dome which, on this painting, resembles those of the sixteenth-century cathedral of Basil the Blessed in Moscow's Red Square, and so on. Another relatively late feature—the breaking of the unconsciously yet universally accepted rule of the unity of time—is illustrated in this example by the inclusion in the icon's foreground of the cave in which the Child was later to be born.

The second iconographic version of the Annunciation is the more usual for it presents the Virgin, if not actually spinning, yet seated and with the Archangel approaching her from the left (*pl. 178*). On this example some of the buildings are linked by a drapery. The Virgin is youthful-looking, but seen to be overcome with apprehension on hearing the Archangel's tidings; he strides towards her, his feet scarcely touching the ground in his haste. Nevertheless his draperies are hardly ruffled by his speed. The buildings in the background are fairly complex in form and include two capitals displaying faces. This unusual detail, seen in conjunction with the architectural styles, with the method of highlighting the faces, the proportions of the figures and their relationship to the sizes of the heads, hands and feet point to a date towards the end of the fourteenth century as the more likely one for this painting.

The third iconographic version of the Annunciation is probably later in date than the two others for it appears to consist of a blend of both. It is found on a late Byzantine icon (*pl. 179*) which presents the two figures standing, not statically side by side, but rather as if the Virgin had just risen from her throne to meet the advancing Archangel. An icon in the museum at Novgorod follows the same iconography, but it also includes the ray symbolizing the immaculate conception, although not the unborn Child. The Archangel's heavy build, the graphic, slightly awkward and essentially decorative presentation of his wings and the highlights on the faces all point to a fifteenth-century date for this icon (*pl. 175*).

The two icons which have just been considered bear little relationship to the one painted in 1408 under the direction of Andrey Rublyov and Daniil Chorny for the Dormition Cathedral at Vladimir (*pl. 113*). They chose to follow the most usual iconography for their painting by showing the Virgin seated with the Archangel approaching her from the left. The buildings in the background, although conspicuous, are simplified in accordance with Rublyov's practice and the style, with its stress on delicacy and linear rhythm, is very much his own.

In the seventeenth century the architectural setting for the Annunciation became very elaborate. In 1652 Spiridon Timofeev, (*pl. 180*), was filling his background with buildings as multifarious as Piranesi's. He not only included the cave associated with the birth of Jesus in the foreground but also depicted the Almighty (shown full-length, which was unusual in early times) in the centre of the sky with the dove descending earthward. Later Ivan Maksimov (*pl. 181*), while retaining the figure of the Almighty and also that of the dove, was presenting the scene in a palatial interior remarkable for its marble slab floor, the baroque decorations of its wall and furniture, and the inclusion of a vase of tulips and carnations. Meanwhile Ushakov (*pl. 143*) was attempting to introduce more naturalistic-looking faces whilst depicting the scene with almost as few details as Rublyov had done. Westernization is even more strongly in evidence in the icon which Matveev, son of Bobyleov, painted in 1696 (*pl. 155*). He chose to give his Annunciation a Western setting, to clothe his figures in Western garments, to include such Western details as the dove and flowers, and to allow the naturalistic treatment to prevail over the iconic in his faces.

The painting of the Veronica or Holy Face which is preserved at Laon (*pl. 41*) and the Novgorodian rendering of the same subject (*illustrated on pl. 95*) are both the works of Slav artists of near contemporary date. It is clear that each followed the same prototype yet each treated it in accordance with his own temperament and outlook. The Laon Face conforms to the facial type of Christ associated with Byzantium's Second Golden Age, although on the icon the severity of expression seen in mosaics such as that at Daphni near Athens is replaced by one of pain and compassion. Regardless of the stress laid on symmetry its treatment is pictorial rather than linear. The almond-shaped pupils are set to the sides of the almond-shaped sockets, the eyes, forehead and cheekbones are highlighted, the colouring is dark. The Russian icon portrays a fair, it might be said a golden-headed Christ, and breaks free from the Byzantine idiom by the essentially graphic way in which the head is rendered. No highlights are used; instead the fused technique is employed to avoid any marked transition from light to shade. The colouring recalls that of the Golden-Headed Angel (*pl. 176*), the pronounced curve of the eyebrows closely resembles that of St Demetrius of Salonica (*pl. 87*), the shape of the eyes and the method of outlining them is the same as on the icon of the Golden-Headed Angel and on that of the Ustyug Annunciation (*pl. 174*). These characteristics suffice to assign the panel to the pre-Mongol invasion period, and more especially to the twelfth century. Its distinctive characteristics appear in a well-nigh contemporary version of the Veronica belonging to the Russian Museum at Leningrad. Another example, this time one belonging to the Tretyakov Gallery (*pl. 185*), has the face similarly outlined by a dark line but whilst the treatment is as graphic as that found in both the preceding icons, the pouches under the eyes have been rendered more geometrical, the eyes have been rounded and the mouth given more prominence. These features point to a slightly later date for this icon than that of the two previous examples, and one in the late thirteenth century is suggested for it by the cataloguers of the Tretyakov Gallery's icons.

At some stage, although it is as yet impossible to establish precisely when, a slightly different facial type came to be portrayed in Russia. The change affected the lower part of the face and resulted from the shaping of Christ's beard into a point with a slight cleft in it. The appearance of both the beard and the moustache has earned for this version the title of The Holy Face of the Wet Beard (*pl. 182*). The example illustrated here displays many fifteenth-century characteristics, notably the large, pouting lips, the elaborate modelling of the forehead, the limited use of highlights in the form of white lines, the inclusion of oval pupils, dark lids and the double underlining of the eyes. The eyes on the late fourteenth- or early fifteenth-century icon of the Prophet Elijah (*pl. 184*) are treated in a very similar manner although the sharp curve in the prophet's eyebrows suggests a slightly earlier date for the Elijah than the Veronica's. The extremely linear, almost geometric treatment of the eye pouches on another Novgorodian icon of the Veronica (*pl. 183*) would, if considered alone, suggest a fourteenth-century date for the icon, but this is a mannerist work and, notwithstanding its strongly graphic character and the somewhat archaic treatment of the eyes, the rather more detailed modelling of the forehead and the pouting mouth suggest a date early in the fifteenth century in preference to a slightly earlier one. The eye pouches receive very similar treatment in an obviously later icon of the Saviour in the Korin Collection, Moscow. The latter is assigned to the end of the fifteenth century.[1]

Few changes other than these are to be noted in most sixteenth-century versions of the Veronica and even in the seventeenth century the original outlines and features were still being closely followed although (*pl. 186*) by then the face had been shortened, the cheekbones highlighted and the forehead rounded. By the latter half of the century Ushakov (*pl. 140*) was to give the face an even more naturalistic appearance by extending the highlights along the sides of the cheeks, but like so many of the early artists he continued to outline its contours with a dark line.

The Old Testament Trinity became a favourite subject in Russia after Rublyov had painted his lovely version of the theme (*pl. 119*), but it had also been depicted in Byzantium and it is therefore interesting to compare a fourteenth-century Byzantine example in the Benaki Museum at Athens (*pl. 187*) with Rublyov's near contemporary one. In the Byzantine panel modelling of the faces is achieved by assembling pale, thin strokes into fan-shaped highlights on the cheekbones. Thick lines as well as thin ones indicate the folds of the draperies but the work is so delicate that it is more reminiscent of book illumination than of easel painting. The setting is very elaborate and elegant, and rich in detail. Although the buildings forming the background are fairly severe they destroy the pictorial space which is such an important feature of Rublyov's composition, yet their role is not a purely decorative one for they constitute an integral part of the composition. The angels, to quote Chatzidakis, have 'neutral faces', whilst Rublyov's angels have celestial ones. The differences between the two paintings are differences of personality, outlook and environment rather than of time.

In the Bulgarian version by Nedyalka (*pl. 45*) the device of indicating an interior by a drapery suspended from two buildings provides no clue to dating. The confused way in which the piece of furniture occupying the centre of the panel is rendered is a better guide, for its muddled appearance suggests that its original shape had become blurred during the passing centuries. The shape of the jug also serves to indicate a late sixteenth-century date and so too does the treatment of the angels' wings which, in the case of the two side angels, look almost like garments.

The artist responsible for the version in the Korin collection (*pl. 188*) was a follower of Rublyov's, but one working a century later than the master. The passage of time is reflected in the schematic treatment of the hills, in the elongation of the bodies of the two side angels and in the heaviness of the feet and hands. It is interesting to find Christ's initials appearing above the central angel's head, thus supporting the belief of present-day scholars that Rublyov intended the central angel in his icon of the Old Testament Trinity to symbolize Christ. On this later work in the Rublyov tradition the modelling of the faces corresponds to that current in Novgorod in the fifteenth century. The use of the fused technique in the faces and the more narrative treatment of the scene on an icon in the Tretyakov Gallery (*pl. 189*), together with the decorative appearance of the hills, the building's rounded porch, the proportions of the figures, and more especially the life-like expressions on the faces of Abraham and Sarah combine to indicate a mid-sixteenth-century date for this icon.

On stylistic grounds the painting illustrated in *pl. 128* could easily be assigned to the fifteenth century for it closely conforms to the Rublyov tradition yet the appearance of its buildings and the shape of its hills point to a somewhat later dating. The three panels which complete this icon confirm such a conclusion for they are painted in the style typical of Moscow at the dawn of the seventeenth century. The side panels are divided into several scenes. One panel (*pl. 190*) depicts the interior of Abraham and Sarah's house, which is in itself a late innovation. On the worshipper's left Abraham is shown asking Sarah to prepare a meal for their unexpected guests; on the right Sarah is seen kneading the dough whilst, in the centre, she is engaged in rolling it out. Members of her household are gathered in a room above the kitchen; this detail represents an adventurous experiment. The town stretches beyond them; its buildings include one which is roofed with the tent-shaped spire which was popular in Muscovy during the sixteenth century, although its diminutive dome rests on a drum rather in the manner of an egg in an egg cup. The rather subdued colours are attuned to the darker ones which characterize the years of dynastic troubles (1591–1613). The interest in genre and anatomy that is evident in this painting dates from the closing decades of the sixteenth century and was to become increasingly marked in the seventeenth.

In order to appreciate the stylistic changes which had occurred in the course of some three centuries or so it is helpful to compare Rublyov's version of the Old Testament Trinity with Ushakov's (*pl. 142*). Ushakov was too sensitive an artist to encumber his painting with subsidiary details likely to detract from the subject's mystical significance and therefore, like Rublyov, he included in it only the bare essentials, yet he provided his angels with faces which are almost naturalistic in appearance. Less sensitive seventeenth-century artists tended to mar their renderings of the theme by an excess of detail, scattering vegetation in the landscape, providing Abraham and Sarah with a large house designed on seventeenth-century lines, seating the angels at an ornate table and serving them from vessels of seventeenth-century shape (*pl. 191*). Such panels often possess a decorative quality which is not devoid of charm, but the lack of unity and balance, the intrusion of worldliness, the incompatibility of the iconic and naturalistic traditions and the inclusion of numerous only indirectly related scenes detract from an icon's quality.

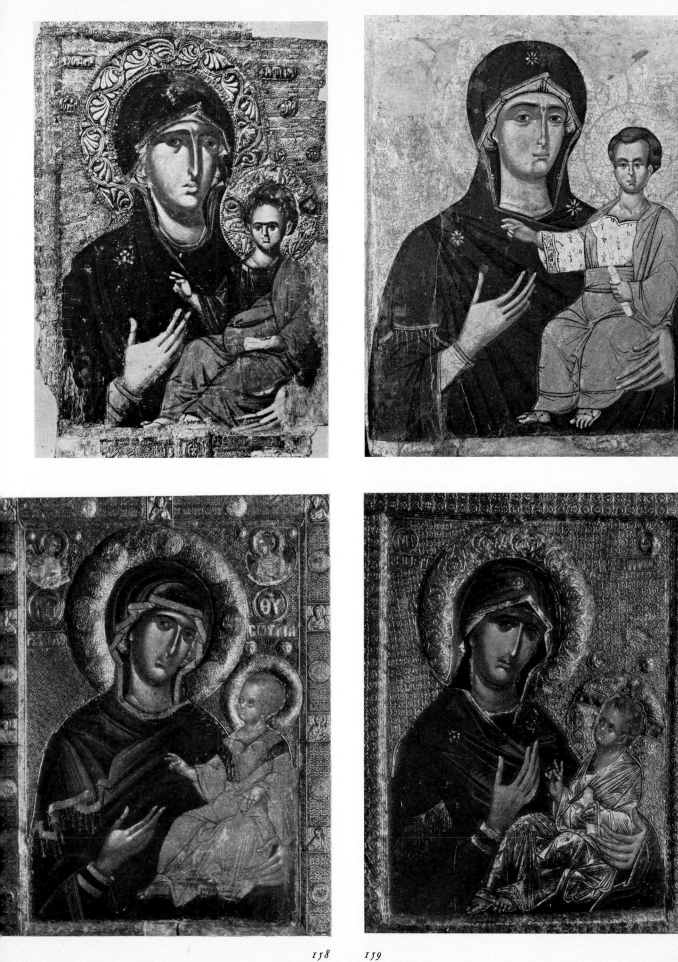

173

174

175

177

176

178

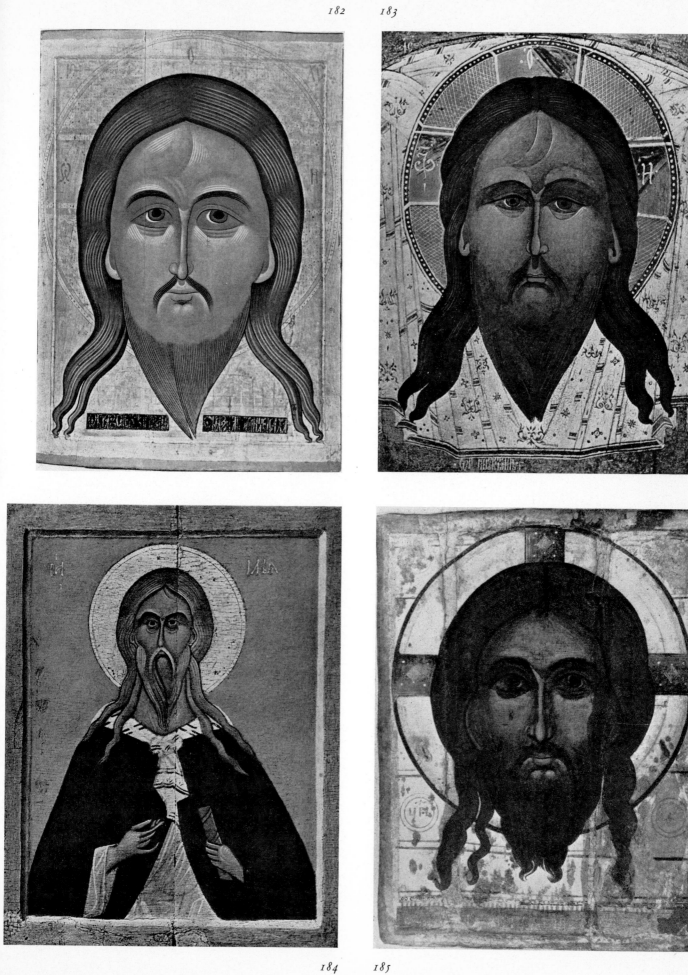

189 190

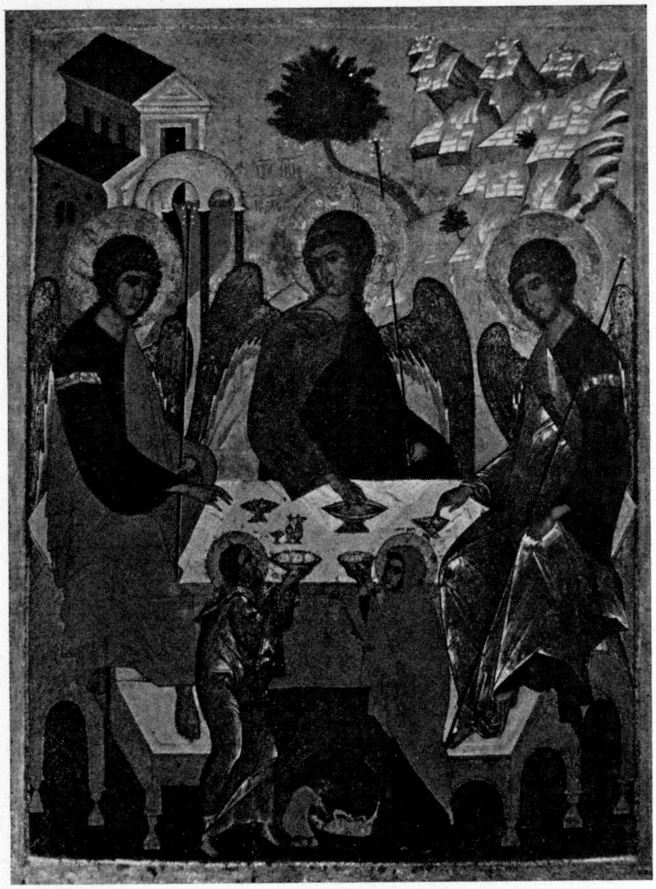

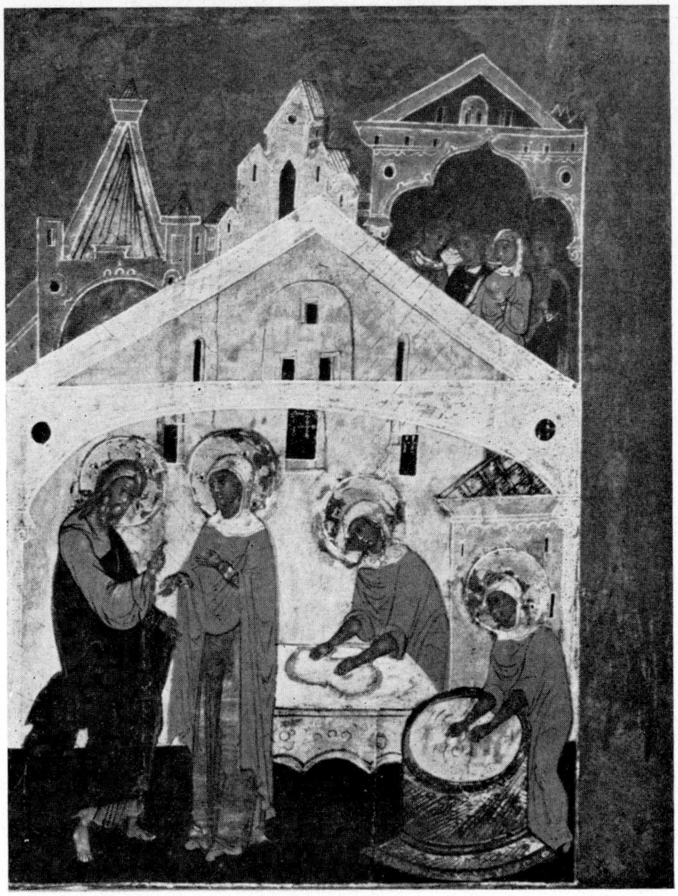

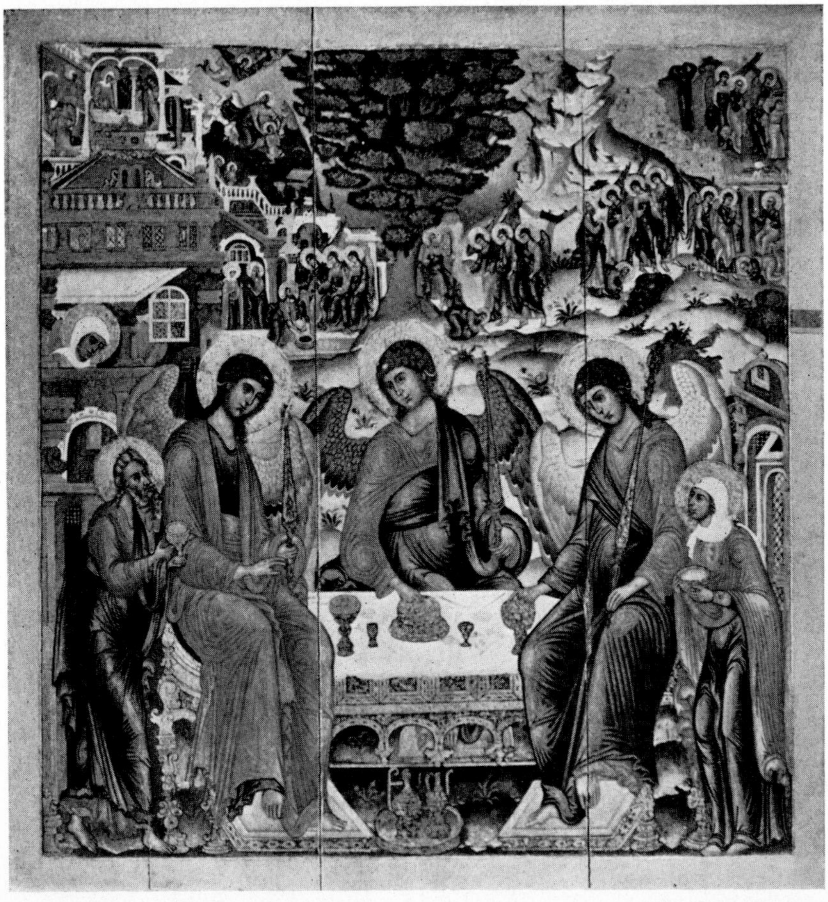

191

156 The Virgin Hodegetria
Double-sided icon with *the Crucifixion* on the reverse
The National Museum, Ochrid.
37 × 23 cm.
Early 14th century

Icons, pl. 178.

157 Virgin and Child Hodegetria
The National Gallery of Ireland, Dublin, cat. no. 2.
82 × 63 cm.
Early 15th century

158 Virgin and Child
The Annunciation is on the reverse
The National Museum, Ochrid.
94.5 × 80.3 cm.
Probably c. 1310. (See Pl. 8a)

Icons, pl. 159.

159 The Virgin Perebleptos
The Purification of Mary is on the reverse
From the church of the Virgin Perebleptos, Ochrid.
Now in the National Museum, Ochrid.
32.5 × 26 cm.
14th century

Icons, pl. 171.

160 Virgin and Child
The Byzantine Museum, Athens.
33.5 × 25.5 cm.
14th century

Icons, pl. 58.

161 Double-sided icon with the *Virgin and Child* on one side
Now in the Phaneromeni collection, Nicosia.
14th century

Published by permission of the Director of Antiquities and the Cyprus Museum

162 The Virgin Hodegetria with two archangels in medallions above, *St Michael* on the spectator's left
San Giorgio dei Greci, Venice.
11.1 × 79 cm.
Post-1574
Signed XEIR MIX . . . DAMAZKYNOY in gold under Christ's right foot.

Venice, pl. 27.

163 (Colour plate IX) *Virgin and Child* with, on the margins, *the Baptist and twelve Prophets*
The National Gallery of Ireland, Dublin, cat. no. 1.
140.5 × 110.5 cm, width of margins 20 cm.
14th and 15th centuries

164 Virgin and Child
Tretyakov Gallery, Moscow.
102 × 85 cm.
School of Novgorod, but with inscriptions in Greek.
14th century

Antonova/Mneva, Vol. 1, no. 19.

165 Virgin of Petrov
Formerly in the Riabushinsky collection. Now in the Tretyakov Gallery, Moscow.
23 × 17 cm.
School of Novgorod. 14th century

Antonova/Mneva, Vol. 1, no. 20.

166 Virgin Hodegetria
Presented by Prince Tumen in 1591 to the Troitse-Sergeyeva Lavra. Now in the Tretyakov Gallery, Moscow.
39 × 31 cm.
School of Rostov-Suzdal. 14th century

Antonova/Mneva, Vol. 1, no. 169.

167 Virgin and Child
Benaki Museum, Athens.
32.5 × 23 cm.
Anatolian school. 14th century

Icons, pl. 53.

168 Virgin Hodegetria with two archangels in the upper corners
From the Troitse-Sergeyeva Lavra. Now in the Tretyakov Gallery, Moscow.
40 × 32 cm.
Moscow school. Late 14th century

The silver oklad is of contemporary Byzantine workmanship. The busts represent the Apostles Peter and Paul, the four Evangelists, Cosmas and Damian. The full-length figures are those of the Byzantine courtier Constantine Acropolitos (late 13th–early 14th century) and his wife. The figure in the bottom margin is that of Panteleimon.

Antonova/Mneva, Vol. 1, no. 221.

169 Virgin and Child
The Icon Museum, Recklinghausen.
Moscow school. Late 16th century

170 Virgin Hodegetria
The Icon Museum, Recklinghausen.
Serbian school. Mid-16th century

171 Virgin of Tikhvin
The Icon Museum, Recklinghausen.
Armoury School, Moscow. Mid-17th century

172 Virgin of Vladimir and the family tree of Moscow's rulers
By Simon Ushakov.
Tretyakov Gallery, Moscow.
105 × 62 cm.
1668

The walls of Moscow's Kremlin as seen from Red
Square occupy the lower part of the panel; beyond them
Ivan Kalita is seen planting a large tree with the Metro-
politan Peter watering it. The tree rises through the
roof of the Dormition Cathedral to display on its
branches medallions containing, in the largest the Virgin
of Vladimir and, on the left, the Tsarevich Dmitri,
Tsar Feodor Ivanovich and Tsar Mikhail Feodorovich,
the patriarch Filaret, the patriarch Job, the Muscovite
Metropolitans Philip, Photius, John, Cyprian and
Alexei; on the right are shown God's fools Ivan and
Basil, Parfunty of Borovsk, St Sergius of Radonezh,
Nikon of Radonezh and Prince Alexander Nevsky.
Below them, within the Kremlin's walls, are, to the
left the kneeling figure of Tsar Alexei with, opposite,
those of his wife and the Tsareviches Alexei and Feodor.
Christ appears at the top of the icon, as do the two
archangels.
Antonova/Mneva, Vol. 2, no. 912.

173 The Annunciation
Monastery of St Catherine, Sinai.
29.5 × 16.5 cm.
Late 12th century
Icons, pl. 30.

174 The Ustyug Annunciation
Formerly in the Dormition Cathedral, Moscow. Now in
the Tretyakov Gallery, Moscow.
229 × 144 cm.
School of Novgorod. Probably between 1119–30.
Onasch, pl. 15. Antonova/Mneva, Vol. 1, no. 4

175 The Annunciation, with St Theodore Stratelates
Novgorod Museum.
2 × 1.5 m.
School of Novgorod. 14th century
Onasch, pl. 23.

176 The Golden-Headed Angel, part of a Deesis group
The Russian Museum, Leningrad.
48 × 39 cm.
Mid to late 12th century.

Lazarev, 2, pl. 10.

177 An Annunciation of the Ustyug type
Formerly in the Morozov Collection. Now in the Tretyakov Gallery, Moscow.
32 × 27 cm.
Late 16th century

Antonova/Mneva, Vol. 2. no. 605.

178 The Annunciation
From the Troitse-Sergeyeva Lavra. Now in the Tretyakov Gallery, Moscow.
43 × 34 cm.
Moscow School. Late 14th century.

Onasch, pl. 81

179 The Annunciation
The Icon Museum, Recklinghausen.
Byzantine. First half of 15th century.

180 The Annunciation
By Spiridon Timofeev
The Tretyakov Gallery, Moscow.
39 × 34 cm.
Stroganov School. 1652

Antonova/Mneva, Vol. 2, no. 801.

181 The Annunciation
By Ivan Maksimov
The Tretyakov Gallery, Moscow.
67 × 71 cm.
Armoury School. 1670

Onasch, pl. 140.

182 The Saviour of the Wet Beard
Formerly in the Morozov Collection
The Tretyakov Gallery, Moscow.
128 × 91.5 cm.
School of Novgorod. 15th century

Antonova/Mneva, Vol. 1, no. 121.

183 Veronica
Formerly in the Ostroukhov Collection.
School of Novgorod. 15th century

184 The Prophet Elijah
The Tretyakov Gallery, Moscow.
75 × 57 cm.
School of Novgorod. Late 14th or early 15th century

Lazarev 2, pl. 25.

185 Veronica
The Tretyakov Gallery, Moscow.
89 × 70 cm.
School of Rostov-Suzdal. Late 13th century

Antonova/Mneva, Vol. 1, no. 161.

186 The Veronica and 'Weep not for me, Mother'
The Russian Museum, Leningrad.
School of Moscow. Mid 17th century

187 Old Testament Trinity
Benaki Museum, Athens.
13 × 23.5 cm.
Byzantine school. Late 14th century

Icons, pl. 78.

188 Old Testament Trinity
The Korin Collection, Moscow.
48 × 36.5 cm.
School of Novgorod. 14th–15th century

Onasch, pl. 30.

189 Old Testament Trinity
Tretyakov Gallery, Moscow.
164 × 126 cm.
School of Rostov-Suzdal. Mid to late 16th century.

Antonova/Mneva, Vol. 2, no. 398.

190 Interior of the house of Abraham and Sarah
One of the three remaining side panels. The Tretyakov
Gallery, Moscow.
159 × 29 cm.
The side panel *c.* 1600.

Antonova/Mneva, Vol. 2, no. 547.

191 Old Testament Trinity with subsidiary scenes
Tsar's iconographers.
The Tretyakov Gallery, Moscow.
133 × 127 cm.

The foreground of the icon is devoted to the main
theme, that of the Old Testament Trinity. It shows the
three angels seated at table, attended by Abraham and
Sarah with wine vessels set in the space often occupied
by the scene showing a servant killing the fatted calf.
The left upper portion of the icon depicts Abraham's
splendid house. Sarah is seen below, looking on the
diners, above preparing their meal and, to the right, in
the porch, being instructed by Abraham to do so. To the
right of the porch Abraham is seen washing his guests'
feet and, above, sacrificing. The space to the right of the
oak illustrates the story of Lot.

Onasch, pl. 141.

NOTES ON THE TEXT

Chapter One

1 Grant Allen, *Evolution in Art*, London, p. 146.
2 'On some icons of the seventh century', in *Late Classical and Medieval Studies in Honour of A. M. Friend*, Princeton 1955, ed. K. Weitzmann, p. 136. For the first publication see Pico Cellini, 'Una Madonna molto antica', in *Proporzioni*, Florence, 1950, no. 3.
3 N. P. Kondakov, *Iconography of the Virgin*, St Petersburg, 1914, Vol. I, pl. III and fig. 90.
4 Now in the Museum of Western Art, Kiev.
5 *Icons*, pl. 3.
6 *Icons*, pl. 9.
7 G. Sotiriou, *Icônes du Mont Sinai*, Athens, 1956, pl. 34.
8 *Icons*, pl. 11.
9 *Icons*, pls. 15 and 21.
10 Sotiriou, *op. cit.*, pl. 47.
11 Sotiriou, *op. cit.*, pls. 43–45; *Icons*, pls. 22, 23.
12 Sotiriou, *op. cit.*, pls. 54, 55.
13 Sotiriou, *op. cit.*, pls. 76, 77.
14 Sotiriou, *op. cit.*, pl. 30.
15 *Icons*, p. XXIV.
16 *Icons*, pls. 44, 45.
17 *Icons*, pl. 47.
18 Sotiriou, *op. cit.*, pls. 126–52.
19 F. E. Hyslop, 'A Byzantine Reliquary of the True Cross from the Sancta Sanctorum', *Art Bulletin*, XVI, 1934, p. 4333 ff.
20 *Icons*, pl. 42.
21 Sotiriou, *op. cit.*, pl. 165.
22 Sotiriou, *op. cit.*, pls. 157–203.
23 Milković-Pepek, 'Les auteurs de quelques Icônes d'Ochrid du XIII–XIV siècle, Mihailo ou Eutychie', in *Glasnik*, I, Skopje, 1954, pp. 23–50.
24 See D. Talbot Rice, *The Art of Byzantium*, London, 1958, pl. XXXIV, or *Byzantine Art*, London, Pelican Books, 1968, fig. 320.
25 Sotiriou, *op. cit.*, pl. 224.
26 D. Talbot Rice, *The Art of Byzantium*, pl. XXXV.
27 *Byzantine Art—A European Art*, Athens, 1964, nos. 200 and 201. That from Mitilini is illustrated.
28 *Op cit.*, no. 186.
29 P. Mijović, 'Les icônes avec les portraits de Toma Preljubović et de Marie Paleologina', in *Recherches sur l'art*, 2, Belgrade, 1966 (in Serbo-Croat with brief summary in French).
30 For a full discussion of the problem of the inclusion of portraits of the living in religious scenes see Tania Velmans, 'Le Portrait dans l'art des Palaeologues' in *Byzance sous les Palaeologues*, Institut Hellénique des Études Byzantines à Venise no. 4, Venice, 1971, especially p. 121.
31 P. Uspensky, *Travels to the Monastery of the Meteora in Thessaly in 1859*, St Petersburg, 1896, p. 130 (in Russian).
32 The case for Bulgaria has been put by Miatev in *Icons*, p. XLVII, and S. Bossilkov, *Twelve Icons from Bulgaria*, Sofia, 1966, p. 6, while S. Radojčić claims it for Yugoslavia, *Icônes de Serbie et de Macédoine*, pls. 58 and 59.
33 *Icons*, pl. 77.
34 'New monuments of Byzantine Painting of the XIV Century', in *Vyzantinsky Vremenik*, IV, 1951, p. 122 (in Russian).
35 *Iconography of Christ*, St Petersburg, 1905, p. 79, pl. I (in Russian).
36 *Venice*, pl. 1.

Chapter Two

1 *Icons*, pl. 157.
2 See especially P. Milković-Pepek, *L'Œuvre de Michel et Eutychios*, Skopje, 1967, pp. 23–50. (Text in Serbo-Croat with a summary in French.) See also 'L'Évolution des Maîtres Michel Astrapas et Eutychios comme peintres d'Icônes', in *Jahrbuch der Österreichischen Byzantinischen Gesellschaft*, XVI, 1967, p. 297.
3 V. J. Djurić, *Icônes de Yougoslavie*, Belgrade, 1961, nos. 20 and 21 and p. 16. See also K. Balabanov, *Icons of Macedonia*, Skopje, 1969, pl. 3 and p. XL.
4 Djurić, p. 18.
5 *L'Œuvre des peintres Michel et Eutychie*, Skopje, 1967.
6 *Icons*, p. lxvi.
7 Balabanov, p. XII.
8 Djurić, pp. 20 ff.
9 Djurić, pp. 20 ff.
10 Even so they are not truly Byzantine, as is evident if they are compared to such a typically Byzantine product as an icon of the Baptism now at Belgrade, which is reproduced by Radojćić in *Icons* (pl. 175). Here the colours are brighter and more polished and the general effect much more enamel-like.
11 Djurić, pl. 16.
12 Djurić, pls. 17 and 18.
13 *Icônes de Serbie et de Macédoine*, pl. 37.
14 *Op. cit.*, pls. 33, 38 and 39. He reproduces the St John in colour. See also Djurić, pls. 30–33.
15 'Die Serbische Ikonenmalerei vom 12. Jahrhundert bis zum Jahre 1459', in *Jahrbuch der Österreichischen Byzantinischen Gesellschaft*, V, 1956, p. 78 and fig. 18. For the Athens icon see G. Sotiriou, *Guide de Musée Byzantin*, Athens, 1932, no. 100, fig. 55, or Sotiriou and Hadjinicolaou, *Guide*, pl. XVIII.
16 *Icônes de Serbie et de Macédoine*, pls. 44, 47 and 48 respectively.
17 Djurić, no. 36.
18 'Deux images de la Vierge dans un manuscrit Serbe' in *Art Byzantin chez les Slaves*, I, Paris, 1930, pp. 264 ff. For the Sinai icon see G. Sotiriou, *Icônes du Mont Sinai*, I, Athens, 1956, p. 235.
19 Balabanov, pl. 61.
20 Balabanov, pl. 62.
21 Djurić, no. 54.
22 Djurić, no. 53.
23 Balabanov, pl. 63.
24 Djurić, pl. 72.
25 Radojčić, *Les Maîtres de l'ancienne Peinture Serbe*, Belgrade, 1955, pl. XLIV.
26 *Les Maîtres de l'ancienne Peinture Serbe*, pl. LII.
27 Radojčić, *Icons*, pls. 210, 211, 213 and 217.
28 Djurić, pls. 84 and 85.
29 *Loc. cit.*, pls. XLVI, LIV, LV, LVI and colour plate F.
30 Djurić, pls. 70, 71 and 81.
31 For a full study of painting in the Catholic areas of the Adriatic littoral see M. L. Karaman, 'Notes sur l'art Byzantin et les Slaves Catholiques de Dalmatie' in *Art Byzantin chez les Slaves*, II, 2, Paris, 1932, especially pp. 355 ff.

Chapter Three

1 *Icons*, pl. 97.
2 N. P. Kondakov, *The Iconography of Christ* (in Russian), St Petersburg, 1906, p. 23 and pl. B. For an excellent coloured reproduction of one of these see *Art Treasures in Russia*, Paul Hamlyn, 1971, fig. 53.
3 See W. P. Gerhard, *The World of Icons*, London, 1971, p. 118, pl. 33.
4 'La Sainte Face de Laon', *Seminarium Kondakovianum*, Prague, 1931.
5 *Icons*, p. xlvii.
6 A. Grabar, *La Peinture religieuse en Bulgarie*, Paris, 1928, pl. 1.
7 *Icons*, pls. 99–100.
8 *Icons*, pls. p. xlix.
9 The actual date is 7106 after the creation of the world. This system was in common use at the time, for calculating dates. See S. Bossilkov, *Twelve Icons from Bulgaria*, Sofia, 1966, no. viii.

Chapter Four

1 *Icons*, pl. 37.
2 A. Bank, *Byzantine Art in the Collections of the USSR*, Leningrad-Moscow, 1967, no. 233.
3 *Icons*, pls. 55 and 65, pp. xxxi and xxxiii.
4 O. Wulff and M. Alpatov, *Denkmäler der Ikonenmalerei*, Leipzig, 1925, aff. 101, pp. 241 and 293.
5 *Venice*, no. 6.
6 Xyngopoulos, pl. 6.
7 M. Chatzidakis, 'The painter Euphrosynos', in *Critica Chronica* I, 1956, p. 273 (in Greek).
8 *Venice*, pl. 48.
9 *Venice*, pl. 31.
10 *Venice*, pls. 50 and 51.
11 *Venice*, pls. 52 and 53.
12 Xyngopoulos, pl. 7.
13 *Venice*, pl. 66.
14 *Venice*, pl. 67.
15 *Venice*, pl. 55.
16 *Venice*, pl. 56.
17 Xyngopoulos, pl. 14.
18 Djurić, pl. 59.
19 Xyngopoulos, pl. 18.
20 No. 216.
21 Xyngopoulos, pl. 19.
22 No. 325.
23 N. P. Likhachev, *Materialy dlia istorii russkago ikonopisaniya*; atlas snimkov, chast' I. no. 105, St Petersburg, 1906.
24 Included in C. T. Seltman, *Exhibition of Greek Art*, Royal Academy of Arts, London, 1947, as no. 363.
25 *Venice*, no. 62.
26 Xyngopoulos, pls. 21, 22 and 20.
27 *Venice*, pl. 70.
28 Xyngopoulos, pls. 27 and 29.
29 *Venice*, pl. 107.
30 Nos. 329, 261, 265.
31 *Venice*, pls. 120, 121 and 122.
32 No. 328.
33 *Venice*, pls. 128 and 129.
34 Xyngopoulos, pl. 23.
35 Djurić, pl. 64.
36 No. 379.
37 Xyngopoulos, pl. 42.

Chapter Five

1 D. Talbot Rice, *The Icons of Cyprus*, London, 1937, nos. 1, 2 and 4. A. Papageorgiou, *Icons of Cyprus*, London, 1969, pp. 34 and 35. These books are hereafter referred to as Rice and Pap.
2 C. Mango and E. J. Hawkins, 'The Hermitage of St Neophytos', in *Dumbarton Oaks Papers*, no. 20, Washington, 1966, p. 201 and figs. 54 to 57.
3 See Rice, no. 9 for the fragment, Pap. p. 38 for the two complete panels.
4 Rice, pl. 11.
5 Rice, pl. 64.
6 *Ikonensammlung Amberg, Städtische Kunsthalle Recklinghausen*, Dec. 1960–Jan. 1963, p. 15.
7 Pap., p. 91.
8 'Crusader Icons on Mount Sinai', in *Transactions of the XII International Congress of Byzantine Studies*, vol. III, Belgrade, 1964.
9 Rice, pl. 102.
10 No. 208.
11 Rice, pl. 58.
12 Rice, pl. 14; Pap., p. 109.
13 Rice, pls. 17, 22, 101; Pap., pp. 103, 93.
14 Pap., p. 96.
15 Rice, pl. 46.

16 Rice, pl. 23; Pap., p. 102.
17 Rice, pl. 108.
18 Rice, pl. 82; Pap., p. 110.
19 Papageorgiou, p. 108, gives the date as 1559, but this is surely an incorrect reading.
20 *The Iconography of the Virgin* (in Russian), St Petersburg, 1914, Vol. II, p. 316.
21 Rice, pl. 57; Pap., p. 74.
22 See Rice, *The Icons of Cyprus*, nos. 35, 34, 36, 37 and 38. For a full discussion of the patterned materials see Ch. VI and text figures 30–40.

Chapter Six

1 Kondakov, *Russkaya Ikona*, Prague, 1931, Part I, v. 3, text pp. 14 and 15, ill. p. 11.
2 I. Grabar, *O drevnerusskom iskusstve*, Moscow, 1966, p. 236.
3 T. Talbot Rice, *Concise History of Russian Art*, London, 1963, pl. 144.
4 T. Talbot Rice, *op. cit.*, pl. 121.
5 D. S. Likhachev, *Chelovek v literature drevnei Rusi*, Moscow/Leningrad, 1958, p. 168.
6 N. P. Likhachev, *Istoricheskoe Znachenie Italo-Grecheskoy Ikonopisi*, St Petersburg, 1911.
7 They provide a very full bibliography of all the icons published in the catalogue.
8 'Ikonen aus Polen', Recklinghausen Museum, 1966, nos. 77 and 79.
9 The prototype—a twelfth-century painting—is now undergoing restoration and cannot be photographed.
10 Antonova/Mneva, Vol. 1, no. 6, pp. 65 and 66, ill. 22–5 n. 4.
11 *Istoriya*, I, p. 496.
12 Historical Museum, Moscow, Khlud. 187, f. 1.
13 The icons from Vasili's iconostasis in the cathedral of St Sophia are undergoing restoration and cannot be photographed at present. For a full discussion of the doors and illustrations see V. N. Lazarev, *Russkaya srednevekovaya zhivopis*, Moscow, 1970, pp. 179–215.
14 With Prokhor of Gorodetz and Andrey Rublyov in 1405.
15 Church of the Archangel in the Kremlin, built in 1399.
16 According to the Troitskaya Chronicle for the year 1395 this was the church of the Virgin's Birth, where some of the murals were executed by Andrey Rublyov, Daniil Chorny and their pupils.
17 For the column see E. H. Minns and N. P. Kondakov, *The Russian Icon*, Oxford University Press, 1927, pl. 26, p. 116.
18 Antonova/Mneva, Vol. 1, pp. 253–4, place his birth in about 1340.
19 Antonova/Mneva, Vol. 1, no. 176.
20 Antonova/Mneva, Vol. 1, nos. 274–9, pp. 329–41, ills. 214–25.
21 Antonova/Mneva, Vol. 1, no. 107, ill. 75 and *Art Treasures of Russia*, Paul Hamlyn, London, 1970, ill. 128.
22 Catalogue of Recklinghausen Icon Museum, no. 71.
23 Among the minor Stroganov artists of importance who made a practice of signing their icons are Stepan Afanasiev, Semeon Borozdin, Stepan Pakhiria, Mikhaila, Pervusha, Ivan Sobol and Spiridon Timofeev. The Tretyakov Gallery possesses examples of their work.
24 For a specimen of Khitrovo's taste see the icon of St Sergius of Radonezh which he presented in 1673 to the Troitse-Sergeyeva Lavra in N. P. Likhachev, *Materialy dlia istorii russkago ikonopisania*, Vol. 1, St Petersburg 1906, ill. CCXCIX, no. 560, also pl. 141 in this volume.

Chapter Seven

1 See V. I. Antonova, *Drevne russkoye iskusstvo v sobranii Pavla Korina*, Moscow 1966, no. 23, ill. 43.

APPENDIX I

Recorded icon painters

(Other artists whose names are known through written sources or through signed works)

AGAPETOS, Michael, early 18th century

Agarastos, Antonios, 1595–1625?

Allovi, Guiseppo, icon of the Virgin and Child in the Delaporte Collection, Athens

Ambrosios, a monk of the 15th century. Is he the same as Ambrogio Monacos? See S. Bettini, *Pitture Cretesi-Veneziane, Slave et Italiane del Museo Nazionale di Ravenna*, 1940, p. 23

Ananias, a monk; an icon dated 1558 in the church of A. Paragonitissa, Arta

Andriapolites, Constantine; icon no. 63 in the Benaki Museum, Athens

Andronikos, ? c. 15th century. See C. Diehl, *Manuel d'Art Byzantin*, Paris, 1925, p. 766

Andronos, ? 17th century

Angelos of Crete, 1604. Robert Byron and David Talbot Rice found icons by him in the Greek Church, Cairo. See their *Birth of Western Painting*, London, 1930, p. 148

Antakos, Stamatos, after 1521

Anthimos, a monk, 1634; is he the same as the wall painter of 1645 of that name?

Apakas, John, a contemporary of Tsanfurnari; an icon at the Lavra on Mount Athos and at San Giorgio dei Greci, Venice, nos. 79 and 80.

Apocaucos, Alexios, went from Constantiniple to Crete in 1421. *Icons*, p. xxxvi

BARDAVAS, Jeremiah, 17th century? Loverdos collection, Athens

Basilikos, Antonios, 1629

Basilikos, ?, an icon of St Philip dated 1528 at Oinodos, Cyprus

Basilios, a Greek working in Italy who, with Eustathios, signed paintings at Carpignano dated 959

Basilius, ? ; he signed a miniature in the Psalter of Melisanda, British Museum, Egerton 1139; c. 1140

Basybozes, John, of Chios, 1502–87; studied on Mount Athos. See *Burlington Magazine*, 1919, 35, p. 102

Biagiakis, Michael, 17th century?

Bizamenos, Donatos, brother of Angelos; an icon of the Visitation in the Vatican Museum, Rome

Bores, Antonios, 1636–59

CALIERGIS, described as Thessaly's best painter; in 1315 he signed works in a small church at Veria, near Salonica. See *Izvestiya Russkogo Instituta v Konstantinopole*, 1898, IV, p. 129

Callinicos, 15th century; icon no. 161 in the Byzantine Museum, Athens

Canzo, Mark, of Candia; noted at Venice in 1534

Chrysoloras, ? , icon of a Baptism, c. 1550, in former Selltman collection

Clotzata, George, c. 1590; two works in the Vatican Museum, Rome

Constantakes, ? , 1687

DANIEL, Ieromonachos, late 15th century; icon of St John the Baptist in the Delaporte Collection, Athens

Danilo, a Serb; icons of 1664

Demetrios of Pera, worked in Genoa c. 1371. See N. P. Kondakov, *Russkaya Ikona*, Prague, 1931, Vol. 3, p. 158

Demetrios, the Zographos, worked in Suzdal and Moscow c. 1385; Kondakov, *op. cit.*, p. 47

Demetrios, a monk, 16th century

Demetrios, ? , 17th century

Demesianos, Theodore, 17th century

Digenis, Xenos, went from Mistra to Crete in 1461. *Icons*, p. xxxvi

Disalvatore, George, a Constantinopolitan who worked in Ferrara c. 1404. Kondakov, *op. cit.*, p. 158

Dominikos, John, worked in Venice early in the 16th century

Doxanitos or Doxavas Panagioti, who may have been the father of Nicholas; an icon of 1660 by the former is in the Delaporte Collection, Athens

Dracopoulos, John, 1580

Dracopoulos, J., at Venice in c. 1600

Drino of Edessa who worked in Italy c. 1330. Kondakov, *op. cit.*, p. 158

EMMANUEL, two icons of his are praised in verses in the Codex 527 Barberini

Emmanuel, painter of icons at Trikkala, Meteora in 1684

Emporios, Beninos, a Last Supper of 1606 in San Giorgio dei Greci, Venice, no. 70

Eugenikos, Manuel, of Constantinople, who worked in Georgia 1384–96. See N. Tolmatchevsky, *Les fresques de l'ancienne Géorgie*, Tiflis, 1931, pp. 27–9

Euphrosynos of Dionysiou on Mount Athos; signed icons in 1542. Chatzidakis, *Crit. Chron.*, X, 1956, p. 273

Eustathios, 14th century. See A. L. Frothingham, *American Journal of Archaeology*, IX, 1894, p. 48

GABALLAS, George, *c.* 1650. Kondakov, *op. cit.*, p. 158

Gastrei, 15th-century Peloponnese painter. Kondakov, *op. cit.*, p. 158

George the Cretan, 14th century. Kondakov, *op. cit.*, p. 158

George of Constantinople. He was in Venice in 1396 and Ferrara in 1404. Frothingham, *op. cit.*, p. 50

Grammatikopoulos, Manuel, 1571

Gregorios, *c.* 1350; he signed royal doors in the Grüneisen collection, Paris

Gremianis, Nicholas, at Venice 1578

IOANNIKOS, worked in Athens *c.* 1600

Ioannikos, signed work at Nisou, Cyprus, in 1670 and 1678

Isias, a Greek who worked in Novgorod in 1338. Kondakov, *op. cit.*, p. 47

JEREMIAS of Crete, a 16th-century icon in the Greek church at Cairo

John the Cretan, worked in Crete 1314–32. Kondakov, *op. cit.*, p. 158

John; the painter of a 13th–14th century icon of the Presentation in the Vatican Museum, Rome

John; worked in Suzdal and Moscow in 1345. Kondakov, *op. cit.*, p. 47

John the Ieromonachos, painted an encaustic icon of St George in the Viano Belvedere, Crete, in 1401. G. Gerola, *Monumati di Ravenna Byzantinos*, Milan, p. 309

John the priest, worked in 1621 in the Meteora district

KAIROPHYLAS, Ioannes of Zacynthos, *c.* 1600

Kairophylas, Peter, was in Crete in 1589

Kakavas, Demetrios, was in Nauplia 1590–1607

Kakavas, Theodosios, was in Naupactus in 1565

Kalerges, Nicholas, the Cretan, 1669

Kalogheras, John, worked in Venice in 16th–early 17th centuries

Kalonas, Cosmas, 16th century

Kanachios, ?, 1621

Kareklas, Nicholas, 17th century

Katellanos, Francos, 1560

Katephores, Paisias, 1657

Kaverzas, Franghias, a follower of Klotzas; 17th century. Painted icon no. 59 at San Giorgio dei Greci, Venice

Kontonis, Antonios, signed a Presentation in the Temple of 1530 in the Benaki Museum, Athens

Koronias, Michael, 17th century

Korensios, Belisarios, 1641

Kortexas, George, signed a Martyrdom of St Demetrius, no. 9 in the Benaki Museum, Athens

Kontogiannes, Nicholas, 1645

Koumis, Nicholas, at Venice in 1600

Krassas, Stephen, 17th century

Krides, Johannes, 1682

Kyprios, Johannes, studied under Tintoretto, but painted in the Byzantine style; some of his paintings are dated 1585 and 1589; see icon no. 9 in the Benaki Museum, Athens

LAMBROS, the painter, 1622

Lamprados, Emmanuel, 1598–1640. He is represented in San Giorgio dei Greci, Venice

Lampsa, Manuel, a signed icon is mentioned by Kondakov, *op. cit.*, p. 159

Laodicea, presumably a woman, worked in Paria *c.* 1330. Kondakov, *op. cit.*, p. 158

Lekharkhos, 17th century

Lombardos, Ioannes, early 17th-century icon of St Gregory the Theologian, no. 18 in the Benaki Museum, Athens

Lombardos, Joachim, *c.* 1602; mentioned in documents in the archives at Zante. Kondakov, *op. cit.*, p. 224

Lombardos, Peter, early 17th-century icon, no. 19 in the Benaki Museum, Athens

Lubrina, George, of Candia, known in Venice in 1546

MAKARIOS; he is mentioned in the verses of Manuel Philos, *c.* 14th century. Kondakov, *op. cit.*, p. 158

Makarios, the Cretan, the monk of Christ; icon of 1663, no. 379, in the Byzantine Museum, Athens

Marc of Constantinople, worked in Genoa *c.* 1313. Kondakov, *op. cit.*, p. 158

Marc, 16th–17th century; icon no. 1653 in the Russian Museum, Leningrad, is by him.

Margazines, George; icon no. 134 in San Giorgio dei Greci, Venice

Mauriki, Loukas, 17th century; icon no. 34 in the Benaki Museum, Athens

Megenas, Loukas, 1672

Melissenos, Parthenios, 1665

Melomos, a Greek painter working in Tuscany *c.* 1212, who taught Guido da Siena. Frothingham, *op. cit.*, p. 44

Metaxas, John, of Kalabaka; in 1665 painted icon of St Nicholas in Trikkala Cathedral

Michael, the icon painter; worked in Crete in 1318. Kondakov, *op. cit.*, p. 158

Mitaras, Anthony, painted 16th-century icon of the Archangel Michael, no. 67 at San Giorgio dei Greci, Venice

Moschos, Leo c. 1648–75, painted Tree of Jesse, no. 26 in Benaki Museum, Athens. Is he the same as Elias Moschos, 1649–86, also represented in the Athens museums?

Moschos, John, the Cretan, 1680–1714; icons dated to 1681 can be seen in the Benaki Museum, Athens

NEGROPONTE, Antoniodi, 15th century. A painting of his is in the church of San Francesco della Vigna, Venice. Frothingham, *op. cit.*, p. 51

Neophite, the monk, a Cretan, son of Theophanes Baphi who did the wall paintings in the church at Kalabaka in 1573. Icons by Neophite are in the Greek Church at Cairo. R. Byron and D. Talbot Rice, *op. cit.*, p. 148

Nicephorus, the monk, 17th century? A Transfiguration in the Lavra, Mount Athos

Nicholas de Gabriel, noted at Venice c. 1560

Nicholas the priest, early 15th century; there is work of his in Venice

Nicholas the Peloponnesian; in 1659 painted an icon belonging to the monastery of St Stephen, Meteora

Nicholas, the Cretan, 17th century; painted a Divine Liturgy which was in Kiev. Kondakov, *op. cit.*, p. 158

OLYMPITIS, Giorgios, 1660

PACHOMIOS, noted at Venice 1520

Pallades, Jeremiah, in 1612 painted an icon in the Patriarchate at Cairo

Panselinos, Manuel, probably worked between 1535–71

Papadopoulos, Antonio, painted an icon in the Vatican Museum, Rome

Paramaniata, John, painter of a 16th-century icon in the Russian Museum, Leningrad

Pavias, Andreas, the Cretan, 17th century

Pegasios, Ieromonachos, an icon in the Benaki Museum, Athens, dated either 1608 or 1680

Pelergos, George, a Cretan, probably 14th century. Kondakov, *op. cit.*, p. 158

Peter the Greek, worked in Novgorod in 1196. Kondakov, *op. cit.*, p. 47

Peter, painter of a triptych in the Russian Museum, Leningrad

Peter, zographos, signed an early 13th-century icon of the Virgin and Prophets in St Catherine's Monastery, Sinai. Sotiriou, no. 158

Philanthropinos, Nicholas, went from Constantinople to Crete in 1419. *Icons*, p. xxxvi

Philip, Ieromonachos, icon of Dormition, no. 10, Benaki Museum, Athens; second quarter of 16th century

Philippos, 17th century

Philotheon, Kudonisios, icon no. 328 in the Byzantine Museum, Athens, dated 1669

Phlorias, Jacobos, 1675

Phocas, Manuel, worked in Crete in 1446. Kondakov, *op. cit.*, p. 158

Phocas, John, brother of Manuel. Kondakov, *op. cit.*, p. 158

Plakotos, Ieronymos, 1670

Platypodis, John, of Candia, in Venice in 1524

Polites, Georgeios, 1515

Porphyrios, 1541

Poulakis, Theodore, 17th century. Of his numerous icons one is at Grotto Ferrata

Pretoris, Tzemios, son of Leontios the priest. Painted an icon at Agios Nikolaos, Cyprus

Propontos, John, icon no. 132 at San Giorgio dei Greci, Venice

Prorata, John, a Cretan, c. 1430. Kondakov, *op. cit.*, p. 158

RITSOS, Andreas, of Candia; a 16th-century icon in Parma Museum

Ritsos, Nikolaos, son of Andreas. See L. Mirkovic, *Actes* IV, Vol. 2, p. 129, of Byzantine Congress at Sofia

Ritzes, Ioannes, 1694

Romaios; an icon in the Loverdos collection, Athens

Romanos of Crete, c. 1571. Bettini, *Frühchristliche Malerei*, Vienna 1942, p. 22

SARAKENOPOULOS, a 16th-century Incredulity of Thomas, no. 9 at San Giorgio dei Greci, Venice

Sclavos, Marthos, in the Loverdos collection, Athens

Scopoula, John Maria, worked in Otranto; there is an icon of his in Naples. Kondakov, *op. cit.*, p. 157

Scordile, Georgios, 1657

Scordile, Antonios, 17th century

Sguros, Constantine, worked in Venice in late 16th–early 17th century. Bettini, *op. cit.*, p. 23

Siropoulos, John, 17th century; an icon of the Virgin in the Russian Museum, Leningrad

Spantoules, Francis, 1606

Stammati the Cretan, 1447; a relation of Manuel and John Phocas. Kondakov, *op. cit.*, p. 158

Stasnios, Theodoulas, 1689

Stentas, Spiridon, 1674

Stergios

TAMARINI, Gregory, of Crete; icon of 1618 of Christ. See D. Wild. *Les Icônes*; *Art religieux d'orient*. Orbis Pictus I, Lausanne, 1947, pl. IX

Theodoros, a signed painting in the Vatican Museum, Rome. Frothingham, *op. cit.*, p. 51

Theophanes of Constantinople, worked in Venice c. 1242. Frothingham, *op. cit.*, p. 44

Theophilos, the priest; an icon of 1576 in the Loverdos collection, Athens

Tsankarolas, Stephanos, two icons, one of 1688, in the Benaki Museum, Athens

Tsaouses, Iakovos, 1590

UPATOS, Ioannes, 1682

VATHAS, Thomas, of Corfu; worked in Venice from *c.* 1581; an icon of the Virgin, no. 61, in San Giorgio dei Greci

Venier, Emmanuel, 1672

Victor, the Cretan, *c.* 1651–72; icons in the Vatican and Correr Museums, also no. 297 in the Byzantine Museum, Athens

Victor di Bartholomeo, noted at Venice 1546

Victor di Giovanni, noted at Venice 1585

Vidales, George; a 17th-century icon in the Loverdos collection, Athens

Vlastos, John, 1606–31

ZANE, Constantine, 1673–94, icons nos. 120–2 in San Giorgio dei Greci, Venice. Bettini, *op. cit.*, p. 23

Zanetto, D., noted at Venice by 1546

Zangavoi, Stefanos, 1688–1710. Bettini, *op. cit.*, p. 23

APPENDIX II
Additional list of recorded dated icons

1156. *The Virgin Bogolyubovo*. Vladimir–Suzdalian school

1169. *Virgin of the Sign*. Novgorodian school

Soon after 1220. An icon at Veria in northern Greece. Byzantine school

1327. *St George*. Moved from Erzurum to the Greek church at Alexandropol. M. F. Lynch, *Armenia*, London 1901, p. 128, fig. 25

1333. *The Archangel Michael*. Moscow school; see Kondakov 1, p. 325

c. 1364. A double-sided icon with the *Georgian Virgin Hodegetria* on the obverse and *Christ Pantocrator* on the reverse. This icon is thought to date from the consecration of the cathedral of the Virgin's Protection in the convent of that name at Suzdal. Rostov–Suzdal school. See Antonova/Mneva, Vol. I, no. 170

c. 1364. Icon of the *Virgin's Protection* from the same convent. It is believed to have been commissioned by Andrey Constantinovich, who became Prince of Suzdal in 1365. Rostov–Suzdal School. Antonova/Mneva, Vol. I, no. 171

1383. *The Virgin of Tikhvin*. Novgorodian school. According to the legend it was found in that year suspended from a tree

1395. *The Transfiguration*. Rostov–Suzdal school. Dated by an 18th-century inscription copying the original one. Antonova/Mneva, Vol. I, no. 176

1395. *The Virgin's birth*. Kondakov 1, p. 325

1397. *The Annunciation*. Kondakov 1, p. 325

1432. *St Nicholas of Mozhaisk*. Commissioned by Prince Ivan Andreievich, who inherited Mozhaisk in 1432. Moscow school. Antonova/Mneva, Vol. I, no. 259

1465. Biographical icon of St Nicholas, Pskov school

1488. *The Entombment*. By Jacob Iel. Novgorodian school. Antonova/Mneva, Vol. I, no. 102

1495. *St Simeon the Stylite*. Museum of History and Architecture, Novgorod.

1501. *The Archangel Michael*. From the Chudov Monastery, Kondakov 1, p. 325

1505. *The Assembly of the Archangel Michael*. Kondakov 1, p. 325

1512. *A Crucifixion*. By Efrem in Russian Museum, Leningrad

1513. Biographical icon of *St Nicholas of Zaraysk*, the copy made in 1513 when the miracle-working prototype was removed to Kolomna as the Tartars laid siege to the town. Monastic school. Antonova/Mneva, Vol. 2, no. 557

1534. *St Nicholas*. From the Morozov Collection. O. Wulff/M. Alpatov, *Denkmäler der Ikonenmalerei*, Leipzig, 1925, p. 283, pl. 73

1542. *Ascension*. School of Pskov. Museum of History and Architecture, Novgorod.

1542. *The Ascension*. Dated by its inscription. S. V. U. Mánes-Svoboda, *Russky Ikony*, Prague, 1948, pl. 22

1543. *The Ascension*. Novgorodian school, dated by its inscription. Wulff/Alpatov, *op. cit.*, p. 286, pl. 79

1549. Icon of *the Veronica*, dated on its metal frame. Kondakov 2, ill. 103

c. 1550. Icon of *the Saviour*, from the cell of Patriarch Jeremy. Kondakov 2, p. 474

1557. *The Women bringing Myrrh*. N. P. Likhachev, *Materialy dlia istorii russkogo ikonoposaniya*; Atlas Snimkov, St Petersburg, 1906, pl. CXXVI, no. 221–4

Prior to 1560. *Constantine and Helena*. According to the inscription on it, it was embellished with adornments in 1560. Rostov–Suzdal school. Antonova/Mneva, Vol. 2, no. 395

1561. *St Nicholas with twenty-four scenes from his life*. Kondakov 1, p. 309

1561. *St Nicholas*. Novgorodian school. Wulff/Alpatov, *op. cit.*, 283, n. 86

1565. *The Raising of the Cross, the Virgin's Protection and selected Saints*. By Mitia Usov, son of Ivan. Rostov–Suzdal school. Antonova/Mneva, Vol. 2, no. 399

1564–67. *The Old Testament Trinity*. By Bishop Akaky, who died in 1567. Tver school. Antonova/Mneva, Vol. 2, no. 641

1578. Double-sided icon—*the Veronica* on the obverse, the *Virgin of the Sign* on the reverse; from Borovici. State Historical Museum, Moscow

1602. *St Basil the Great with sixteen scenes from his life*. Moscow School. Antonova/Mneva, Vol. 2, no. 515

Early 17th century. *The Rich Fruits of Learning. Basil the Great, Gregory the Evangelist and St John Chrysostom conferring*. By Nikifor, son of Istom Savin. Antonova/Mneva, Vol. 2, no. 793

1608. *The Saviour*. A Prince Galitzin gift to the Troitse–Sergeyeva Lavra. Kondakov 2, pl. 15

1630. *The Metropolitans Peter, Alexis and John with Bishop Leonty of Rostov*; presented to the Troitse–Sergeyeva Lavra in that year. Likhachev, *op. cit.*, pl. CCXI, no. 380

1635. *The Virgin of Molchansk*. From Putivl. Kondakov 1, p. 290

1639. *Sts Cosmas and Damian*. Stroganov school. Likhachev, *op. cit.*, pl. CCXLI, no. 460

c. 1645. The memorial icon painted on the lid of the coffin to which the Patriarch Joachim transferred the remains of Prince Gregory Vsevolodych (1187–1239) in that year. It was exhibited at the Victoria and Albert Museum, London, in 1929. Antonova/Mneva, Vol. 2, no. 858

1654 1. *The Virgin of Tikhvin* with *St Minna* in the margin, and 2. *St Nicholas, the Apostles Peter and Paul and St Ignatius*. Both icons are inscribed and dated. Likhachev, *op. cit.*, pl. CXIV, nos. 204 and 205

1668/9. Biographical icon of St Paraskevi. Russian State Museum, Leningrad. E. S. Smirnova, *Zhivopis drevney Russi*, Leningrad, 1970, pl. 53 and 54

1672. *The Veronica*. The icon was given to the Troitse–Sergeyeva Lavra by Prince Trubetskoy in that year. Kondakov 2, pl. 24. In the course of the same year the Moscow merchant Nikifor Bezsonov also presented the Lavra with a triptych of the three central Deesis figures; each is in a different style, probably by a different hand, St John the Baptist being the more accomplished. The Virgin follows a Greek prototype, Christ is rendered in the contemporary Muscovite style

1674. *The Veronica*. From the Novospassky Monastery at Khlyudovo, near Viatka. Kondakov 2, pl. 82, 2

c. 1680. Icons of *Longinus* and *St Theodore Stratelates*. By Feodor Zubov. In the church of the Saviour behind the Golden Lattice, the Kremlin, Moscow. M. A. Alpatov, *Khudozhestvennya pamiatniki Moskovskogo Kremlya*, Moscow, 1956, pl. 165, and Kondakov 2 refers to one—Zagorsk Treasury no. 473—on p. 65, ill. 106

1685. *The Saviour*. Museum of History and Architecture, Novgorod.

1686. *Parsunya* of Tsar Feodor Alexeevich, commissioned in 1685 from Ivan Maksimov and Simon Ushakov and painted a year later, possibly, it is thought, with the assistance of Ivan Bezmin. U. Malkov, 'Iskusstvo Parsuny' in *Khudozhnik*, no. 12, 1970

1692. *The Virgin and Child*. Kondakov 1, p. 290.

1693. *The Resurrection of Our Lord*. Likhachev, *op. cit.*, pl. CCCXXXVI, no. 530

INDEX

Numbers in *italics* refer to plates and notes on the plates